The Last Five Dollar Baby

The Last

HARPER & ROW, PUBLISHERS

New York   Evanston   San Francisco   London

1817

Five Dollar Baby

Nancy Wood

FIRST EDITION

STANDARD BOOK NUMBER: 06–014739–3

LIBRARY OF CONGRESS CATALOG CARD NUMBER: 71–156568

For Andy and Peggy Marshall
and their Ft. Union Ranch
where this book was born

The author gratefully acknowledges a debt of gratitude to Norman Sams, who produced the character called the Stranger and who spent countless hours in preliminary editing. To her editor, Ann Harris, the author owes particular thanks for bringing the manuscript into its final form. And to Judy Noyes of the Chinook Bookshop special appreciation for a critical reading of the manuscript.

The Last Five Dollar Baby

Because I know that time is always time
And place is always and only place
And what is actual is actual only for one time
And only for one place
I rejoice that things are as they are and
I renounce the blessed face
And renounce the voice
Because I cannot hope to turn again
Consequently I rejoice, having to construct something
Upon which to rejoice

T. S. ELIOT

1

He had left the town forever and his throat felt dry. There was a numbness in his left arm and his intestines were full because he had not taken a crap in a week. He was a doctor and ought to have known what to do for himself but over the years he had let his body fail him so that now it was worn out and in step with his mind. He had nothing to live for but he would go on living because there was nothing else to do. If he was lucky they would take him on at the clinic near Kayenta and he would live out his life with the Navajos. If not he would just keep on going and maybe head for Mexico and find himself a place on the beach and live out his life as a catcher

1

of fish. Either way it did not make much difference for he had done what he had set out to do and that was to stay with the town till it died.

It lay before him now in a smoking heap with not a single soul around to tell him what had happened the town had simply disappeared in the forty-eight hours since he had seen it last well the town was dead all right and there was nothing to be done except clear out of Yellow Bird Colorado where he was born fourteen years after the century turned and fourteen years before grownup men started to cry over what had happened to the price of gold.

On Sunday the nineteenth of October Eli Wetherill adjusted his spectacles and got out of the car at Holdup Hill just where it wove into the gulch where the Swede hanged himself with a bridle and Bessie Pilcher at the age of eleven paid a quarter to see a boy have an erection. The railroad from Coronado once ran along the bottom of that hill on the last straight stretch of ground before it crossed the bridge and deadended at Yellow Bird bringing in pickaxes and pocket watches fresh oranges and oil for the lamps and hauling out the uncouth ore to be processed at a mill which never shut down. It was so long ago and there is an end to everything and now the track is all torn up and the grass is pressed down into two symmetrical lines going nowhere anymore.

What is gone has a way of leaving its mark on men and mountains the hard rock stiffs still have callouses fifty years old and their eyes have never lost the bleariness from a life of underground dust nor has daylight improved their sallow skin after a half century ruined it in a shaft that never felt the sun nor got roughened by the wind nor was made bearable by the seasons shifting that sort of tempering happened to the thirteen-thousand-foot mountain towering above the town.

The mountain had as bad a case of acne as he had ever seen. Its stoic face had begun to bleed in 1878 when the United States of America Pikes Peak Platte River American Desert Gold

Seekers had run out the first poor prospectors and attacked the mountain with a savagery reserved for enemies. They gouged it beat it scraped it performed a thousand lobotomies on it and took the spirit from it. The mountain however was not dead yet. Its life was already eighty million years old and it had a way to go so in its own slow inexorable way it went on living. The mountain of course could do nothing for itself although at times he had seen it rear up and swallow whole a man who had offended it by sinking one more shaft into its worn and sullen countenance. Or part of that countenance would break off and come hurtling down on those who liked to witness the mountain's crippled state he preferred to think of its revenge as a giant tooth dropping from the mountain's weary head because to him that thirteen-thousand-foot monstrosity was as alive as any child of nature and thus to be feared respected and never trusted. Just like a female. What else was so stubborn vengeful and a perennial candidate for rape?

The old girl's scars would take a thousand years or so to heal and in that time only one inch of new soil would settle over the wounds the shrieking winds coming down from the north would make only slight new configurations in the mountain's distorted face the avalanches which already had alleys to call their own would wear only slightly deeper into that brooding granite façade. New scars caused by wind and water and shifts of gravity would become marks of dignity and old age unlike the man-made acne which to him had always been synonymous with indecent liberty.

The exchange between man and mountain was now favoring the mountain for which man had no further use. The same was not true of other mountains but it was of this one. Indeed its insides had been gutted its bodily wastes stood in shameful heaps at the base its face was scarred and its skin punctured but noble stands of ponderosa and aspen were still intact and numerous streams which oozed from the top of the mountain became clear and gurgling torrents emptying into the river.

3

The forest had not felt the lumberman's axe nor the streams the campers' spit and shit there was they said air up there that had not been breathed before and it was possible Eli Wetherill said to just go up and breathe trees. The slopes of the mountain were not right for skiing and so the bulldozers would not come the tilt of the land was bad for building and so the developers would not come the trail to the top ended at the thirteen-thousand-foot summit and so the climbers of fourteen-thousand-foot peaks would not come. Asked what the mountain was good for Eli Wetherill would always reply it's good for itself.

And now because it was left alone the mountain went about healing itself and burying the indecent liberty taken with it. The blade of a saw the ore bucket dangling on a cable the bit of a drill the stamping machines the discarded pieces of equipment once shining and new were now the property of the mountain and were being disposed of with a generous dose of rust. The shaft houses scaffolding outhouses gallows frames and miners' shacks had been bleached by the sun brought down by the snow rotted by the rain and claimed by the earth. And who could say whether the wildflowers did not grow better because of what the mountain was taking back to itself or whether the particular peace of the high place was not due to the fact that man had used up all his chances with nature and now the mountain was having her turn?

And had perhaps another eighty million years to go.

Eli Wetherill learned what made them come to the mountain when he was only nine and was sweeping up the floor of the Britannia a multi-purpose edifice for theatre legislature formal balls wrestling matches opera and large-scale drinking. Using a whisk broom and a turkey's wing for a dustpan he had gleaned a total of $14.57 in gold dust enough to buy Buddy Ralston's nickel-plated revolver. In his gold pan he had also found two unused theatre tickets cigar stumps tobacco cuds a silver buckle and a crumpled note which read Dearest Sid my husband started for Cripple Creek yesterday and if agreeable

4

please call around ten this evening yours anxiously Flora p.s. knock at the back door three times.

For years he kept a gold nugget in his pocket to remind himself of what it had cost to bring it out and how vain was any man who thought it possible to keep steam trains hard rock mining a matched pair of Kentucky bays or the Bull Moose party going forever. He wore the nugget smooth with his thumb and forefinger and wore out the pocket of every pair of pants he ever had it in and finally he had lost it while taking a nap in one of Thornburg's caskets waiting for the coroner to report which bullet had killed Bliss Majors the only desperado he could ever remember in Yellow Bird Colorado. He had been shot a week after Pearl Harbor by Sheriff Jim Wilson who found him in bed with the wife of the blacksmith who had just enlisted. An escaped murderer from the Kansas State Penitentiary Majors was shot six times by the sheriff who mistook him for a Japanese.

He was in fact half-Indian.

If you couldn't live off the mines you could always live off the miners was what they said in Yellow Bird and so it was for nearly sixty years from 1888 until things got bad then they lived off each other. And there in the smoking heap was what he had lived off of for thirty-three years the common colds stomach aches silicosis tuberculosis lung cancer rheumatic fever broken bodies dead babies and what he could not diagnose nor treat he called Black Ass. It was what made Katharine Phillips jump out of a third-story window with her five-day-old bastard boy child and what made Tom Pazulla walk into the path of a Denver and Rio Grande Western locomotive and the Irish washerwoman drink a tumblerful of lye and what made a miner called True blow himself up with dynamite on Christmas Eve. The lives of these people had a way of leaving their mark lingering in the air also and although there was now scarcely one brick standing upon another nor one chimney blowing coal smoke nor one sign of life along the empty shattered streets he saw Katharine Phil-

5

lips' Buick roadster tearing up the hillside with a laughing young man in the seat beside her a yapping Yorkshire terrier in her lap. He saw Tom Pazulla's big hands nailing a shoe on a horse's hoof his back permanently bent his legs encased in leather chaps and a dirty Stetson covering his bald spot. He saw Mary Feeney Murphy's winter wash solidified on the line the miners' union suits bent like some crazy fracture of the elbows and knees and he saw the school children laughing when the sheets blew off frozen stiff like sails made out of cement. And he saw a pair of boots that belonged to True which he removed before he blew himself up and which were carefully polished and shined with bee's wax so that you could see your eyeball in the tips.

They had cost forty dollars and were the only thing of value he had besides his wife.

Eli Wetherill sat down on a rock and put his legs in front of him and leaned one hand back in the parched dead grass and did not seem to notice the red ants which crawled through the hair on his arms. His watch was too tight on his wrist and that seemed to bother him more so he took it off and shook it once or twice it no longer kept good time and after some consideration he hurled it into the gulch thinking of how he had failed to win two bits from Bessie Pilcher because his penis had simply quit and she had laughed and called it a dead balloon. And she hoped it fell off. Well to hell with her she paid out a fortune in quarters there in the gulch the boys of Yellow Bird would do anything for money even let an old man touch it or some miner's wife grab hold but nobody married Bessie Pilcher and she died with a reputation as a religious fanatic who ordained herself a minister and converted the heathen by chewing up the Bible page by page in front of them. She had eleven Bibles to the credit of her stomach by the time they carried her out. Among her belongings they found a box containing snapshots of nude men and concluded she had confiscated them from the heathen.

Bessie Pilcher was known as a woman of virtue.

The doctor's hands were no longer steady and in order to steady them he went to the car and got a six-pack of beer from the cooler which also contained a chunk of ham and a wad of bills to take him wherever he might happen to go now that the thing was finished. There was no ice in the cooler and so the beer was warm but it tasted good as it trickled down his throat and it would serve as a laxative besides. He went back to the rock his mind being on nothing in particular not wholly on the town which lay in ruins before him because that was no longer a part of him just as he was no longer part of the town. He had given out he was in limbo and it was not altogether unpleasant. Watching the smoke drifting up from the demolished town he felt an enormous relief it was like having school behind you or the army or like seeing the last of your children gone. But he had had no children and his wife was dead and the loneliness with which he had lived for so many years attacked him suddenly and prickled his skin with something like fear.

But it was not fear. He had seen the end of a time and a place and knew himself to be among those men who would with tiresome regularity relate what had happened and what did not happen it would run all together in his mind and come out as half fiction and half truth and he would not know which was which and it would not matter nor would anyone care. He would tell his stories of mine disasters blizzards and cattle drives the shooting of Bliss Majors would multiply into a dozen killings witnessed by him in Yellow Bird he would tell of weary miners giving them a little glory and raw courage mixing them up with the prospectors of a century ago but who would know he would tell of saloons and poker games that lasted a week of fat madames and slim prostitutes of engines roaring up and down the canyon carrying gold and silver ore he would speak of ordinary men and give them their dreams of bravery and omit the truth of failure he would make jokes about the stupid sheepmen and the ass-addicted lumberjacks and somehow no

7

one would ever know that he was not to be believed.

His mind was crowded with incidental things the pages of his Sears Roebuck catalogue and they did not amount to much. So he would forget. Even then looking down at what was left of Yellow Bird he could not remember where Sweeney's grocery store had stood or where Josie Stringer had her hotel or even which heap of smoldering rubble represented what had been the hospital. The place was gutted except for a few houses which stood on the edge of town his own and that of Meridian Muldoon plus a handful of others which had been closed up anyway waiting for the bulldozers to come. And all of it was to have been accomplished with the plodding on-time scheduling of the Army Engineers who had planned to tear down the buildings one by one a slow and painful death for anyone to watch and now it had happened all at once a mercy killing Eli Wetherill said to himself maybe Yellow Bird has screwed the Army Corps of Engineers after all maybe they have found some courage at long last.

Maybe.

But he did not know if they had not dropped a bomb instead he only knew that a time and place had ended and there was just the river still untamed and untroubled the way it was in the beginning.

The West Bountiful River was what had put Yellow Bird on the map in the first place and it was what had already begun to take it off. The river was not much where it flowed through town just a muddy stream that now and then flooded in the spring but was otherwise docile containing no fish since uranium tailings had been dumped into it some miles upstream where the boom of the fifties had brought one last gasp of prosperity to Yellow Bird. The river was a vulgar display of nature taking off her underwear it was a dog with its tongue hanging out a nuisance when the old bridge collapsed and a new one had to be built raising taxes one hundred percent. It divided the town socially as well as geographically and that was its sole distinction. If you lived to the east of it where the ground began to bulge toward the mountain it meant that your father or grandfather had whacked off a piece of land there before the century turned and had probably fleeced the mountain of gold or it meant that you had surprised everyone by making something of yourself the way Eli Wetherill had.

He grew up west of the river in a suburb called Stringtown where the houses were all of split logs the streets were of mud and manure and daily garbage and the value of the Monday wash was less than one good mule. He had coveted the house that belonged to Ratsey the mine owner from the time he was five and spent the dark winter afternoons in the attic pissing out the window into a snowdrift twenty feet high. Each time he pissed out the window he watched the Ratsey house christened it in effect and coveted it and in time signed his name to the deed. Then he watched out of Ratsey's leaded glass windows and did not piss into the snowdrifts anymore but stared at Stringtown crumbling across the river and was not sorry to see it go.

The river had filled a few pans of the placer miners who scrambled over the divide in their restless lonesome search for gold and satisfying their pans as well as their longings for a new and unnamed place named it and moved on. And did not keep their mouths shut. Nor stay to watch the river milked the mountain murdered or the hard rock stiffs become glazed in the eyes weak in the lungs and driven with a greed that the pay dirters never learned about. The river having served its one brief purpose got in the way of the railroad the mule skinners freighters whiskey drummers and the soft girls in silk skirts who got muddy when the wagons bogged down in the river's evil sucking mud. So it was cursed. And bridged. And had a tree where they hanged people as late as 1915. The West Bountiful River was never bountiful it served no purpose whatsoever its banks were not even used as a place to fish or to lay good she-stuff the banks were steep and ridiculous with gravel and red dirt and except for the hanging tree there was not a cottonwood which did not grow crooked and haphazard and often with its roots exposed if not bled dry from having its trunk pictographed by the whim of Yellow Bird's untamed youth.

The river was in short as useful as a callus on your working finger and as difficult to remove. Ironic that the town which never claimed the river was now to be claimed by it. It happened when the government back in Washington said there had to be a dam so that all the good water would not go running off into Utah and make the Mormons think they had a right to it. And besides what good is a river flowing with nothing to stop it? And what are we to do with the essential Army Corps of Engineers god love them? And there is this money to spend in a fund called reclamation so let us reclaim and not wonder how we had the right to claim it in the first place.

For twenty-five years there had been talk of a dam and the people of Yellow Bird had always laughed and said it would never come to pass what good would it do to have a reservoir thirty miles off the beaten path who were you going to get to fish in it some mountain goats an importation of polar bears no motor boats will ever make it up the road from Coronado a sin to put a lake where the Lord didn't intend to have one a crime to take our houses out from under us suppose we don't want to go?

Sorry about that we have set up a committee and the committee has made a study and the study proves that a reservoir at Yellow Bird Colorado proves the greatest good for the greatest number it proves the risk/benefit principle the land-of-many-uses principle the pork-barrel principle the dam-the-last-river principle. We shall proceed and we regret that due to unforeseen circumstances the name Yellow Bird was inadvertently removed from the chamber of commerce road map this year and so the town does not exist in fact or principle we shall proceed.

We object your honor we object to the unfair prices paid

10

for our homes where we lived and loved and laughed and raised our kids we object to the fact that we cannot replace what we have lost we object to the fact that we have no choice we object to our destruction.

Objection overruled we shall proceed.

And Eli Wetherill who was mayor for twenty years saw them go down fighting over the prices paid for their homes fighting among themselves over one man's getting more for his house than another and he said what he always said that if you want to see a fellow have a real hemorrhage stick your knife in his pocketbook.

So just below Yellow Bird not far from the rickety old bridge where the railroad used to run they were going to build a dam which would be made from the guts of Yellow Bird itself a two-hundred-foot-high collective corpse put together from all the streets sidewalks backyards vegetable gardens and open fields where you could fly a kite or a boomerang or lay your girl in the moonlight all of this was being scraped up from Yellow Bird to be put into the earth-filled dam. The buildings or what was left of them would be stuffed into the gulch where Bessie Pilcher and the Swede had given themselves in different ways to different causes and the gulch would be filled with the rubble and covered with dirt so the water could not get to it. There was no sign of the dam yet but there was a tombstone a two-hundred-foot-high water intake tower which loomed above the town and bore the castle insignia of the Army Corps of Engineers and the word CUNNINGHAM the name of the water politician who had pushed through Congress the $60 million to keep the river from going its own way in its own time the way it had always done.

And Yellow Bird which had not done much in its lifetime except produce over $125 million in gold was giving its life for the sake of the dam and did not have its name on the tombstone. Irrevocably denied the privilege of dying on its own the town had not fought against the government committees or the

11

bureaucrats or the Congress of the United States or all the wonderful principles they had learned about it boiled down to that magical word Progress which made it imperative reasonable and right that Yellow Bird pass from the scene like so much excess landscape. Yellow Bird had never bothered to incorporate and so the government was under no obligation to build another town they simply came in and put prices on the houses and told the people to move or if they didn't want to they could lease back from the government their own homes and stay there until the first of June when all the power would be shut off and Josie Stringer's liquor license would expire and the U.S. government property signs would go up on all the houses that had not been knocked down with the bulldozers.

But now of course it was only October and he sat there wondering what exactly they had done to it and why and where they had gone since he left them two days before to chase wild horses with Matt Brittman and all of life had truly come to an end though he could not understand any of that either and he began to consider that he was suffering from shock and that what he had done was not real and the demolished town was not real and he would presently find himself in his canopied bed on High Street trying to think himself into an erection because he was fifty-five years old and had drunk himself into impotence long before his time and so just maybe it would all pass and he would fuck Josie Stringer yet because he had to. But Josie Stringer had vanished along with the rest of them and her hotel was blown to bits and the old bank building where he had his office was down there somewhere in the mess and he had nothing except his house the clothes on his back his Plymouth automobile one quart of bourbon and the gun with which he had just killed a man yet had not killed him because the man was coming up the road on horseback waving his hat and the wild stud was haltered and on a lead rope tied to the saddle and he was the goingest concern they had ever taken fourteen hands high the color of good alfalfa his long head high and jerking against the rope.

12

Eli began to tremble he could not get his legs to raise him could not get his voice to call out could not make his eyes to see or his ears to hear the hoofbeats or the hollering and then he passed out on the cold ground and stayed that way for a long time until he came to and had no recollection of anything there was just this blankness about himself an anesthesia of time.

He finished the last of the beer and got to his feet. He was no longer shaking but his stomach felt bloated and he knew he had to do something about his condition or face nausea until he did. He opened the trunk of his car and found his medical bag crammed in with dirty clothing a sleeping bag spare tires and the portraits of his family piled in a box. He had they said the hands of his father a jeweler who did not believe in unions Teddy Roosevelt foolishness taking a bath mining engineers spitting on the floor or wearing an undershirt to the table. But he was as good with his hands as any surgeon and he made fine jewelry and fixed watches and repaired the fancy pieces of machinery they brought to mine the gold easier and faster and better. He called it balderdash the strongest word he ever used. He preferred mules and men to any machine and he was the first to proclaim that automobiles would never catch on that airplanes would never fly and that any woman who needed a machine to wash clothes in was just plain lazy.

The picture of his mother appealed to the doctor she was the kind of woman to rear a neighbor's child or take in sewing to help out or to raise a few chickens in the backyard. Only she didn't. She had an everlasting case of the vapors and she stayed in bed most of the time with the shades drawn and the room reeking of ammonia which she said kept germs away from the house in a town that was so filthy it was a wonder they didn't shut it down. Well no matter she was a good woman and she would have done all those things she talked about if she could. He had his mother's eyes. Where his disposition came from he did not know. His mother would have blamed it on his father's side.

He gulped down a bottle of castor oil it was not much worse

13

than Josie Stringer's coffee and would have the same effect. Perhaps she had gone to Kansas City after all to set up shop all over again. She would not like it there and he sort of wished he had told her just once how much he needed her but she would have taken it as a proposal of marriage and spoiled their friendship of three decades a miracle of craps played with horse dice samples of all the new vitamin pills and antibiotics a quart of cream per week and the kind of straight and simple talk that seldom came from a woman she had said the week before as she was washing dishes and taking the postcards from the mirror she said to him the only way we can survive dying is not to be reminded of it. So they talked instead of the men who had gone to the moon and she said it was a bad thing going so far to bring back rocks that any fool could tell you were no different from the ones they had spent their lives seeing blasted and crushed and melted. Besides which when you interfered with heaven hell was not far off. Her mother had said so half a century before the government decided to waste its money getting a man on the moon. I can think of a lot better things to do with cash than that but you know what doc if they needed a café up there I'd go to see the view. But I would have to be back in time for Christmas.

They were all gone from Yellow Bird now Josie and Britt and Killeen and the girl only one of whom had ever understood really understood about the mountain the secret places that you went to when life was breathing hard down your neck and you had to go out and find yourself in a cranny that nobody knew about and you would stick your fingers in the ground and feel the roots going a long way down because the earth was where you came from and it would take you back and reclaim man and mountain alike they will be as one and Yellow Bird will also be one with nature when the dam is finished and two hundred feet of water lies over it and what will its mark be? Nothing. The mark is on us who lived here who knew the mountains and the mines and the secret places but not each other. No. We never knew each other. Some of us tried. What was and what might have been. What was not and could not be. What should have been and what there was no hope to become. It's all there for them to scrape up. An epitaph which reads at last I've bid the knaves farewell ask not my name but go to hell.

Then the doctor's thoughts began to run all together like ice cream left too long in the sun he found himself in the ludicrous position of being exactly between before and after with one stretch of time already completed and the next too terrifying to begin. You had to begin somewhere. You could not sit forever on a rock contemplating the visible remains of your life. It is time to go it is time to go it is time to go he said to himself and the words repeated themselves in his mind like a chant from the Navajo. A wasp came along and stung him above the eye he could not feel the pain. He shivered in the cold sun and let himself be frozen at nine thousand feet frozen until his head was swimming and coming up the hill he saw a squadron of citizens from Yellow Bird naked with the mistakes of his surgery carrying the babies born dead through his poor judgment the mutilated miners he could not paste back together again the wailing women whose husbands he could not save the grim-lipped men whose wives he could not save. In the diamond-hard brilliant hot sun they came silently without faces only the bodies which he had bungled moved upward toward him on one leg and two carrying his surgical tools which consisted of a hacksaw a screwdriver a monkey wrench a jackhammer and a salad fork. They were to perform on him an amputation of his third leg the dead balloon that was not even worth a quarter. For an anesthetic they had remembered to bring a fifth of Jack Daniel's and he smiled thinking they were not so vicious after all.

He began to thirst and he went to the car after some more beer and finding none unscrewed the top of the whiskey bottle the last one left from the wild horse hunt the four men had brought a case in all and mixed it with apricot brandy and they

15

had gotten very drunk together. But he remembered nothing about it as he went down the hill toward the wreckage of the Yellow Bird Hotel where Josie Stringer had dispensed potatoes and philosophy with the same degree of importance.

2

He had promised himself he wouldn't go looking for any of it let the magpies strut among the anonymous debris the enormous anthills where they wept and slept and posted their bills this property is condemned no trespassing forgive us our trespasses I must have one last look at it before rigor mortis sets in.

A stranger in a jeep drove up from the river and stared at the doctor whose fly was unzipped whose left eye was swollen shut and whose growth of beard was three days old. His teeth however were set in a good-natured smile and his white-maned head was thrown back and he walked evenly steadily with a

17

sense of repose. But he was mistaken for a bum by the man in the jeep who pulled up in front of him pushed down the lock of the door rolled the window down a crack and said hey buddy what happened to this place they tear it down? The doctor looked at him out of his one good eye appraised the Colorado license plate and the shiny jeep with a trail bike strapped to the fender the man wore a baseball cap and sunglasses a bumper sticker said is thy heart right with God and another America love it or leave it and an American flag was flying from the radio antenna. It was not in him to hate anything so he said softly no mister it fell down all by itself.

And more would come he knew and ask questions and he did not want to be there so he hurried along toward what remained of the church the coal stove used for forty years before they installed a furnace the brick steps leading into thin air the panes of broken stained glass scattered over the dirt and catching the sun like a field of flowers somebody had sat down on. He could not feel God's wrath coming out of the debris for the desecration of his holy house he felt certain that God was glad to have vacated that stuffy little freight car of safe conduct into heaven.

I must be going he said to himself wondering why it was the church carcass he'd come to and not the hospital which though shut down for eleven years had always had his best interests unlike this edifice of an intellectual enema. He turned back again and rested on the steps and put his head between his hands and knew that it was barely six weeks ago that the yellow brown of the earth had darkened with the bubbling spit of Nate Houghton whose wife Rose was coming head first out of the butcher's truck into the church. Anno domini 1889 Holy Ghost Episcopal Sunday Worship 9:30 A.M. Holy Comm 3rd Sunday Jesus saves George Washington Lacey Vicar. Houghton clutched his hat and bowed his head stood close to her feet size 6 what will I do with the bedroom slippers?

I am the resurrection and the life. We brought nothing into

18

this world and it is certain we can carry nothing out.

He hadn't been able to bring her in the old discarded school bus where she always sat in the seat behind his cleaning her teeth on the lunch menu bubble gum mud stuck on galoshes insides of the seats dangling white sneezy fuzz too much heat they never did fix the thermostat. Sweeney's truck carrying whole carcasses bloody new slaughtered dead.

For I am a stranger with thee and a sojourner as all my fathers were

lost in the Baritone Wonder 6 July 1922 second shift all lost what a funeral that was leave it to the Baptists what do Episcopalians know of grand uninhibited burials only church in town now they have more power than the Pope in Yellow Bird Colorado.

One by one they filed into the antiseptic interior used only once a month and scrubbed with Mr. Clean the buckets were still beneath the places where the roof leaked. A gold-plated crucifix made by Joseph Wetherill stood on an oak table donated by the BPOE to replace the handcarved altar carted off by souvenir hunters the summer of sixty-three. The doctor seldom went to a funeral unless it was the result of one of his mistakes and then he went to square off with God and make himself presentable to a town which no longer believed in his ability they said he could not tell the difference between aspirin and an ass burn and that if you went to him with a tumor he would deliver it nine months later. He noticed that the paint was peeling off the wall that Nate Houghton's shoes were worn through the soles and that his limp was worse that Mattie Leger's arthritic fingers were now so bad that the organ sounded like a fish moaning in shallow water that the minister so gray and lifeless seemed prime for immediate dissection and that Gus Jones's mongrel had found itself a place in the middle of the aisle.

He stumbled over it and sat down beside Matt Brittman whose huge frame was at right angles to the pew the unfamiliar

19

Book of Common Prayer grasped between the fingers of a brown and roughened hand that was more at home with the texture of a rope the smoothness of a rein and the flesh of a newborn calf. Rose Houghton had once kept house for him in forty-eight the year his wife Billy Deere couldn't take it anymore and left him with a four-year-old kid and the bitterness of five long years recorded in a document that summed it up as mental cruelty when in fact his only crime was that he much preferred the company of his cattle and his horses to that of a human heifer who never once shut up.

The doctor and the rancher had known each other so long and so well that even in that alien surrounding they acknowledged each other the same way with a dusty boot placed beside a dusty boot two sizes larger their feet touched and moved away. Neither man looked at the other man's face each heard the other breathing in familiar rhythm as a little pile of dust fell between two pairs of boots.

Houghton crouched on the edge of the wooden waxed oil-of-wintergreened pew looking at the casket. Five hundred dollars' worth of shining metal all pink inside she'd like that if only she knew maybe she does they painted a smile on her lips Cherokee red a mirror above her head just in case the eyes come unstuck because of the florist's poor embalming. The six pallbearers' faces hollow blurred remember her mourn a little so used to death and funerals reflected like ghosts in the shiny top open it for one last look. No. I should have got the burnished one a hundred dollars more was all six months to pay I could have done without cigarettes and beer I don't need them anyway. Does she know will she know once ascended into heaven the final act says what never could be said in all the years I love you Rose and I'm sorry we never got to Paris like I said and walked along the Seine you had the chance and didn't even go to Denver on the Wednesday train. I'm too old to go without you Rose I never will except to Coronado Saturday night you never minded that.

20

Portly disdainful Edgar Purvis the ex-principal of the now-closed Yellow Bird High School examined his white unworked hands. Rose the lunchroom cook forty-seven years of age she was a woman of compassion Jello Quaker oats resourcefulness she saved five dollars a week with powdered milk margarine cracked cups and beans until the place shut down last year we had five kids that graduated and then she was so simple. You wondered how her mind worked when school emptied out every time the mine whistle blew and running up the hill was bad news somebody's father or brother or sweetheart dead like her she liked school kitchens where it smells like flour and bacon grease stuck on everything the pans are too big we only had thirteen kids who stayed for lunch imagine that. No.

What shall I do? A retired principal with no school after half my life spent in eleven smelly rooms where the goddamn kids learned as good as in the city went on to college and the world escaped from here thank God oh she understood me how it felt to face a job alone no help no credit no kindness but for her a student in eleventh grade bursting out of all her clothes she told me things I liked to hear comparing me to Clark Gable the same kind of mystery and toughness she said my hair was the best she'd ever seen so thick and lush like native grasses. I had it all then she touched it once. Her hand was rough and smelled of Clorox. She never forgot my birthday Christmas my granulated eyelids hurt so much she'd smile and say mother had it too you suffer and for what nobody loves you when you're weak. Oh I never did a thing for her the way I felt revealed in dollar chocolates cheap perfume fifty dollars from my pocket the year Nate took sick poor child she worked nights at the Almighty Dollar it was so long ago I wish I had closed the windows it's going to rain then what will become of me I'm sixty-two years old. I always thought I knew myself could pull the trigger when the time came.

for a thousand years in thy sight are but as yesterday when it is past and as a watch in the night as soon as thou scatterest

21

*them they are even as sheep and fade away suddenly like the
grass*

is getting browner because it's fall another fall will I live to
see another spring you poor bastard vicar trembling like a leaf
in the wind.

George Washington Lacey in rotted black vestments belonging to the last vicar smiled and smelled the mothballs and
urine on the altar. You could not keep them out the dam workers' kids from Coronado. Screwing right here in God's house oh
yes he'd caught them twice they only laughed and said fuck you
on the door too with red paint oh my just like Los Angeles the
very day in fact he'd seen it on television. You could try locks
but they'd rip them off what were you supposed to do stand
guard over the Lord's edifice well the good Lord had ter-
minated the lease moved out and left a shell so let them screw
I mean where can you go when it's cold and snowing and there's
this pressure building up and up and

up mine eyes unto the hills from whence cometh my help

help me to get it over and done with so I can go fishing
goddamn nuisance to be burying the ungrateful dead well this
is the last time I shall set foot in the place I shall conveniently
take sick. Yellow Bird is hell.

The elderly vicar who came up once a month from
Coronado wished he did not have to come anymore to adminis-
ter to the heathen they did not like him and never came to
church they laughed behind his back and called him a horse's
ass he was bow-legged and his hair lay in strands sideways across
a misshapen skull he had been forgotten in that remote part of
Colorado which spills off from the west side of the continental
divide and cracks up and levels out toward Utah. He had been
there for five years a penance for having crossed the bishop and
there was no hope now for a transfer because he was sixty-four
and would retire in another year. He hated the town of Yellow
Bird and its mean little people who had been Baptists and
Methodists and Lutherans and Catholics and who had lost their

22

churches one by one except for this decrepit wreck of the Holy Ghost to which he came from Coronado the third Sunday spending the others in Lodestone and Cross Mountain and Missouri Gulch. Well another nine months and then they'd tear it down let the water come and cover what ought not to have been born in the first place and to think they had predicted he'd be a bishop ten years out of seminary failure was one thing bad luck another and bad luck was all it was thanks to indifferent illiterates like these who did not give a damn about their souls.

He cleared his throat and tried to bring a little warmth into his voice oh look at them not one good Christian amongst them a miner never thought of God just gold all pensioners now not worth saving not worth one good funeral *to everything there is a season and a time to every purpose under heaven a time to be born and a time to die a time to plant and a time to reap a time to kill and a time to heal a time to break down and a time to build up a time to weep and a time to laugh a time to mourn and a time to dance a time to love and a time to hate for that which befalleth the sons of man befalleth beasts all go into one place all are of the dust and all turn to dust again.*

In the beginning God created heaven and earth and chaos.

Look at the rows of people come to reassure themselves the open books contain no further promises no new thoughts it's too late they can only wait with faces like a platter of turnip greens to which

Thou hast set our misdeeds before thee and our secret sins in the light of thy countenance.

Bald ash-gray uncertain Fred Sweeney the butcher grocer worry wart stood on one foot only. He used to call her Blossom held her hand in the afternoons when she came for soap with coupons in the boxes. The wash is still in the basket. The mud beneath the drainspout still has her footprint from the last time she came on Monday of this week when Sigman's Mile High meat truck stopped the movie changed Sunday's Denver *Post* delivered trouble horror dreams futility only faced on Monday

23

man has gone to the moon there are so many dead in Vietnam riots over niggers I cannot grasp it all. What will I do with six dozen cakes ordered special Tuesday was her birthday-death-day the same date on a gravestone means you will never rest in peace my mother said.

Clumsy vexed untidy the doctor shifted in his seat aware of Houghton and his family opposite. The gotch-eyed youngest son looking up said under his breath you bastard you let her die and let a tear roll over his acne brushing it off his plaid shirt the only thing he had to wear. One by one the Houghtons turned and gazed across the expensive gleaming crate that held the light gone now from all their days uncomfortably remembered they had not told her of their love and with strange uneasiness knew they could not remember her face encased in steel already flaking off one shred of dust. They could not remember what she wore the dresses looked alike drab gray dull long unfashionably long they would have liked it if she'd fixed herself up just once the way she was now in a dress bought for the eldest's wedding October first. You have seen to it she's not going to the wedding she's not getting her house in town she never got the apples picked or had a trip to Paris they were taking after all these years they were oh yes in spring she always liked it then she didn't want to see the water come.

Eli Wetherill clasped his hands and dropped his head as if to pray. It's better today Mary. A man came to see me passing through smashed his finger in the car door letting a kid out to pee. Nearly forgot how good I am at setting bones it's been so long three years in fact I could do it in my sleep I don't sleep much the nights are so long the loneliness gets to you I read in bed and watch TV cleaned out the basement it's time I pasted the old pictures in and sold the goddamn furniture you like so well. Last week I was going to plant some bulbs and then remembered there's no time left to plant or do anything except get ready the dam is started you know Mary it's going to cover this place all but the cemetery on the mountain the road is getting moved to where we always sat and watched the town at night and lights reminded you of diamonds you never got from me I only gave you heartaches in the fall it always was my restless time having to do with the winter coming on cold and endless white a long fear spelled out what I'd hoped to be.

What could be said now to Nate Houghton looking his way with hatred? I did the best I could after all you can't keep somebody alive who doesn't want to live who's plain wore out and feeling useless. She used to say she was tired she used to try and find some way to do some little thing to make you notice her you treated her like shit. She loved you yes well you'll never know she died with it all locked up inside that was the way she was. I know. I alone know the way it was with her seven babies ugly as skinned rabbits three would have died but for me. I felt good each time I yanked one out her hole I said you hairless wonder you had no choice from the prick to the fifth finger dilation it wasn't up to you so breathe and know I could have saved you from learning what you'll eventually know it's harder going out than coming in. Except when the choice is yours you screwdeathfategodfutilityrealityballs remember when I lost my head and said lay open for me Rose and she did. The brood mare with a good stud in her never moves or cries out she takes it cold impassive silent not mistaking instinct for passion. The only reason she kept on having children was so that the instant one of them came out of her she could look it in the eye and say here is the youngest person on the earth.

The youngest was the hardest to get born she never said if he was mine or not. He has a cleft in his chin like me but looks berserk around the eyes like Nate so maybe oh hell they grow up hard in Yellow Bird.

The life of a man and the life of a town are as one the town's mistakes are a man's mistakes the glories of a town are the accomplishments of a man and the accomplishments of a man are reflected in his town and that is why the death of Yellow Bird does not mean much nobody to mourn for it like they sit and mourn for Rose Houghton a poor soul at best and would we look and feel so shabby had poor Rose got her name in lights or won the Miss America contest or revolutionized the world of sport no in that case her death the town's death would get written up in *Time* magazine and become a permanent record and what we were would grow even better with time a hundred years would give us a distinction we could have earned with one significant citizen who made it big.

Well nobody ever did not one not even Casey Stubbs who fell off an ocean liner and was adrift for two whole days before they picked him up and he was famous for a couple weeks and even got to meet the president. No we shall not be remembered for him or for Daggett the only man in history to carve God's face in a granite cliff some thirty feet in height took him half his life and he was on the verge of fame and fortune there in forty-two when somebody from the newspapers came and wrote him up as having carved a likeness of Adolf Hitler in the Colorado hills and so it was mysteriously blown up. No we shall not be remembered for him or for any act of nature like the one that helped Pompeii along if only the mountain had fallen down or the town been swallowed up in a San Francisco earthquake we would have gone down in history but now we are just going down you cannot even find us on the map they just forgot that's all.

Eli Wetherill was wholly himself on that bright September morning listening to the Reverend Lacey trying to sound sincere as he stood above the gleaming container for Rose Houghton's worn-out remains the minister's little pig eyes were aimed at the peeling patched-up ceiling last repaired by a jobless one-legged carpenter drunk with cheap Chianti wine. The doctor turned his head and observed the firm profile of Matt Brittman the best male specimen he'd ever run across he was the one person left in Yellow Bird with something to live for only one pasture of his ranch was going under water the rest would continue to be a credit to a man whose whole life had been

26

pretty much the way he wanted it he'd been able to call his shots he'd built a minor empire with nothing but his sweat he'd held on to himself when things got rough had not let the people get to him the way the doctor had. Matt Brittman was too much of a man for that and the doctor felt suddenly ashamed realizing the difference between himself and his friend of thirty years one was a failure and one was not one was weak and one was not one had something to look forward to and one did not.

When you got right down to it there was only one thing he could do with his life and that was to go on living it and only one thing he could do for the town and that was to stay with it till it died. When he got back to the silent empty office he would have nothing to do no patients to see there was a time when the waiting room was full the telephone was ringing and there was one emergency per hour to keep him in the throbbing split-guts two-fisted world that once was Yellow Bird. But no more. Rinsing his mouth in the lavatory after steadying himself with the bourbon he always saw the town and not himself reflected in the mirror. You have weathered badly and what has rotted out was not essential age becomes you but the years have not been kind you are sagging in the middle wrinkled deaf and blind out of step and don't give a damn the time you knew is long since past and you must exit as graceful as you can not listen to what they say about you kind of quaint you are a curiosity a symbol that is not important well if the end brings you out all right what is said against you won't amount to anything as Abraham Lincoln said.

Matt Brittman was dreadfully out of place in church had been there only twice before once when he buried his father the other when Eli Wetherill had married Mary Walsh a stuckup Boston girl whose nose remained forever in the air and her feet planted so solid you could not budge her opinion and her opinion was that everything connected with Yellow Bird was bad including Eli and himself. They raised a lot of hell in those days Eli fresh out of medical school and practicing in the hospital on the hill while he himself was trying to fulfill all that his father had failed to do making a promise that the land would not slip through his hands as long as he drew breath and there it was at last all that he had ever hoped to become and looking around he saw that it was a great deal more than any one of them had accomplished well you could not blame them now for not being what they never were and never promised to be. They were honest hardworking people like his father Big John a wrangler who came north from Oklahoma in hopes of buying a little land right after the First World War and had hired on at the very same ranch that Matt Brittman now owned without a cent against it. Big John had hired on and saved and married a good woman and they had lived for years in a little house without electricity or running water and all the while Big John had kept on hoping. One hope for every dollar saved was what he said and finally there it was enough to buy a couple thousand acres and a couple hundred head the money banked a dollar at a time over twelve long and dismal years.

In twenty-nine the dream had died Britt was seven at the time and it was the first time he'd seen his father cry well he hadn't jumped out of any window the way some men did nor took a gun to his head Big John just picked himself up and went at it all over again and what got him this time was not the banks failing nor himself failing for lack of trying it was his health that quit the first year Matt Brittman went off to agricultural school. And it had been Eli Wetherill who'd broken the news Eli Wetherill some eight years older than himself and not his childhood friend Eli Wetherill who had covered his father's debts and put bread on his mother's table Eli Wetherill who had begged him not to marry Billy Deere the rich young Texas girl who summered in Yellow Bird and was sought after by every young man from Canada to Mexico she fancied him above all the rest and so the summer he turned twenty-two he made the only mistake of his life he married a woman for the sake of her money and it was enough to get him started.

She would have bought him the manicured lush showplace Zapata ranch ten miles out from town but for some reason she did not understand he bought the rundown ranch he had been born on all overgrazed and cursed with crossbred cattle that did not bring a price it was a poor man's ranch she said a Texan would have traded it off for a yellow dog well he had his reasons and she never understood not once in the five years she stayed married to him then ran off with a rodeo cowboy leaving him a four-year-old who wet his pants and sucked his thumb and cried for two whole months for his no-good mama.

Well Harley had grown up more or less on his own had gone to college and done his duty with Uncle Sam and had toured Europe for the summer and was ready to come back and settle down and that was the one thing that kept Matt Brittman whole the kid coming back and falling into what had taken him twenty-eight years to build up. The land was better than he'd found it he was a man of considerable wealth yet that was not it at all the value of the land and the animals was strictly in itself and each year he found himself growing deeper into it shutting out all that displeased him he was an extension of the land and subject to the same forces that shaped it he had no time for sentiment with the cattle they either measured up to the standards he had set for them or else he marked them for slaughter no he was not brutal he was practical and he had had a goal and reached it there was no more to be attained either with the land or the cattle and maybe with himself as well.

As he squirmed uncomfortably in the oaken seat noticing that Eli Wetherill was beginning to fall asleep and that the faces of the people were old and worn and tired and that the Reverend Lacey was actually picking his nose he felt that his life had not turned out exactly as he'd wished it and it had to do with women. Oh he'd had plenty enough in twenty years had gone off in search of a mother for Harley a couple of times and found that all of them were stupid or ugly or after his money and so he always fled contenting himself during the last couple of years with an occasional out-of-town bang at the cattlemen's conventions where the wives flocked around him and tried to seduce him but what he called it was an intellectual massage of the genitals it didn't mean a thing and so the kid was really all he had and he'd been without him six years now and what he wanted was to set things straight between them and somehow fix up the gulf that separated them that was what he wished with all his heart wished it because he had some notion he was not going to last had it especially when the winter wind was howling and he tossed in his bed alone feeling that nature was too much with him and he had no human contact.

At forty-seven he was afraid that his place and time were nearly done that the range cattle business as he had known it had another thirty years to go and then would vanish into the nostalgia of all those things that were no longer necessary in the West fur trapping longhorns boom towns gold cattle barons buffalo Indians steam locomotives and squatters' rights. His memory was crowded with line camps and cattle drives blizzards and drought plugging fences and pulling calves getting up with the sun and going to bed with it going almost broke and finally making it. The wind always stayed within his ears the taste of salt from his sweat was always on his lips a bit of the earth was always beneath his fingernails and the preservation of his time was always with him in the form of what he hoped to leave. The weather cracked along with his bones and if he believed in anything it was that he had done right. And wished he had more time. A new urgency possessed him and he had waked to it every morning for a year and found himself listening to the ticking of the clock paced against the ticking of his heart and thus he began to think in terms of how long he might have the sound to listen to and how long he could keep his cattle good and nonskid soles on his shoes for the downhill plunge.

He had had enough of church and buzzing flies coughing women and chirping ministers he had an urge to get back to the ranch and then to check his mail to see if there was any word from Harley and maybe drive to Coronado and cure this spell of loneliness he could not sit still for very long and so he nudged Eli who sprang to life and adjusted his spectacles his face was very red and he smelled of last night's bourbon but Matt Brittman had long since ceased to notice. He whispered in his ear I'm cutting out can't stand this circus want to come along?

The doctor did not answer right away his bleary eyes were on a young slim girl tiptoeing down the aisle to the last remaining seat two rows ahead and as she made her way the length of the church a low murmur went through the crowd. Even the Houghtons looked around and the minister cleared his throat the old women lifted their prayer books high enough to whisper it's her Meridian Muldoon the nigger lover you wouldn't think she'd have the nerve lookit the way she walks once a you-know-what always a you-know—what's she doing here she was in Denver last I heard yeah well maybe they run her out like we did.

—Britt said Eli with a quiver of excitement it's the Muldoon girl ain't she growed up pretty?

The rancher was also watching Meridian Muldoon and remembering how he'd lifted her on his own horse when she was barely old enough to walk a long time ago he thought it was about the year he got rid of Billy Deere in forty-eight was she going on twenty-five no it couldn't be not her after nigh on ten years well she hadn't changed she had the same blond hair the color of fresh oats and skin that kind of glistened like it was always wet and she was forever chasing Harley down with her quarterhorse it was good in the old days with Marcus Muldoon owning the adjoining ranch drinking up a quart of whiskey every other day damn good in fact until Marcus had tried to get the bank to call his loan had sued him over water rights and then had taken an old Brahma bull and turned him in with Matt Brittman's registered Hereford heifers just once. Well he'd bided his time and then he'd got him where it really hurt he took after Frieda Muldoon who whaled with every man in town

31

Meridian was her mother's image all right he wondered what else she was and what had brought her back his hands were sweating and he could not take his eyes from her slender figure turned part way toward him as her high-heeled shoes stopped clicking on the floor and she stood next to Josie Stringer and tried to climb across that vast unmoving shape.

—Eli old man said Britt that is one hell of a powerful ass.

Grotesque shrill and pompous Reverend George Washington Lacey went on *all flesh is not the same flesh but there is one kind of flesh of men another flesh of beasts another of fishes and another of birds*

Britt let out his breath so hard that it stirred the feather on the hat of Cora Wagner who had once danced in a vaudeville show then married a miner and had six kids all grown and gone she had for company half a hundred cats in a house that had not had its windows open since 1945 the year she believed the atomic bomb had sent unknown poisons into the air kept out only by living in as tight a vacuum as one could create.

—Behave yourself Britt she's probably just passing through

the resurrection of the dead is sown in corruption is raised in incorruption

—Remember Frieda Eli remember how she looked.

the first man is of the earth earthy

—Shut up Britt.

—No Eli I ain't going to shut up.

O death where is thy sting?

Meridian Muldoon wished she had not come to Rose Houghton's funeral. It was stupid to sit there and listen to that dreary old man go on and on and watch the Houghton family shed its tears and recognize all the old faces she had never liked much to begin with. It was just that Rose Houghton had practically raised her and it was in her father's house that Nate Houghton had nearly lost his leg when the chain saw went through it while chopping wood in the backyard and Eli Wetherill had worked three days to save it and finally did but Nate was forever crippled and blamed the doctor for his misfortune not once admitting that without the doctor's skill he'd have been an amputee. Well that was the way they were in that town and she had grown up with it and despised it and when she was forced to leave at fifteen she was liberated and did not come back for almost ten years would not be there now except for the fact that she needed the money and needed to prove herself.

She had more or less gone dry she had not written a good thing in a year she had once been good and wasn't anymore you could just lose whatever talent you had and maybe never get it back well there was a chance thanks to Mike McAdoo who ran the Denver paper he said get in there kid and give us a couple yarns on how a small town dies you grew up in Yellow Bird didn't you kid well it's no sweat then you know the mob and morals just get the goddamn punctuation straight the trouble with you is you have never learned to write a sentence in the English language it's like a nonstop dictionary too bad Mike I'll try but Jesus you can't imagine what a place it is I mean nobody's human the place is broken down I'm glad it's going to die Mike there's not one reason to keep it alive. Not one reason Meridian? No not one go on up there anyway kid I'll give you a couple weeks goddamn it Mike it just won't work I hate that shitty Yellow Bird I just can't go back what did you do there kid oh nothing Mike it's what they did to me you've got till the first of the month I'm sorry kid but this is the last chance I can give you.

She climbed over the feet of Josie Stringer the apelady who ran the hotel and the feet of Edgar Purvis the frail and false-teethed principal who made a move as if to kick her in the shins and over the feet of the Coyote the crazy gold miner still wearing his metal helmet and carrying a lunchbox and a transistor radio and she saw the rows of faces frowning knit together brows straightlined above eyes that never saw beyond Yellow Bird's horizon and she knew what they were thinking that ten years before she had been caught in this very church screwing

33

with Squash Jenkins the son of the coal-black janitor from Purvis' old school. And that was just too bad. She would have a time of it with them she would not be able to write anything because there was nothing to write about who gives a shit if you all drown and there is the purple principal and red-eyed Doctor Wetherill poor man and oh my god Matt Brittman is still handsome but cold as ice look at them Mike McAdoo you yourself could not write one decent line.

Sitting there in that hot and stuffy church she needed a drink more than anything yes a drink was what she needed and so she climbed back over the feet again and caught their little sighs of irritation and felt the heads turning as the warty little preacher was winding up his prayers and it was time for the old reed organ to get cranked up and the wailing to begin and for a hundred pairs of eyes to give her killing looks oh to hell with them and she half ran through the unhinged door still faint with paint fuck you in loving memory of Albert G. Larson 1881–1929 rest in rags and rotting wood both now and evermore amen.

The sunlight blinded her and she fumbled in her purse for her sunglasses Jesus she said Jesus what a dump. And the ugly little wood and shingled houses all in rows along the dusty half-deserted streets had never looked more ugly to her nor had they ever reminded her more of where she came from and what she had finally become. And then she felt a hand on her waist and there was Matt Brittman with a cigarette pointed in her direction and saying hello girl it was me that first gave you one of these remember?

—Hello Britt she said and what struck her was that he was more of a giant than she remembered. He was at least six and a half feet tall with shoulders like a bull and she could see the hairs on his chest sticking out of his shirt and the sunlight striking his burnished face where the whiskers were beginning to poke out even though he had just shaved.

—What brings you back he said leaning against somebody's pickup as if it were a fence.

34

—Nothing much she said letting out the smoke just came to have a look the old house is still standing thought I'd put up there for a week or so.

—That dump's not fit to live in girl come on out to the ranch Harley'll be home in a couple days you two can have a reunion.

The smell of him standing so close was like raw meat and the way a saddle sweats from a man's muscle-bending thighs encased in Levi's he was a hunk of man by God yet somehow wholly animal and repugnant to a woman. Oh no thanks Britt she said I have some things to do around the house before they tear it down mother wants some things out of there guess you've seen my brother he comes up every year from Texas.

—I've seen him said Britt sharply where's Marcus?

—In hell or somewhere in Wyoming.

—Figured.

—He's a bastard Britt I haven't seen him in five years and never will I found out what he did to you my God I never knew.

—We did a lot to each other reckon he hates me just as much as I hate him but a man's got to bury his hate sooner or later else it eats him up.

He looked at her sharply and saw she was tanned and healthy and beautiful and he had an urge to run his fingers down her arms she was all grown up now he could remember the time she rode through town naked on a horse like Lady Godiva she was about thirteen and wild she also loaded up her gun and took out after a man from Pennsylvania who'd shot her thoroughbred having mistaken him for a deer. And she'd winged him in the shoulder when she could have plugged him through the heart. There was the time she took her baby cousin and tied him to the railroad tracks because he would not shut up and the time she drove her father's pickup through Del Branson's herd of bulls because he had not kept a promise to her father to sell him two sections of grazing land. She was all grown up before she ever learned geography and algebra and how to

35

dissect a frog but what she learned instead had always seemed to him more suited to her kind.

—What have you been doing all these years Britt she said pleasantly the smoke curling around her young and beautiful face the way it would before a campfire he said to himself feeling powerfully drawn yet knowing he was a fool.

He scraped his boots in the dust and sucked his teeth oh you know girl the usual stuff a cowboy does to stay alive you breed and calve and brand and ship and hope to god the bottom of the market don't fall out.

—I thought you would have remarried by now she said avoiding his startling blue eyes and oh she had felt rape with the eyes before and she knew she had him sweating if not hard on and it pleased her to know she could do it to him like a stud he was you could tell from the way he pranced and shook his head and from the way he could not keep his legs still and she had seen it in animals and now in him and she laughed inwardly knowing he was different from all the rest he was crossbred with his cattle a man who now as when she knew him last resisted all human contact. And yet he was so handsome so vital and alive how could a man look like that and be so cold inside?

—Remarried he said forcing a laugh what the hell do I need with that?

—Oh I imagine it gets pretty lonely.

—Lonely he said pushing his Stetson back on his head what's that and even as he spoke the lie he felt it coming on as it so often did a thing he could not control a pure and simple longing to belong a terrible need to be held like some baby sucking milk and he closed his eyes and remembered the dark of twenty years well he had beat that down along with everything else and he would not yield now not after this long a time.

—Don't you ever need company Britt she said her fine blond hair blowing across her face and he had to hide his hands behind his back to keep from touching it and he made himself move away from her the minute he became aware that her

36

perfume was not like the smells he was accustomed to.

—The trouble with the world he said is that it says you ain't normal if you choose to live alone you got to have company when you take a crap excuse me girl but that is what it comes to.

She threw back her head and laughed I know what you mean but still I wonder if you haven't missed something.

—Like what?

—Oh getting to know a person.

—Bad medicine he said feeling the need to lie down.

—Coming back here she said looking around at the half-empty silent town gives me the creeps I realize it was all some tremendous act we played not letting go just putting one foot in front of the other and I grew up thinking it was best to stay your distance.

—Saves a powerful lot of trouble he said looking now at her dress and how tight it was across her breasts and she was not very big a cow with an udder like that would have to get the axe.

—You remember Squash she said yeah the whole town does well he heard the rhythm see he listened to a voice which said just be.

—Squash he said looking away to the mountain and feeling a lump rise in his throat girl that was the one mistake you ought not to have made a nigger yet.

—Oh Britt she said throwing up her small hands I wouldn't have cared if he was purple.

—Goddamn it Meridian I know you're a rebel and all that but there's some things you just don't do.

She looked him square in the eye and he felt himself tremble and he stuffed his hands in his pockets oh to ball her on the run like Worthington his prize bull who could service twenty heifers in an hour if he had a notion.

—Like what she said defiantly.

—Well that thing you did sure caused a lot of grief.

37

—Because Yellow Bird is so strait-laced evil bigoted backward inbred puritanical and I raised hell.

—That you did and what did it prove he said suddenly realizing that the pain was starting again as it had a habit of doing these many months and he had to get away and hide himself so she would not think him weak.

—Prove she said incredulously prove that I am better than they are.

The pain was tearing suddenly at his middle and he resisted the impulse to take hold of himself and push it back he would not give in not now presenting himself to this lovely vision not now with the sun at his back and so much to be done he would just ignore it and pretend.

—Maybe not he said in a voice that startled her maybe you're just the same and she thought she heard him groan.

—If I thought that she said I'd put a bullet through my head.

Pain and desire and loneliness and fear and sweat and pure grief were all around him and he saw himself coming through a tunnel the voice was not really his any more than his body was really his and he wanted her and did not want her wished for human contact and longed to be in his bed alone screamed out to be noticed and desired to fade into the rock and what was happening to him at the age of forty-seven a stupid fool wishing he could telescope his life into one brief and happy moment. And did not know how to begin.

—The cattle he said at last I have got to go and see about the cattle.

—I want to see you Britt come up for dinner tomorrow night.

—Oh no Meridian he said I can't do that.

—Why not?

—The cattle he said uneasily the cattle—

—Britt she said her eyes on fire her hands placed on her hips are you some kind of talking bull?

38

—No he said turning crimson.

—Then come for dinner Britt.

—No.

—Well I'll come to your place then

—Oh no it's all a mess.

She shook her head so I'll clean it up.

—Ah the end of a day I'm really pooped I ah—

—I'll come at noon.

He was trembling and trying not to his heart was pounding and everything in him ached for this lovely slender girl and yet he heard himself say and was disgusted you will not come at all.

—Oh she said coldly watching the way his face muscles quivered and how he had to stuff his hands in his pockets to keep them from shaking poor Britt what else do you love besides yourself and dead things?

He turned on his heel and walked rapidly to the truck hoping his legs would carry him and that the wave of pain and nausea would not knock him flat as it had before in the privacy of his own home and he had to watch himself in public and not go out anymore than he had to or else someone would call him weak. Weak. And up against a thing he could not control. And was losing ground daily. The irony was he had never felt more wholly human than in those last few weeks human and vulnerable and with a physical ache to fit into somebody's lifetime puzzle. Well he had chosen the way a long time ago chosen it over human alternatives was stuck with it and realized it was just too late. He would get through the best way he could and give up wishing for what he had no right or reason to possess. The land would as always fulfill all he allowed himself to desire.

Meridian watched his truck disappear in a cloud of dust no Matt Brittman had not changed and never would he was as human as a tree stump small wonder that Billy Deere had run off and Harley grew up like a field mouse shivering in the wind small wonder that a physical attraction was the limit of her response and she had made a fool of herself with men like that a time or two before they had taken from her pure sexual gratification nothing more was possible within a framework of utter steel and she wondered as she walked along Yellow Bird's sad and empty streets what it was that prevented a human being from reaching out and letting himself fall toward another well you would get hurt if you did hurt as she had been so often in the past. It hadn't been so bad at first the search for love had led her up some pretty interesting alleys and she had learned you never really found it even when you did and so she had buried what others called sentiment and what she called sensitivity well it was gone all right and she had been numb for some years now. And blamed it all on Yellow Bird.

Crooked streets potholed dogshitted pushed up in the middle like somebody trying to get out cracked curbs split sidewalks bricked by a mason named Hugo who laid them end to end in Yellow Bird the graffiti goes like this Ida and Bill forever '48 fuck you D.U. '54 Jack was here. Oh you cornhusked shabby shacks of a hopeless few deserted now the roof caved in a sheet of flowered wallpaper blowing in the wind the porch rocker rocking you can almost see the old man smoking his pipe and reading a newspaper and he was going to plant a potato patch but didn't you see they never did anything but talk and they would have done better if only if only if only . . .

Just look at what they have left behind the artifacts of Yellow Bird tell what they missed and why. A rusted automobile. A washing machine that never got fixed. A Sears Roebuck catalogue 1959 they never ordered from just looked at the pictures. A baseball glove. A wagon with wooden wheels. A bathtub with a hole in it. One rubber overshoe. A miner's cap. One wool stocking. A scrub board. Rusted metal bedsprings. The head of a kewpie doll. A coal-burning stove minus one leg. A boot with a hunk of rubber tire for a sole. A framed picture of the Last Supper. A stack of assay sheets. An ore bucket and the discarded pathetic hunks of machinery torn apart. And the melting snow from an early storm drips off corrugated metal roofs into a wash bucket plink plink plunk the simple outdated love song of a town that never knew itself and didn't care. Not quaint or pretty or important in a single way unredeemed by the name of a famous man we walked in the shadow of the better gold camps the ones that had tradition and reputation even if it's bad but us we lived in solitary indifference for so many years it was like eternal senility. And now it has to die. Well good. It never ought to have been born in the first place and I wish to God I could have come from Santa Fe or Cripple Creek or even Leadville spunk guts quality that's what they say if you come from there but Yellow Bird? Isn't that some two-bit burg that nobody ever heard of? And aren't they going to tear it down and build a reservoir? Well at least some good is coming from that horseshit hamlet after all.

She walked faster now closing her eyes to the ruination around her the memories of her early uneasy years when the place at least had a beating heart came back like the pages of a bad book she never meant to read again and she choked on every word she could remember every word and every face every mundane life and it was not much different except now it was near death. She did not pity it nor wish its life to be saved looking over her shoulder as she wandered down toward the river she felt only a sense of relief that she did not have to come back there anymore. The grasshoppers stirred the grass in the fields the wind blew her hair in her face and raised the dust all along the road where few cars came or went. Up the hill toward town the ghosts had already set in but the wash was still on the line.

3

To be forgotten is to be lost and what is lost surely becomes forgotten we reckon a tombstone won't do Rose any good either said the four old gravediggers piercing the earth with their shovels brought from home the handles worn smooth by their fathers who had labored underground and did not see the light of day except on Sundays the shovel tips were all bent and rusted and caked with what ought not to have been disturbed the unwilling mountain forced to yield against its will to so many shovels and so many picks and so many drills and so many sticks of dynamite you couldn't count it all. If you did to a man what you did to a mountain he'd be a hollow corpse and you'd get out the shovel again and pry open a hole in the mountain for a different purpose and the mountain would not mind so much if you laid a man to rest within it somehow that was right and just. If anybody else wants to get buried here they better hurry up and die the government says nobody can be buried here after October on account of keeping the records straight about who lies here and who doesn't a list is going to be sent clear back to Washington an honor roll of dead looking out over the goddamn reservoir a few years hence one grave to face another forever and ever as long as the mountain stays put and the river keeps on flowing maybe they will rig up something to show where we buried our dead a sign with lights on it or one of them historical markers along the road.

And what makes you think we are so important is there a man buried here whose name got written down in any book none except Saunders who in eighty-nine was launched in a gas balloon soon after announcing he was going to fly to California on the prevailing wind and got blown north instead landing on the railroad track where the noon express cut him right in two. You'd think they'd want to make some sort of park for all the kids wiped out in the typhoid epidemic of ninety-four and buried right over there alongside the stream wooden markers mostly that you can't hardly read no more William Abbott Gray October 11 1893–1894 we loved him. And look some of the iron fences around the graves are falling down and the markers have fallen into the weeds and some are busted even marble don't last it seems and see how many there are with nothing at all to mark them just a little lump in the earth growed over with flowers I buried my mother someplace up here in thirty-one can't find the marker no more me and Clyde carved it ourselves from a rock well she knows where she's at my mother does even if we have forgot. The winter is just too hard it pushes down on what is dead and what ain't.

A hunnerd years or so and you won't hardly be able to tell where any of it was who will look after the cemetery? Nobody.

Somebody has always looked after a cemetery yeah well not in a town that died a town that ain't even on the map hell could you go and find where Fossil was or Dime Box or Hangman's Tree they all started up not far from here once upon a time and died sooner than expected now there is only their dust blowing up the canyon. Not only are they missing but their cemeteries as well covered with nature's grief they are buried above and below. It's as simple as that. Makes you stop and wonder why a man gets born in the first place. And the gravediggers spit into the palms of their hands and made an effort to turn over the earth a little more carefully now that they understood what life was all about.

The sun hot at ten A.M. bathed the old church steeple in luminous rays the breeze stirred the dust in little clouds around the shoes of the pallbearers gently shoving her feet into the butcher's truck which bore a faded bumper sticker we eat Colorado beef not LBJ baloney. Nate Houghton came limping out followed by his children he passed by the doctor his hat clenched in his hands his face bloated with grief and said in a low voice you son-of-a-bitch I'll kill you. Then he bowed his head and accepted the condolences of those who knew and loved a simple gentle woman born and raised in Yellow Bird who like the rest did not want to go but offered no resistance because such was not the nature of the woman or the town she was in a way like the pensioners some of whom it was said died on purpose rather than be made to leave the ugly little town in which they had been planted and had become one with. The doctor shook his head and turned to Edgar Purvis who with a smile of satisfaction said did you see Meridian Muldoon Eli she had the nerve to come back.

—She has a right to come back said Eli watching Houghton drive off with his wife's coffin in Fred Sweeney's butcher truck.

—Well yes but you wouldn't think she'd have the nerve.

—It was a long time ago Edgar you might just as well forget.

—Forget her and that nigger boy well I just won't forget

and neither will the rest of us we'll make things tough for that Muldoon bitch just like her father bad blood never runs its course.

—Whatever business she's got here is of no concern to you or them.

Edgar Purvis went away pouting and among the crowd getting into automobiles to follow the surrogate hearse to the cemetery on the mountain there was the whispering of voices and the doctor knew what the whispering was about and he wished Meridian Muldoon had not come back. They would not be kind and he had no control over them anymore they had turned to stone. Well that was the way things went in that town and in all towns he guessed where people owed so much to you that they paid you back in hatred or indifference or worse yet with deprecation once they saw you were going down after you had been up so long. They spoke to him in patronizing tones they were careful to leave him out of all poker games dinner parties and fishing trips they borrowed money from him and knew he would not ask to get it back they took their ailments to the clinic in Coronado and left him with nothing to practice medicine on. He was a mirror of their own decay and they knew it because as his mother had told him long ago he would never get wise to himself and as his father told him long ago he was one of those persons to be forever sandwiched between two loaves of life what he wanted to be and what he had no hope to become.

They were drawing to a close the town and himself and while the town's death was physical his was of a different nature. He began to realize it on that early September morning at nearly the same moment that the mounds of raw earth were carefully heaped on top of Rose Houghton's gleaming crate and the four old gravediggers sat down for a beer under the aspen trees their shovels stuck in the ground beside the sprays of plastic forget-me-nots. He felt tired and no good anymore he tried to remember the exact cause of Rose's death and could not he had difficulty recalling the symptoms of ordinary ailments of a community exposed not so much to disease as to discomfort you could not live with ease at nine thousand feet where there were just two seasons nine months of winter and three of reality no you could not accept the isolation the winter sun disappearing at two in the afternoon the hellish roar of avalanches at night that made you sit upright in bed and breathe a little harder. The altitude was accountable for nearly everything from taking one drink and going down for the count to getting pregnant regardless of precautions you could blame the altitude if your business failed or if you got fever blisters skin cancer an enlarged heart worn-out lungs baldness in women and nosebleeds in the young.

But he was no longer sure how to treat these simple things no not positively for sure. He was slipping had slipped and he wished for a test to prove to himself he could still function as a doctor. He had set a pretty good fracture the day before. And diagnosed infectious hepatitis in the man from the Bureau of Reclamation. And spayed Gus Jones's dog for free. Oh well those were not real tests real challenges to his mind and hands and training as a man to heal the sick which was what in his lucid moments he believed himself to be. There was however another side which was blank and cold and strange it had to be contained and brought to heel and must not be shown to the people who still had confidence in him. Like Purvis. Like Josie. Like Matt Brittman. And he knew he would be himself again if he put his whole mind to it and beat back this thing which seemed to latch onto his balls that morning. He must not lose hold must not seem to falter or look unwise or presume upon their friendship or seem anxious about himself. All this he understood and failed to act upon there lurked within him the beginning of despair a word he would not have used but would have named it Black Ass a slow yet terminal case.

—Damned dog in the doorway somebody ought to give it a kick or else a home you can't expect people to fight their way into this saloon said Eli to Josie Stringer who was frying a couple of frozen T-bones on the grill behind the bar at the Yellow Bird Hotel.

—Susie's got as much right as you doc to lay where she wants. She's a human breathing thing like you I can't see no difference but she's got four legs and you got three is all.

He laughed sloshed down the beer which Josie set in front of him a luncheon appetizer going on thirty years. He raised his eyes to the crack in the ceiling which was growing longer every year curling like a serpent's tongue through the grease accumulated from minute to minute day to day month to month year to year. That was a symbol of Josie Stringer's life a serpent in the grease. No that's not it at all. This is where we come to reassure ourselves there's still contact before we go out the door to God knows where. That all-important contact with Josie Stringer and the Yellow Bird Hotel we don't have to go to church have meetings clubs parties games love affairs or war the Yellow Bird saloon is where we come to verify God in overloaded flypaper twisted neon rusted linoleum cracked cups beatup cowboy hats and manured boots the smell of leather coffee beer bacon grease men's sweat undeodorized Josie's good humor never failing. We are alive as long as we remember this time and place and take it with us inscribed on our foreheads in her we trust.

To look at her you would have thought she was part rhinoceros the way her head hung forward on a very heavy neck a solid rump and legs as thick at the thighs as at the ankles below which her feet were encased in rounded shoes just like a pair of hooves. Her hair had turned gray in the last few years since her husband died and she wore it in a braid held fast to her head by a row of heavy-duty paper clips going from her shoulders to her crown. She stood barely five feet tall a bulky solid hulk and when she walked it reminded him of an armored division moving across a battleground. But her face was sweet. Two big dots of red stood out on her cheeks her eyes were hot marbles and she had lips of equal size. His heart beat fast at the familiar sight of her fanny pushing shut the silver drawer he whistled and said somebody's got the hots for you kiddo.

—Oh doc she said waving a banged-up spatula the awfulest thing happened to my baby. You want to see the corpus delicti? She wiped her hands on her apron and came over to the table.

—Poor little Susie she almost died the vet said he don't know how she ever carried them around so long. She shook the plastic medicine bottle and dumped out the gallstones all in a heap around his beer glass. Four bucks each I never thought I'd spend it on a dog they get to you like people only worse because they can't talk I would have known if she'd only of talked. She shrugged gathered up the dachshund's gallstones tucked the bottle in her pocket and went back to the grill where the T-bones sizzled.

—Two T-bones medium well what you want doc you know yet you been reading the menu like it was the medical journal. Hello Mister Purvis haven't seen you since Labor Day sick or something?

The principal came in and sat down opposite Eli shook his head topped now not by the magnificent black patch of yester-year but by a blob of white which gave him the appearance of having just been squirted by whipped cream from an aerosol can.

—I am suffering from diverticulosis said Purvis plaintively drawing in his cheeks to make himself look gaunt.

—That so said Josie molding the hamburger patties well I expect you'll survive it somehow what do you want to eat?

—Nothing fried my gall bladder tells me just toast and a little marmalade I brought my own teabag Josie so just hot water please.

—How's the stew said Eli studying the menu the typed words did not seem to register.

—Terrible doc you had it yesterday you ought to know it's bad.

—Fry me a steak then Josie there's nothing wrong with my gall bladder or the other bladder either so give me another beer. One for you Purvis?

—I don't think so said Purvis drinking his tea with the spoon in the cup alcohol gives me a rush. He folded his arms across his chest and leaned back in the chair appraising the man across from him. His voice was like ice. By the way Eli you were not in your office yesterday afternoon I came by for the Erythrocin I always keep on hand you promised to give me some you weren't even there and it said on the door you would be well where were you as if I didn't know?

The doctor was used to him by now. You don't blame a man for what he lives by or for what he can't live by. He wished he'd mastered that fact of life while there was still time.

—That reminds me Purvis when are you coming in for a blood test?

—For my diabetes oh yes well Eli I was down in Coronado the other day and had it done routine you know I didn't think you had the time Eli you are so terribly busy. The principal smiled with satisfaction and picked his nails with a fork. My nails not too bad too round the cuticles grow fast over the halfmoons the hands of a gentleman my auntie always said I could have been a concert pianist fondled only two tits in my life with these hands she said my nails were sharp making marks on fat soft flesh liver spots now I guess it's truly age coming on now oh God my hands are going along with my hair.

Eli Wetherill said nothing. He got up and touched Purvis on the shoulder took his empty glass behind the bar and helped himself to another beer noticing himself in the mirror he needed vitamin C yes and more rest yes and a good lay yes and to make up his mind about the future no. I could still pass for fifty if I'm careful I could get away with it another five years oh what the hell am I saving it for

Mary Mary Mary I miss you in the fall it was good in its way we toughed it out achieved a proper balance broken when I had to go to Denver to the hospital there to study hematology surgery cardiology what can you learn in Yellow Bird so far away from scientific thought you forget if you don't keep learning. But I was afraid to learn as if learning would lessen my impulses my uniqueness my certainty of the world as I wanted it she made me learn. From Rosemary in a brass bed on Downing Street twice a month or whenever I could get away it was so hard to lie to you to try and cover up even here in Yellow Bird where I laid them left and right you never knew you proud and haughty bitch I loved you in my way I just never knew you were so cold withdrawing from my prick like it was infected with the syph. Galina Galina Galina with tits like cement and a lovely vagina I said I never felt the likes of it not even the Mexican whore I nearly married three weeks straight up and down goddamn impotent lecher fifty-five and not a lay in six months I think I ought to go to Coronado and make a fool of myself one more time.

He grasped the glass remembering the firmness of her thighs Galina Jordan's thighs the slender legs spread out wishboned in the stirrups of the delivery room in the Yellow Bird Hospital white sheeted his hands wresting the tiny head wishing he'd taken it after six weeks the way he'd done before this time she wanted the child something of her own at last she said. She died after seeing it once a smile on her lovely lips she had birthed a wretched baby boy a five dollar baby the first of many born to the good-time girls up here I never had the heart to make them charity five bucks was all that stood between them and dignity five bucks was all they charged to make a man feel good I did the same for them else charged five dollars to abort.

And he had gone on practicing medicine though he was dead inside and remained that way with neither hope nor desire the five dollar babies were to him a symbol of his failure as well as a manifestation of an honest mistake by any woman who did not want a child or having produced one out of wedlock proved that reproduction was just one more bodily function. And he went on implanting his sperm in those well-trod vaginas turning out a bastard on occasion he never claimed a single one it was his belief he should not become involved.

—You could do a chest x-ray however said Purvis when Eli sat back down. Purvis frowned the man seemed distracted far away. It was becoming more and more obvious the doctor was not living in the world. I presume said Purvis making an effort to be humane that you are still interested in tb and emphysema and lung cancer not that I smoke or that the air is foul I just am near asphyxiation a good part of the time.

The doctor drained his glass his eyes remained fixed on the bubbles in the bottom he felt something pressing down on his head the place was hot he lowered his voice and said pleasantly Purvis you old faggot you think I'll get it wrong a blood test mixed with piss and tell you by Jesus screwed his mother you got cataracts up the ass.

Purvis did not smile his face turned crimson. He sat rigid in his chair chewing a pickle and accepting the cost of acid indigestion. Thirty years and he gets no better I mustn't think ill of him perfectly useless man no breeding background skill imponderable you wonder what would happen if the word got out I used to help him practice on a dog the night before an operation.

The café began to fill up as much as any place can which only seated twenty people there was the Coyote who hunted for his gold mine which was covered up when the uranium company blasted the entire hillside there was Dixie Pogue the only lady gold miner in Yellow Bird's existence all dressed in gold lamé there were the Chilson brothers former blacksmith and mucker respectively now in their eighties and nearly blind there was T.P. the so-called garage mechanic who once crossed the Arctic with a team of dogs there was the assayer Thompson who only came on Thursday the day that Josie didn't bake and there was Alice Crowley the teenaged fourth wife of Jason Crowley a burly ex-Marine who lived on unemployment checks

51

and veteran's compensation having been wounded in Korea his excuse for remaining constantly in bed and drunk was his fear of the field artillery alleviated by fucking off as often as he could.

Alice Crowley was chewing bubble gum her full dress just cleared her panties she tossed her matted head of hair and headed toward the doctor who had cut her mother open some seventeen years before to get the stubborn she-goat born. Purvis turned his face away she was a dropout from the eighth grade and wrote in lipstick on the girls' room mirror the prince can't prick. The prince. That was what they called him short for principal of course but he liked to think they had noted his princely characteristics a noble frame of mind. But no. They meant it as a joke. And he had ordered her to wash the mirror and not use lipstick anymore.

—Hiya doc she said blowing a bubble in his face. Hiya Mister Purvis.

—Hello Alice what's the good word?

—Nuthin's good doc you know that not in this dump. And she spit her wad into her fist and began to play with the salt shaker. Well shit doc I guess somethin's good I'm peegee going to lay the egg in November and I don't even show.

—That's real nice Alice reckon you ought to stop by the office soon.

—Hell doc I can't do that Jason says she stopped and ran her tongue around her mouth and stuffed the bubble gum back in.

—Jason says what Alice now out with it.

She squirmed and giggled and shoved her tiny pointed breasts out. Purvis shuddered and got up and said the Erythrocin Eli remember I'll be by after a while after a while Eli.

—I heard you Edgar I'm not deaf.

—I know I know said Purvis irritably it's just and he glanced at Alice who winked at him and roared when he blushed to the roots of his snow-white hair.

—All right Alice behave yourself said Eli when Purvis was gone. What did Jason say?

52

—Jason says a lot of crap you know I thought to quit him but guess I can't now well Jason says you are a walking bunsen burner all filled with alcohol so he says I gotta go to Coronado for the kid which is just shitty I'd take my chances with you but Jason says—

—To hell with Jason.

—I know to hell with Jason but I gotta do like he says.

—Now Alice I can fix it with Jason god knows he's stubborn like a mule but I knew him when.

—No soap doc Jason says you kilt the girl he had by Flossie and he's not likely to forget such.

—There are a lot of stories floating around this town pure bunk Alice pure bunk.

—You think I don't know that doc I told Jason everybody is jealous of the doc cause he knows more than we do and been to medical school and all such but Jason is a hard man well doc what I came to ask is this specialist Jason sent me to in Coronado he knows Jason is out of work and don't pay his bills so he says in order for me to get took care of he needs a hundred dollars down.

—A hundred dollars down?

—That's right doc and a hundred dollars more when the watermelon busts and we ain't got a hundred right now Jason says he's going to help build the dam he says—

—Never mind what he says Alice money talks. And he took out his checkbook and wrote her out the sum and she kissed him on the head and said I'll pay it back my own self doc right after I get on my feet again I'll get a job.

The doctor finished his beer oh forget it Alice I can make it tax deductible.

—Sure sure she said bouncing in her miniskirt tax deductible you won't be out a thing how come I didn't think of that well so long I'll bring it by whatever it is a horseshit monkey prob'ly.

Watching her go out the door he felt better she had been his first caesarian performed under the influence of alcohol and it had been one of his best deliveries and as fine a piece of surgery as he was ever again to do. But he had taken a risk and had known for seventeen years that by all rights Alice Crowley ought never to have been born alive nor should her mother have lived to become the manager of a motel in Elko Nevada. That's the way it went sometimes when luck was with you.

He was finishing his coffee and the thoughts of Alice Crowley and Galina Jordan were getting all mixed up in his mind and he could not remember which was which or what he had done to whom and he tried hard to recall whether Galina Jordan had had a baby by some acne-faced young kid one of those from town who thought Yellow Bird girls an easy fuck five dollars was connected with each of them a five dollar baby of one sort or another was what he kept delivering up to three months ago it was all that kept him in his tiny office those girls who came from as far away as Salt Lake and Albuquerque Phoenix and Cheyenne his notoriety was such that he thought of raising his fee to ten but that was not it at all no his was a service to mankind no matter what the law and the A.M.A. said but really there had to be an end there had to be a last five dollar baby and when there was he finally would be through finished and used up an end to all that he had become. So lost was he in his flaking thoughts that he did not notice the young man who had sat down across from him and was ordering lunch even though the other tables were empty. I beg your pardon said Eli taking off his glasses and wiping them on the shirt he had worn for three days straight.

—I beg yours the stranger said the folks at the bar don't look too friendly thought you might be different.

He liked the way the stranger looked he was no more than thirty with reddish hair and sideburns that came to the lobes of his ears he wore tight Levi's and cowboy boots his face was brown and open and not without some humor.

—Passing through said the doctor.

—Nope.

—Here to stay?

54

—For a while.

—A while is all we got this town has a nine-month gestation at which time it will be delivered by the Corps of Engineers who will subsequently kill it. I am Doctor Eli Wetherill and have diagnosed its ills going on thirty years.

—I see said the stranger studying the plastic-covered menu with a map of Colorado on the front.

—Nobody in his right mind would come and stay unless he likes to watch things die which ain't a pretty sight.

—No I don't imagine it will be. He sprinkled salt in his beer and ate his way through three hamburgers and a plate of fries and two bowls of soup.

The doctor watched him with interest. The stranger kept his eyes on his food and did not look up while he ate. Eli said you like to eat.

—Yep.

—Not ate for a while?

—Nope.

—You sure put away the food look here son where you say you're from?

—Didn't.

—Well you ain't from here.

—Yeah I am.

—I ain't never seen you around and I been here all my life.

—I was little when I left.

—That so how little?

—Don't know exactly come to find out.

The stranger wiped his mouth with a napkin and pushed back the chair and looked the doctor in the eye and said if you're a doc maybe you whacked my ass the minute I got born.

—Me said the doctor finding himself greatly agitated oh I doubt that Mister—

—Killeen Joe Killeen.

—Nobody by that name ever lived here said the doctor with great relief.

55

—Course not. See the orphanage named you A through Z Adams Baker Cooper Davis Evans Fisher and when they got to K it was Killeen and that was me had I waited a couple weeks I might have been Smith would have liked that better a hell of a lot easier to spell.

—What orphanage Killeen?

—This place in Denver St. Anne's Home they called it well it never was a home nor a house either the girls were kept separate from the boys forever and ever and ever.

—St. Anne's well a lot of people grew up there said the doctor feeling vaguely uneasy. He had to play it cool.

—You don't grow up there you grow up on your own you get fed and clothed and twice a week bathed and for conversation there is the rosary and the seven deadly sins and the Baltimore catechism number two who made us God made us why did God make us God made us to love the Russians and hate the Jews and Japs and Nazis until they became the Jewish the Japanese and the Germans whom we now love and hate those traitorous Russians see—

—Listen Killeen the doctor interrupted with fear in his craw what makes you think you came from here a lot of kids grew up at St. Anne's from all parts of the West.

—Well now look here doc said Killeen patiently and he took a piece of newspaper from his pocket and unfolded it and shoved it across the table at the doctor who saw it was a clipping from the Denver *Post* personal column it said anyone knowing of a male born May 20 1939 raised in St. Anne's Home Denver please contact R. Houghton Yellow Bird Colorado.

Joe Killeen bent over and the doctor caught the agony in his voice as he said I know I was born May 20 1939 in western Colorado well I just thought I'd mosey out to Yellow Bird and have a talk with R. Houghton whoever he may be.

—She said Eli softly Rose Houghton we just buried her this morning. Oh God May 20 1939 I thought I had forgot.

The stranger's fist came down on the table and the dishes

56

jumped and the men at the bar turned and stared and Josie Stringer's half-moon eyebrows went straight up.

—It's not true.

—I'm afraid it is Killeen those men at the bar put her under and over there is Reverend Lacey who said the service and you're looking at the man who pronounced her dead. May 20 1939.

Joe Killeen's mouth tightened and he ran his hand across his forehead and a bitter laugh came through his teeth well it figures he said get a thing in your pocket and discover you got a hole well doc what about her husband?

—Nate? Nate's a bitter man Killeen a mighty bitter man. Owes his limp to me likewise a son with faulty vision he claims his wife would not have passed had I got to her in time. May 20 1939.

—You sit there and admit to that what kind of doctor are you?

—Except for me Nate Houghton would have no leg at all his son would have no vision and as for Rose she just up and quit not even God could save her she was a phenomenon I've seen a lot here lately them that die because they don't want to go on living. The doctor was perfectly in control he had his world intact his mind was operating on all eight cylinders for once he felt secure.

—I don't know whether I like you or not.

—A lot of men don't.

—You live alone?

—Yep.

—No family?

—None to speak of wife died in sixty-three never had a kid. May 20 1939.

—Been all your life in Yellow Bird?

—Born here like I said.

—Knew your father and mother did you yeah and had a brother yeah and two sisters nice little family you got raised in

57

doc well then you don't know what it's like to wonder about the color of your mother's eyes or if she was pretty or not or the clothes that your father wore did they hang on him right was his hair long or short your sister was she smart and your brother was he strong enough to whip you I've wondered about those things a long time doc and sometimes I go down the streets in Denver Cheyenne Albuquerque Tulsa Phoenix all those nice houses with nice people having dinner I see them through the picture windows and I watch them in the park with their kids on Sundays and I think that's me yours truly Joe Killeen all nice and middle class with a name that people know a face they don't forget and maybe I got a kid in school and a wife to come home to and I can talk for hours about going fishing with my old man and how I never tasted the likes of my old lady's cooking. I'm no sentimental slob not me I was in the army two years and everybody thought I had a family outside Denver old man a minister of all things was what I told them my sister is engaged to the son of a university president and my brother is studying for his Ph.D. in physics even gave them names Electra for a typewriter I saw in a window and Shane for that guy in the movies who never did come back hell doc I got no business here after all guess I'll just shove off.

He reached in his pocket for some change and stood up he was tall and bronzed from the sun a Navajo belt held up his Levi's a turquoise watchband was around his wrist.

—You like Indian stuff Killeen said the doctor strangely touched by the young man.

—Yeah I dig it worked for the Navajos one summer on a road-construction job got to know some other Indian cats down near Santa Fe working on a ranch this guy named Silver Hand saved my life one time a flash flood hit when we were working cattle in a draw never heard it coming till Silver Hand rides up and grabs me off to his saddle lost my horse and saddle and a .30–30 won from a guy in Roswell doc I got to go.

—Where to?

—Just keep moving doc me and Daisy.

—Your girl?

—You bet my four-wheel-drive V-8 stripped-down girl purrs like a kitten her name is Daisy and she's fifteen years old enough past puberty to be nice and ripe and dependable Daisy just got all painted blue is her favorite color did a valve job on her she's good as new. He was smiling for the first time two nice rows of white and even teeth between two squashed caterpillar lips just right for a man.

—Listen Killeen why don't you stick around said the doctor suddenly anxious that Killeen not pass from his life.

—Got no reason to with Rose Houghton kicking off.

—Well maybe we can check out some other stuff the old hospital is all shut down but I got a key and maybe a few connections.

—Doc did you deliver me now out with the honest truth so I can go with nothing on my brain.

—Wish I had Killeen wish I had but I'd have remembered that date for a reason sure can't figure what Rose Houghton was up to running an ad like that a little off her rocker at the end so it's nothing but coincidence Killeen just a goddamn coincidence you probably got born in Tucumcari.

The stranger looked at the doctor fumbling with his tie his eyes on a pool of catsup on his plate and what he felt was what he often felt in the places he found himself and there was this terrible urge which kept presenting itself and made him think he was weak because he gave in so easily to it. So he said as he had said so many times before when he knew he ought to get up and leave this looks like as good a place as any to settle down.

—Can't do much settling down it's going to drown we all got to move out before next June.

—Yeah read that in the paper too doc maybe that's what drew me here I got a morbid fascination with what's going to disappear I think I must have been a beaver trap-

59

per or some goddamn prospector when last I lived I sure was never anybody that had a future.

A grin spread over the doctor's face and he pumped Killeen's sprawling hand goddamn good to have you old Josie here can put you up and maybe you can find a job what do you do?

—Anything swing an axe drive a spike wrangle cattle cleaned out cesspools one time and collected garbage three bucks an hour and all you could eat are the engineers hiring for the dam?

—Dunno go down and ask for Frank Robinson they still got to work on the intake tower but what in God's name you want to do that for? We got no use for dam builders.

—Pays good that's all I worry about doc a little cash in my pocket a broad on my arm and Daisy gassed up and ready to roll.

—Sounds like a pretty good way to live Killeen.

—Suits my fancy doc I got no ties at all.

He went out the door with his hat tilted back a faint arrogance in his stride the eyes of every man were on him and the same thought was running through their minds who was he and what was he doing there and they would not rest until they found out quietly and with feigned indifference they would watch each move he made and speculate about the ones they did not see.

It's nearly time for the weather report. And to break the news to Vera Hayes. And to see about the light bill. Allaby will recover but not for very long. I must dig up the iris for the last time. Go see how the Williams' house is and nail up the broken door. Everything will go on the same as it always has. There are certain inflexibilities and certain certainties that need to be taken care of.

They watched him go through the door slightly stooped slower than he used to move a little more unsure.

—He's still a good man a good doctor too I don't care what said Josie Stringer solemnly. He delivered all of mine I like to

60

have bled to death but for him I'd trust him with my life.

—That's more than a lot of people would they say he could have saved Rose Houghton with adrenaline in the heart he didn't do a thing just let her pass.

—Are you a doctor well shut up he knows his job.

—He gave Willie cough syrup last week thought it was an antibiotic.

—And Vera ain't been right since he took that tumor off her head.

—He did a good job sewing up old Franzoni's stud the fool spick tried to geld him with a knife.

—Let him take care of critters then he ain't no good with people.

Across the street the stop sign shot full of holes the Stars and Stripes saloon boarded up the light bulb still dangling outside the signs in the windows fading after twenty years. Draught beer one dime we never close bring a buddy home tonight girl wanted kitchen good wages time off U.S. savings bonds mule sale cheap see Jesse ladies' aid bake sale July 26 1946 firehouse ken ennybody help Joe Dugan hay Wensday call 328 grub $1.95 day. Extract Mac played craps with a hand blown off until the shock wore off and they carried him out with his hand on a plate like an order of eggs covered with a napkin to keep the dirt out and I sewed it back on good as new and twice as useful. Antlers sleeping rooms 50 cents furnished clean please ring buzer quiet pleze. Slanting Annie was okay just twenty and all the time thought it was gas I said you ever seen gas look like that she said no I wish I knew who its father was it seems a shame not to know its last name for sure.

Thornburg's Funeral Parlor stood underneath that heap of brick next to the Almighty Dollar you could drink and watch the goings-on through the plate-glass window. Old man Thornburg embalmed in the back with the door open and every now and then came out and we handed him a beer it's all he ever drank. The avalanche of forty-one named Gertie nineteen dead

I hauled them down on sleds Thornburg he just stood 'em up outside all froze stiff they didn't thaw for two months the town came by to have a look any time it wanted the longest viewing on record it seemed a shame they couldn't talk just leaned against the wall like after a bad night at the club the altitude paralyzed us all one time or another.

And when the Glass Eye blowed sky high that Thanksgiving I had pumpkin pie still in my mouth going down the hill they came so silent fifty odd trapped in there we got 'em out dead all but Finney and Plummer poor Plummer his brains hanging out of his head the first time I ever played God gave him morphine enough to do the job twice over it only made him bear the pain I never knew for sure why he lived too bad he didn't die but lingered on in awful dark must be like that with dumb animals they can't tell you anything it's all in their eyes I never will forget Plummer's eyes you don't play God twice on the same man I never could. I never could.

—What ails you Purvis he called to the principal who was running up the street his pallid face contorted his thin frame shaking

—Eli Eli the most awful thing they took Rose from her grave and propped her between Nate and all the kids Christ Eli so that man from Coronado could take her picture he was late Eli three hours late they just had to have it done oh I tell you I will never be the same.

—You went and looked?

—Couldn't help it Eli I went to decorate her grave with an American flag the old one with forty-eight stars from the school I thought she'd like to have it resting above her head but there she was Eli like this and Purvis began to shake violently.

Eli took his arm and pushed him across the street keeping up a line of talk they had grown used to over the years which did not offend or matter or question. Things like the weather being what it was winter would be a month deceived and how it was at the calf pulling on Sunday and how the start of hunting season was not far off.

Edgar Purvis and Eli Wetherill had lived in Yellow Bird so long they did not notice the heifer chewing grass in the empty shell of the Dennison Dry Goods store or the three-legged dog lying in the middle of the street or the top of the Fairchild Block 1891 which had since the day before lost four panes of glass out of the dormer window onto the crumbling sidewalk. They did not notice the horse tied up at the gas station or the swings of an empty playground banging together in a park filled with tin cans and trash. They did notice the freshness of the air and the brutal blue of the sky and the white jet contrails going across into the blinding sun. They said it was a shame to mess up the sky like that. The mountain rose in splendor above them and they noticed that too and how the first snow had already fallen at thirteen thousand feet. Winter came early in that part of Colorado and they shivered thinking of the cold ground into which Rose Houghton had once again been plowed.

4

The September sunset was one of those rare ones in Colorado where instead of sinking as a brilliant white ball the sun burst into orange and set fire to the clouds and turned them orange and pink and then to mauves and blues the mountain was similarly aglow as were the aged boards and roofs and porches and false fronts of the town. The people who lived there noticed the beauty of the evening and went about their chores a little happier a little more alive for to them small pleasures were all that stood between themselves and feeling blue and so a sunrise or a sunset the rain coming down on the tin or tarpaper roofs or the first snow falling or the smell of fresh earth in spring always brought joy to them in a way that was hard for other people to understand. Those small pleasures accompanied by the success of a rose garden or a bumper crop of squash and cucumbers and tomatoes or the first son's graduation or the first daughter's marriage and the grandchildren whose pictures stood in frames on the television sets were among the things that made life in Yellow Bird tolerable. The whitewashing of the picket fence the seed catalogues the homemade bread and pies the dances in the firehouse the church suppers and the Fourth of July picnics the music lessons and the trumpet bought with money saved from returnable bottles the house plants exchanged with neighbors and the pots of homemade soup on a winter's night the garbage-can lids used for sleds and tin cans used for skates these things also made life tolerable and some of them had had their day. The firehouse was torn down along with city hall the churches had been demolished except for the Holy Ghost the grade school had shut in sixty-six and the drugstore where the youth had gathered for lemon phosphates before they took to beer was now a heap of rubble between the heaps of Ruby Moore's beauty parlor and Jack Washburn's garage and general store. If Yellow Bird in September resembled nothing less than a war ruin its people had nothing less than the dispirited solemnity of a people who had likewise been bombed out.

But Meridian Muldoon did not notice the sunset and did not remember any of the small things that had once made life tolerable for her in Yellow Bird. Her mind was on herself as she walked back toward town having spent the afternoon brooding beside the river knowing that before long she would have to get to know them again and try to find some good in Yellow Bird and write her story and get the hell out of there without getting further involved.

She pulled her coat around her neck as she turned up the street toward the old house that Marcus had bought with his first ill-gotten money she saw it standing ghostly gray and melancholy in a yard that was overgrown with weeds the fence was falling down and on either side of it the houses had already been demolished. Across the street a light was burning in Eli Wetherill's decrepit house and she saw his car parked in the garage and for an instant she desired his company then changed her mind she had seen him at the funeral his face all bloated and ashen his eyes like a road map of America and she knew he had not changed in ten years he was a sad pathetic parody of a doctor whom one would not trust to remove a hangnail oh she could write a tale on him all right that blundering fool and how he had messed up nearly everybody's life not knowing a liver from a larynx and got away with it because apathy was a symptom of Yellow Bird and they would tolerate most anything rather than rise against it or make a change that would require their collective necks stuck out.

To hell with Eli Wetherill she said to herself turning the key in the door and switching on the lights in the dark damp mouse-droppinged cobwebbed horsehaired living room where the mice scrambled behind the walls and there was a clammy chill that made her turn and walk out and catch her breath in the rapidly darkening night. And just where would she go if she didn't stay in the house since she did not have a friend left in Yellow Bird did she go from door to door asking for bed and board or how about the hotel which smelled of awful nameless things and creaked and groaned in the wind that nondescript pile of rotting rooms called the Yellow Bird Hotel in which she had not set foot since that night so many years ago when she went there and climbed the fire escape to visit the farm-machinery salesman a fellow by the name of Goodnight who was drunk and stank of motor oil his hands were dirty and his breath was garlicky he slept in soiled long johns and had a set of dentures he put in a glass of water the only good thing about him was that he gave her something to remember and that was more than most of them did. She had not experienced another like him for almost a year and she had only been fourteen at the time and Goodnight was her third experience the other two being the Mexican foreman at her father's ranch the other Millie Adams' father a brakeman on the Rye-O Grande her last in that town being Squash Jenkins the good and gentle son of Willie Jenkins the coal-black janitor at the school the only blacks ever to live in Yellow Bird were Jenkins and his family the boy was nineteen and had never had a girl well he had her all right at fifteen right there in the church and she had been sent away and what they had done to hurt him was to rape his sister aged eleven and leave her dead in the ditch behind the waterworks and Squash had come into Josie Stringer's saloon looking for the bastards who had done it and they had only laughed and laughed and laughed and gone right on playing poker.

So he went home and hanged himself with an electric cord a gentle coal-black boy named Squash too shy to appear in town except for that fateful night he went to account for his sister's death to try and make them pay for what he had lost and found he couldn't niggers don't have guts was what they said afterward deciding that his death was no fault of theirs. What made the rapists poker players faceless nameless unaccountable sons-of-bitches was the simple fact that they had been born with the essential pieces missing and I am not so sure ten years later they remember what they did or how or why they always had a tendency to forget what they did not want to remember a habit acquired right after the last mine shut down and they had no place to go and be somebody Yellow Bird was the grave into which they were born nobody and lived nobody and died no-body the irony is that it never could have been otherwise you see they had been born with the essential pieces missing.

She had to have a drink and so she went back in the house and found what her brother had left from the summer before a full bottle of vodka and she poured it straight in a glass turned the furnace up and sat with her coat on staring at the Currier

67

and Ives prints on the brown walls of the living room those depressing brown walls that she had once been made to turn her face to oh it was not a good house anymore it was old and worn out and everything that had been new when she was small was worn out the piano was cracked in the middle and the keys were split the pattern was off the rug the stuffing was out of the chair the lining of the white damask drapes had rotted the shiny kitchen range was rusting the door knobs were worn smooth the stairway creaked the roof leaked the barn had collapsed the toilet would not flush the sink would not drain the bathtub ran rusty water the flocked wallpaper was peeling the mahogany paneling was cracked the dishes that her mother had left had the pattern worn off the kitchen stank of flour and grease the four bedrooms smelled of old newspaper eleven panes of glass were broken and the chimney was stopped up.

She hated the house. Rose Houghton had tried to keep order and couldn't her mother had endured as best she could she had made her learn piano and forced her to read the complete works of Dickens Shakespeare Twain Balzac Conrad and Teddy Roosevelt. Frieda Wheeler came from a third-generation Colorado family railroad people who ran a short line to half a dozen gold camps they had until the Depression been successful freighters bankers wholesale grocers financiers had married well except for Frieda who at twenty-one was teaching school in Denver when Marcus Muldoon walked in one day and announced that the only way he could avoid the draft was to be married by midnight and so she had done it and survived for twenty-seven years she was what held Marcus together cooled him off and turned him on and upside down he was untamed except by her he was impossible to live with except with her he fumed and spit and cursed except with her.

But Frieda got her licks. She turned her back on her son Stanley when he was sixteen and she caught him with a boy his age had turned her back on Meridian when at thirteen she had taken a twenty-four-year-old bull buyer around to the back of the house and tied him to a tree he'd had too much to drink and did not care that Meridian unzipped his fly and felt her way around until her mother saw her. And gave up. So she could do anything she pleased except come home and that she had not been able to do after Squash had knocked her up well it was just too much for Frieda who took her to Chicago to get rid of it and they spent three months in Florida waiting for Meridian to reform well she hadn't and never would and she guessed it was in her blood and in Stanley's too.

The house was still cold she turned up the thermostat to eighty-five it was hard to believe the house belonged to the Bureau of Reclamation now and that when the town surrendered next summer it and all the rest would be knocked to the ground scooped up and stuffed into the canyon for fill and the water would come over the houses and stores and schools where so many lives had played out and dreams had failed along with the price of gold what was there worth saving one man's shithouse one man's poorhouse one man's slaughterhouse one man's cathouse she closed her eyes and pushed her mind back to the first bad thing she could remember her mother in the cool dim bedroom her father out of town I have to take a nap her mother said so play outside but she had climbed up the fire escape and peered in there was this large white ass moving up and down fascinated she pressed her face against the window the ass flipped over and she saw for the first time what a man used to make a baby it was all fat and ugly red all dripping and shrinking before her eyes she put her hand across her face wondering why Matt Brittman had come and done such a thing to her mother she was no more than eight at the time and it took her a while to find out.

And the second bad thing she remembered was being pushed out the door to Sunday school and forgetting her purse the door was locked and so she climbed through the window

69

and tiptoed to her room and in her very own bed was her mother without any clothes on and Matt Brittman without any clothes on and they were just lying there all stuck together and they neither saw nor heard her as she slipped down the stairs again not wondering any more how a man did this thing to her mother she was no more than nine at the time and from then on she did not have to find out.

And the third bad thing she remembered was the way Stanley took after the thin asthmatic son of a steel worker who had come out from the East to give the sickly kid a chance to breathe Stanley was tutoring him in math and English and went there every day with his books and pencils and a notebook full of paper he was just sixteen and had never liked a girl he liked the Dugan boy in some mysterious way she was determined to find out and did she was no more than ten at the time. And had squealed to Frieda when Stanley quit paying her to keep her mouth shut a quarter at a time paid out over the weeks and months until he had pushed her in the face and told her to drop dead. He had been sent away for therapy and the whole thing got hushed up but Stanley was hooked for good and made no bones about it he toured Europe with a faggot and lived in New York for a while his college days disgraced the family the army would not take him he had no money and no job and finally drifted down to Texas where some Lone Star fag had given him a business opportunity and some divorcee had given him a bunch of kids a bank account a presentable façade well screw them all Marcus you were no angel either buying out the suckers for a song the goback land wasn't worth a nickel till you cozied up to a couple of bureaucrats who knew the score and told you where the dam was going and so you bought up the land and hung on for all those years until they gave you fifty times what you paid for it and that's how come you made a million dollars off of Yellow Bird and tried to put poor Britt out of the cattle business by getting the bank to call his note. Well

I guess he got even with you by laying Frieda good when I was just eight peeking through the window at him giving her a two-cog framisator meat-injection lily-livered sugar-coated gumdrop advanced algebra Cuban cigar so you know what Squash you know what I am going to do don't be scared now please don't shake how else you expect me to get it hard for you Squash poor thing just close your eyes yes right in front of the altar what the hell is it good for oh don't you know anything I swear it's a resurrection that's what it is my god Squash is it diet or were you born this way oh stop oh stop oh stop oh again yes again and again.

She had sworn she would not go down to the town tonight but there was nothing to eat in the house and something urged her along the broken sidewalks and made her heart beat fast as she saw the familiar hotel so forlorn in the yellow light and there were the pickups and the jeeps of the poker players rapists they still came and the night was still black and lonely and oh so cold and you could hear the juke box clear down the street and the wind coming up from the river a cold tongue licking a wounded town and she felt an eagerness to see them again to look into their inscrutable faces to hear their cynical laughs to try and find some way to immortalize their degeneracy on paper and oh she would she would and maybe not feel guilty about Squash Jenkins anymore.

Joe Killeen was whistling to himself as he came out of the Yellow Bird Hotel having had his luncheon with the doc he felt the eyes of the faded-out men upon him and he knew he was okay as he listened to the way his Levi's rubbed together as he strode rapidly toward Daisy.

You take a man and stick him in a pair of Levi's and you know what you got all the stuff a man ever thought he was made of crammed into a pair of pants it's not any pants mind you you can go around in army twill or navy wool it just don't feel the same as blue denim the first time it's washed and shrinks down to curve around the vital spots and when you walk and your knees just naturally rub together and you feel the seam there and the tough old cloth you straighten up real fast and if ever you thought less of yourself it's not then with Levi's on and the pockets cut so you can't lose nothing out of them your billfold is pressed right in there and anybody knows seeing you from behind just how much cash you carry and the billfold gets worn too and curves around your ass just so sandwiched between those two folds of jean.

And the way you tell the difference between a drugstore cowboy and the real McCoy is how long his Levi's are if they come below the heel of his boot and even drag the dust he's an honest to god cowboy but if his Levi's hit him at the ankle or above you know he's an imitation no matter how good he struts. New-bought and stiff they got a pleasant odor like a country store in the good old days where they baked potatoes in the pot-bellied stove and you just helped yourself I saw that once in Texas but I reckon it's all gone the smell of new Levi's brings it back though that little country store with the Levi's piled to the ceiling and a row of boots you'd buy if you were rich me I got mine at the army surplus store it's all I could afford but hell boots don't improve your disposition the way those Levi's do no sir you can have all the boots you want and they are just boots but Levi's are like a man's tobacco or his horse a personal thing that comes in contact with an earnest part of himself and the smell is one of those things you never quite forget like the forest after it rains pitchwood burning good fresh manure and your own stink. Coming out of the drawer all fresh and clean you think of some incredible cotton that they mill there is nothing in the world that smells like a pair of Levi's smelling better if they're wet soaked through they smell well they smell blue yeah blue and you mix that wet smell with a little mud a little manure a sour mash is what it is and add some steer piss it brings

72

out a whole new fragrance and makes you think by god there's still this one thing they haven't found a way to improve one thing women don't do justice to one thing that's the way it always was a man can still feel good wearing them what else can he feel good wearing well maybe his hat maybe his beatup Stetson creased the way he wants it not his till he's soaked it through with sweat and rain and grit I've seen a man ride half a day to find his hat I've seen a man tangle with a bull to keep his hat and if it wasn't for the ladies he'd never take it off. The hat and the Levi's make the whole world seem right you can have a fuss with your wife get fired by your boss and walk away with the rustle of tough cloth between your legs you ain't whipped then there's not a thing can get you down not a thing they can take away from you as long as you keep your Levi's on.

It's funny though you see a drugstore cowboy sitting on a bar stool or walking down the street or in a used-car lot or swaggering into the movies with some long-haired broad on his arm and he's got these hot-shot Levi's on too short to make him real but he walks as if he's the envy of every man there it's all in his head and that's cool because when he takes those Levi's off he's just another man living in the dark fighting his ass off to make a buck and getting shit on and knowing he's never going to make it well those Levi's coming to his ankles give him a chance to pull his stomach in and say man don't you know I'm going to find my own way and my way may not be your way and don't blame me for what you haven't lived up to. Me I just live. me I got a pair of Levi's that are such a part of me that when I take them off at night they stand up in the corner knees bent and real ass-riveted pockets with a red handkerchief hanging out my own true self is standing there I consider Levi's are just not broke in till they stand up by themselves and I'll wear them out till new ones have got to be worn in it just comes natural like making love or cutting down a tree.

Joe Killeen had been in Yellow Bird exactly two hours he

drew a cigarette out of his shirt pocket and struck a stick match on his Levi's yeah Daisy this little old town is just cool. Hell of a lot better than Shirley Basin Uravan and some of the holes we been to right and that old doc you wonder what he carries around that makes him look so sad they all got faces like somebody chopped out of the goddamn mountain never crack a smile maybe it's that way in a town that's gonna die kind of subdued you know like Tall Grass with leukemia down in Window Rock didn't say a thing only his face got shrunk of all emotion the way those Indians do hell Daisy we got no business here ought to keep on moving to a new place that's alive with people in it and some broads I haven't seen one good ass that's under sixty what you want to stay here for the altitude is bad for your carburetor know that well maybe this is as good a place as any to be from it doesn't look so hot but it feels good you reckon they got anything here that's worth our time?

Daisy bumped along the street that was full of holes and would not be fixed having been removed from the worklist of the Carbon County road-repair crew. He drove up and down the streets rising toward the scarred-up mountain with a miners' boardinghouse still clinging to its face and a waterfall gushing not far from where the men used to enter the Glass Eye mine now blasted shut forever he liked the look of the place he had never been very long in a mountain town before and its impending death intrigued him as much as the origin of himself and by and by he would find out what he had come to find out and when he went away he would be complete and not worry about his background anymore. There was the name Houghton on the mailbox of a green-shingled house with a broken chair on the porch the window shades drawn the chimney had a hole in it and in the back the privy was on its side. Well some other time for Houghton some other time to talk to them one by one and try not to get involved because when that happened there was trouble and so he just kept moving the way he had for a

74

dozen years going his own way on his own terms a desert rat a river runner a man who kept silence with the mountains for weeks at a time in British Columbia where it took him ten days to ride across the ranch and back but he could raise hell too like the time he got blind drunk and took his gun and robbed the bank in Sheridan of four thousand dollars cash fancying himself a modern Jesse James making his getaway in Daisy who blew her fuel pump two miles outside of town and it had cost him two years in the federal penitentiary hell a man was better by his wild lone any way you looked at it and so whenever he found himself moaning about who he was or where he came from or what he might have been he hightailed it for some new place and stayed just long enough to straighten out. But not this time not when he was thirty and figuring he was maybe halfway to his end he had to find his beginning and would have put it off except for that thing in the paper except for what was settling in his bones and stirring him about Yellow Bird now two hours into his acquaintanceship and luring him in a strange and not unpleasant way.

He turned Daisy toward the river he would go and hunt up Robinson and get himself a job and then a room assay the whores down in Coronado he had heard from a hitchhiker he'd picked up on Wolf Creek Pass that Coronado was loaded for bear if you went about it right and weren't particular hell the best he'd had in recent months was a sixteen-year-old diesel in Colorado Springs a quivering girl who bit her nails and said he was her first well from the way she acted he guessed she might qualify for the entire Fifth Army division she relieved him of all his cash and he slept the rest of the week on the ground and ate chocolate bars until his face broke out and then he drifted out toward Boyero Wild Horse and Kit Carson and found a ranch that took him on just an old man and his wife near blind he would have liked it fine except when the granddaughter arrived from Canon City and stirred his blood he could not help

75

himself he tried to sweat himself out of thinking about her moving about the house in miniskirts and heaving out her breasts and lying in the hammock with her long bare legs dangling and she would ask him to come and sit and have a cigarette and play his cheap guitar the only song he knew was Shenandoah her name was Scarlett and she bathed with Lifebuoy soap and wore her hair in wire rollers until noon then teased it out in a wasp's-nest hairstyle by International Harvester she said I only like the Beatles don't you know anything by them? Well he didn't and in his creaky voice he tried to sing Streets of Laredo which made her laugh and pull his hair and bite him on the ear after which he carried her to his dirt-floored bunkhouse and had her then and there. And was fired the next day by the old man who had stood and watched from the upstairs window with a shotgun in his hand and never fired because he'd remembered he'd gotten his wife in the same damn way. Did Killeen want to marry the girl no he did not and so he found himself in Daisy once again going nowhere and with nothing on his mind just this urge to keep moving with the wind to a high place and then in some dirty café he picked up a week-old Denver *Post* and happened to turn to the personal column and there it was and so here he was screwed up again the story of his life.

But he kept on singing off key with the radio because nothing bugged him for very long life was a bitch and there was nothing you could do except run away or kill yourself or roll with it. He counted up the other places he had been to places where he thought he'd find out about himself establish maybe one strong root with a person he was related to he would have liked a place to just come home to now and then and maybe an old maid aunt to cook him supper it wasn't so much for a man to ask and he had gone around trying to find it all the way from Missouri to California and from Canada to the Mexican border and a couple times he thought he had and wished he had and imagined he had and then he had to wake up. You always had to wake up. Wake up and run. Well maybe he wouldn't run for a while maybe he would just let things be.

The afternoon did not turn out the way he had hoped it would. Robinson had stared at his sideburns coming to the lobes of his ears at the way his hair curled over the collar of his shirt had noticed the way his Levi's fit and the particular way he carried himself like he was somebody big and wanted the world to know and he was chewing gum all the while he talked to Robinson seated behind a messy desk working a dead cigar around his lips there was dirt underneath Robinson's fingernails and he wore a heavy ring the sleeves of his bright plaid shirt were rolled up and Killeen noticed a tattoo on either forearm one was the screaming eagle from the 101st Airborne Division the other was a heart entwined with roses and the words MOTHER GOD COUNTRY. Robinson was shorthanded all right and was running three weeks behind schedule he had an opening for a hod carrier and Killeen said I'll take it and then Robinson's heavy lids came down on his eyes he screwed the cigar into the ashtray and a cruel smile formed on his lips as he said coolly to Killeen I don't hire hippies you longhaired freak go find a circus you Communist infiltrator we don't need the likes of you. And he had almost punched Robinson in his overfed face which was exactly what Robinson wanted him to do as he sat on the edge of his chair his fists clenched and a look of utter contempt in his eyes. Killeen rose slowly and put his hat on flicked some lint from his jacket nodded his head toward Robinson and said evenly I'll see you around corporal. Sergeant said Robinson turning red Master Sergeant Robinson. Too bad said Killeen closing the door corporals have all the savvy.

Robinson had blown his cool all right running after him and making threats and trying to provoke Killeen into hitting him but Killeen just walked on out to Daisy whistling his little song a toothpick stuck in his mouth his thumbs stuck in the pockets of his Levi's and Robinson was still shouting as Killeen started Daisy's moto stared him in the eye and slowly raised his arm in salute at ease he said and drove away watching Robinson in the rear-view mirror shaking his head in rage and the dam intake tower was directly behind him an appropriate combination that tower and that man. Maybe someday he'd let Robinson know how he felt about the whole asinine idea of building dams and highways and more and more better and better bigger and bigger and if you just looked around at the earth you knew it was considered wasteful unless man was doing something to it and what good is a lot of land just sitting there and a river just flowing and trees just growing and the wind just blowing what we need are jobs yeah and a jackhammer on every hunk of concrete and a bulldozer in every building knock it all down and start again and when you have paved the forests drained the swamps preserved the prairie in asphalt wiped out the wilderness killed the air and water and made the world over with your computers and your atomic energy and your super-sonic jets and the people are still crying more well I guess you can just have them send in a boxtop and a quarter for a do-it-yourself annihilation kit orange lemon or lime.

He drove all the way to Coronado and there was nothing for him there except to dun the poor for unpaid bills to take away their cars and television sets if necessary and let their children starve and that's what happened the finance company man said when you give them a little they want a lot people must be kept in their places. Screw you. And he had fled in Daisy back up the road toward Yellow Bird counting the money he had left just twenty dollars was all so he turned around and went back into town and pawned his turquoise belt for five bucks and bought himself a bottle of the very best Scotch and then he had just fifteen dollars left and a credit card which had expired two years before but they took it at the gas station anyway and gave him a free balloon. He kept the Scotch in the brown paper bag and sipped it as he went along he was feeling somewhat better at least he did not have the urge to go out and smash something the way he had done in Lubbock hurling a brick through the window of an oil company whose ocean drilling rig had just busted and spread a sudden death to birds and fish alike.

The hell of it was the fucking establishment had you by the balls no matter what you tried to do you could escape if you had the dough if not you sooner or later had to resort to compromise a word he hated more than any other in the English language a word that made him think less of himself when he submitted to it for economic reasons. Compromise is a dirty word it means you have sold out. And gotten your belly filled up. And left your principles somewhere back behind a dung heap called necessity. And the dung heap is what you'll lay down your principles for since you stood too long telling the motherfuckers where to go. So where does it get you Killeen does it make you feel good knowing you ain't got but one pair of socks and Daisy needs a ring job bad and your tooth has got a hole in it and when was the last time you felt reckless enough to blow yourself to a real good steak?

Killeen was driving fast along the road sipping the Scotch from the paper sack and wondering why life had cast him as a misfit and why it was so fucking difficult to find yourself a place where you belonged and could start liking yourself the way you used to before you learned that the world was hard up for simple things and always would be and you gave up your dream and crossed the line. He had never seen all he had meant to see or done all he had meant to do he always itched to have more behind him and the whole earth before him but things never worked out he always found himself in doubt or debt or love or loneliness and eventually one thing or the other fucked him up and he was exactly where he started from. And when that happened he would tell himself as he did that very minute that you took it and went on whistling or if you couldn't take it you whistled anyway.

The sign said Happy Hollow Mountain Estates a totally planned community lots $100 down choose from six exciting model homes designed with you in mind fishing riding golfing tennis free club membership act now.

Four miles from Yellow Bird they were cashing in on the benefits of a reservoir still five years from reality and the bulldozers had already carved a swath through the forest so that the cars could have someplace to go and there were the plastic survey ribbons fluttering in the breeze and the lots marked SOLD and then the person's name and the Brooks Brothers-suited real-estate agent sitting in the luxurious A-frame said yeah we could use you as a carpenter provided you don't mingle with the ah customers we wouldn't want them to ah. Go up to number five the Mountaineer it's called and ask for Curly he's the project foreman tell him I said you're hired what's the name oh Killeen pleasedtameetcha hope you like our little town all the conveniences of the city we have a potential investment of forty million dollars here expect to build a ski slope condominiums townhouses going to make it another Aspen the money oh our investors are all from Texas bigtime Killeen bigtime boys who know what the people want and we'll give it to 'em eh Killeen?

And so he was hired as a carpenter and he would create as he destroyed. In the beginning was the word and in the end was bullshit.

Having completed his compromise more thoroughly than ever before he drank some more Scotch and drove on back to Yellow Bird just as the sun was going down and though he was slightly drunk by then and the houses looked pretty much the same he found the green-shingled one with the name Houghton on the mailbox and he whistled all the way up the crooked broken sidewalk to Houghton's solemn house the drawn win-

80

dowshades soaked with a greenish light a limping figure moving back and forth and then the figure stopped bent itself in two a jackknife closing up. A wail which carried with it a whole lifetime of despair stopped Killeen in his tracks it was a cry he had not heard since he went to tell the foreman's widow that her three boys had drowned in the reservoir each in his turn while trying to save the other.

And he came out of Houghton's feeling no better than when he went in the poor man was eaten up by a grief consumed with a fury that made Killeen's blood run cold and so he did not believe him not a single word he likewise considered Houghton's threat to murder Eli Wetherill nothing more than that and so he left the insane and blithering cripple hammering on the wall his four small children standing in visible horror all crying out for their mother who was now six hours into the cold and comforting earth and he knew he should not have come at such a time. He apologized to Houghton who did not hear he continued pounding on the wall and his words came out like a phonograph record run on the wrong speed Killeen shuddered and went out knowing that he had no further reason to stick around had no use for the job he had just accepted no love for the people he saw moving along the street the place repulsed him and yet drew him to it in its helplessness. So he took a room at the hotel for seventeen dollars a week brushed his teeth and went downstairs wearing a fresh shirt and Levi's his dark hair combed and with the last of his after-shave lotion splashed around his ears he nodded to Josie Stringer who was cooking hamburgers on the grill and to her jack-o'-lantern son who was mixing drinks behind the bar and looking around he saw that the same men who had been there for lunch were back again seated around a poker table and he nodded to them as well and got no response whatever they stopped talking for the time it took for him to find a table in a dark corner of the room they resumed their chatter and their laughter and the slapping down of cards.

—Whatcha want Mister Killeen said Josie with a smile happy to have rented the room for the first time since last year's hunting season. The stew ain't bad but it don't have onions I run out yesterday and so did Fred over there he's the grocer and he don't have an onion tells me garlic will do and I says Fred you think I am so dumb I don't know garlic from an onion well he's out to make his dollar same as me you going to be here long Mister Killeen?

But Killeen wasn't listening his eyes were on Meridian Muldoon who was sitting quietly at a table about twenty feet from his and he felt the hair on the back of his neck stand up and the palms of his hands grow sweaty who is that he said to Josie.

Josie swiveled her head around and frowned oh her that's Meridian Muldoon born here father was a big rancher a lot of trouble in that family Mister Killeen.

Killeen rubbed his chin and saw the girl lower her head to a magazine. Does she live here said Killeen.

—Her live here said Josie with a short laugh oh that ain't likely considering.

—Considering what?

Josie shrugged her huge shoulders I don't like to talk about people it ain't nice I just take it out in thoughts.

—What are you thinking then said Killeen.

—She should have stayed in Denver well she left here ten years ago and this town ain't got over it yet.

—What said Killeen.

Josie glanced back at Meridian heaved a sigh then bent her enormous body so that her mouth was against Killeen's right ear and then she stood back triumphant her eyes sparkling waiting for Killeen to say something but his expression had not changed and all he said was fry me up a chicken please.

—A chicken said Josie her mouth flying open.

—That's what I said have you got a chicken or not?

—Sure but—

—That's what I'd like and a salad and some fries coffee later right now I'd like a beer.

—Mister Killeen said Josie helplessly.

—What?

She ran her tongue around her lips and looked disgruntled oh never mind she said and stamped across to the bar drew a beer from the tap and slammed it down in front of him twenty cents she said you pay it now it don't come with the meal.

With his beer in his hand he made his way to where the girl sat picking at her salad he stood there for several minutes before she looked up and then her eyes were cold she said what do you want?

—May I sit down?

She waved her hand toward the opposite chair and said why not they'll make it out much worse than this no matter what you do.

—Who he said unable to take his eyes from her face.

—That bunch over there the poker players who come night after night for a hundred years and mostly talk but now and then they see that justice is done.

—What did they ever do to you?

—Nothing much.

—Then how come you hate them?

—I don't.

She went on eating her salad and Killeen took his time lighting a cigarette and letting out the smoke in a little cloud he studied every feature until he had memorized her face memorized her small white hands with short fingers and the way her neck was long and graceful she was one hell of a hunk of woman all right and he wanted her then and there but he would take his time with this one and puzzle her out a bit before he made his move he drummed his fingers on the table not really knowing what to say to her she seemed neither pleased nor displeased to have him there.

—Uh look he said finally I think we are the only two people in this town under thirty years of age and I don't know about you but me I aim to stick around a while we might as well get to know each other I'm Joe Killeen.

—Meridian Muldoon she said turning the pages of the magazine and don't tell me you don't know who I am Josie spilled the beans.

—Just some of the beans he said with a grin and what the hell?

—Yeah Killeen what the hell?

He sat thoughtfully chewing on a toothpick and she had her head buried in the magazine and he was getting exactly nowhere and Josie was coming with his food so he got up and said uh what do you do Meridian?

—It depends on the time of day.

Well that was that and in a big hurry too. He sat eating his food in silence watching her eat hers and not look up and it bugged him really bugged him that she was so uptight and after the bitch of a day he'd had all he wanted was somebody to talk to for Christ's sake you'd think he'd committed rape. After a while she got up and put on her coat and passed by his table and said nice meeting you Killeen.

He scrambled to his feet wiping his mouth with a napkin yeah Meridian same here will I be seeing you around?

—Maybe.

—Well I'll buy you a drink.

—You don't have to she said I can buy my own and she went over to the bar and sat there talking to Josie and Charley who suddenly became subdued and scarcely replied to her questions and it made him mad to see them treat her like that and he gulped down his dinner as fast as he could and made his way to the bar and sat beside her and ordered a double Scotch.

—Right friendly town this he said under his breath.

—Isn't it she said smiling sweetly.

—This place gives me the creeps he said let's have a drink in my room.

—That is not what we would have in your room she said getting up and laying a dollar on the counter I'm tired Killeen and I'm going home to try very hard to remember what I came for and do it and get out I don't have the time Killeen I'm sorry if I'm rude.

And she was gone leaving him to hunger after her leaving him so wound up that even after drinking what was left of his Scotch he could not sleep and tossed in his bed seeing her face before him.

Three o'clock. What do you do when you have not slept when the world is pressing against the windowpane the brown chair in a corner of the room looms like a spider scuttling toward its prey the light cast from the street lamp reflects the sadness of the room in which have lain a thousand despairing men raising and lowering the shade turning off the hissing heat fumbling with the lamp above the bed spinning beneath the camphored sheets lumps rise from the mattress the same as in a million cheap hotels.

Joe Killeen counted the stripes in the wallpaper it was a cage a jail five hundred and sixty-eight straight roads leading nowhere you always counted numbers were important then the number of ties in a mile of railroad track telephone poles how many blades of grass in a square inch the number of peas on your plate the sidewalk sections in one block how many cars passed in the night measuring the distance you could piss your height on the door frame your dick computed on a stick meant for arithmetic. Mine was the longest and then there was the rubber hose they used to tie our hands behind our backs for stealing wax we only wanted to see if you could make a mold of a double dick Barber's and mine.

He got up sat on the windowsill watching the coal smoke drift along the deserted street touching the stone-faced buildings in the dark. The smoke turned yellow in the street light wrapped around the iron lamppost rose on a puff of wind discharged its solemn obligation as a living presence the holy ghost the conscience drained out of a sleeping town slow inexorable gone with the first breath of life.

The milk truck. It rolled down the street trespassed the coal smoke rendered it invalid dropped two cases at the door of Sweeney's and moved on. The hunters' bug-eyed jeep swung around the corner one got out to piss against the lamppost crying I baptize thee.

Four o'clock. The wind restless to begin the day starts with a gasp the birds come out of the eaves the sole inhabitants of the street a cat passes slowly sure of itself there is plenty of time. What am I doing here? What am I doing undressed in a hot room drip drip drop drip drop footsteps in the hall the guy in number three going to the can.

The ceiling sheds its skin ungracefully. The striped walls cannot contain the secrets of this room secrets shared by perspiring women bent in two getting it good enough to last a lifetime in the grave are women who had intercourse 9,608 times each the average number computed one day while I was waiting for the bus in Laramie.

Smoke a death stick coffin nail you will not die of cancer before you die in a traffic accident smoke choke croak Marlboro country is where the flavor is it's better when you do it together it's better at both ends more smokers prefer lung cancer than all other kinds of recreation put together. There was a time when you picked up tips from empty tables robbed poor boxes newspaper racks even took a blindman's cup to buy yourself a pair of gloves it was so cold in Denver the morning the train pulled out of the stockyards reeking of beef to feed a nation. Four dollars in an inside pocket lying on the rods on a platform of boards the grit of a thousand miles between your teeth and in your eyes they never found me until Pittsburgh Pennsylvania I was only thirteen and that was the end of my freedom more than most have ever known. Burnt-out cigarettes in ashtrays is the earth corrupted by one moment of passion? For each man it goes so fast and leaves you with no taste. What if passion reconsidered saved us all from ashes the light still burns at the end of a cigarette enough to read by to illuminate a face to see the ugliness of rooms rented for the last time.

Five o'clock. We sneaked out and sailed the boat at dawn it was made of a fence post pulled up one night from the garden a pillowcase taken when they forgot to lock the linen closet the string was saved up from the cord around Mother Immaculata's mail. Poco held by his heels over the trash can got it out along with tin cans for soldiers' helmets magazines we had a new car pasted up every week and things to eat with their names in French. The titty magazines we cut up and put under the bed springs facing down you only had to lie on the floor and see it all bursting out glorious.

They never knew what became of Barber let out at the legal age he could have been a doctor the way he cared for sick birds rabbits stray cats when he wasn't in the closet fucking with Gonzales who did it for a penny I only touched Gonzales once enough to know he wasn't worth it we got the rubber hose for that Mother Immaculata was always spying. The softest thing I had was the rabbit's tail from Barber's dead menagerie the cook poisoned everything said it was unsanitary sick animals in the pantry we trusted her we liked the way she smelled of womanly secretions titty bags full she never let us near.

Six o'clock. The fragile first sunlight spilling on the tops of buildings dated 1889 1892 1899 I wonder if the buildings spoke would they object to going down toward no purpose whatsoever and how come they couldn't let this burg die of natural causes the way most places do and god I feel like busting something but there's not a thing to bust.

Here comes a woman hurrying down the street her hair in curlers beyond repair she is old and dry harming no one I do not know why I should dislike her but I do. The garage man Pope jumping out of his pickup with a dog better qualified than he says he'll just go fishing when the place is done an honest man you'd think he'd zip his fly.

Seven o'clock. The old Yellow Bird Hotel creaked and groaned in the wind its ancient radiators hissed and clanked there was the odor of all the cabbage that had ever been cooked in the kitchen and all the beer that had ever been spilled on the barroom floor and the miners' odors of sweat tobacco disinfectant took up what was left of any clean air.

In addition to Joe Killeen the only other lodger at the four-room hotel was an old man by the name of Tom Smith who was always called the Coyote because when he was young he made his living stealing sheep then became a mule skinner then invested all his nickels dimes and quarters in a claim halfway up the mountain mined it without success for twenty years then sold out for a song to a metals company in 1950 which proceeded to remove nearly a million dollars' worth of uranium it had never occurred to the Coyote to buy himself a Geiger counter his whole mind was set on gold.

He was in his seventies now toothless friendless penniless except for his Social Security checks which he turned over to Josie Stringer in grateful payment for room and board he passed the time of day listening to the radio his dearest possession or when the weather turned fair he put on all the clothes he owned took a lunchbox and walked up and down across the mountain hunting for his mine the uranium had long since played out and his mine was no longer recognizable there was a tailings dump where he remembered it and the company had scraped away the entire hillside and the trees and earth and grass had eroded away leaving gullies deep enough to hide a horse in if he had a horse but he didn't he only spotted the wild ones from time to time racing toward the mesa oh to have caught one and broke it and save himself the long walk oh to be sixty again and there were sheep or even mules he could catch a mule sure.

The Coyote was thinking about catching himself a wild horse as he lay in his bed in a tiny room next door to Joe Killeen's he had his radio on and was listening to Western music he sang softly with it and in his heart he felt only gladness the radio was a good thing to have he turned it up and chirped in a creaky voice and then Killeen rapped on the wall shut up old man. The Coyote got out of his bed and shuffled to the wall and said you got no friendly spirit young feller now listen here and he began to croak sixteen tons of number nine coal I owe my soul to the company store shut up shouted Killeen I get no rest because of you and that damn radio how would you like me to come and smash it? The Coyote pondered that holding the radio in his hands the sweet music so full of joy filling his empty hours with the best of all worldly pleasure he would have first forsaken his tobacco or his sour mash before the radio he turned it low and went back to bed and did not sing anymore ever.

Killeen's Levi's were seated on a chair the legs crossed the handkerchief billfold key ring still in the pockets the legs were a little flat but the folds and creases were all his the knees exactly bent like his own legs hell man I wouldn't have shouted at you had I had my pants on a man don't think right without his Levi's on like a tiger without his tail I'm sorry do you hear and maybe I just ought to go yeah look at Daisy all lonesome in the street steamed-up windows and in need of a bath oh honey I treated you better than this yes sirree I don't neglect my girl you want to cut out is that it you want to roll on down the highway heading west speak out now girl before it's too late.

And while waiting for the answer he slipped into his Levi's and put on a clean shirt and combed his hair he looked okay in the mirror better than when he came oh hell he would just forget what Houghton said or didn't say and how the Muldoon girl had made him feel for the first time in his life. He'd just go on out to the project and work awhile and tell himself that yesterday was one of those things that didn't happen even if it did 'cause man there is no way you are going to trap yourself between a rock and a hard spot you got to go along like a log rolling down from the highest mountain and when it hits the river it's going to float on down to the sea that's the way it is hotshot that's the way it's always been for me.

As he was opening the door to go to work he saw her standing there in the sallow light from the overhead bulb dangling on a cord and she seemed so small and fragile that it took his breath away and he took her by the hand and led her in and said gently what's the matter?

—Couldn't sleep.

—Me neither he said reckon it's the altitude.

With her hands at her sides she did not move at all but stood looking up at him and very quietly she said no it's you Killeen.

—Me?

—Yeah how about that?

He made no answer but drew her to him gently and stroked her hair and touched it with his lips and she smelled so good and was so soft that he felt all tightened up inside and he wished it wasn't time to go to work and time to think about how he was going to eat and time to report for duty and time to compromise. Screw it. He would be an hour late and maybe get fired and maybe go hungry and maybe tomorrow would never come and what did it matter anyway just to make a buck when all of him seemed to be going into this girl so that he was without all his usual defenses and he damn well didn't feel like making her another mark on the wall and he had to do it right

90

nervous and fumbling as he was and trying to stand up and not fall down and not rush her too much and then there she was taking her clothes off in that wretched room and looking at him with great sad eyes. And so there was nothing he could do except give her what she desired and she desired one hell of a lot and could give it too and kept on giving it every damn day when he got back from the project hangdogged and pooped she revived him and made him feel alive in a way he'd never been and he found himself saying after only two weeks had passed I love you. And he did and would and there was no help for it and he would have asked her to marry him but it was the wrong thing it involved a future and the lack of future was what they had in common and what the hell did he want to put a leash on her for? Because she had said on the very night he knew he couldn't have her anymore she had said with tears in her eyes I love you Killeen I love you too.

Time past and time future
Allow but a little consciousness.
To be conscious is not to be in time.

5

    At night vast stretches of land are as lonely as
the sea and the form of the sea is the form of the land also and
there is a terrible void connected with being out on the land at
night just as there is a void at sea. At night the sky presses down
on the land like an enormous bowl and the blackness of the land
is made bearable only by the Milky Way and the constellations
and the moon even if man has been to it and back the moon
retains its mystery especially on a winter night deep in the
Colorado high country and from your place on the wet cold
ground smelling the smell of frozen earth and touching what
has shriveled up and died and hearing only the sound of your

wild heart beating the night sky overhead disturbs the loneliness of your soul. The beauty of such a sky in such a place is dreamlike and unnerving one feels drawn upward at the same time the stars press downward there is no motion and one becomes desperate for motion demanding of the universe some sign of life and maybe if you are lucky out there on a winter night a star falls or a man-made satellite twinkles along on a straight course yet even this does not take away the emptiness the illusion of time suspended nor being so far removed from civilization that perhaps there is none after all and you are just adrift on a voyage from dark to dark again.

The sound of one's own voice becomes essential. And gripped by a primitive terror of the night there comes an involuntary whistle from one's lips soft and tentative and unheard by other ears and it is also like a sailor humming with the wind at night on a lonely watch but on the land at night the wind is not so great a force. Under usual circumstances it comes and goes a breath from the universe chill and melancholy deadended somewhere out there against a sheer rock wall.

Matt Brittman had spent the night on the land and felt himself to be as much of an animal as any man could be. The land had made him so. The land was what he worshiped and felt beholden to the land was what he would have given his legs for and bled for and given up all earthly delights for. He felt himself to be a measure of the land when it was strong he was strong when it failed he failed when it did not yield he did not yield when it reaped he reaped and when he saw it ravaged felt himself ravaged also. He hated builders and highway engineers hated developers and road pavers hated men in jeeps and the slobs on wheels who roared across the land leaving a trail of beer cans candy wrappers cigarette butts noise filth and tire tracks. When he caught one on his land it was all he could do to restrain himself the urge was strong to kill him and in another time another place that would have been his right.

The land put everything back into you and took you down

94

a peg or two. When you were feeling mighty big it made you small when you thought you could make it do what you wanted it would rear up and let you have it. You did not push the land the land pushed you making you grow to its size a thing you'd never do but struggled manfully to attain. You never injured land. If you dug a hole you covered it up if you had to chop a tree you felled it in such a way that it did not hit one that was growing straight and tall when you laid a fence and pounded the poles and posts into the land you apologized to it else the fence would fall down the land would not hold it. The land was good to you and you were good to the land. Nature could make it suffer but not you. Nature could give the land too much rainfall or not enough rainfall too much cold or too much heat too much wind and too much snow nature could strip the land and waste it but you could not. You had a solemn obligation as strong as to any god or country to kin or friend or foe the obligation to the land was to leave it better than you found it else you did not deserve to have the land. The land comforted you when you were sick picked you up when you were down the land verified your nothingness and quickened your pulse the way no woman could and when you died it was your hope that you would go quick the way the land went when it had to.

Matt Brittman stood in the mirror shaving thinking about the land and what was to become of it. The land had never failed him though he had failed the land and not listened to it when it was clearly understood that two things he'd done in his life were against himself and therefore against the land as well. One was selling twenty thousand acres when he needed cash the other had to do with marrying a woman when he had no comprehension that you did not treat them like men or like cattle you treated them like well women. You had to strain yourself at every moment to be what they wanted you had to play a sort of game with them in which you had to admit your weaknesses in front of them and make yourself out to be help-less and entrust yourself to their care you had to humor them

95

and pamper them and make them feel important when in truth they weren't well were they? There were some things they were good for some things they did that you could hardly do for yourself some times when the only way you felt at peace was with a woman some way you had to get rid of the pressure and a woman solved that a woman could trick you and you didn't mind provided you understood the rules a woman was often handy to have around and talk to a woman could make you feel pretty damn good. There was a place for the land and a place for women and you could not mix the two.

All these years had passed his whole lifetime really and he had fought back and pushed aside all that a man ought to have been able to give a little tenderness a little understanding and love whatever that was he could not be sure until now and now was too late he knew that as he finished dressing it was just too late he would go and find out just how late it was and put his suspicions to rest and confirm what he had already known for some months now and would not believe until Eli Wetherill told him and then he would make his plans and stick to them and there was just no time left and goddamn it all to hell he had really blown his life the only thing he had to show for it was the land and the cattle that had always been enough until now when he knew there was something more important that he could not name it had to do with starting over with digging up some long-buried emotions and laying them on the line. Now. When all the time was used up. Now. When Harley was all he had left and he couldn't tell him of his feelings just couldn't undo all the years and years of putting the kid down and telling him he was never going to make it as a man.

Well he had made it all right and without his help he'd been away for two whole years and he'd come back a person that Britt really didn't care to know and all the old sores had been opened up the kid asking for money his father saying no the kid telling him he couldn't stick around much longer and just what the hell was on his mind we don't have a thing to talk about the kid had said I just came back for a visit and I'm moving on dad going to look for a job in Washington or maybe L.A. And Britt had said what kind of job Harley you never worked a day in your life just like your mother. The kid had gotten sore all right and disappeared for two whole days leaving Britt afraid that he was never coming back and also that he'd made an awful mistake and owed the kid an apology and would tell him he was sorry and would explain what was happening to himself and why he needed the kid so bad so bad that he broke out in a cold sweat every time he thought of all his years going down the drain. Sure spill the beans and have the kid see him weak see him asking for help swallowing all his pride and putting his life in the kid's hands so the kid could kick him in the teeth then what well he had certain things he was not letting go of no matter what and he would try and use some patience and persuasion with the kid and bottle up his anger and his dislike of the way Harley had turned out he would just grit his teeth and level with the kid and Harley would come around the way he always had sure and it would be okay the whole thing dumped in Harley's hands and maybe it would take a year or so for Harley to really like what he had to do for his father but after all a man's son has certain obligations and how the hell does he know what's good for himself? He doesn't. You got to point these things out and get rid of all these silly notions a kid has nowadays nobody in his right mind would turn down what I got to offer Harley.

The kid had come back the day before and not spoken a single word he was sulking that's what he was doing like he was seven years old and couldn't have a brand-new pony and like he did at sixteen when he couldn't have a car no goddamn it Harley you don't get stuff handed to you let me see you work a little do you appreciate anything I've done for you do you do you? Like what Dad exactly what have you done for me? Now Harley you know I've done the best I could bringing you up alone I reckon you could have had a worse father than me I could have beat you up or run off the way your mother did but hell we've had a lot of things just you and me. Like what Dad just name one thing. The trouble with you Harley is that you have failed to recognize your advantages. What advantages? Look here Harley I have busted my gut trying to make this the goingest bunch of cattle in the West and it's all for you boy. Thanks a lot Dad but I don't want it. Why the hell not Harley give me one good reason. You remember old man Buckley dad who had that huge place right outside Montrose and for fifty years or more he was like a king it was yes sir Mister Buckley and no sir Mister Buckley and nobody made one move without the old man's okay he was in absolute power and control down to how the last blade of grass was used and then he died at eighty-three and people found out he had a son who'd been there for forty years working with his father only nobody had ever heard of him and never knew his name they just saw him around for all those years and figured he was a hired hand. Now Harley that is an extreme example Buckley was a fool you think I'd do that to you Harley why hell I ain't going to be around that long. Oh yes you will dad you'll live to be a hundred. I swear to you Harley I ain't going to reach half that. Even if you died tomorrow I don't want this place on your terms. What am I to do with it then? Sell it give it away I don't give a damn I'm going to do what I want to do and that's that. Listen to me you son-of-a-bitch you will take over this ranch and run it like I say. I can't. You mean you won't. All right then dad I won't. You are just like your mother was Harley selfish and no good so run away then and don't come back. I'm not running away dad I'm not. But he had for two whole days and came back during the night and there he was now sitting at the breakfast table as if there was nothing wrong.

Harley was going on twenty-five but could have passed for sixteen his face was like putty Britt thought pouring himself some coffee and sitting opposite the kid and he has his mother's soft hands and her mouth with a drooping lower lip how come

98

I never noticed how weak the damn kid looks.

—Dad said Harley holding a fork between his fingers I'm sorry I took off like that I figured I ought to get out of your sight a couple days and let you cool off.

—Me cool off why Harley we ain't come to blows yet said Britt evenly though his hands were trembling.

—I've been thinking dad and maybe you're right I ought to come and work with you.

Britt tried not to show his excitement he slurped his coffee and felt himself get warm inside well Harley that's right nice of you to come around I figured you'd come around I figured you'd see it my way sooner or later.

The kid's steady blue eyes penetrated his father's he was considerably smaller than Britt with longish yellow hair that Britt thought made him look like a hippie a hippie cowboy is all I need I'll make him cut his hair. But on one condition the kid was saying leaning back all nice and relaxed.

—And what might that be?

—You let me run this ranch the way I see fit.

—You Harley you?

—That's right.

—You must think I'm stupid or incompetent or plumb out of my mind.

—You want me or not?

—Now listen here Harley that is the most unreasonable outlandish impossible thing I ever heard tell.

—That's the only way it will work.

—And what am I supposed to do take up knitting?

—Get away dad enjoy yourself you've never been any-where or seen anything you've spent all your life in Yellow Bird I think you need a rest.

—Oh you do do you well that's just dandy and what do you reckon I'd come back and find everything all nice and pretty hell boy you don't know where to begin.

—I grew up here the kid said ignoring the rising anger in

99

his father and you taught me well I could do everything that you do.

—And no doubt better.

The kid's blue eyes were soft around the edges and when he smiled they crinkled up like Billy Deere's and a little dimple appeared in his cheek just like hers. Harley wiped his mouth with a napkin and his teeth showed up all white and even like a woman's teeth he was beginning to grow a mustache and that made Britt kind of mad too and the first thing you know he'll be smoking pot he said to himself watching the way the kid took his time to reply. What I want to do said Harley slowly is crossbreed this herd add some shorthorn blood or maybe Charolais.

—What said Britt coming out of his chair in stunned fury crossbreed a purebred herd?

—I've looked into genetics dad and I know damn well you could cut out some of this fancy stuff and get down to the business of raising food that's all ranching is dad isn't that really so?

Britt's head was splitting the pain had come and gripped him he thought he could explode or have a stroke he turned and saw that Harley was facing him his hands on his hips looking very sure of himself. Harley he rasped his breath coming in short gasps I put my life into that herd and you want to turn it into a bunch of mongrels.

—Bigger better beef is all who cares what they look like.

—I do said Britt and every cattle buyer in the West does.

—Well they're wrong.

—How come Harley how come you know so goddamn much all of a sudden?

Harley shrugged his shoulders and looked as weak as he ever did confronted with the truth oh I don't know so much dad he said slowly it's just a hunch.

—A hunch said Britt furiously you are telling me to run this ranch on a hunch.

Harley was squirming in his seat well he said staring at the floor people say—

—People say well to hell with people *I* know what is good for this ranch and what is good for this ranch is not a stupid son-of-a-bitch like you.

Harley's shoulders drooped and in a barely audible voice he said well that's okay too what I really want to do is study law.

—Law said Britt sinking back into his chair law?

—That's right.

—Now listen Harley you will never be a lawyer hear and you will never be a rancher you will never be anything but a bum.

The kid seemed to cower then just like Britt had so often seen him do and he saw his advantage and pressed it in a voice that was pure hate he said Harley you are the biggest disappointment of my life worse than that Harley you are a disgrace to the Brittman name you have inherited your weakness from your mother and let me tell you boy some of the worst blood ever to run through Texas ran through the Deeres halfwits crooks scoundrels not one honest straight true man ever drew breath in the Deere family and by some freak of nature you have inherited it all.

Harley was slumped in his chair and with his hands over his face he was beginning to sob the way Matt Brittman knew he would and a smile of satisfaction crept over Britt's face and he relaxed a little and said now Harley tell me why you don't like my cattle.

—They're not good enough said Harley with a sudden fury.

—Not good enough not good enough and before he knew what he was doing he had hurled himself at Harley and with his fists doubled into weapons tore at the kid's head and his middle and the chairs broke and the dishes cracked and there was blood running out of Harley's nose the kid did not fight back at first and then with one powerful blow he sent his father spinning to the floor. Britt hit his head on the table leg and felt it opening up the hurt feeling good and the blood warm in his hair he was nearly out cold and it was so godawful he wished he could just die. Then he felt Harley's arms around his chest and the kid was saying I'm sorry dad I'm sorry.

Britt's foot came up and the tip of the boot connected where he wanted it to and Harley staggered back against the wall grabbing himself between the legs and howling.

The sweat and the blood and the tears were all mixed up on Britt's swollen anguished face he had only one thing to say to the kid and the words cracked in the stillness of his mind get out of here Harley get out of here for good I never want to lay eyes on you you bastard not as long as I live.

And Britt left him crumpled on the floor and did not look back as he put on his jacket and his hat and let his boots take him clanking out the door into the bright September sun he felt drained and hollowed out he was fighting nausea and an urge to take the gun from the back window of the pickup and put it to his head his world had gone up in smoke and there was nothing left nothing at all just a hole where his heart ought to be and an ache that was impossible to describe festering inside of him and it was weak weak that he was and without courage or decency he ought to take the gun to Harley was what he ought to do and the fire boiled within him and set his teeth to chattering and he sat hunched over the wheel of the pickup for a spell unable to move or think until the foreman drove up. He was a sober silent man who'd been there thirteen years he'd come from someplace outside Calgary and was as dependable as the wind Bob Wingate never asked what was not his business and so he only said you okay Mister Brittman?

And Britt who was without feeling in his hands or feet shook his head and saw the foreman in a prism the light splintering and going into needles what oh yes Bob I'm fine.

—Got the last of the bulls ready to weigh Mister Brittman.

—What oh yeah Bob the bulls well I got to go to town.

—Go to town Mister Brittman when you got the bulls to weigh? The foreman leaned out of his pickup and looked closely at the man whom he'd worked for all these years and never really understood well it was not his place to get involved he did his job and got good wages and what more could a man expect.

—You go ahead and do it Bob I just can't today.

—Without you Mister Brittman said Wingate oh I couldn't do that.

—Well goddamn it man you do it or you're out of a job.

The foreman hung his head the soiled and stained Stetson rode on his brow as if it were part of his skin no he would not ask about the blood on Mister Brittman's shirt nor try and reason why the boss was acting strange he only said yessir Mister Brittman I'll do the best I can but—

—But what Bob said Britt sharply.

—Well sir it's a two-man job you reckon Harley could—

—Harley is no longer part of this ranch you got that straight Bob he is no longer here.

—Yessir Mister Brittman.

—And one thing else Bob.

—What's that?

—Tomorrow you dehorn.

—Tomorrow Mister Brittman why it's my day off I'm planning to take the wife to town.

—Some other time Bob.

—All right Mister Brittman. And his tired eyes filmed over it wasn't right to do a man that way not when he'd given the best years of his life to a job and got rewarded only with extra pay you had to give a man more than that to make him feel like a man well you couldn't hardly blame Mister Brittman no more ever since Harley come home he ain't been right always cross and brooding like he's figuring to get Harley mad on account of he ain't a kid no more he's all growed up and trying to find out how he fits in well he don't I guess and that's one godalmighty shame.

—What are you looking at Bob?

—Nothing Mister Brittman.

—You were staring at me like I was a dirty bastard.

—Just thinking to myself Mister Brittman.

103

—Do it on your own time Bob he said and threw the pickup into gear and tore down the gravel road bouncing over the cattle guards and not really seeing the land the way he always used to it was gone out of him all right his dream his hope and now his ability to see. The drive to Yellow Bird was just two miles and he knew every inch of it the barbed-wire fences and the padlocked gates the grove of crooked aspen and ponderosa pine the ruts in the road that got deeper with the rain the black rocks along the first arroyo with its caked banks like elephants' feet the deep cold stream running under the wooden bridge the stream he'd nearly killed Marcus Muldoon over and then the windmill beside the road he'd named Big John after his dad the blue spruce where an eagle lived for years and years until he'd found it dead one morning shot by some lunatic he'd have killed if he'd caught him at it. The land between his ranch and town was as familiar to him as his own face and it picked him up each time he drove along noticing each small thing and each small change the way no man could unless he had a practiced eye and took pleasure in finding a meadowlark some morning or a jackrabbit hightailing it into the brush or a pair of bucks come down to drink at dusk all of that could steal away the loneliness or the staleness or the just plain tiredness yes that particular stretch of land could always make him glad to be alive. But not that morning because that morning for the first time he did not see the land did not see the porcupine scurrying to get out of his way he ran it over without noticing he was going seventy miles an hour and the tires barely held the road he came to the pavement and went through the stop sign causing the bread truck headed for Sweeney's to swerve into a ditch but he did not see or hear that either nor was he aware of the little boy on the bridge over the river whom he narrowly missed as he roared into Yellow Bird's Main Street.

Eli Wetherill's office was once the bank which had shut down the same year as the hospital and so after they had stripped it of its paneling and huge old rosewood desks

104

removed the safes and tellers' cages Eli had moved right in partitioning it in half. Even so it was too large and somewhat dreary with just one window and the walls almost the color of the cash that stank up the air even now long after it was carted off. The venetian blinds in the front window were pulled at a rakish angle and several slats were missing so that the sunlight fell in patches on the rusted linoleum floor illuminated the brass spittoon that sat beside the straight-backed chairs from Sully's Snooker Hall and the half-dead palm donated by Mrs. Thornburg after her husband retired from the undertaking business.

Matt Brittman rubbed the dirt off the window and looked in his heart thumping a little harder than usual it had taken him all these months to bring himself to the doctor's door and the doctor was not there well he would put it off until he was and give himself one more reprieve then the pain struck again and he knew there was no time for reprieves or anything else and he straightened up and tipped his hat to Robinson's wife one hell of a dandy gal married to the superintendent of Yellow Bird's unnatural death the U.S. Army Corps of Engineers' own personal executioner. Well now that is quite a wiggle lady and if you don't get out of sight Harley Jesus Christ I will never see you again hey lady come back come back I forgot to introduce myself Harley you bastard how could you and God my whole head is coming off and there is this tremendous hole opening up and it is dark filled with fresh manure sheepmen with drawn guns and nobody ever thanks you anymore.

—Britt what the hell are you doing sitting on the steps and bellowing like a cow said Eli noticing the blood on Britt's white shirt.

—I wasn't bellowing Eli.

—Like a bull moose now get in here and sit down.

The inside was chilly and smelled terrible a single lamp was on and shone on the puke-green walls a calendar for 1967 was hanging lopsided and a mangy elk's head held a cigarette between its teeth and the doctor's hat on its rack on Eli's littered desk there was a human skull an Indian artifact he'd found near Mesa Verde many years ago. He'd refused to give it to the Park Service along with an ancient femur he said was crippled with arthritis he sat in his chair and fingered the skull as he stared at his friend and whistled man you have tangled with bear.

Britt looked at his shirt and felt the lump on the back of his head it's all over Eli between Harley and me he's a stranger with a lot of bullshit in his head he had the nerve to tell me to get out and let him breed the cattle to a bunch of sheep.

—Sheep?

—Well practically tell me something Eli have I done good with the cattle?

—As near as I can tell I ain't no expert though.

—And the land why Eli you can see with your own eyes it's better than it was.

—That's true.

—And ain't I done the best I could with Harley raising him up without a ma?

—You done a good job Britt nobody could complain.

—Sure and I been proud enough till now and now I just don't give a damn.

—Aw Britt you just got Black Ass is all let me clean up your head we'll go have us a drink.

But the rancher shook his head that ain't what I come to see you about he said and could not go on.

Eli put the skull in its place and folded his hands well if it's about Harley don't worry I talked to him last night and I know what's on his mind Britt now maybe he's a radical and young and crazy and maybe he'll go wrong but goddamn it man so were you once upon a time remember the first Mexican steers you bought and they all died within a year.

—That's not my fault Eli sicker cattle you never saw.

—Let the kid have his mistakes.

—At the expense of my entire herd?

—Give him a section and a couple dozen head what harm can it do?

—Eli you don't know a damn thing about the cattle business and nothing about Harley either he's vicious and ruthless and he'll kill me if he can yes he will Eli he wants the ranch real bad to destroy all that I have done well I'll kill the son-of-a-bitch before he gets to me.

—Britt!

—I mean it Eli.

The doctor came around and shook the rancher hard so hard he finally said you're hurting me Eli.

—Just trying to get some sense into you is all said Eli angrily now settle down.

Britt sat straight in his chair the fire had gone out of him and he was pale so pale and not well thought Eli in alarm wanting to take his pulse or listen to his heart they were getting older the two of them and crotchety Britt's face looked puffed out and aged for the first time. Eli Wetherill felt a lump rising in his throat and he saw the two of them as bookends to a shelf of obsolescence and he did not know how to put it into words so he merely said you up to a game of two-handed pangui I got four bits to get reckless with.

Britt stood up his fingernails were cracked and one was gone entirely his hands were large and firm and would have matched in color a roan stallion of the finest order. The way he was put together with his big raw bones hung with taut brown flesh and a carriage that was tall and straight and limber reminded Eli of a noble Douglas fir you could not look at him and think he was not an extension of the land that had sprung up and taken human form pouring as much back into the earth as he had taken out. And had done it right and well and on time and Harley would never match him. But it was not for him to say and he resolved to keep his mouth shut.

—I better not gamble today Eli you got time to look at me right quick?

—You ailin'?

—Indigestion is all can't stand my own cookin' you know anybody'd take up with a poor lonesome cowpoke?

—Josie maybe. She's getting on.

He shook his head and smiled she's got it all doped out. Me I just need a heifer to roll with in the grass a piece of ass like that would make me feel inferior.

—What else besides indigestion you old fart?

—Nothing much some colorful piss is all.

—Pain?

—In the ass.

—Drop your socks you revolving son-of-a-bitch.

—Right now?

—Hell yes you think I got all day?

So they went down the long hall to the examining room together those friends of many years and they did not think about time future but only of time past and they speculated about where it had all gone and how and decided it was good not every man had the chance to do what they had done and to themselves they attached the same kind of individualism that had made the West and dwelled upon it and felt good and laughed as Eli was turning on the lights and saying hell Britt we're not rugged we're ragged.

—We would stand out right well in the Smithsonian.

—A place of honor next to the stegosaurus.

—Thought I'd keep the dodo company.

—They got a dodo?

—I aim to give 'em one that lives inside this skin of mine and refuses to behave itself has got some notion to make itself extinct along with me.

—The symptoms being what said Eli laying out the steril-ized tools of his trade.

—Cantankerous constipation gas around the gizzard the pain is in the ass blood is in his piss don't ask me why he hates to let me ride a horse can't tolerate the bounce.

—Lay him out said Eli won't take long I'd like his piss some fresh manure his blood an x-ray wouldn't hurt him none you think he'd swallow that?

108

It took a while all he had to do was complicated he wanted to be sure he hadn't overlooked a thing all his skill and concentration never failed him he even recollected what he thought he had forgotten.

—So what is the verdict on the parasite said Britt getting dressed I want to get him buried before hunting season starts.

—I got to send the stuff to Denver with the x-rays said Eli with a lightness he did not possess. Listen you son-of-a-bitch why don't you drop him off at Colorado General they can take a look at him with all the right equipment specialists and such I'll call them up and get him in maybe the end of the week how's that?

—To hell with it said Britt you get him in a hospital they'll screw him up but good he'll be worse off than he ever was and that's not what he needs an enema might do the trick blast him loose with dynamite.

—You want something for the pain said Eli fingering the bottles on the shelf.

—Pain he doesn't give me much I can outlast him there you fart I just use my brain he hasn't got to that yet and never will said Britt putting on his hat. I got some bulls to ship Eli after that let's you and me go up around old Marvine Creek get us a ten-point buck. Henderson's got a cabin the last week in October can you get away?

—I think I can said Eli. Had planned to go down around Kayenta investigate the situation guess it can wait.

—Everything can wait time is standing still for us imagine two old studs balanced just right can you see any reason why we ought to worry?

—Nope said Eli I can't.

He watched him go tried not to think of how he walked like no man he had ever seen tried not to think of how they'd been together in another stage of life tried not to remember anything at all he was not a sentimental man he had no time for that which was thoroughly in the past. He rushed the x-rays through

109

they told him a questionable story he was not sure could not be sure as he packaged the film and shipped it off to Denver with the tests when he went to get the mail.

He had not slept in so many nights that the insides of his eyeballs ached and his head felt swabbed out with tongue depressors. He was a wreck and knew it knew he ought to take better care of himself but for what and for whom? Nobody that's just the trouble. And loneliness struck him along with the midmorning light coming over the brooding disfigured mountain and spilling across the rooftops oh how he loved that poor dilapidated town and the blue sky and the fringe of low mountains off to the west and the hugeness of it all and there was the goddamn river to put an end to it oh the Lord giveth the Lord pisseth the Lord fucketh and the Lord taketh away.

Because he could not face his office again that morning he went on down the street to Josie's place again noting the sudden prickling freshness of the air and the cobwebs in the windows of the old Yellow Bird *Herald* and the coal smoke pouring from the chimneys it was beginning to get cold by God the seasons kept on coming no matter what and that is all it is the seasons marching across your life and pretty soon you are no more.

The drainspout had fallen off the side of the Yellow Bird Hotel and lay on the sidewalk no one would ever fix it or carry it away they would not heed what fell at their feet between now and the day of doom. Josie Stringer looked relaxed a toothpick in her mouth at the same time she smoked a cigarette and fried hamburgers with onions on the side. The doctor swung onto the stool and studied her from behind she still had pretty good hips and breasts her shoulders had not sagged too much from all the work four kids and a husband who'd died after a lifetime in the mines and left her penniless but proud. He wished he could have laid her as a token of his esteem but his heart wasn't in it he would have spoiled a very important relationship.

Her elbow in a puddle of beer she was arguing with Beetle James the dude rancher over what was wrong with the country

110

he said it was the goddamn kids she said it was the goddamn President he runs the nation like it was a sewage-disposal plant and we are just raw shit.

—Is Susie better said Eli studying the shape of Josie's breasts still round and high beneath her uniform.

—Sure and you know what doc it don't hurt her none to pee. Josie opened the corner of her mouth and let the toothpick fall into a potato chip box which held the trash. She did it without letting go of the cigarette stuck firmly between her teeth on the other side.

—Her sex life good said Eli noticing Josie's somewhat mulish ankles.

—Fair she's going on thirteen for a dog that's like seventy-eight so she hardly breathes hard when those he dogs come to call soup doc?

—What kind?

—Split pea made it myself including a lemon meringue pie got tired of all your bitching doc a person'd think I never saw to it you ate right. She was in charge of his stomach and looked at him with pure pleasure there were times when a look like that from a woman made him erect right then and there but he never had screwed her she only made it jump and then fall still.

The café was filling with the regular noontime crowd the dam construction men the road gang from the highway maintenance department old Pope who closed the garage from twelve till one Andy from the liquor store the ones who had no wives or homes to go to Josie saw about them all implacable and dedicated as a nun.

She pursed her lips and counted heads silently fourteen not bad she hoped the stew would hold out and that the beer was cold there weren't homemade biscuits she hadn't time the coffee was especially good the meringue had set just right. Her heart was full she whistled The Battle Hymn of the Republic slammed shut the silver drawer with her goodly thigh kicked the Drano can out of sight and inhaled the marvelous burning

111

crust of her grill sweated over these many happy years.

Eli stirred the soup he wasn't hungry he didn't want a drink after all he sipped his coffee and found himself with fear gripping his throat and spreading down until he could no longer feel the tightness of his shoes. He had always been able to control fear talk back to it and make it disappear.

Oh come on come on you don't know for sure the x-ray wasn't definite it's for them to say they could operate cobalt treatments he'd have to stand for that if I had to knock him in the head to get him there. In one year he'll be dead. Oh stop that talk in one year we could all be dead. Well he has no choice in this predicament. True true and yet I've seen a man survive by will alone. But how long can you prolong certain processes certain loathsome growths certain responses to what you cannot control. I've seen worse thought worse and been wrong you know that medicine makes more mistakes than government.

—You haven't heard a word I said doc. Josie banged on the bar with a soup ladle dropped it on the floor and put it in the soup. Tony wrote and asked me to come to Kansas City.

—What for Kansas City said Eli trying to remember who Tony was.

Josie's hands flew in the air a peal of laughter shook her noble bosom.

—Honestly doc a person'd think you was deaf. She spoke the words slowly enunciating each syllable as a nun would with a catechism for six-year-olds. Tony is my sister's husband owns a wholesale grocery business in Kansas City she said. Kansas City Missouri which is better than Kansas City Kansas. He says there's a place for sale cheap. Good neighborhood. Lots of customers. Good will. Lady died or something. You think I ought to go? Tony wants me to.

Eli mopped up the coffee in the saucer using a paper napkin.

—You should go Josie if that's what you want.

—I got to make a living doc only— She looked around at

112

the men who were eating laughing playing the jukebox reading the Denver *Post*. She came close and whispered.

—It's not Colorado.

—Pretty flat.

—Yeah and the people and noise and traffic and filth I think I wouldn't like it.

—No sky.

—No anything what do they do for air it's all contaminated.

—No mountains.

—Not a one it's just like eastern Colorado only worse. She chewed the end of a pencil. They'd think I was a yokel.

—You know better than that Josie.

—Yeah they would doc it's kinda like a zoo. You know me doc I'm as local as that sagebrush and twice as tough to kill that would do it all right me stuck in the wrong dirt.

He put his other hand over hers it was the closest he'd come to communion he didn't care what anybody thought he leaned across and kissed her.

One week passed before he knew one week in which he did not sleep and the edges of his life got fuzzy and day passed into night without his knowing there was no light and the day came when he got the word and word was passed to Matt Brittman exactly as it should have been.

Eli had a bottle and two glasses on the table he poured the whiskey steadily and said you got your debts paid and books balanced?

—Yep.

—You're checkin' out.

Matt Brittman's face betrayed no emotion. Got to sooner or later I reckon he said in a husky voice.

—I made arrangements for you to be in Denver next Monday we are going to get some of it out of you at least.

—No Eli I am not going to any damn hospital ever.

—Well then you won't be around long.

—How long?

—Oh a couple months maybe depends on how you behave yourself.

—And how fast the booger grows that right?

—Yep.

—I don't want Harley to get wind of this.

—That's your business.

—Harley's gone Eli took off a week ago I ain't heard a word.

—You want me to try and find him?

—Hell no I don't he'll be around as soon as I push on.

The doctor looked at the way the light fell across Matt Brittman's face and how the man was tough so tough you'd think he'd never break you got guts you bastard any other man'd be in pieces after what I just said.

Britt got up and put an arm around Eli's shoulders I knew a little while back went to some fancy specialist but I didn't accept it Eli not till I heard it from you and now it's okay it's as true as winter coming on and likewise can't be helped.

There comes a time when life becomes too delicate for words when all of what a man is or isn't hangs on what he doesn't do and Eli Wetherill knew better than to let himself break down and cry or get all worked up and not do either of them any good but one thing was for sure he hadn't slipped this time he could still function as a doctor and friend to a man he felt a sense of satisfaction knowing it was his word that Britt had been hanging on he was of some good after all.

—Eli?

—What?

—Got something I want to tell you to do will you promise to do it?

—Depends.

—No you got to promise first.

—How can I promise what I don't know I can promise?

—We been friends pretty near forever right and I never asked you to do anything bad right and you and me have always understood what a lot of people don't remember Plummer Eli remember what you did to him?

114

—Give him morphine enough to kill him twice over only it didn't work he lived on like a vegetable Jesus Britt don't ask me to do that.

—That's what I'm asking Eli only do it right when the time comes.

—I can't.

—I'll do it myself then.

—You can't.

—One of us has got to you or me which is it?

Eli filled his glass walked to the window where the day had just bled into the low hills to the west the street was deserted only one car rolled by and there was only one person walking. He said I can't do it Britt that's the most terrible thing you ever asked.

—The most humane now Eli you always said and I always agreed that a thing gets to be where it is no longer useful and it becomes a liability then it's got to go and it becomes the responsibility of the person closest to it to see it goes fast and clean when the proper time comes.

—That's okay for sick animals but not humans Britt.

—What about Plummer and there was another one that man from the sawmill who cut himself in two.

—That was different I didn't even know the sawman and Plummer was just a crazy miner we're speaking here of you.

—Then Eli you will watch me waste away little by little month by month and then one day you'll see me and I'll be a shadow of myself and what will stick in your mind is how you let me rot how you did not have the decency to chop down a diseased and falling tree said Matt Brittman with such control that Eli was amazed.

—I would never let you come to that.

—I would never let myself come to that but the question is which of us knows best when that moment comes when I no longer know right from wrong light from dark life from death when I can no longer think straight when I no longer care about the land yes that's a fair and final test.

—I couldn't live with myself.

—The way I see it Eli this would help you out you'd have to leave this place that's the other advantage giving you another start.

—Burdened with guilt.

—Doing for one man what he cannot do himself.

—Neither of us has to do it you could just—

—Just what? Get juiced up with pain killer fed through a tube feel my own mind splintering my body rotting watch the pity in their eyes the endless vigil and when it's over it's all the same.

—Maybe there's a chance.

—There's no chance and you know it.

—They'll find a way to cure it.

—Not on this old stud.

—I could never practice medicine again.

—You don't want to practice medicine again you know it's all past my kind of ranching your kind of doctoring nobody wants it anymore it just ain't practical.

—And if I didn't practice medicine what would I do?

—Travel plant those tomatoes in Israel like you said you wanted to.

—Hit the jug is what I'd do.

—If you had a notion to but Eli I reckon deep down you know you'll never let the bottle put you in the grave.

—What's a man to do when he's finished?

They were silent for a while the perspiration ran down both their faces the smell was mixed with whiskey and antiseptics the stark white light overhead lit their features with garish imprecision.

—Christ Britt said Eli with his arms stretched toward the ceiling.

—It finally makes sense doesn't it?

—I'm just getting tight is all everything makes sense.

—You or me Eli?

116

—Jesus Britt.

—I could be out hunting with you make it look like an accident happens all the time I just don't want to know exactly when.

—How could I know either? I'm slipping Britt I don't always know what day it is don't remember if I ate lunch or not can't be depended upon.

—You set a mighty fine fracture couple of weeks ago.

—That oh I could do it half dead just the way you could pull a calf with the last breath you ever drawed.

—Maybe it will be easier if your mind's not altogether there.

—What and let McTavish pick me up for murder Christ I got to know exactly what I'm doing can't be on the sauce got to be functioning all the way oh Britt this is terrible to plan it like a tonsillectomy no I won't be able to do it right I'm sure I won't.

—You damn well better if I'm counting on you and you never come through then what do I do wake up some morning a blithering idiot unable to even reach the gun much less use it?

—I can't play God again I can't.

—Not even for the sake of Galina Jordan?

—What? Britt had not spoken the name for twenty-five years or more.

—Remember that spring Eli remember how she died and what did you do because you bungled the job tried to kill yourself drank up a whole bottle of Lysol or some damn thing and who found you Eli and poured milk into you and made you vomit yourself inside out who cut you down when you tried it again in old Salazar's barn and when you laid your head in the river Eli who yanked you out three times saved your stinking hide and has never mentioned it for nigh on thirty years who did that Eli who?

—You Britt you but I loved her I did love her.

117

—Loved her hell you loved a lot of women in those days she was nothing special.

—I let her die.

—You did no such thing.

—I was drunk when I delivered her.

—An accident an accident your day off the horse doctor's patient as I recall not yours at all she couldn't have been because—

—It's come back to haunt me Britt the kid has turned up after all this time.

—What kid?

—Her kid the five dollar baby I took to the orphanage in Denver remember.

—The hell he has.

—He has I tell you.

—How can you be so sure?

—The goddamn date Britt May 20 1939 the night she died you think I could forget that date oh Christ Joe Killeen is his name came to town couple weeks ago with a clipping Rose Houghton put in about a kid born May 20 1939.

—Rose Houghton what'd she know?

—Beats me Britt 'cept as I recall she was working in the hospital a lot of nights maybe the night I let Galina die I just can't recall and he dropped his head into his trembling hands.

—You think he's your kid Eli is that what you think?

—He could've been Galina never know for sure she had a lot of men well he ain't never going to know you think I'd ever tell him what his mother was and look at me go on take a look you realize I'm all through.

—Bullshit Eli you got a ways to go.

—No I ain't got far and that's why this kid has never got to know what you and me know he's got to be just one of them five dollar babies born in this state from Central City down to Creede from Breckenridge to Cripple Creek to Yellow Bird and Telluride Ouray Silverton Durango you name it Britt there was

118

a happy horde of bastards laid out from camp to camp.

—I'll have a talk with him Eli.

—The hell you will.

—Not mention your name I swear just welcome him to town is all.

Eli Wetherill shook his head please don't do that Britt.

—Hell man you realize I ain't got a son anymore you realize he's good as dead?

—I'm sorry Britt there's nothing you can do.

—There is maybe this Killeen kid would like a million-dollar ranch maybe he would like a herd that's taken nearly thirty years to build maybe he would like what nobody in his right mind would turn down except that bastard Harley.

—Don't you do it now back off Britt and listen.

—I'm listening Eli what about our deal you going to do it or not I got to get a move on.

—Hold on Britt you expect I can give you an answer just like that?

—Yeah I do and you got exactly three minutes in which to decide else I do it myself and I have the guts to do it Eli. Thought about it plenty of times what the hell you just go into night is all.

The whiskey was getting to him and the awful specter of what was happening to his friend was too much he felt close to complete disintegration it was like leprosy and he might as well give in.

—Britt he said at last I have a better idea what if you and I was just to say we got us a contest you get me or I get you whichever comes first and we lay out some ground rules dependent upon our dissolution into night.

—I couldn't do that to you Eli you plumb crazy?

—I'm washed up Britt like you just said when a thing is no longer useful it's got to be retired.

—Retire then.

—And stare at the wall.

—Go someplace do something.

—No place to go nothing to do.

—Eli what's a man to do in a case like this?

—Jump out of an airplane but I hate to waste the ticket.

It struck them as funny then and there they had lived with life and death so long that the business of their own dying was what they called their face-up time and it would come to them in the same way that all of life had come head on and without much room for sentiment.

—Eli Britt said after a while feeling pleasantly drunk I will have to try and get you first else you will have no reason to get me second and what if I never do?

—Oh I'll give you a reason make you mad enough to pick up your .44 and plug me in the head.

—You silly son-of-a-bitch.

—Got to work on it a while Britt figure out a plan you got a plan?

—No plan.

—Me neither s'pose we can't think of one?

—Avalanche pray for a god a'mighty avalanche.

—Not a prayin' man Britt.

—Nor a god-fearin' one.

—Nope we just a couple old salmon goin' up the river to spawn.

—What we goin' to spawn?

—Bullshit same as always.

—Let's shake on it Eli to make it legal like.

—You got my word since when you doubt my word?

—No notice of foreclosure posted beforehand Eli no warning whistles alarm clocks or flashing signal lights agreed?

—Okay.

—One other thing it's got to be outside.

—Outside?

—On the land.

—What land?

120

—Any land just so it's land.

—Okay.

—Now Eli we never speak of it again we'll just drink to what we had when we were young and the place was good.

—You revolving son-of-a-bitch.

—You lousy bastard.

—Eli remember the time you ran out naked in the street to watch the fire down on Main?

—They forgot to use the new fire engine.

—And poor old Mister Higgins the retired preacher who ran the novelty store he snatched up an armful of skyrockets and ran outside plumb forgot his wife who was sleeping in the back.

—And those seamstress girls from Alabama who dragged their reed organ six blocks to keep it from burning up.

—Yeah and Pinky Johnson had to interrupt a winning hand when he felt his feet were getting hot ran out with the cards and they played there in the street under the lamplight.

—Oh Britt and I never will forget the time we were up at Boone's place hunting elk you put that dude to work gathering dung to start a fire with.

—It burnt okay now didn't it?

—Stunk like a sewer fresh shit was what it was.

—The hell it was you think I can't tell between fresh and mummified shit?

They were like a couple of brothers who were very close or like two veterans who had shared a war they laughed as they remembered and the past grew richer as they remembered for looking back they plucked out only that which was rich and therefore serving its rightful purpose to make the future able to be faced.

Here is a place of disaffection
Time before and time after
In a dim light: neither daylight
Investing form with lucid stillness
Turning shadow into transient beauty
With slow rotation suggesting permanence
Nor darkness to purify the soul

6

By the end of September the sunlight did not strike Yellow Bird until nine o'clock in the morning and people began to mumble as they always did that getting up in the shadows was the first sign of winter and getting up in the dark. The relentless white sun was what made life at high altitude even remotely tolerable and on the days when it did not shine the moods of the people matched the gloom of the sky. In the winter when heavy banks of clouds shrouded the top of the mountain and held back the sunlight and the sky spewed blizzard after blizzard the town was not at all like the picture postcard that visitors said it was. It was a town in hibernation a town betting that the one paved road which connected it to Coronado would remain open at least half of the time it was a town which quietly yearned for the ski trade which had restored so many Colorado mining camps with another kind of gold or for a summer tourist business to give it yet another shot in the arm.

But because Yellow Bird was going to die because it was so remote and so far off the beaten path and because not a single new public building had been erected since 1945 tourists simply passed through gawked and went on to towns which had melodramas steam trains tours through the gold mines and souvenirs made in Japan. In 1951 when nearly forty feet of snow fell on Yellow Bird in a single winter four people committed suicide. In 1964 when there were thirty-six consecutive days without sunlight the retired station master went to Pueblo and committed himself to the asylum four marriages ended in divorce there was one murder and ten new babies born the following fall double the normal annual crop. Cakes fell when the sun did not shine none of the newspapers were bought off the stand the purchase of whiskey went up people stopped writing graffiti on T.P.'s service-station walls and there was a general sullenness among friends. It had been that way for eighty years in Yellow Bird for as the generations came and went the weather did the same there was a time of course in the days before automobiles that the people of Yellow Bird were sealed off for the winter and sent teams of dogs down to Coronado to bring in a few supplies. But no more. That final September people began getting out the coal-oil lamps in case the power failed took the down comforters out of the hope chests washed the long johns in extra-strong detergent chopped firewood and stacked it on the back porches tanked up the cars with antifreeze tacked sheets of plastic around the storm windows and took down all the signs which said welcome tourists camp here free drinking water here stood Bat Masterson's saloon this steam engine made its last run November 29 1947 RIP gold paning (sic) 50¢ per hour.

In late September the air was as cold as the inside of a refrigerator it smelled clean however and was so cool that noses which had not run since spring began an eight-month drip. The wind came down from the mountain carrying dust from what hadn't healed up and when the dust was no longer airborne it meant also that winter had truly begun. They looked to the mountain for everything for signs of spring and signs of winter for changes in the weather and for the time when the sun began to slip past the summit notch that meant the day had exactly five full hours of sunlight to it if they could see the top of the peak upon arising it meant the weather might hold off if not then you could expect most anything from hail which ruined the roses in July to a cloudburst that set the goddamn river on its ear they also looked to the mountain as a symbol of what they'd lost a chance to make a fortune in getting out the gold to be minted into coins stamped IN GOD WE TRUST.

That final September in Yellow Bird had an anxiety about it that was not entirely due to winter coming on and the sunlight growing scarcer and the air more insistent to be felt. It had to do with the last three hundred residents the hangers-on the entrenched citizens of that town the native sons and daughters the yokels the country hicks the ones whose isolation had bred indifference to the outside world it had to do with those typecast individuals getting ready to move out. Since winter in Yellow Bird was merely to be tolerated with a distant promise of spring in a punch 'n' grow flower box there was not much use in staying on if there was nothing to hold you. So a number of families took their pet cats and pet dogs and their children carrying dolls basketballs model rockets saddles and their unfinished 4-H projects and loaded them into vans and automobiles being careful to leave the houses clean and the gates shut and utilities disconnected they even scrubbed their bathtubs and burned the trash which included all the things related to life in Yellow Bird and now were no longer necessary. The parties given for those who departed before the gun were dreary sentimental affairs with nothing to talk about except what had been and how they would not have traded it for living anywhere on earth old Yellow Bird was good for kids it was a shame to expose them now to a different sort of life well time marches on everything has got to end sooner or later don't forget to write I bet it's hard to leave well Grand Junction's not so bad you'll forget us in a year.

The anxiety or communal Black Ass as Eli Wetherill would have called it was hard to put your finger on even if you lived in Yellow Bird you wouldn't have known exactly why you didn't feel like getting up in the morning or why you fought with your wife or screamed at the kids or took to burying yourself in magazines with ads about cruises to Greece or the Galápagos Islands and for once believed you might really do it. Or maybe the beer suddenly didn't taste good anymore or you couldn't stand the sight of the oatmeal you always ate when the mornings began to turn cold and although you knew this was the last fall and winter you'd ever spend in Yellow Bird some part of your mind conveniently blocked it out and you'd say with a smile *next* year I am going to put a Coleman heater in the bedroom so my feet are not like ice when I get up.

As Yellow Bird headed for its final stay on earth it was hard to know exactly what was happening to a town which had for all these years of its existence displayed an outer calm often mistaken for serenity by outsiders who believed a special kind of mysticism emanated from life at high altitude. The people of Yellow Bird were not profound nor were they sophisticated or especially versed in social graces good grammar appreciation of the arts higher education and deep conversation they would go unnoticed anywhere in the world except for one thing they were unmistakable Westerners and better yet unmistakable Coloradans and better yet unmistakable gold campers most of whom could remember when the mines were running most of whom could remember one actual killing one narrow escape with a wild animal one brawl with a drunken Indian one ordeal in the treacherous throbbing brooding mountains which were the source of their impulses inhibitions faults failures successes hopes dreams bold deeds that never happened except in their imaginations brought to life on cold winter evenings in front of a fire. Shut off as they were from civilization locked in at nine thousand feet attracting no newcomers for over twenty years the people of Yellow Bird were very much at home with one another and when the summer tourists happened to find them they did not like it and said as little as possible when they were made to feel like freaks that walk on all fours kiddo was how Josie Stringer expressed it. Except for one old mucker who charged a quarter to take tourists through his dilapidated played-out mine the people of Yellow Bird remained aloof from most strangers.

Among themselves they were like members of an old established club they joked a lot and made fun of themselves they loved to drink and gamble and make love they were earthy unpretentious hardworking souls with an abiding love for children horses dogs and neighbors they helped one another with everything from canning peaches to roofing a house or branding five thousand steers and if you laid a hundred-dollar bill in front of them as payment for haying your field you'd have insulted a man and strained a friendship some might have said they were in a boring inbred rut but if that was the case it was also a good rut harming no one in that little club where the only rules were that you remained honest loyal helpful considerate of your friends as long as you could keep in mind the little marked-off clans in that small community you never talked about your own you only talked about the *others*. As Yellow Bird got smaller and smaller there were no *others* and the lines between the clans were hard to find and people drifted in and out of days and years not knowing how it had got so mixed up but only that it was getting harder and harder to get a real feud going or to make some husband jealous or to find your girl in bed with another man or to bear grudges against people who had moved away or died it was everyday things like that which kept the talk alive and talk was what broke the monotony now monotony was breaking them. Each day seemed longer than the last. There was little to gossip about except that Meridian Muldoon had dared to come back and was going around asking questions in order to write some story or other she'd been around for a couple of weeks keeping mostly to herself in the big old house and they wondered and placed bets on how long it would take her to make a fool of herself once more and you could feel the tension rising as the temperature went down.

It was not just the terrible monotony which accounted for the anxiety which settled over Yellow Bird that final September although the shrinking of the town and its impending doom had something to do with it. The so-called calm which always seemed to be there was replaced by a restlessness which grew to dissatisfaction and an urge to destroy and they began to ask one another what could be destroyed that wouldn't really matter or hurt anyone they were not especially vicious or vindictive yet deep within them was a feeling that somebody was to blame for the town being taken out from under them and although they blamed the government and hated the Bureau of Reclamation and the army engineers you could not take it out on them so vast and cold and impersonal were they and besides what could you do shoot them kill them then you'd go to jail no the government was just too big and besides this was helping America was it not to have a fine dam that could generate power all the way to New York City or so they said now you could not fail to be impressed by that kind of big thinking.

Still they were sad and miserable over what they were being forced to do and it dawned on them that one man was responsible for all their misfortune and that was Eli Wetherill whose list of sins was long but what topped it was that he'd been mayor for twenty years during which time some very hush-hush deals were going on between himself and the bureaucrats coming in and out appraising things and boozing it up with the doc and you knew damn well there was some hanky-panky going on

128

the doc had sold them out and then pretended to fight the dam when all along he was getting his pockets lined. Oh he was they said it for years thought it when looking up at him from the operating table and felt it when the hypodermics were going into their fannies Eli Wetherill had the best house in town once drove the only Cadillac in Carbon County had inherited money from his wife did not pay any income tax fought Medicare voted for Johnson when all of them supported Goldwater drank more than any man in history was privileged well-connected called the governor by his first name he was guilty of assorted sins they only suspected but could not prove and the more they thought about what he did not do the more certain they were of what he did do and had gotten away with forever.

How it all began no one ever knew for sure but by the end of September Eli Wetherill had become the most unpopular man in Yellow Bird he was to blame for all their misfortunes for all their misery for the fact that they had to give up their homes and be cast out into the cold penniless and afraid while he they'd heard had bought himself a fifty-thousand-dollar house in Phoenix with all his ill-gotten cash he was responsible for the gas main breaking on a night when the temperature was ten below he was at fault when their cars did not start when the sewer backed up and the electricity failed for two straight days. The only ones who still spoke to him were Josie Stringer and Matt Brittman he had no patients now not one and reduced his office hours to Wednesdays from two to four but they would rather have bled to death than come to him for anything. He did not understand them at all and puzzled over why they had suddenly turned against him on the street they looked the other way refused to speak to him in the bar hung up when he called when they did not so much as acknowledge his presence or importance he thought it strange quite strange of these his friends of thirty years.

He concluded that the strain of giving up the town was just too much the mail from the Bureau of Reclamation was more frequent now and more specific the deadline for moving had been pushed to the first of May and the town was divided into quadrants for demolition the burning was to be May fourth by which time the dam was to be begun.

The reality struck hard and sudden with antique dealers coming in offering hundreds of dollars for furniture they had not been able to give away to married daughters the junk of maiden aunts was worth enough to buy a fur coat freezer color television a down payment on a car they were besieged by loan sharks moving companies realtors from retirement villages an undertaker came and offered free cemetery plots for a funeral plan that cost two thousand dollars their days were truly numbered they complained that the calving would not be over that the trees would be in bud in yards they'd have to leave the birds would be building nests to be sent sky high. Their lives were interrupted confused and irritated they felt pushed and hurried they cursed the antique dealers and took their cash they felt unclean unwholesome unredeemed they had to fix the blame on someone and so they blamed it all on him in a variety of ways some subtle and some point-blank like the time Edgar Purvis slipped on the ice and broke his wrist on his way in the back door of Sweeney's. Eli was inside buying groceries at the time and rushed outside to help but Purvis hit him with a rock and screamed at Sweeney to take him to the Coronado hospital at once.

Every night when he went to Josie's place the conversation and the laughter suddenly ceased and the men lowered their heads and slunk away like dogs simple Charley served him with his perpetual grin and said a two-word sentence Josie tried to make amends by chatting with him as long as she could but she was wise to what was happening and could not afford to offend the other men who would keep coming in as long as they knew that although her sympathy was with the doc her loyalty was to them.

And so unless some construction worker wandered in and

130

bought him a drink Eli was all alone with his thoughts focusing on Britt who had known about his coming death for about a week and was taking it in stride he showed no weakness yet he was a little thinner a little pale the pain was not such that he could not endure it without the aid of drugs his one telltale sign was that he tired easily and the lines in his face began to grow deeper and he was losing a great deal of his youthful appearance that made him pass for a man of forty and his hair began to show some gray. Still he licked Eli every poker hand was a better shot at trap and skeet they did not plan to go for elk or deer Eli let him say it was because of paperwork piled high at the ranch what kept him going seemed to be the annual ritual of the wild horse hunt the middle of October. The hunt had taken on a fantastic importance it was all he talked about he counted the days until it would take place just Eli and himself the same as for the last two dozen years he did not know that Yellow Bird was getting itself worked up about the doc.

It all began when Nate Houghton took to drinking and blaming the doc for Rose's death he said it to everyone he met and those who would not have taken him seriously a year ago listened and were convinced this was just one more thing Eli Wetherill had got away with there were rumors of it at the funeral who was it said why Mister Purvis our principal I believe it was you know he used to sit up at night with the doc and help him practice the next day's operation on a dog so I guess he ought to know Rose Houghton could have been saved. Did you ever wonder why there was no inquest into Skinner's death that mucker who went in for an appendectomy and died on the table a young man too the doc must have been polluted then too it's drink that's got him every time how come Missus Webster's malpractice suit was dismissed in fifty-nine he was clearly at fault letting her fall off the operating table he has pull somewhere along the line don't think he don't oh what's he ever done for us we could've got more for ourselves if we'd done the dealing sure and who got the idea for the dam in the first place

131

him I bet he's going to put up a big resort on the lake make a ski run on the hill and what about us what do we get ain't we got as much right as he. Always was too good for us peasants put us down stifled us he's why we're in this mess and he must pay let's don't ever speak to him again no worse than that wreck his office no he don't care about that wreck his house then no that was always her house he don't give a hoot for it. Well what does he give a hoot for except the jug? And they thought and thought and finally concluded Eli Wetherill didn't give a hoot for one damn thing and they would think some more and figure out some way to put him in his place.

By the end of September a kind of madness united Yellow Bird in a way the neighborliness used to and to the deliverymen mailmen salesmen and the scroungers who came there the people seemed determined very distant very set in their ways not at all like other times when they had been called easygoing jovial polite and often sentimental wishing no harm to anyone yet now said one liquor salesman they're all on edge got blood in their eye.

Those who saw what was happening in Yellow Bird said it was because a little old hick town was dying and the people couldn't stand the fact they had to go where would they fit in those hicks unless it was another hick town and all the other hick towns had their resident hicks you couldn't just go and join them they'd just be homeless hicks and they went batty just dwelling on it. And so the reports drifted back to Denver Montrose Grand Junction Colorado Springs Pueblo have you been to Yellow Bird lately well those folks have all gone loony up there don't speak a word and have a look like wolves maybe they ain't going to move maybe they are going to fight the army when it comes to call. You reckon they'll use tear gas and beat them with clubs just like Los Angeles oh wouldn't that be something we could watch it all on television. Yep that's what's going to happen I know I been delivering produce there for forty years and I lay my life on the fact that them people have made up up their minds they are never going to budge I bet you they are buying firearms to defend themselves with. Well how would you like it if the govmint come and told you to git out and a lake was put over this here house you ain't no fish so I guess you'd fight 'em too like any ordinary person would. One thing is for sure them yokels up at Yellow Bird is ordinary ordinary as all hell.

One night in early October the men gathered the same as usual at the Yellow Bird saloon there were a dozen poker players cowboys a couple of dam workers the retarded garage mechanic the man who wore a saddle once to Sunday school the old Illinois pig farmer who had always carried a pistol until he fell and shot off one testicle the druggist who had good business sense but no business the Polack from the Coronado sawmill who specialized in railroad ties and Dixie Pogue the only genuine gold miner left in all of Yellow Bird and the only female devotee of the Yellow Bird saloon for fifty seasons running. They were all inside they always came early right after the news and made themselves at home with stockinged feet on the tables and one round of drinks on the house the jukebox outscreaming the television until someone turned off the TV sound and they watched the Westerns finding fault with everything but lapping it up just the same they often swapped stories the same stories year after year always the same except the details got better. To hear them talk you'd think the citizens of Yellow Bird were the bravest toughest most hell-raising bunch west of the Arkansas their memories were the most important thing they had. There was laughter in the bar they were getting roaring drunk carrying on as if they would always be there under the elk head with Josie Stringer's piebald son grinning like a fool and the old lady herself taking pleasure in the dirtiest jokes a man would ever want to hear.

They nearly lived up to what they thought they were it was easy to do as evening gathered round and the snow began to fall so far from civilization you could hardly suspect that civilization

133

was closing in no they would not think of that now but later there was still time the notices had only come last week telling each and every one he had to be gone by the first of May oh my that was such a long way off. The notices were stuffed in with unpaid bills circulars for boots and saddles fruitcake Havasu City where they were getting the London Bridge piecemeal free life insurance for one year a high school diploma at home oh hell who needs any of it we are going to live forever that is what we've always done verify it verify it only one of us has died since Rosy Houghton old Allaby checked out today too bad what say we hunt the Rye-o Blanco forest up around Cow Creek is real good get your license yet hell no I can't shoot straight nohow what about them tires T.P. you fixin' tires naw he's fixin' to leave ain't you T.P. hey look at the Marlboro man his spurs is upside down. Hank McIntyre the retired barber unofficial gravedigger and gregarious buffoon became suddenly serious spit tobacco juice and to Floyd Rumsey the retired druggist raiser of orchids children and youthful hell said I believe this place is dying to which the druggist replied well the bugs have left.

Remember back in forty-one when the Baritone Wonder was going strong before the war he had them labor racketeers them dudes in from the East not to mention cattle buyers from every place 'cept jail and salesmen for farm machinery stayed here along with senators and movie stars they made a movie once right there on Main Street and there was an English duke what come with fifteen servants to haul out the game he shot 'cept the cost of shipping all that wildlife was so terrible he just made a pile and burnt it all buffalo and cougar sixteen-point elk black bear and wolves and other such of course that was in the prehistoric days when we had a shoot-out near every night there's bullet holes behind the bar and that gap is where some maniac throwed a hatchet at his wife missed her by this much.

—Would you marry a fifty-five-year-old stud with half his teeth conjunctivitis neuritis bronchitis halitosis encephalitis tonsilitis a short way from pasture he don't need much hay oats agua fria to get rode once in a while he says his life is not por nada said Eli Wetherill climbing astride the bar stool looking into the glass eyes of a ten point buck.

Josie Stringer mopped the bar with a rancid rag pushed her hair out of her eyes and gave the dog a kick.

—Has he got any money the old stud she said.

—Nope said the doctor leaning on his elbows and letting the bourbon run between his lips. The place was full that Friday night in Yellow Bird which meant the dam construction crew and Yellow Bird's citizenry were getting tight.

—What would I do with a brokedown stud if he hasn't any money? Josie Stringer pursed her lips scratched her chin waved a finger watched two poker players dancing while another played the square grand a Sears Roebuck catalogue for sheet music. Look at that sweet corruption she said it's like the good old days but it ain't enough to keep me in Sweetheart soap warm galoshes a new nighty now and then. Hell doc I'd trade it off for a welfare check I sure don't need no stud.

The elk looked down a dead cigar between his teeth one ear gone from mice or had they cut it off one night he couldn't remember it was so long ago. Beside the elk hung a black bear the last one taken from Maverick Mountain he'd brought it down one shot was all slung it on the back of old Red Mule that ornery beast you had to hit him on the head to let him know and there was the bobcat from the San Juans right where the Forest Service built the road through alpine wilderness those damn campers ruined it the motorbikes too there ought to be a law a .22 is all you'd need to keep the wilderness intact.

The big-jowled poker player got up from the piano picking his nose banged on the bar and shouted Charley you got two coming up straight? Charley was Josie's second son thirty-five never married a little touched in the head he was the postmaster by day tended bar nights for his mother's Yellow Bird Hotel the clientele was what you'd call irregular he hadn't seen a business suit in the bar since last the piñon bore nuts five years ago he didn't mind the dam construction crew they spent with a certain frivolity he hadn't seen before. The miners had more savvy though came right from work lunchboxes in their laps and never shaved except on Sunday you'd have thought it was Christmas the way they spent on payday they were all gone now twenty years now twenty years gone in fact it hardly seemed so long.

Joe Killeen had for the past three weeks been working for the developers at Happy Hollow Mountain Estates had worked from sunup to sundown and deadened all his senses and pushed his body until he could feel an exquisite ache creep from his shoulders down to his thighs each night. He told himself he was getting rid of a lot of hostility that he might otherwise take out on some poor slob like Robinson the dam super and spend the night in jail. Something was changing his life all right it bothered him and wouldn't let him rest even when his bones gave out it was something he couldn't explain except that he knew he had a craving to go half blind into the future and plan for it and work for it and hope to hell he could stick it out. He wasn't running anymore and it took some getting used to he found himself content to shack up with Meridian Muldoon yet uncontent with some of the conditions she was putting on him. Like being there by six o'clock sharp for dinner. And not liking it if he took off for Coronado by himself and hell it wasn't to whore around or anything but she didn't like it no siree. She was a pretty good cook though and he kind of liked that and she was good in bed and could make him feel all sorts of things he wasn't accustomed to. And he loved her and it scared him because he had never loved a woman like that his whole life long and what if he should lose her what if she should just up and leave him? That bugged him too although in a way he wished she would so that he could go back to his nothingness again although he knew he'd never run in a straight line now he'd run in circles.

Well today he'd had it with the Happy Hollow predators

and he found he could not hammer another nail and watch them hack up another tree he had to eat but he also had to live with himself and so he'd said screw it and come out hopping mad so mad he'd accidentally bashed in Daisy's right fender coming into town and screw it he said again not going to Meridian's place but to the Yellow Bird saloon where he was getting good and drunk. They had pretended not to notice him when he came in and took a table by himself and Josie who was unhappy about his leaving the hotel after just one night stuck her nose in the air and sent Charley to wait on him. He'd been there a couple of hours sitting in his dark corner and listening to them they were okay a lot like what he'd been used to over the years in a lot of little towns strung out across the map. He wished he could remember where it was he'd balled some minister's daughter and where it was some old lady had let him sleep in the woodshed and where it was he'd busted off a tooth fighting with a truck driver and where he had picked lettuce with the migrants and where he had had his first love and where he had once tried to buy a little land to put a cabin on and lacked the money. The small towns were nearly all alike. When first you came the people generally friendly till you took a notion to stay on then they became like bank examiners and made things tough in one way or another small towns were designed to remain that way the people spoke of Growth and Progress and Friendliness but what they meant was for you to keep on moving unless your credentials began with a birth certificate from there.

No wonder the small towns of America were passing from the scene. He had witnessed what was good in them and what was bad and what big cities did to you was even worse the small town at least let you breathe and told you when to quit in the cities they didn't give a damn and that was what he couldn't stand except when he wanted to lose himself entire and be caught up in the anonymity of the crowd and let himself be carried down the street with it and into one-night cheap hotels

137

letting his mind rest easy while putting his body to every test he could think of and always winning. That meant a lot knowing he could not be licked not physically at least and as for the rest of it well that intellectual shit was just no good not when you did your thinking on your feet and didn't dwell on anything too long nor let it get the best of you.

What he had you couldn't set a price on except now and then he wished he had a thing to call his own the land stayed always and forever on his mind and whenever he got a little money he stuck it in a sand bank some spot or other where he dug a hole and dropped his money in not believing in the other sort of bank well no sooner had his money got planted safe and sound than something came along and he had to dig it up he had spent every damn dime he made but he'd had a good time and that was the main thing or had been up to now Christ did a man hit thirty and get infested with a case of settling down if so he ought to hightail it out of town and quit this sentimental baloney that would get him absolutely nowhere even if she did respond what difference would it make in the way he had to live his life no difference just a complication was all and so he would do what he had always done just let his feet take him where they would at the same time he put his mind at ease.

—Buy you a drink he said walking over to the doctor at the bar who turned and stared and stuck out his hand to be shaken.

—Sit down said Eli warmly where you been hiding figured you left town.

—Not yet.

Charley Stringer put a shot of whiskey in front of him and said hear you been out to the development getting to be a right good hand.

He swallowed the whiskey and felt it burn all the way down. It tasted good and he began to realize that working for the predators for three weeks running had left him a little on edge. Maybe so he said to Charley who was not used to people who did not talk. And he knew that every man in the bar knew

138

exactly where he had kept himself for three weeks and that he had quit at sundown and had a hundred dollars in his pocket his entire worldly wealth and maybe he would get tight and blow it all at poker he was not good at cards it made him mad that he wasn't sharp like that he might have been had he lived a century before.

—I've been thinking said the doctor about what you wanted to know and I did a little research and what I came up with is that you couldn't possibly be from here there's not a chance I went through all my records and those of Simpson the horse doctor who was at the hospital when I came found it all in an iron box in the hospital you want to come up and see?

—I believe you said Killeen swallowing the bourbon he was going to get good and drunk before the night was through. And what's more it doesn't matter he murmured remembering his wild encounter with Houghton the day of Rose's funeral.

But the doctor had not heard him.

—I've come to the conclusion that you were just one of those five dollar babies born anywhere in the West said the doctor firmly.

—I was a what?

—That's my name for illegitimate kids that's all I ever charged to deliver one or else abort it was all the same to me.

—Why five dollars you could have charged a lot more.

—Most of them were the bastards of the whore ladies and that's all they ever charged me so what the hell.

Joe Killeen set down the empty glass and threw his head back and laughed until his entire body shook and he wiped his eyes with his hand the doctor went on drinking with a straight face while Josie Stringer only shook her head and looked circumspect the stranger was a little crazy you had no trouble telling that.

—I'll tell you something doc said Killeen at last that is the best one I've heard in a while did you ever make it a fair exchange?

139

The doctor shook his head. I was pretty careful in those days I set the same rate for everybody they knew they could depend on me just like I or any man could always depend on them it was sort of mutual.

—And what happened to the five dollar babies the ones you delivered?

—Hard to say some got adopted out from here a bootleg operation if you know what I mean some went to state homes or private ones depended on what the mother wanted to do a couple of them just kept those kids and raised them on their own it was a common practice not just here but everywhere from the time the miners first hit pay dirt and the whore ladies followed suit it never did no harm and I have always believed were it not for the five dollar babies this state would still belong to Mexico.

It was the kind of story Killeen liked and the doctor was the kind of man he kindled to and he wished that Eli could have been his father after all just like crazy Houghton said. It wasn't true not the doctor and a scrubwoman no she was not the kind of mother he could accept but the doctor yeah now there was a man that would have raised him as good as he was. Killeen ran his tongue around his lips and looked sideways at Eli who had not taken his eyes off the elk with the missing ear. The old man's face was good Killeen decided with thought lines about people running across his forehead and the flesh only a little bit loose his eyes were a lot like a map of secondary roads but what could you do in a place like this except drink yourself into some sort of state or other and then he noticed that Nate Houghton and all the other men at the bar had suddenly moved away and were playing poker at a table with a lampshade hanging over it and they had not asked the doctor to join in nor did he share in any of the drinks they bought one round to a man and Killeen thought it odd to treat a man that way and he edged a little closer and touched the doctor's sleeve.

—Listen he said a little bit self-consciously you know any-

140

thing about hunting you been staring at that buck like it was your second cousin.

—I've done my share.

—Yeah well what I was thinking was maybe you know a place that's good for deer I haven't been hunting for years.

The doctor shifted on the stool it was hard not to let his feelings run away with him and hard to remember what year it was and what he was to do about getting rid of his house and closing the office things like that were getting harder all the time. He swallowed half the glass of bourbon and said I gave up hunting long ago you ask yourself what it really is you're after.

Killeen munched ice and ordered another drink. What does it matter I mean a man doesn't need a reason for every damn thing he does.

—If you take to hunting you do I'm not one of those sports that come up here with a dirty shirt and a ten-dollar bill and don't change neither one.

Killeen sat thoughtfully with his drink and after a while he said maybe I ought to have a reason to hang around this place since I really don't give a shit who my parents were I got no excuse to stay.

—You don't need a reason said Eli you just stay because you want to.

—Like you?

—Me I'm different I'm Yellow Bird's one paved street its running water its skin and its contents I flatter myself with that and go on living.

—What's this about living said Matt Brittman thumping him on the back Eli you old fart you didn't come out for dinner.

—Was I supposed to?

—Hell yes man I rang you up this morning did you forget?

—Must have said Eli wishing he did not have to introduce him to Killeen whose name he suddenly could not remember reached back in the shadows of his mind for it and finally the words formed on his lips Marcus Muldoon.

141

—What cried Britt looping his legs around the stool has that bastard come back to town I'll bust his head.

But Eli was not even aware he had spoken the name of the man who had pulled the rug from under Matt Brittman and left his life in shreds the man Britt had once sworn to kill then backed down it was not after all the nineteenth-century West when you could take evil and plug it dead so he had just gone along all those years thinking not so much of good and bad and right and wrong but of something in between that he could tolerate. A man could put himself in hell believing in extremes.

Joe Killeen went on drinking and listened to them talk the tall rancher sitting on the other side of Eli had a pair of hands like a man he'd worked for in Wyoming he could swing an axe with just one of them or lift a newborn calf he could grab one whole watermelon and bust it open with one hand or scratch the dog's belly all over just by moving his fingers the same strong fingers could squeeze a beer can in half or pluck feathers from a duck in about two shakes fasten easy around some reins or lift a bale of hay he was so interested in watching Matt Brittman's hands that it was only after a while that he began to study his face the forehead white above where his Stetson came his eyes deep set in crinkled pouches his jawline running like a crack in a rock his skin was the color of the desert and so tough that if you ran a fingernail across it might come flaking off you could not produce a face like that except with sun and wind and rain the same imprimatur that gave the mountains class. He stuck his hand in front of Eli Wetherill and it disappeared in the rancher's hearty grasp I'm Joe Killeen call me Britt what'll you have whiskey straight up Charley give the lad some brandy for a chaser this is a real occasion.

Across the room the men were playing cards the haze of smoke drifted around their faces giving them a softness they did not possess they had abandoned the square grand and the pinball machines Josie Stringer marched around the room her hands behind her hips her laughter masked the fear she had about closing up but what stood out the most in that dank and smelly saloon was the way in which each man fit in a slow and easy way all that is except the doctor who seemed an outcast among his brethren. It occurred to Killeen then that what was being lost was not so much the town itself as what had held it together all those years a nameless something running through them all and linking them together as they would no longer be linked once the town went down. The doctor had surely been a part of them a strong link in that chain but they did not need him anymore and it puzzled Killeen as to why.

—Tell me about yourself Britt was saying looking past Eli's gradually dissipating face the doctor's nightly journey into oblivion was gathering speed there was hardly any pause between one night's journey and the next Britt had begun to notice with some alarm.

—Not much to tell I've been a loner all my life had jobs from Texas to Timbuctoo don't worry a whole lot don't work unless I have to don't much care where I lay my head and that about sums me up.

—What brings you here said Britt playing it as cool as he could.

Killeen scratched his ear that's a good question Britt what brought me here is likely not what'll keep me here I reckon.

—And what was that?

—Personal business.

—I see said Britt nudging Eli's cowboy boot with his own and getting no response.

—Yeah some personal business that's been attended to I guess that right doc?

—What said Eli coming out of his daze just long enough to glance at Britt's face and know that he was in pain and it was getting worse and in his mind he saw what appeared to be a large potato growing in his friend and he saw it being sliced and growing back together again sliced and growing even larger sliced and turning colors it was hopeless to try and do anything

143

with a potato he ought to know that he'd been a doctor long enough to know not to fool with potatoes.

—Eli the lad's talking to you.

—What lad?

—This lad Joe Killeen you recognize him Eli?

—A potato.

Jumping up the doctor took hold of Britt's huge shoulders and nearly fell as he shook him and cried the the potato we have got to get rid of the potato.

—Eli settle down.

—Now Britt we got to do it now.

—Do what asked Killeen puzzled.

—Get rid of the potato.

—What potato is he talking about said Killeen feeling a sharp plunge to his innards the doctor was out of control.

The sweat stood out in beads on the doctor's forehead his eyes were red and tortured he opened his mouth to speak and no sound came out his lips were dry and cracked his tongue coated and hanging between his teeth he seemed confused as he searched Britt's face for some answer some clue as to what they were doing there.

—Now Eli said Britt gently why don't we take you home?

The doctor pulled away and straightened himself with difficulty the words came out as if he had a clothespin between his lips don't want to go home Britt you know that.

—Suit yourself Eli but at least sit down before you fall.

He staggered to a booth and collapsed on the seat his hands trembling his white hair lay in wet strands across his head without a word Josie Stringer set before him a double bourbon the men playing cards did not speak or pause what they saw was familiar to them and happened nearly every night they only shook their heads very slightly drew up one corner of their mouths exchanged their deadly glances and went on playing.

Killeen looked at him and made a move to go to him but Britt laid his arm on his he'll be okay he said just leave him be.

—He's a wreck said Killeen frowning.

—He just looks that way he really ain't.

—Well why don't those bastards over there do anything to help him?

—Oh they don't hardly see him.

—But there he is.

—They still don't see him.

—What kind of crazy place is this I've been to lots of places and when a man is down you try and help him you don't just sit there.

—Well this is Yellow Bird.

—Jesus said Killeen whirling around on the stool a tin shit Jesus Xavier Christ sons-of-bitches.

—Have a drink Killeen.

—You known him long?

—Long enough.

—How come he drinks like that how can he run his practice and all why he must have a hospital full of patients don't they—

—Want a job Killeen said Britt cutting him off.

—His patients see him like that they'll sue him for malpractice we got to sober him up.

—I said you want a job Killeen yes or no?

—Britt that man is sick why does everybody stand around?

—Boy said Britt sharply his blue eyes cold as steel you want me to learn you your first lesson about Yellow Bird the hard way?

—Hold on a minute no sense getting mad.

—Your first lesson about Yellow Bird is you don't ask questions the second lesson is you pay no mind to what you see the third lesson is you learn to keep your mouth shut now you want a job or not?

—Doing what?

—Cowboying.

—Sounds good I've done a lot of it before.

—Yeah Killeen I know said Britt coolly.

—What else do you know about me?

—All I need to know.

Gazing into the other man's eyes Killeen knew it mattered more who he was with than what he did and he would learn a lot from this man and ask nothing except to have the sun at his back and to lose himself out there for a little while at least and then he would be moving on to try and find himself again. The pursuit was what took his fancy and he could not imagine what he would do if he ever struck pay dirt and the thing was over with well he'd come close in Yellow Bird really close and with a sigh of relief he was glad Rose Houghton had died he reached in his pocket and took out the newspaper clipping and set a match to it and watched it turn to ashes then he said to Britt yeah I'll come and work a couple weeks okay?

The big man's eyes narrowed the pain was welling up again not bad but he could feel his legs draw up he brushed his hand over his eyes you okay Britt Killeen was saying anxiously jeez don't you go out on me too.

—Got a bad stomach Killeen don't pay it no mind you got it straight that whatever happens to me you keep on going is that a fair deal?

Killeen did not understand any of it the doctor slumped over the table out cold and nobody paying him mind the rancher acting odd and him supposed to hold his tongue and hobble his feet well it was plain out of sight what was happening in that town maybe that's what altitude did to you slowed down the blood going to your brain he said it's the goddamnedest deal I ever made Britt it's a dude.

—Want to bunk out to the ranch tonight?

—I'll come on out tomorrow where do I find you?

—Across the bridge go left a quarter mile you'll see the gate.

—That place said Killeen that's quite a spread.

—I'll show you around said Britt with pride the kid was

146

going to be okay just turn him loose he'll eat it up Harley can go to hell.

He ought to go home and get himself to bed fatigue had busted him below the belt a pretty good swat and he was all in he caught his breath and saw the room begin to tilt the goddamn son-of-bitching parasite and he calmed it down with one of his pills but he knew he had to get off his feet maybe he should ask Killeen to drive him home no and let everybody know there was something wrong and Eli was no help over there trying to come to and the bullshitters playing cards kept looking at him funny like well he never lost a thing to them hey Britt Josie was saying anxiously you okay? Sure said Britt I'm okay but mind if I lay down in the back a couple minutes? And he was up from the stool as steady as could be and walking as strong and straight as ever toward the cot in Josie's little back room and he would not falter as long as they were looking at him Matt Brittman was never going to show one sign of dying because when he did the time was up and Eli would move in and that is all he would ever know.

Killeen sat by himself mulling over his good fortune the town had set him on his heels with its indifference yet here was a man giving him what he could not define he only knew he felt a bond that he had not known before. His friends were like his life he liked the new and different he did not let himself get close you just moved through life and moved through people it was all the same till now.

He took his drink and went over to the doctor who had roused himself and had his head thrown back against the wooden booth as Josie Stringer appeared with a pot of coffee and set it at his elbow he was coming round the way he did each night before he went on home and struggled with the dark. His bloated face lighted up when he saw Killeen approaching through the smoke he sat up straighter and smoothed his coat he did not want Killeen to think he was untidy or a wee bit off his feet he grinned and said what you been up to?

147

—Messing around how about you?

—Me why I'm ready for bear you know any bear?

—Nope but I know a girl.

—Named what?

—Meridian Muldoon.

The doctor let out a long low whistle her boy she's dynamite you tame her Killeen and you got one fine woman she's a lot of gas a lot of shit a lot of temper what gal ain't her pa let her run and her ma was strict but there was a woman with no heart at all oh she did in the beginning but Marcus spoilt it all I guess he didn't know how to handle a woman do you boy?

—I try but it doesn't always work out right.

—Seldom does unless you marry a cretin or a mule.

Killeen laughed and let his hand rest beside the doctor's fingers steady now as he was drinking his coffee and said doc I'm a happy-go-lucky fool 'cause I'm happy just going around.

—Me too Killeen.

But Eli was not happy and it became suddenly important to Killeen to make him happy and he wondered how he ought to do it and why it mattered to him at all you could go just so far with another man's life. But he could not think of anything and so he lapsed into silence and watched Eli sink into a world he seemed comfortable in and let it go at that. Killeen glancing over his shoulder was not comfortable the eyes of the men playing cards were upon Eli their faces were pale and expressionless their lips were fastened together and their bodies were rigid and stuffed with scorn. They were not like men at all but like some dreadful committee of robots with cowboy hats set up to decide how many rats and how many matchsticks and how much coyote poison you would use on the children of the world. He did not recognize any of them except for Houghton whose glazed eyes sat like marbles in his head unblinking and unrelenting in their hate one tooth hung out over his bottom lip and he worked his tongue around it and laughed with such malice that Killeen shuddered and turned away the doctor was not

148

aware of what was happening he was sipping his coffee and seemed absorbed in the progress of a fly pushing its way through the crumbs on the table and then suddenly there was Houghton limping across the room his eyes bulging a strange and eerie cackling coming from his throat he thrust his face close to the doctor's and said for the second time you son-of-a-bitch I'll kill you.

Killeen sprang up and pinned Houghton's arms behind his back the card players began to rise as a body and then sat down as Killeen relaxed his hold and said get the hell out of here Houghton if you know what's good for you. Houghton shook himself free and said who the hell are you? Remember me said Killeen sharply sure you do. Houghton screwed up his face yeah ain't you the one that helped to murder my wife along with this bum he said jerking his thumb toward the doctor who only shook his head and murmured aw Nate now cut it out.

—Cut it out said Houghton his voice rising so that everyone could hear sure I'll cut it out when I got you six feet under and the card players began to pound the table and shout yeah six feet under six feet under oh doc come quick we are having a heart attack bring a toothpick doc and a fifth of gin whatsa matter doc you out of Band-aids get him Nate right between the eyes and they laughed and hooted and beat the table. Josie Stringer shouted for them to shut up and they replied you old bat bring us some more booze and she did muttering to herself how could it come to this she was on the verge of tears her heart went out to the doc who sat implacable and serene you had to hand it to him he never blew his cool.

Killeen was sickened by the shouts of the men and the curses and abuse they were heaping on Eli c'mon doc let's go he said and tried to take his arm and get him up but the doctor would not budge he merely raised his hand and said sit down Killeen don't you realize it's what they want.

—Huh said Killeen scratching his head you going to take this shit?

149

—A man don't run from mice the doctor said.

—Houghton's got it coming.

—Let him be.

—He's crazy enough to try and kill you.

—Maybe so I ain't going to worry though.

Killeen looked puzzled. What keeps you here doc I just don't understand.

A smile flickered across the doctor's face all haggard and unshaven and blemished with a lot of little red things fuzzy like spiders beneath the skin. Oh Killeen he said if that ain't obvious to you I don't know what is.

Suddenly the room became quiet and Killeen looked around saw that the card players had shut up and swiveled their heads around to watch Meridian Muldoon coming through the door dressed in a pants suit her long hair tied back with a scarf. Her eyes traveled the length of the room and then she saw the doctor and Killeen and began walking toward them.

—Uh-uh said the doctor she ought to know better than to set foot in here.

It's Meridian Muldoon said the poker players yes it's her again thought she got the message last time she was in and picked up that Communist bastard Killeen yeah well more power to him any niggers yet not yet well she'll get herself one she always does ain't none left in Yellow Bird what's she doing here all this time that's what I'd like to know how come she's back we run her out in fifty-eight or was it nine Marcus run her out remember it was him that lashed her with a bridle right there in church we ain't never made her welcome and don't intend to start now look she's headed for the doc and that bastard Killeen fellow that stays to her place well just keep on playing don't let her know we give a shit I mean we are respectable folk we don't want none of her or him.

She had not been in the hotel in three weeks and had avoided the doctor knowing that he had little to do with the story of Yellow Bird a drunken fool who had let Squash Jenkins'

150

sister die and done so many awful things that she felt only contempt as she looked at his sodden face his trembling hands his shaggy hair and his seedy clothes she shuddered and tried to catch Killeen's eye what was the matter with him not showing up for dinner well maybe she was getting bitchy and had made him mad so let him cool down off she'd have him back where he belonged. The writing wasn't getting done because of him and it didn't matter she was drifting along with him wild and improbable and today was for one day only to be felt to all its depths and tomorrow might come or might not with Killeen you learned not to worry to just share in his dreaming and his sheer pleasure of a natural world that to her had seemed so alien well she was learning about the way he saw things and she was learning not to hate he was cooling her down and doing it with such grace that she wondered how she'd get along when he up and left and he would she knew a man like that you did not tie down a man like that was a free spirit always on the move.

—Buy me a drink she said to the doctor who was sipping his coffee with the spoon in the cup.

The doctor frowned you ought to stay away from here.

—No doubt.

—Uh said Killeen rubbing his nose you two are uh friends from way back?

—Hardly said Meridian sitting next to Killeen and pressing against his leg.

The doctor shrugged ten years since I saw her last and she's still in a huff women never change.

She smiled in spite of herself feeling Killeen's hand on her thigh and she was determined to make an effort to be nice to the doddering old fool how's the Band-aid business she said.

The doctor rubbed his hands together. Slow he said thanks to only slightly putrified air I got no bronchial patients the pill has lowered the accident rate and Medicare has carried off what would have died under my stethoscope I can cure a pretty good hangover however.

151

—The doctor has always been something of a mystery around here she said to Killeen we used to wonder if he was practicing medicine or the violin.

—Meridian said Killeen in reproach.

—Well it's true she said we used to say does he deliver babies or newspapers or milk.

—Hush up said Killeen sternly but the doctor was smiling jovially he seemed to hear only that which he wished to hear and the rest he turned off like a radio.

—Killeen he said raising his coffee cup this girl is going to be very big at the United Nations highly recommend her for the Paris peace talks the Veterans of Foreign Wars and the Mothers March on Polio not to mention the Red Chinese Red Cross.

—Oh shut up said Meridian lightly you see Killeen the doctor is also a clown.

Killeen sloshed down his drink the room was going around he said I'm going to the can and he staggered through the smoke past the poker players the juke box blasting just call me angel he was whistling and watching them out of half-shut eyes good evening he said solemnly as he passed by and watched them freeze like naughty kids caught in the fucking act and it made him laugh to see grownup men behave so odd.

—What a dump said Meridian in disgust and those creeps over there have never changed.

—Don't be hard on them said the doctor defensively. It was time to begin the next act and he signaled Josie for a drink pushing away his coffee cup and feeling his brain begin to alter course for what was coming up. You don't understand what Yellow Bird is all about.

—No I don't she said and she looked so young and pretty and innocent it was goddamn hard to believe she fucked with the dirty nigger.

He felt his poor undependable prick rise and fall a dead balloon said Bessie Pilcher well Frieda Muldoon had called him a grade A stud and here was temptation again and he wanted

152

to tell her now go away because if there's two things I can't stand it's pain and temptation but what he said was well you ought to learn.

She smiled sweetly at him and shook her head he felt himself getting hotter by the minute he was relieved that Josie set the drink before him in the nick of time it was all that stood between making a fool of himself she did not seem to notice his discomfort reached in his pocket for a handkerchief and finding none wiped his nose on his sleeve she turned away disgusted the man would never change she could remember going to him once when she was small and he dropped the tongue depressor on the floor and picked it up again and went right on jabbing it down her throat.

—Marcus okay he asked fitfully wishing that Killeen would hurry up.

—Marcus is a crook.

He nodded. Frieda?

—Same as last you saw her.

—Ain't seen Frieda in ten years.

—She hasn't changed a little fatter peroxided her hair had a face job and two abortions since she left. This town is a cesspool of corruption look what it did to me.

—You weren't so bad he said nodding his head Marcus ought to have paddled you.

She looked around the room the poker players glanced sideways out of their reddening eyes she smiled and blew a kiss they lowered their heads and began a sudden conversation she laughed look at those self-righteous sons-of-bitches.

—Just because you have been away and got yourself educated and tuned up don't mean you can come back and find fault he said irritably.

—I certainly can she said and I mean to do worse than that before I'm through.

—What are you going to do missy that you ain't done before?

—Enough she answered and banged her glass on the table they will wish they had left well enough alone.

—You mean he said leaning on his elbows and staring into her blazing eyes you mean that nigger thing well missy you asked for that you sure as hell did getting into trouble like that I have never said a word till now but damn it girl you offended more than just this town you offended your own self ever think of that?

—Bullshit doctor bullshit you know what they did that very bunch that's sitting at that table playing cards they killed that girl and got away with it because she was black and no good and inferior like some dog or other they had the right to kill or was she really dead when they brought her to you was she dead or did you let her die doctor did you stand there and do nothing?

—I don't remember he cried.

—Yes you do and you remember cutting the black boy down when he had hanged there long enough to be dead then how come the Jenkins' house got burned to the ground? How come that poor old black man could never work again?

—You should have thought of that before you done what you done.

—Look at them doctor she said waving her hand toward the poker players they'd do it again and so would you everything is the same as it always was in Yellow Bird.

—But not for long it's dying missy and you ought to leave it alone because when a thing is dying it ain't accountable.

—Like you she said bitterly.

—Like anything which has got a soul.

—Put it out of its misery then look how much it suffers.

—It ain't time.

—Oh are you planning to put it to sleep after all how humane doctor how humane.

—Under the proper conditions.

—Meaning what?

154

—The disease has got to be incurable and painful.

—The conditions are properly met in this case.

The doctor wiped his eyes and lowered his head I'm afraid so he said hoarsely

—Then what are you waiting for?

—The patient must be beyond hope he must be on the other side of the line drawn between life and death he must be negative in all respects to earn a painless death said Eli with tears running down his cheeks.

Suddenly she felt awkward and ashamed he made no attempt to conceal his emotion just sat there with it all dribbling out she took his hand in hers and whispered oh come on doctor it's only a town.

—Missy he said with enormous effort to control himself it's life.

The poker players began to howl and Josie was banging on the bar with her shoe the juke box blasted yeahyeahyeah two poker players got into a friendly brawl over the price of a drink Meridian closed her eyes and said oh god it's awful.

—What's awful said Killeen returning with Matt Brittman who did not look well at all. The two men sat down opposite Meridian and the doctor and ordered drinks. Britt crossed his legs and dug his fingers into the seat the booger was rampaging all right well he'd given him a real fight this time he heard himself in a strange and choking voice saying to Meridian I've missed you why ain't you been out.

She lighted a cigarette and drummed her fingers on the table avoiding his eyes oh I've been trying to write a story Britt just haven't had time.

—What kind of story?

—A history of Yellow Bird.

—I didn't know you were a writer.

—I'm not.

They all laughed and Killeen said this girl's a mixed bag a

man don't rightly know what she is or isn't till he gets her all choked down like a wild horse.

—You know anything about wild horses Killeen said Britt suddenly.

—I've seen them in Nevada went with a guy who used an airplane and shot 'em dead it kind of turned my stomach I never went again.

—We got a herd about thirty miles west of here we don't kill 'em just try and catch us a stud that's right Eli and I have caught exactly four in twenty-odd years just using ourselves and ropes no guns or brush traps or trucks or airplanes you might like it we're fixing to go in a couple weeks.

Killeen did not take his eyes off Meridian he felt like crushing her to him then and there and with his boot he touched her leg and felt her quickly withdraw a peculiar woman if ever there was one he closed one eye and looked at Britt through his glass sure I'd like to go he said if I'm still around.

—That would be nice said Britt okay with you Eli what ails you Eli wake up hey Meridian what did you do to poor old Eli here he's kinda turned to stone.

He gave the doctor a poke and Eli Wetherill fell face down upon the table his head landing in a puddle of beer the poker players began to cheer and Houghton was getting up Josie came running interference and Killeen said they're after his blood let's get him out of here and he hoisted the doctor to his feet and began to carry him toward the door as the poker players all lurched toward him fists clenched saliva and booze at the corners of their mouths wetting drooping cigarettes their feet shuffled across the wooden floor and Houghton shouted kill him kill the son-of-a-bitch.

At that instant Matt Brittman rose with his feet planted solid and his huge frame commanding and severe he reached beneath the leather vest he always wore and drew out the nickel-plated revolver that his father had brought from Oklahoma and he fired it into the ceiling just once it was enough the poker players went back to their seats and picked up their hands drank their drinks and went on playing.

—Just like on television said Meridian let's go home.

7

Eli Wetherill never remembered how he got from the Yellow Bird Hotel to his bed that cold October night he had no recollection of Killeen and Meridian dragging him up the stairs and dumping him into bed he had just gone to sleep the same as always and the sleep cleared his brain but not his memory the night was the same as all other nights when he rose at 4 A.M. automatically poured the bourbon in a glass certain of himself in the darkness let his fingers slip along the rosewood railing down the well-worn stairs into the parlor stuffed with his wife's antiques he hadn't touched a thing since the day she died not even moved the magazines from the rack nor turned the pages of the sheet music on the piano the bric-a-brac was the way she'd left it even though he hated Dresden figures cuckoo clocks English pewter embroidered pillows Limoges and Wedgwood teacups silver spoons collected from every state they'd been to twenty-six in all. He sat on the green velvet settee and put his feet up she'd have frowned at that he'd done it so long now the velvet was wearing thin the horsehairs sticking out scratched his legs he plucked them out and threw them on the floor. Mrs. Craddock came on Saturdays complaining of the mess his clothes in heaps ashes on the Brussels carpet the fine old mahogany dining table scarred from his carving soap a hobby he'd taken up to do something with his hands. Twenty-nine years he'd lived in that house the finest one in town he'd bought it the year he got out of medical school for two thousand dollars half the fortune inherited from his aunt in Louisville where he'd studied medicine. She had a wooden leg he fancied cutting off to throw at the niggers across the tracks had scared them once with a human head from his autopsy class tossed from a trolley in a burlap bag.

He drank to Auntie Nat's wooden leg and what he always thought she had v.d. his maiden aunt was so discreet her rooming house attracted the best horse trainers she was very fond of them and so was he living in the attic of his aunt's establishment meant he could hear her cries of pleasure coming up through the heat duct she was laid by every man who walked in the door it seemed the sole condition of her place.

Next he drank to his old house built in ninety-nine he poured the last of the bottle in the glass and raised it to his wife whose portrait above the fireplace he could remember in the dark the high-necked collar framed a face beautiful in youth but time had severed her connection with a sunny disposition and placed instead on her countenance a nervous disillusionment.

The government had paid him eighteen thousand dollars for his house and land a price he felt inflationary he'd declined to sell it off for scrap let it drown in peace with memories of tearful nights and sullen days a house bereft of children's laughter the footsteps of a dog no daughter's marriage solemnized by the preacher no cakes with champagne drunk from crystal goblets the dinner guests were chosen from her tiny list of acceptable acquaintances Yellow Bird was so gauche she used to say the friends he liked he'd have to meet for poker at the Elks Club or city hall or the hotel sneaking out to play the slot machines at the Almighty Dollar meant he had to claim an emergency operation else face her terrible frown.

Eli got up feeling dizzy he'd had too much to drink he had to watch it what if at that very moment the telephone rang for him to sew up the victim of an auto accident perform a tracheotomy on an old friend or deliver some baby after all. He would not be able to hold a needle or a knife or to make the right decisions for a woman giving life it hadn't been the first time he'd sat fearful of a call nor would it be the first time he'd answered one in this condition two malpractice suits in twenty-nine years both dismissed for lack of evidence they didn't know the evidence was he'd come to this against his will the devil had got hold of him to use a phrase his mother used with every other breath.

He stumbled over the rocker and the footstool knocked a cut-glass ashtray on the floor it broke oh never mind I didn't like it anyway let me have some air he tore the lace curtain off the door and staggered to the porch.

Not a goddamn person alive at this hour need a little company tha's all call old Mortimer no he's dead le's see Preston what became of him oh gone Tucson year ago Thomas Johns too sick near dead in fact what about old Gus Watson now there's a man hunted every fall with fished every damn trout stream with 'tween here an' Wyoming yeah ole Gus is who. But Gus Watson was in a nursing home he couldn't remember where. And that left only the man who was the other half of himself.

He made his way back into the house switched on the Tiffany lamp with a savage pull he hated it and unsteadily dialed the well-known number 'lo Britt it's me yeah me what doin' come'n over have a drink Jesus Christ Britt only a frien' wantin' a little comp'ny's all okay okay you go to hell yourself.

He put the receiver down mopped his forehead with a sleeve he felt his skin draw tighter every year and sink into the pouch beneath his chin. I need a woman. The realization struck him frustration raced through his body he could feel all the she stuff pressed into one as if there had been only a great monster of a woman looking like a giant squid.

What was there to lay in Yellow Bird he scratched his head there was Josie Stringer age fifty-three she'd gone through the change last year he was familiar enough with her cocoon had felt it while doing yearly pelvics and delivering her flaky children there was a lot of her all right so warm and moist but the logistics perplexed him did he mount her and run the risk of collapsing on a mountain of heaving flesh did he go in from behind and if so would he reach no the goddamn thing is out of commission kaput a dead balloon well the Muldoon bitch stood it up tonight go give her a plow you think she'd turn you down a slanting Annie if there ever was one and Frieda hollered and said I hurt imagine in those days I had a cucumber it shrunk out on me it's just a little old dried-up mushroom damn son-of-a-bitch he said yanking open his pajama bottom to have a look I'm old he cried I'm finally at long last old.

He hung his head in desperation a gun in the upstairs drawer you shoot from right to left above the temple not very clean what would Mrs. Craddock say about the mess outside then in back of the house. Messy messy still they would have to clean it up remarking on the condition of my brain. A bottle of barbiturates inject myself with air. No. The river then yes like glue they'd think I fell not enough water at this time of year however you only need a thimbleful it would not look right my body in the mud. No not yet there is something left to do.

A smile spread across his lips he dialed again. 'Lo Josie yeah me watcha doing up this hour can't sleep me neither come have

161

a drink with me Josie what the hell's the matter you talk like some lunatic I'm not bad off you think I'm what what crazy you say Josie now quit that moaning take a Seconal one is all do it you old batty Hattie. Nighttime is so bad so bad so bad.

He stuck his finger in the bottle and swished it around and rubbed his gums they were getting sore he ought to have his teeth attended to and send himself somewhere to be cured there was still in him enough desire for self-preservation that he could not see drinking himself to death. Yet. There was a time for everything and now was not the time for that no now was not the time to face combat with his liver he pondered his current state of usefulness or uselessness and tried to think of one single thing he was good for one person who needed him and his mind which had become a stranger to him produced an inventory of fifty-odd years clear back to when he practiced first aid on his baby sister and made up his mind to become a doctor the faces came up out of the blue-black depths of a typhoon the names on cards he could not read sometimes he identified the people by x-ray only or by EKG a death certificate birth certificate for the howling skinned rabbits who grew to something human.

But that was the past. What am I good for now with no hospital no patients no skill no desire to try another place where they'd take any old doc even one like me the Navajos are hard up likewise the Tex-Mex likewise the cannibals in New Guinea you want to give them a treat as well as treatment? No. If you can keep your head when all about you are losing theirs and blaming it on you exactly exactly that is what is happening so who needs me who gives a shit gimme the roster of the shitgivers society. Josie. Ah loyal to the end and what an end I tell you one lay is all that stands between us maybe she wouldn't mind at this late date to remember me by so who else? Britt. Behold the grinning executioner who with stealth creeps up upon the chairman of the shitgivers society oh God if you haven't died and are speaking English I will give you the rest of all my years

162

if you will take him while he sleeps take him herding cattle take him branding doing what he loves but take him yourself why should I do your job answer me that God. You appoint me your hangman of heaven I'll proceed to weed your garden how many times have I seen you in a hospital or a sickroom taking what you oughtn't to have taken like some common trashy thief heisting candy from a kid but this you got a right to do because I tell you true I cannot do it I cannot lift a hand oh yeah God there was Plummer and Skinner and the sawman three times I wore your skull and crossbones I figure you owe me one speak up you damned idiot you got horseshit between your teeth?

And as it began to get light he staggered back to bed ready for a duel with God the foremost adversary in his life the one he blamed for what was or what was not. God was a devil a deceiver a fake a spook related to Lyndon Johnson Karl Marx Santa Claus Charles de Gaulle and Pope Paul the Twelfth people went to church and paid good money to keep the monster in business and prayed to it and didn't understand when it turned around and wiped out whatever they were praying for didn't understand all manner of evil things it did to them called it fate or His divine will or some such lamebrain excuse. Why not bomb all the churches execute all the bishops rape all the nuns dismember the Pope burn all the Bibles and nevermore allow that name God to be spoken. At times he had to deal a straight deck to God regardless of his opinion and once in a while God dealt a straight deck to him but they were enemies God and he. And as he lay in bed raging with the bottle and bellowing up to God it became apparent that the monster was not listening or speaking he was indeed dead just as all the rumors said and if he was dead there was no way to make a deal he would have to attend to the beheading himself God would not have done it right anyhow he almost never did.

With that in mind Eli almost decided to get up and dress having discovered one reason for his being alive was to murder the one true friend he'd ever had a thought which struck him as not wrong at all if the cards were dealt that way. But no there was another thing to consider the town over which had fallen some rigor mortis along with the first snow he could make neither head nor tail of what possessed them yet it reminded him a little of what happened to Harry Mason a friend he'd gone to medical school with. He'd once stopped by Yellow Bird and told a remarkable tale of how he'd practiced medicine in Bolivia for twenty years in a small native village where there was so much sickness so much death so much infanticide so much utter filth and pestilence when he arrived that he took one look and decided to leave. It was a group of nuns working there who persuaded him to stay and help them build a hospital and he said all right when that was done he'd ask for a replacement it was his hope to amount to something he would amount to nothing there and so the hospital got built and he had his bags packed and the nuns implored him once again to stay just one more year there was money for a school and if he'd just stay to help them build and so he did and when it was time for him to leave again the nuns were very clever they said look around at what you've done is there any more you'd like to see accomplished so that we may do it when you're gone. And he saw the shabby huts in which the natives lived and the open sewers in which they bathed and washed and drank and he saw the filthy rags they wore and the flies on the open sores and dogs being cooked for the evening meal and he saw a great deal to be done that was not in the construction of buildings.

But he wanted to do it himself and so he did feeling very much like Albert Schweitzer as the village took shape under his hands and some of the children he'd given up for dead went away to school and some of the men went to the next town and learned a trade and the women stopped killing their babies and he saw what he'd done was to make the human condition bearable and nowhere could he have done that better not even in New York where he had wanted to go not there with such evident success and with himself the center of their lives. Harry

Mason grew fat and content with his life and in his attitude toward the natives he became permissive and paternalistic. A village girl came and lived with him and bore him children others built him a fine house and staffed it and saw to his every need his happiness was great in that quiet steamy village and so he was not prepared for what finally happened. He had been there twenty years without incident and then one night without warning the villagers burned his house down burned the school burned the hospital killed two of the nuns and tortured the other and he escaped with his life only by sacrificing the girl to his pursuers and hiding in an old mine without food or water for six days then slowly working his way across the mountains to where the railroad came. And when he told his friend the story he was bald and fat and a little lost but he was not bitter he explained it thus:

That when one man gives to a society or to a community or to a family not one's own all that it is indebted for the debt must be paid by the destruction of that man's work that man's gift or that man's life. In that way the one thing that is left to the society the community or the family is itself and that is all one individual has the right to bargain for.

Eli Wetherill had not thought of Harry Mason's words for many years but he remembered them then as if they had just been spoken and pondered them long and hard and knew they were not true of himself and Yellow Bird he hadn't tried to change them hadn't built a hospital or a school or cured much disease or even made the human condition bearable he had only done the best he could that was the truth and the truth sank in and he felt that he was closer to understanding himself than he ever had been. And very nearly at peace.

The doctor was not aware of himself as a man he had regarded himself as a functionary expecting no reward he did not suspect that he like Harry Mason had placed the people in bondage to himself had acted a little too self-righteous in their presence dismissed their opinions as irrelevant he had invited

165

them to his house expecting homage and when he went to theirs he expected deference he did not notice that they kept him in their living rooms never once invited them into their kitchens he never asked himself why they were more at ease with potato-faced faggot Fred Sweeney a groceryman native of Yellow Bird than with himself the most educated well-connected family-treed man in the entire community. He could not see the reason why he had at some point fifteen twenty years before tried to come to their level deliberately debauched himself imitated their rough uneducated talk tried to cure his feeling of superiority and had he not become less of a doctor less of a man less of a citizen in the process and as he played with the animal in himself become wholly animal? To all of this he would have answered no for he saw himself as an unthanked humble man in service to mankind. Mary his wife always nagged him for his lack of interest in his appearance refused to admit his so-called friends to the house and saw that he would always remain outside of them in spite of what he did to himself in spite of what he tried not to be. She was born and raised a lady she spoke flawless French and understood the theory of relativity she liked Bach and Modigliani and could discuss intelligently nearly any subject open to civilized man she was mismatched to him and Yellow Bird and that was part of the reason she up and died on him when she felt herself drawn into the same web when she saw that his degradation had curdled her milk so to speak.

And he thought he understood himself felt very sorry for Harry Mason and saw no resemblance to their situations for Harry Mason had escaped his fate returned as half a man unable to live within the confines of a society not made by him was unable to adapt to medicine in a large Midwestern town was unable to clearly see his role in any capacity and so leaped out of a window less than a year after his return from Bolivia. His saving grace was that he understood it all and after that corrected what ought not have been an error at all.

166

Yes Eli Wetherill at last was at peace with himself as he lay relaxed his heavy arms rested like discarded weapons on the outside of the quilt the legs upon which he had stood in love in vanity and in disrepute were prone and not drawn up in the pain he experienced from arthritis in the knees. The mental solitude more barren than any desert drew around him now in comfort and he would not have been interrupted for anything the warmth of his bed his preoccupation with grasping the meaning of his life awakened in him a feeling of overwhelming love a freshening of his spirit that would sustain him a good many days. The overwhelming pangs of loneliness which had gripped him all these years were no longer there for which he was grateful was this what they called mysticism finally coming to his aid he asked himself for he knew that neither God nor the Holy Spirit had come to him in the night conveying assurance as it were. The peace was unattributable unless it could be that in some final phase of life man is allowed one consuming look at himself. Eli Wetherill believed he had seen what was the essence of himself and it was all beneath the skin as it should be he would never realize that it was his outer appearance the world would continue to judge him by he looked debauched uncouth bloated lusterless the way any vagrant or cheap wino would he did not care. To him cleanliness was not next to godliness it was a prerequisite for surgery the unsightliness of himself was something he'd got accustomed to.

A small noise broke his pleasant reverie and he opened his eyes slowly and focused on the room as best he could without his glasses the wind was howling and the day was cold and demeaning to the spirit he glanced toward the window and wondered if a shingle had come off the roof no time to fix that now so let it go. And then he heard it again. A footstep on the stair. Who's there he said without fear for he always kept the house unlocked and thought perhaps it was Mrs. Craddock his cleaning lady coming a little earlier than usual. There was no answer and he listened for some time and did not hear the noise

167

again but he knew with whatever sixth sense a man has about things like that that someone was in the house.

He slipped quietly out of bed put his robe on and slippers it seemed unnecessary to take the revolver from the drawer after all he had no reason to fear anyone in town. He decided against turning on the light and made his way along the wall then across the room ever so quietly turned the handle of the door and braced himself for a human being on the other side but there was no one in the gloom of the hallway and he could not see beyond the top of the stairs. Who's there he called again and thought he heard the rustling of clothing. He held his breath he heard the clock ticking downstairs the wind banging a loose shutter the furnace kicking on and then he heard something else the breathing of another human who had also been holding his breath and let it out in a long sigh.

—I am going to kill you.

From out of the darkness the shape came toward him moving slowly and limping his back was to the wall the hands that had served him so well in the past were now his only defense against this apparition he spread his fingers his legs ached but would support his wretched body and then he recognized the thin and whiny voice and was not afraid only annoyed he said Nate what the hell do you want?

—Goddamn you goddamn you Nate Houghton said almost sobbing his body was bent like a reed rooted but waving in the wind. The faint light from the street lamp illuminated a haggard half-crazed face it also illuminated the metal of a gun held in Houghton's trembling hands.

The doctor was strangely calm he welcomed death in a certain sense had wished it many times something sudden and painless was what he saw his end to be an end not mourned nor noticed it would give him dignity to go that way or so he once believed and now that he was faced with it and saw Houghton drawing himself up not ten feet away he knew that death had to be delivered properly else lost its meaning and Houghton was not even so much as a foot soldier in the death army that stalked the world of the weak and weary anxious to be signed up and so he said in a clear voice Houghton you're a fool.

—I we trusted you you butcher I lived with your mistakes nigh on thirty years can't take it no more she's gone ain't never coming back what I got to live for now they took away my house my house is gone can't see nothing of my life and he began to choke on his words the emotion which had dragged him down and curdled all his reason now impelled him to destroy the very cause of why his life was all used up and if only his eyes did not burn so much and his bum leg would just stop wobbling and if he could just pull the trigger and get it over with this plan which had been building in his mind so many sleepless nights and seemed the only thing to do but first he had something to say he cleared his throat and shifted his weight to his one good leg seeing in his mind the night the doctor was going to cut it off right there in Mercy Hospital if it hadn't been for the fact that Eli Wetherill did not know how to do it right he'd be an amputee but as it was the doctor was to blame for the fact that he never had one day without pain he could not walk the hills again could not dance or plow his field alone he was a crippled man in every sense of the word.

—Go home and cool off Nate said the doctor impatient and unafraid I got to get some sleep now run along and he moved in the direction of his room.

—You ain't going nowhere except to hell said Houghton.

—Now be reasonable Nate after all you can't bring Rose back.

—Rose she was a good woman.

—Yes she was Nate you remember that.

—You done her wrong you bastard like you done me and a hunnerd others wrong now you got to pay you know what she said just before she died you know what she told me after all these years twenty-three years married never any secrets and there she is dying thanks to you and she says to me I can't carry

169

it around no more I done a terrible thing when I was seventeen I had a kid right here in Yellow Bird and I said well that's not so bad it's before I knew you she says yes well I gave it away he made me and I says who knocked you up none other than Eli Wetherill you a doctor a honorable man you ain't such after all he said with a bitter laugh.

—It wasn't me Nate I swear you got it all wrong.

—Did she have a kid or didn't she?

—That's part of her medical records I can't reveal.

He felt the gun against his ribs and knew that he could not move his only hope was time time to throw Nate Houghton off balance time to pull the gun away from him.

—Tell me goddamn you or I'll blast you to hell and gone.

—All right she did.

—When?

—I don't remember Nate I'd have to look it up.

—Liar and as for the kid she tried to find him she run an ad in the paper all she wanted was to see how the kid growed up it was all she talked about before she died you heard her doc.

—She was delirious then said the doctor putting things together in his mind.

—Like hell snarled Houghton stepping closer you lousy son-of-a-bitch you killed her when she began to open up about the kid you was scared she'd tell a lot of things she had on you oh a lot of things you got away with but no more no more.

The doctor swallowed and felt his legs go weak he shivered and said okay Nate she talked about the kid but he wasn't mine I give you my word.

—Your word sneered Houghton don't make me laugh your word is a pile of shit.

The doctor leaned against the wall trying to get hold of himself he began to hear them calling to him from the operating room and what they were saying was Pepsi-Cola hits the spot twelve apostles that's a lot.

The sun was beginning to come up it coated the hall with

170

a dingy light that made both men look like a faded photograph no solid lines or color their vague and shadowy images were gray and somewhat grotesque Houghton hunched and lopsided the doctor with his head hanging forward as if on a broken spring what was happening seemed not to be happening at all. He remembered the clipping that Joe Killeen arrived with and then it all came back to him how Rose at fifteen had slept around. Her mother was a waitress her father had died of cancer from a lifetime in the mines and so Rose had turned to an easy way to make a living it was no disgrace considering there were some seven mouths to feed. Rose matured early and passed for twenty-three thé ones she catered to were men from out of town the railroad crew turning around at the end of the line the truck drivers evangelists who were the best of all she said how well he remembered her shining eyes the first ten dollars that she made she spent on shoes never having worn anything except the heavy boots belonging to her father the carnival came to town one summer and stayed a month it was just before the war and the money was good Rose fell in love for the only time in her life with the ferris-wheel man she was planning to get married then found out he had a wife and five kids in Oklahoma it nearly broke her heart her first love was her last she said and so she produced his son paid Eli Wetherill five dollars to deliver it the same godawful night Galina died. He could not remember where it went from there he thought she gave it to some Mormons from Salt Lake but wasn't sure it could have been that Mullins girl who had a set of twins. Then it struck him hard that Joe Killeen could have been Rose Houghton's son or Galina Jordan's he was not certain then nor would he ever be which of the five dollar babies delivered that same horrible night was Joe Killeen and for once he was thankful his memory was bad allowing Killeen two perpetual possibilities.

Houghton was sweating and smelling like pissed-on wood his jaw was clamped shut and his rheumy eyes reflected the dullness of his mind Rose could never love him he had made a respectable woman of her and she had to give up living out of gratitude for what she did not deserve oh she slipped off now and then and had her fling what woman could be content with just one man if that man happened to be Nate Houghton and he suspected that three of the Houghton children belonged to another father.

—What's done is done said Eli as kindly as he could to Houghton whose mouth was growing harder all the time he had backed off a couple of steps but the gun was still in his hand and pointed straight at Eli Wetherill's heart. The kid she had was not mine I swear that do you think that by killing me you'll ease your mind about what she done you can fix the blame on me and go on living well I tell you Nate that even if you don't go to jail you can't live with yourself you're still an honest man.

Nate Houghton's bony head shot up no I ain't he growled.

—I've known you long enough to know you'd never kill a man it just ain't in you Nate now give it here.

—Well said Houghton slowly if it wasn't you who knocked her up who was it she said it was you with her dying breath she swore it by God you call my poor dead wife a liar?

—She was pretty sick Nate she didn't know what she said.

—She wouldn't lie to me she never did nothing to be ashamed of she loved me she did she loved me a whole lot.

—I know Nate.

—She didn't love you she didn't love nobody else but me. Tears glistened in his eyes his voice broke and he began to go down on his bad leg a look of terror came over his face and it was in that instant that Eli Wetherill knew what he meant to do as Nate turned the gun on himself. The doctor leaped forward and grabbed his arm but not before the terrible sound of splintering bone rang out instantaneous with the shot.

Nate Houghton lay dead at his feet in a pool of blood the gun was still in his hand a crooked smile on his lips there was nothing at all to be done. Eli leaned against the wall looking at him and his mind began to play all its familiar tricks of late and

172

what he found himself not doing what he actually thought he did what he thought he did was to telephone the police who were not in and he was told to take care of the matter himself the way he had always taken care of everything in Yellow Bird or thought he did and so he wrapped Nate Houghton in a blanket and dragged him down the stairs and through the kitchen stopping now and then to make sure the blood was not coming through and messing up the rugs so Mrs. Craddock would have to clean it up oh it was so heavy and he was so tired why didn't they send assistance was it because Yellow Bird was not on the map and did not exist did they think the people did not exist oh you had to do everything yourself if you wanted it done right do it and expect no thanks do it and keep right on doing it.

—Eli what in the hell are you doing?

—It's Houghton he's dead said the doctor impassively.

—Did you kill him Eli Britt said gently noticing that the doctor seemed in another world.

Eli took his glasses off and stuffed them in his pocket he could not see anyway he felt dizzy and he heard Britt's voice coming through water through a tube he saw what Yellow Bird really was the people lived in cardboard boxes stamped with unpaid bills hanging dirty wash out the attic window their false teeth sitting on Coke bottles bed pans wired for sound.

—Eli you better sit down and tell me what happened.

But he could not remember what had happened could not remember whether Houghton shot himself or not could not remember dragging him down the stairs and Britt was saying again did you kill him Eli?

—I don't think so it's a blank an honest-to-God blank.

—If you didn't kill him Eli who did?

—He done it himself.

—Now come on Eli why would he do a thing like that?

—Depressed about Rose.

173

—What was he doing here Eli think for God's sake what if they find him here?

He was seated at the table with Britt's strong arms pinning him Houghton's body was in a shapeless mound on the floor covered by the blanket bloody at one end the doctor stared at it was Houghton really dead was any of this happening at all he had a splitting headache his eyes felt as if they would drop from their sockets he said God Britt I don't know why he came maybe if I think.

—You haven't got time to think man we got to do something.

The doctor turned his baleful eyes to his friend what do you think we ought to do?

Britt ran his hands through his hair and shook his head call the police Eli it's the only way.

—No Britt no.

—Come on Eli you got to.

—Listen Britt it's the last straw they're waiting to catch me on two malpractice suits what if they exhume Rose Houghton's body do an autopsy know what they might find I think I made a mistake Britt it wasn't no crime.

—What did you do Eli said Britt who was suddenly gripped with fear.

—Oh Britt cut it out you know I tried to save her God it wasn't like—

—Eli what did you do?

—I'm not sure that's the trouble I just ain't sure I think it was adrenaline maybe it was penicillin I stuck in her heart but I don't know the coroner signed the death report he didn't suspect anything I just couldn't bring myself I just couldn't run the risk you see all I got left is my license to practice medicine that's all I got Britt and if I lose that I'll be like him he said nodding toward Houghton's corpse.

—Eli you goddamn fool.

—I didn't mean it Britt I swear.

—Now Houghton's dead and you don't know why. You realize they'd get you for murder in spite of how he said he'd kill you last night in the bar.

—It wasn't murder he turned the gun on himself Britt.

—Bullshit Eli if Nate was going to kill himself how come he did it here?

—Well it had to do with Rose he began and lapsed into silence.

—What about Rose said Britt softly and Eli opened his eyes and moistened his parched lips and said oh you know the way she died.

—He was suspicious is that what you mean accused you of letting her die came to kill you and had a fight the gun went off and there he lays was that it Eli?

The doctor nodded yeah that's the way it was Britt.

—Nobody will believe you.

—I reckon not.

—So what do we do?

—What can we do Britt?

—Just hold on a minute I'm trying to think well we could dump him out on the road someplace or leave him here and get you out of town oh hell Eli either way they'll track you down the only thing to do is call the police you got nothing to hide tell the truth you'll get off Eli I'll get you the best lawyers money can buy.

—Nope it just won't work that way I got a hunch time's run out I used up all my wild cards Britt that's the goddamn way it is.

Matt Brittman jumped up and said move your ass Eli we got to do this fast you take his front I'll take his feet and put him in the trunk.

—Where we going said Eli dazed and struggling to his feet he needed a drink in the worst way he was shaking bad so bad this time and God it was just no use.

—I'm taking care of you Eli just shut your mouth and move.

175

The garage was attached to the house and so they were not seen loading their curious bulky cargo into the trunk of Eli's car the sun was coming over the mountain and bathing the sleeping town in a warm and golden light it was cold with a hard blue sky that meant autumn was done and peeling off into the dark and lonesome days of winter. Matt Brittman drove the doctor's car calmly and with ease as Eli sat with his head against the seat he closed his eyes and balls of color exploded in his lids it was pulling him around and around so that he began to feel dizzy and nauseated he said Britt I'm going to puke and so the rancher stopped at the edge of a field across from the Yellow Bird Hotel and Eli staggered out of the car and retched into the grass unseen by anyone in the still sleeping town.

The road was meant for jeeps but they took it anyhow grinding up the steep incline and going around the hairpin curves through the aspen grove where the leaves were turning brown. Up on the mountain there was a patch of ground crisscrossed with burro trails scarred with abandoned diggings slag heaps from the dead mines epitaphed with gallows frames stark against the sky it was a sodden sullen mountain with its face cut up and hacked out its insides in such disgraceful heaps that it made you sore to look at them the mountain had been good to man but man had not been good to the mountain and so if you were like Matt Brittman you ached for it and felt it moving beneath your feet as you committed a body to it as one committed a body to the deep. It had taken all his strength to drag that terrible load across a bare patch of ground and to find what he was looking for an eruption on the mountain's face a gigantic open pore that was once a running sore with gold ore coming out of it. It went straight down down to the mountain's guts or so he hoped as he let Nate Houghton drop into the mine shaft and listened for a sound and there was none nothing at all just the wind howling and the clouds making up for a storm.

He went back to the car and Eli Wetherill was out cold all doubled up on the floor his shirt was filthy his trousers torn and bloodstained he had not shaved in four days his mouth was agape and he was snoring and all the while part of his face was twitching and it occurred to Britt as he stood over him that Eli would not be able to perform that final act would not be able to keep the bargain he was just too far gone for that and so he forced himself to think of what he had not allowed himself to think his end had to be one other man's end there remained just one way to accomplish that one way to get himself gunned down.

But it was only October and he had a while to go the thing had been dormant giving him some borrowed time he added and subtracted time until he was certain time was no longer subtracting him.

8

The West Bountiful River begins at the top of a rugged chain of mountains that are a spur of the Continental Divide and as it makes its way down from a windswept desolate rock face fourteen thousand feet high other streams feed into it and give it courage as well as depth and breadth. From the wild and brooding tundra which is its place of birth down through alpine meadows and stands of struggling spruce blasted bare on one side because of the prevailing wind through groves of aspen hunched over from too much snow resting in depths of twenty feet on noble trunks that do not always make it through till spring but break in two away from this savage battleground where nature always wins and there is no place for man the river is soft and sparkling clear plunging with a clean and pure sound over rocks and around bent elbows of river banks all washed and ever changing. The change is subtle and slow and on its own terms except in those places where the Forest Service has bridged it to make a campground accessible or where some logging company has gone in and chopped down what it felt like chopping down. It is only for a short distance that the river has not been tampered with and where it remains as it was a thousand years ago without the garbage and the sewage of man or his footprints or his motorbike or the tab pull tops of his beer cans.

Coming down the mountain slashing through trees and rocks and earth the river is joy and if a man believed in rivers he would say that up there in a high place the river is truly itself wild and free and lovely and as it should be in the company of the awesome pale plum-colored savage pinnacles stretching vertically jagged uneven walls that twist and turn and have pockets of snow in them that never melt not even in the summer. Up there where the tiny plants perform a two-month miracle of life then die and where even the eagle seems lonely and the scurrying pica seems frantic where death is spelled out in nature's boldest letters the river is almost merry and surely the only gentling influence in a landscape so harsh that eighty million years have done almost nothing to change it.

From where it begins to where it runs through Yellow Bird the river covers a distance of eighty miles winding its way down until it levels off at a bend in the land called Red Eye. There the fur traders rendezvoused the Indians made their camp and the prospectors first began to pan for gold working their way down-river throwing up tent towns and log-cabin villages of which no trace was ever found after the river arched its back and went on a rampage. But Yellow Bird being a hundred feet or so above the river was never flooded and only had its bridge ripped out on two occasions the first one having drowned the bank presi-

179

dent the second the only honest assayer in the county as well as a widow and five children living in a boxcar at the river's very edge. From Red Eye to Yellow Bird is less than thirty miles and along this stretch the river has been molested by every kind of act of man including slag heaps spewed out by the stamp mills and railroad tracks torn out and dumped into the water and uranium tailings which somehow or other rolled off the slopes near Fossil and ton after ton of entrails from the hills along the river which were assailed by every miner for forty years and then finally all the tin cans garbage broken glass aluminum foil plastic bags piss and shit from the slobs on wheels who said that West Bountiful was Colorado's last remaining pure river wild and remote and you just had to leave your mark on it somehow the way you left your mark on the forest by carving your initials on a tree or painting a rock with your high school monogram and so the river was blessed with what had passed through the mouth of man and come out the other end and by those recreational artifacts that nobody but nobody ever carts home.

What flowed under the bridge at Yellow Bird was the river's humiliation unrelieved until two more rivers and countless streams emptied into it on its journey into Utah by which time its clearness and its swift and purposeful course had been restored in a rebirth that the stretch between Red Eye and Yellow Bird had done its best to prevent. The river was at Yellow Bird as near death as the small and sullen town and although there was hope for the river there was none at all for the town the river would in time assume another form and fill a reservoir while the town would simply die and have its body stuffed into all the crevices that the river was not meant to fill. And the earth upon which the town had stood would make something presentable of the river at long last a dam to stop its flow and back it up into such a fine body of water that the river could it speak would surely say how come?

—Bullshit said Eli Wetherill irritably as he picked his teeth with a pocket knife. The trees along the river had lost their

180

leaves and he sat under one of them his sore legs stretched out in the gravel. The day was sunny but there was an October bite in the air and in two weeks the hunters would start coming up the road in jeeps from Coronado and fan out along the mountain and the forest and the sound of their guns would be heard echoing down the slopes and across the river and ending in the broken hills beyond. The killing of the elk and deer was a practice he had grown used to and even enjoyed at one time considering himself an expert marksman who brought down his quarry each and every time but this year was different he had no desire to kill anything he wished to be left alone ever since the night Nate Houghton died and so now he did his drinking at home occasionally with Matt Brittman or Killeen or the Muldoon girl for company they formed a group that had been out of place in Yellow Bird ever since that night a week before when they had come after him in the bar and then Nate Houghton—

It was just not clear that's all not Houghton nor the rest of it he had lived in fear for many days and could not sleep at night. He no longer went to his office and when Killeen had come in for something to cure a sore throat he had sent him to a doctor in Coronado without a word of explanation about why he could not would not should not treat another human patient as long as he lived he would not run the risk again he was finished wiped out and had no place to go. As he watched the river dirty and exhausted and degraded he smiled at it and folded his arms and said to it only the innocent and the blind could love you you crawling along on your belly heaped with what a man don't want or care about and what if you could just flow upstream for a while until you were all rolled up back where you came from and could choose a different course know what you'd do come right on down the same way because the way has put its dibs on you ain't that right you yellow son-of-a-bitch that ain't no good for anything except your own godforsaken self. Bullshit he said again and hurled a rock into it noticing that it sank halfway into the mud.

—What are you doing said Meridian Muldoon coming up behind him from a sea of yellow aspen I've been looking all over for you. She was dressed in Levi's and sneakers and a heavy black sweater and she crouched beside him noticing that there was a half-empty whiskey bottle on top of a frayed leather jacket.

—I have caught the most amazing fish he said it talks.

—And what does it say?

—I haven't the faintest idea it only speaks Hebrew but it has drawn a certain picture with its fin.

—And what is that she said laughing.

He took a stick and drew four circles in the dirt and said the first is spring the second summer the third fall and the fourth winter or maybe the four stages of a man's life or a town's life innocence and childhood discovery and youth success and maturity misery and old age you can only avoid the last if you are lucky. Winter is a prelude to death as far as I'm concerned you know it's coming round the bend when the river freezes up along the edges and you got no wish to sleep in a cold bed you crunch up dead leaves in your hands and wish the clock had only forty minutes to it because when the fourth circle starts forming you got no place to go your calendar is all used up. I saw Yellow Bird's last circle start forming twenty years ago when the last mine shut down and the first man drew an unemployment check you got to know when a thing is no longer good and now we're stalemated and antiquated and going into the fifth circle of eternity not having done half of what we wanted to.

He rubbed out the circles in the dirt and pulled the top off the bottle and offered it to Meridian who took a sip feeling it burn all the way down and she felt relaxed there with the ragged man with the watery eyes who was mumbling I got diarrhea of the mouth pay no mind to me.

—I'm not sure the circles are so clearly defined she said some people seem permanently in winter.

—That's true he said and some are born dead.

—That's the way I feel sometimes and at other times so alive and wanting to take big gulps of life and getting frustrated because the more I take the more I want and the more I want the more I know I can't have.

Eli Wetherill was slipping along with the sun to a different place in time he waved the bottle and avoided Meridian's thoughtful face.

—I am he announced jovially going to release upon the world an enormous catshit bomb.

—And I she said am going to run away.

He closed one eye and squinted at her. Run away once more missy and you've had it stay here and face up it's time you done it time you got to know the second circle of your life.

—It's not important. You of all people ought to know what it's like to be trapped in one circle that's not summer or spring winter or fall a season suspended above all the rest.

—Yeah he said slowly rubbing his eyes his glasses no longer served him well yeah I been there most of my life I reckon.

—That's what you've meant to this town she said abruptly an extra season an extra circle.

—Me he said startled no that's not it at all I tried to be a doctor to this town and failed. He took a long luxurious drink from the bottle smacked his lips and turned his face to her failed he said again emphatically.

—Oh no she said gently it's not you that's failed the town it's the town which has failed you I realized that the other night in the bar.

—That he said oh they were just letting off steam.

—You're a good man you're not like what I thought.

—I'm just plain vanilla.

—The hell you are.

—Now missy he said patting her hand don't get all wrought

183

up I aim to pull out before long and get a fresh start I got some good years left.

But she knew he hadn't and she knew moreover that he had been kidding himself for so long that he did not know what he was or was not. He was playing a role he had played for so long that he had become his own creation. He rocked gently back and forth and a tune of some sort rose from his lips and he appeared content watching the river flow and the sun shone on his dissipated face and seemed to heal him with its warmth and she sensed that he was off in a world that was familiar and comfortable to him so she let him remain that way for some time without interrupting his enjoyment. Then the purpose which had brought her there the fear with which she had approached him an hour or so before began anew and she had to handle him just right and not mess up the only chance she had to know the truth.

—What's the matter with Matt Brittman?

—What said the doctor rousing himself and feeling his heart start pounding.

—I said what's the matter with Britt is he sick or what?

—Of course not fit as a fiddle same as he always was. He avoided her disbelieving eyes and turned his face to the sun and began to hum again.

—I don't believe you because Killeen says Killeen says—

The doctor drew himself up straight and snapped Killeen says what?

—Britt's deathly ill.

—Killeen is full of shit.

—Britt fell off his horse the other day he passed out last night right on the floor Killeen says there's blood on the sheets and that Britt takes a whole bunch of painkillers he says there is hardly a night that he sleeps and he says you better go find Harley because Britt can't run the ranch anymore.

The doctor's eyes were suddenly open and intent. He smoothed his soiled shirt and adjusted his wrinkled tie he

184

cleared his throat and forced himself to stare calmly at the sky where a dragon-shaped cloud was moving west now missy all that ails Britt is that like the rest of us he's getting old.

Was the doctor in or out of his senses the bottle was nearly gone and she could smell his breath as strong as the whiskey itself. She felt an urge to give up and go home but instead she said firmly you will just have to face it doctor whether you want to or not Britt is headed toward the fifth circle no matter what you'd like to believe can't you admit he's one patient you are never going to save?

A strange look came over the doctor's face don't get involved he said harshly.

—Involved she said I just feel sorry for him he has no one at all.

The doctor knew he had to go and he got unsteadily to his feet his legs were weak and his feet had gone to sleep yet he felt in control of himself as he reached down for his jacket and said to her stay away from him missy it's all I'll ever ask of you. Britt is over the hill he's run the race plumb out of steam and vinegar for God's sake don't go and complicate his life at this late date.

—He's half dead with loneliness if you really want to know she said I want a chance to do something about that.

—You in love with him said the doctor suddenly.

—No.

—Then why?

She shrugged and looked away oh I don't know maybe I've got an urge to be useful to a lost cause just like you.

A smile flickered across the doctor's face he murmured that's ridiculous considering.

—Considering what?

He was shouting now and waving his arms considering he's got no time left considering his potato crop considering he is resigned to what has got to happen.

—What cried Meridian shaking the doctor's shoulder what

185

are you talking about you crazy old fool what's wrong with him?

—A right tender scene drawled Jed McTavish standing in the brush above them his hand resting on his hip holster his sheriff's badge gleaming in the sun. He blew his nose into an enormous red handkerchief and said Eli I got a couple questions to ask you mind walking to the car?

—To hell with you said Eli sitting down again and picking up the bottle if you want to talk Mac come and have a snort I ain't in no condition to walk up that goddamn hill. McTavish glanced at Meridian who was crying and said excuse us Miss Muldoon we got business to discuss.

Eli held up his hand whatever business you got with me Mac she can hear on account of she's going to write us up for the paper how nice and polite and homebody we all are.

—Eli said McTavish this is a serious matter.

—This said Eli waving the bottle is likewise a serious matter now sit down Mac and quit acting like the law.

—Well said McTavish spitting tobacco juice and scratching his girth what about her?

—We're all of us having a friendly little snort sit down here missy and quit tuning up like a symphony orchestra.

And so they sat awkward at first and then Eli produced another bottle from his jacket and McTavish broke into a grin and took off his gun belt and said I hope nobody sees us Eli my goddamn job.

—I'll get you another one Mac what the hell you worried about?

—I ain't worried Eli he said taking a long and splendid drink and letting out a belch you ain't too popular around here.

—That so?

—That's so Eli and I don't wonder the town is all stewed up they got to leave the place where they growed up and it ain't easy for a man to walk off from what he built with his two hands and where he raised up his kids and married his wife I know that's what's behind it Eli.

186

—Behind what Mac?

—They don't want you around no more.

—Bullshit.

—A fact Eli I got a whole list of complaints and one I can't hardly ignore they want me to take you into town and put you in jail.

—In the hoosegow Mac now that is really nice but I got a bed and roof over my head and I tolerate Josie's cooking no thanks Mac I don't need a room that bad.

—You don't get the picture Eli ain't you been around for the last week ain't you heard the stir?

The whiskey was all inside him now and the landscape was moving and the sun was hot and the girl's perfume was getting him all shook up and he giggled what stir?

—Nate Houghton disappeared Eli and a lot of people seem to think you know where to.

—Oh said Eli feeling all his strings tighten up of their own accord Nate up and left town?

—Looks that way Eli or maybe it was foul play I haven't got a single lead all I got is rumor some people in this town would like to have your head Eli and I reckon if it was a hundred years ago they'd string you up on evil thoughts alone.

—I'm telling you Mac I don't know a thing about Nate saw him a couple times since Rose passed on he was grieving and sad you know as well as I do how a man acts when his woman passes on.

The sheriff looked across the river toward his own land beyond the first row of hills and he remembered his own Bessie who passed on a year ago come November and he wasn't over it yet and never would be a man seventy-two years of age married to one woman for fifty ain't likely to get over the emptiness of his life once she has been taken from it and he felt himself choke up and that would never do.

—Yep said the sheriff Nate was hard hit same as you and me.

187

—Exactly and so he could have wandered off in the woods or maybe took a bus to California a man does strange things when he finds himself alone.

—But he left the kids behind and never said a word there's three at home and his pickup's still there and all his clothes I dunno what to make of it.

The whiskey was calming him and at the same time placing him out of context he felt adrift as he so often did adrift and sinking fast I wouldn't worry Mac he said thumping him on the back.

The sheriff rubbed his scrawny neck he had held the job since forty-nine and it gave him a certain stature in the town until they tore down the jail and made him take his problems to Coronado where the constabulary treated him with an air of good intentions and the very best of Western tradition.

—What was the ruckus in the hotel all about Eli they say you had a little run-in with Nate and—

—There was no run-in Meridian interrupted. Houghton threatened to kill him and then they all tried to jump him and if anybody should be arrested it's the bums of Yellow Bird.

The doctor closed his eyes and saw darkness he was thirsty and there was nothing to drink but whiskey and his tongue began to feel like a thick-napped rug and he could hardly swallow. His hands lay open on his dirty trousers and he examined them seeing the dirt beneath the fingernails and that they were trembling very badly and he wondered vaguely how he could hold a thermometer let alone a scalpel no no no and God maybe he would just fall off a horse and kill himself or maybe he would just take a turn for the worse and be put away.

—Oh Mac he heard himself saying I don't recall a ruckus I just don't recall much of anything anymore and he tapped his head with his finger this old brain of mine is rusted out.

The sheriff frowned and you could see that he liked the doctor as much as he liked any man and that he was at a loss for words because the job was no fun anymore and why did he

188

have to sit and question Eli in the first place if there ever was
a man who had done good it was Eli and he could go just so far
to protect his friends before those Yellow Bird bastards started
beating on higher doors.

—Eli he said sternly now listen to me this town has gone
plumb nuts like a bunch of sheep in a thunderstorm at timberline they're scared stiff and Eli I got to do something to keep
the thing in check now what the hell did Britt have to shoot at
Houghton for?

Meridian got up her eyes blazing that's a lie Mister McTavish Britt shot a hole in the ceiling go and look for yourself.

—Now hold on girl I know there's a hole in the ceiling and
I know Britt put it there but they say there were two shots fired
and Britt himself don't remember and Josie don't know either
there was so much noise she says she wouldn't know if he had
fired off a cannon.

—Go look at his gun then said Meridian.

—Did that girl and all the chambers are empty on account
of Britt has been plugging away at tin cans saw him myself this
morning a damn good shot like he always was.

Eli stirred himself now Mac he said Britt don't waste his
time shooting at tin cans.

—Well that's what he was doing said McTavish spitting
across a log into the tawny-colored grass recalling the day in
fifty-one he'd won hands down a spitting contest held in front
of City Hall he'd spit twenty feet and three inches a solid squirt
of tobacco juice a record still unbroken. So where the hell is
Houghton he said to Eli who seemed about to fall asleep.

The doctor bit his lip and said nothing just stared down the
river and the nightmare unfolded itself in his mind in Tech-
nicolor snatches and maybe he should tell Mac to have a look
in the mine shaft and get the thing off his chest once and for all
he'd never sleep unless he did and he wished for the first time
in his life to pay for whatever he had done he could not go on
the way he was because he no longer liked himself and wished

189

to clean up his blank and hollow room and he would wish to be sentenced publicly to the worst of prisons and maybe they would let him do one useful thing and he could learn to live with himself a little bit at least. He opened his mouth and was about to speak and then he realized that Britt would be implicated too and likewise found guilty of a crime he did not commit and oh god who would believe either of them.

—Well said McTavish impatiently.

Eli shrugged and said I wish I knew.

—I know said Meridian suddenly and the doctor felt his heart going to his feet had they finally been discovered after all he held his breath and heard her say Nate Houghton came to see me let's see a week ago tomorrow the day after I saw him in the Yellow Bird Hotel and he

—Wait a minute said McTavish pulling out a notebook and moistening the tip of a pencil with his tongue got to write it down else I'm likely to forget all right Houghton came to see you and what was the time of day?

She frowned and drew in her lips oh it was before breakfast maybe seven or eight o'clock he was greatly agitated said he didn't know where to turn well as you know my family helped him out for a long time both him and Rose and all those kids he liked my father and it was at our place that he uh had his accident and so it was natural for Nate to come to me being the only Muldoon within five hundred miles.

—What'd he want said the sheriff scribbling away.

—Money.

—Money?

—That's right he said that what he had to do was get out of town there were too many memories of Rose and he had to go away you know on account of the dam but he'd spent all his money they'd given him for his property and he was broke all he wanted to do was take the kids and strike out for a new place and start all over again now don't you think that was a fine idea Mister McTavish?

190

—Yep yep said McTavish scarcely looking up as he wet the pencil and kept on writing so what did you do?

—I gave him two hundred dollars.

The sheriff stopped writing and gazed steadily at Meridian can you prove it he said.

—It was cash because he had no place to cash a check and anyway he was in a hurry he went out the door and then an hour later he was back and asked me to take him into Coronado so he could get some things but I don't have a car and so that's the last I ever saw of him.

The sheriff snapped shut his notebook and stared down at the river gnawing on a stick he had picked up he pondered the situation for several minutes and then took out his notebook again and thumbed through it talking to himself with words neither Meridian nor the doctor could understand and then he stood up fastened on his gun belt and turned to Eli with a grin. Case dismissed he said.

—Yeah said Eli how's that?

—A man answering Nate's description got on a bus bound for Rapid City South Dakota about Saturday noon so that ties in with what she said I guess he just blew town and left those younguns to make it on their own. He shook his head it don't make sense for a man to up and leave his kids but like you said Eli a man acts strange when his woman has passed on well I guess this ought to satisfy the boys at Josie's place I never thought I'd live to see the day they'd raise up against you Eli I'll try to settle them down.

—Don't waste your breath Mac.

A look of sadness spread over the old man's face and his rheumy eyes filmed over it was a good town he said once upon a time don't know where it all went or why. He started up the hill mumbling to himself and when he was at the top he turned and shouted down hey Miss Muldoon I got no reason to believe one word you said you ain't never told the truth to any man alive.

191

The doctor ran his tongue around his cracked swollen lips and forced himself to smile at Meridian if you were a man and this was a hundred years ago you could plug him dead for calling you a liar.

—Well I am she said.

—Figured.

They were silent for a while and then the doctor said how come?

—Because I want to know what's wrong with Britt.

—So that's your real true purpose that's how come you lied for me you figure I owe it to you now.

—Yes.

—Bitch.

—Will you tell me or not?

—I'd rather be dead.

He got unsteadily to his feet and his whole body was quivering and he slipped and fell down the hill rolling over and over in the red gravel tasting it between his teeth and feeling it go up his nose he saw the trees and earth and sky in a crazy mixed-up ball and the sun was bursting inside his head like fire it was and liquid and then the thing stopped spinning and he found himself against a log and tasted his own blood he closed his eyes and went out and the next thing was Meridian Muldoon kneeling next to him wiping his face with a Kleenex.

—Are you hurt she said anxiously do you want a doctor?

—I am a doctor.

—Do something with yourself then you're all bloody.

—Leave me be.

The girl was near tears again and chewing on one nail oh you she said and put her foot down hard in the gravel Doctor Wetherill you have got to get up from there.

The ground was not too cold and he was not uncomfortable although his head hurt and feeling the gash on his head he knew he required a small suture but the sun was coming out from behind the clouds and there was a strange peace settling over

him so that he felt quite at home where he was. Go get the
bottle he said to Meridian.

—I'll do no such thing.

—Please.

—You've had enough.

—Goddamn bitch he said softly go get Mac and have me
arrested now go do it you don't understand you don't know
what it's like to kill somebody.

—Oh Doctor Wetherill she said trying to lift him up don't
talk like that.

His face was bruised and the cut stung and he could not
keep from quivering and he was ashamed for the girl to see him
like that and he simply had to try to pull himself together and
go find some comfort in his bed.

—Leave me be missy please leave me be.

—It's turning cold and the wind is coming up you'll catch
your death of cold.

—What the hell he growled.

—Don't you care she cried don't you care about yourself at
all?

He shook his head gave that up years ago.

—Well I do will you please get up for me?

It was the first time in a long while anyone had spoken to
him like that and even if she didn't mean it how nice to hear
some words that made you feel good for a change and he
reached out and touched her face he saw that her profile was
as delicate as those portraits that Mary always had around the
house her hair pale gold caught the light and he wanted to
touch that too and did so very gently and she did not pull away
and he remembered similar hair that belonged to Galina Jordan
oh Meridian took him back all right and nearly nudged him
backward into a circle already finished and the inside of him
was crying for what he had had and would not have again it had
taken him fifty-five years to understand his own mortality and
one could not expect him to accept it overnight.

193

He stuffed his hands in his pockets and turned up the collar of his coat letting his head sink into the warmth of the fleece lining he was feeling pretty decent all of a sudden and if he had just one more chance left he'd lay it on Meridian Muldoon who had grown up okay after all and he felt quietly proud that Yellow Bird could claim her even if she wasn't willing to claim it and perhaps the incident with the nigger kid was no worse than any of them had done himself included. And he wanted to tell her it was all right that he wasn't judging her anymore and if those sullen screwballs did that was their misfortune he wanted to visualize himself walking down the streets of New York City with her him a tall and dignified gentleman with an elegant-looking girl he wanted to come out of his shell and take her and spend what money he had on her. But time had worked itself like a screwworm upon him and he felt that only part of him was left standing the rest was eaten up and what he had to offer was exactly nothing.

He sighed deeply and gazed with affection upon the girl's patient face sure he said getting to his feet this is about all I can do for you get my poor and failing carcass up and headed back to town where I will buy you the best that Josie Stringer has in her peritonitis parlor.

They began walking up the embankment grabbing at the roots of trees and holding on to each other until they came out on top and stood there with the wind blowing from the west and the dry fields shimmering in the sun the jet contrails bisecting the absurdly blue sky the yellow leaves clacking together on the aspen trees the town so still and silent that you knew it had already died and was waiting to be buried there was not much of it and it occupied only a small space in a landscape so vast that north or south or west you could see a hundred miles or more just sky and earth that looked untouched until you got up close well it made you kind of subdued standing there taking it all in and thinking for one split second that you could comprehend it all.

194

—Oh look said the doctor here comes the Coyote remember him?

He was a little man not over five feet tall and he had a gold tooth made from his diggings a tooth in which he had once had a diamond set to pay for his burial but one night after he had passed out in Josie Stringer's saloon a couple of men had picked it out and now there was a small hole in the middle of his gold tooth through which he whistled or spat. When the Coyote was very young a team of mules had run over his feet and left his brain strung out in little pieces so that he was given to certain peculiarities such as wearing a straw hat in winter and galoshes in the summer he was also fond of collecting cigarette butts and went around with the snipes carefully arranged in his hatband. Other than his six-transistor radio the only thing he loved was his lunchbox bought for him by the doctor who after seeing how the Coyote's lunch usually dropped from his pockets and he went hungry the rest of the day gave him the gray metal oblong box with a Thermos in it and two clasps that the Coyote loved to open and shut and so each day when he set out in search of his mine he carried those two treasures the radio and the lunchbox. He approached them fairly dancing along the road down from the mountain he wore a faded Eisenhower jacket his straw hat and plumber's overalls and his gold tooth shone in the sun as he spread his mouth in a grin and waved his arms one hand held the lunchbox and on his back there was an army surplus knapsack.

—Hello Coyote the doctor called and waved.

—Hey doc yelled the Coyote and danced along the ground until he was in step with the doctor and then he said I found her.

—That's nice said Eli absently not knowing what he meant.

—Yessir said the Coyote tucking his lunchbox under one arm and reaching for a snipe from his hatband I found her right where I been looking and you know how I knew it was her?

—No Coyote I don't.

195

—The red aspen to the left of her turns that color every year so the only chance I have to find her is October and I always missed for some reason or another but there she was today and here he began to cackle and do a little dance on the road up toward the town his ancient legs moving in quick irregular strokes almost like I left her more'n twenty years ago and there's been this here landslide that has pushed away what them uranium fellers thought they covered up and pretty soon and once more he whirled and his radio came on with a Western tune that he liked so he turned it up and made himself heard above it I am going to dig my way into her doc see how bad they left her and where she needs shoring up a lot of gold left in her a lot of gold doc I know right where I left off.

—Well Coyote said the doctor looking solemnly toward the mountain the uranium boys have probably blowed her up inside and anyway it ain't worth no man's time to become a hard rock stiff these days.

—What else I got to do with my time said the Coyote baring his gold tooth as he carefully took his snipe pinched out the end with his fingers and put it back in his brim. And anyway doc I got me a little help. He put down his radio and his lunchbox and removed the knapsack from his back and set it on the ground untied it and opened the top flap he was nearly bursting with excitement as he stood back and said have a look doc go ahead.

Eli Wetherill peered inside and his first impulse was to get away from there as fast as he could for he had been around dynamite long enough to know what it could or could not do stashed away for God knows how long freezing and thawing and ready to go off. He swallowed and stepped back and said calmly to the Coyote is there more?

—Oh lots more doc and caps too. Enough to blow us off the map.

—What are you going to do with it Coyote?

—Save it.

—For what?

—For my mine what else?

—Then you should have left it where it was.

—No doc I got to test it out.

—Now listen man you'll blow yourself to kingdom come.

—I been around dynamite for sixty years and I ain't never had an accident ain't never done it wrong why doc I could set it off in my sleep.

—That's what worries me the stuff is old it could blow up in your face while you're standing there now damn it Coyote leave it where it is I'll call somebody to come and get it you come along and show me where the rest of it is hid.

The Coyote backed away and held up his hands the stuff ain't that old doc look we never used that kind of casing the uranium fellers left it I figure and I ain't scared of it doc I ain't scared of nothin' and with that he sprang nimble as a cat and wrapped his dynamite and put it in the sack and hoisted it to his shoulders while Eli held his breath and Meridian moved to the very edge of the road and headed across an open field toward town.

—Promise me one thing said the doctor you won't take it into the hotel.

—Never intended to do that doc you think I'm crazy I got respect for people's lives and property no doc I got a place to hide it.

—Where Coyote?

The old man shook his head and pushed his straw hat back ain't tellin' he cackled ain't tellin' nothin' you think I want my claim jumped once more?

—Nobody is going to jump your claim Coyote.

—No tellin' what a man might do for gold.

—They ain't been jumping claims for fifty years said the doctor those days are gone.

—Nope not gone gold he said quietly then gold he said with awe and finally gold the way a man would whisper the name of the woman he loves.

197

The doctor could think of no way to persuade the Coyote to do anything he had always been on the stubborn side and wayward like a mule on its own so all he said was be careful old man.

—Sure sure said the Coyote grinning and waving his radio and his lunchbox Annabelle Lee she lives again.

The doctor hurried through the field after Meridian glancing over his shoulder at the Coyote who was ambling along the road his radio blaring his lunchbox held snug against him and the deadly pack fastened to his back and he would not have been surprised to see the old man blown up right then and there. He ought to get Jed McTavish or sign some commitment papers and have the Coyote locked up where he couldn't harm himself or anybody and then it occurred to him that if the Coyote went that way it was the way he would have wanted to go out in the open with his gold mine and the comfort of his endeavor.

—Madness murmured the doctor mopping his brow and feeling himself sweat so badly that his glasses were steaming up and he could smell his own stink coming through his clothes and then he heard the guns going off some .22's and he looked up in amazement the start of hunting season was several weeks off and what could anyone be doing now except plugging away at birds. The sound was coming from back of the Fairbanks block which was just an empty shell with the wind whistling through it and he began to run because he felt something terrible had happened and then he saw Meridian Muldoon hurrying toward him her face white as chalk. She was waving her arms and talking incoherently what next he thought what next and pretty soon he saw them all the poker players from the Yellow Bird Hotel standing in a ring with their guns and some were laughing and some were merely standing legs apart cruel smiles on their lips as they held their guns close to their cheeks and fired into the dirt.

They spotted him and turning like plastic robot soldiers

they seemed about to fire at him standing helpless and unarmed amidst the last of the asters and the dandelions in a field of weeds they were poised and ready and there was nothing he could do even if he ran they'd shoot him in the back or get him if he flattened himself on the ground cold fear swept over him far worse than the night Nate Houghton had come they had him all right and he did not know what they would do but he knew what he must do. He stopped and let his arms drop to his sides straightened his back and lifted his head and called to them go ahead and shoot.

—The town lush and the town whore one of them said let's get both of 'em boys.

There was a moment of utter silence and then they turned and opened up at something on the ground and it was then that he heard above the blast of guns the pitiful cries of an animal cornered and Meridian was tugging at his sleeve and weeping and he was running toward the men who fanned out and slunk away and there on the ground was what was left of Susie Josie Stringer's little dachshund and pet of thirteen years.

—Oh God cried Eli and kneeling took off his jacket and covered the small body.

Meridian Muldoon said I saw what they were doing and tried to stop them they only laughed and called me nigger lover.

—Why did they do it why?

—Because they didn't know what else to do.

The doctor looked up at the darkening sky and felt the cool air strike his moist cheeks and felt pain in his legs and an aching in his heart and relief was coming to him like the approaching winter the relief of his mind giving out and leaving him in welcome twilight.

He needed a drink more than anything else in the world and he would have to go and break the news to Josie and come back and bury the dog himself and after that he would not have anything to do except play back old movies of himself in slow motion. He began to walk with Meridian up the half-deserted street realizing himself as he was a long time ago when they said to his father that kid is going to amount to something and be a credit to us all the pride of Yellow Bird was what they said he was and who among them had so fine an education with two important letters after his name? But he was not a credit to anything and so he felt a sense of failure each time he walked through a town that turned its back on him.

The girl was walking along with him holding his hand and sharing his sorrow she could not cry anymore and she had seen him cry for the first time and she felt like destroying for the first time and there was the coal-black boy hanging and his coal-black sister in the ditch and who was there to pay for any of it?

They were nearly to the hotel when it got to him about the dog and what could he say to Josie poor woman who had seen much suffering in her time who had just the dog and Charley for company and was the sort of person you wouldn't harm even if you could. Every one of those men standing in the field with a .22 had been helped by Josie in one way or another over the years had accepted her food and drink often on the house had no cause to offend a woman who was the glue of Yellow Bird no he would never understand it he had seen a lot of brutality in his time a lot of offenses committed in the name of alcohol or pressure or rage or jealousy but not with cool hands and heart's blood running cold as a mountain stream and twice as fast. And what of the men whose faces were not distinct who had a line of mouths like mail slots and eyes of glass and when they took off their hats and set them in a row they were all alike the sweatbands sweaty enough to know they were for real and the boots with square toes made in Texas caked with the identical mud and they have worn down their heels on Yellow Bird's streets and sidewalks and public saloons. It's not too odd is it that when one gets mad the rest follow likewise and when one decides to kill a thing the others don't say no. Could he really blame them for doing what they did they were so fired up and frustrated and had to take it out on a helpless creature that couldn't fight back or get away. Men trapped by life have got a way of becoming ignoble like an animal in captivity running contrary to what nature intended they get boiled down to some pretty basic instincts to hell with the goddamn reason.

Eli Wetherill sat down on the broken curb across from the Yellow Bird Hotel and from there he could see down to the office he had not opened in more than a week and he could see the men filing in for lunch like nothing had ever happened and he made up his mind then and there not to tell Josie at all. He got up and with the girl following in puzzlement went back to the field and found a rusty shovel among the junk and buried the dog beneath a bush that had berries on it and found a piece of bleached-out fence that more or less resembled a cross and hammered that with a rock above the tiny grave he did not believe in God but Josie did and that is what she would have wanted.

The girl was beginning to understand and the chill that went down her spine was because she knew that the doctor was neither good nor bad he responded to a town that itself was inconsistent and moody as recalcitrant as the weather and they were all twisted into one melting pot that could not be classified nor defined in black or white. Maybe you had to go back and know that the kind of restless lawless greedy goodness that presided over Yellow Bird's birth was in attendance at its death as well.

She felt like crying but did not she felt like putting her arms around the doctor but could not she felt like telling him she understood but would not. You just stood off by yourself in a little pocket and kept your emotions covered and disguised your vulnerability with indifference.

The doctor seemed to read her mind he sighed wearily and said this is what it adds up to missy.

—Yeah she said slowly.

—It's never going to be again not in any time or place.

201

—I know.

—They used to have some harmless vices.

—I remember.

—Like all of us at one time or another.

—Yes.

—The devil twists the arm of fate my mother used to say.

—And opens the window on despair.

—It can't be helped no matter what you say.

—I wonder what would have happened had we lived differently.

—The condition heredity and problems of the patient indicate a miscarriage.

—I'd deliver it if I were you and see what happens.

—One hell of a five dollar baby.

—Deliver it.

—I'll see.

He picked up a stone and turned it slowly in his hands it was smooth and white and shaped like an egg and the stone was his receipt for services rendered. He put it in his pocket and turning his head to the west he said I got a certain patient that's checking out a couple months from now so I don't rightly think it's a proper time for giving birth.

—You mean she said and her hand flew to her mouth.

—A doctor is obliged to keep his mouth shut that's all I got to say.

And so she knew what she had really known all along and he had done what he had said he would never do they had a bond between them now that did not need words words were a bad thing unless she could confine them to paper and make believe they belonged to somebody else.

By the next morning she had made up her mind what she had to do and she packed her things and got Charley Stringer to drive her to the ranch it was nearly noon and she knew that Britt was home alone working on his books.

He did not look well bent over his ledgers with the light

striking the side of his face he removed the glasses he used for reading and seemed disturbed to find her there. Looking for Killeen he said he won't be back till dark.

She shook her head and said lightly Killeen and I have busted up.

He drew in his breath. Ridiculous that is one hell of a man.

—And so are you.

—Horseshit.

—Well you are.

—Old enough to be your pa.

He sat playing with the pencil and she knew an idea was slowly forming in his mind or perhaps had been there all along a male animal was ready anytime or so she was willing to bet. She perched on the edge of his desk and ran her fingers through his hair and she would have to be awfully clever for him not to suspect that she was there to make a sacrifice she could not wound his pride nor his ego she was there to give him whatever he might have wished for in his most secret longings and it was so delicate and so hard to assume maybe he did not want the contact after all maybe he wished to be by himself maybe his body had played out and suffocated all desire.

—Meridian he said at last you are a mighty attractive gal.

—Oh Britt you're just trying to make me feel good.

—Sure he laughed always flatter a heifer makes them gentler and more likely to wean a healthy calf.

—A calf I don't need she said playing his game but maybe I need a bull.

—There ain't much demand these days for this particular breed.

—That's hard to believe considering the beast is hardy fertile and has a record of productivity.

He shifted in his chair and dropped his hand on her leg

203

well he drawled you know how it is you can have one hell of a record year then whammo the beast goes dry and you got to knock him on the head while he's standing there looking into the purple sunset.

—I am interested in the specimen nonetheless she said if it is allowed to have a second chance.

—Not the usual procedure around here to let anything have a second chance the herd was built on ruthlessness.

—Surely once you dropped the rules.

He shook his head nope not once in all these years and that's how come I reached perfection no second chances ruthlessness and nature give me what I have to have.

—And do they?

—Never failed me yet but having reached perfection I ask myself where do I go from here.

—To a second chance.

—Against my principles.

—To nature then letting instinct prevail.

He rubbed his chin and took her small hand in his Marcus taught you a couple things about the cattle business he said too bad Harley never caught on oh well now what about this instinct thing you think I ought to trust it?

—Oh Britt she said why not?

—It makes sense Meridian by instinct you mean the survival of the fittest.

—That's what Marcus used to say.

—That's been my belief my whole life long and now I say what's fit who is to determine fitness?

—Let nature define fitness she said isn't that what you've practiced?

—Yep he said somewhat surprised that she understood I've let nature do it all.

—So in this case she said dropping her arm around his broad shoulder I think you ought to leave it to nature and see what happens.

He got up and held her at arm's length the weeks of pain had left their mark on his handsome windburned face desperate now in craving what he had needed for some time and as he stood there looking over every inch of her in the same way he could appraise a healthy cow he knew he had to put his body to the test of copulation the test for any bull of his that did not get marked for slaughter. If he just kept her in that context a damned fine hunk of heifer and nothing more then he would be okay there would be no commitment no need for explanation she would just be to him one more proof of his system one more tangible proof that he was strong and had done right and so without another word he picked her up she weighed no more than a sack of feed and carried her to his small and cluttered room. He was very calm and sure of himself and she stood there not really caring that he took so long to undress he was clumsy and fumbling at first and then he was at her hard and fast and was out in less than a minute for him the sexual act was a pleasure not to be drawn out any longer than necessary and having come he rested on his side and silently cursed the pain that had waited until now to present itself. His breath started coming in short gasps and he pulled his legs up to his chin can I get you anything she said worriedly and he answered in irritation there's nothing wrong goddamnit.

She closed her eyes and fought back the tears that's the way it was to be he took her on the run with neither tenderness nor finesse his desire was brutal and quickly satisfied and she often bit her skin and drew blood waiting for him to finish the ordeal. He would never have understood that he had failed her as a man for in his mind he saw that she supplied the missing link he proved himself even in the midst of death and he would go down just like his finest bull contaminated with some affliction.

He never asked what brought her there with all her things why she stayed to cook his meals and clean up after him why she read to him in the evenings until he fell asleep or if he could not sleep why she stroked him until the desire flowed so strong that he could not deny it in spite of what it cost him the pain was constant now and it was a triumph each time he stuck her with his prick and that was his sole ambition to screw Meridian Muldoon with his dying breath like no failing dying bull had ever done in the history of the West.

She never spoke to Killeen about what she had done or why. He only knew that she had become Matt Brittman's woman for some reason he could never figure and so he stayed his distance from her hurt and puzzled and wanting her more than ever but she remained aloof she gave to the dying rancher as she had never given to Killeen and it amazed him that she could be so fickle with no earthly cause.

9

Harley came back right after the first big blizzard in October and where he came from only Eli knew who had got him there and told him a thing or two because it was suddenly apparent that Britt was slipping fast it was with supreme effort that he got himself out of bed each morning and only made it halfway through the day before taking to his bed. But each day he saddled his horse and rode alone across the pastures opening the gates and pushing still higher until the cold and the steepness became too great and he couldn't take it and doubled back to the ranch to criticize Harley for what he hadn't done right. The kid took it okay but his nerves were always on edge his sudden appearance at the ranch he explained to his father was because he couldn't find a job and his old man took a certain pleasure in that confession it was as he suspected the kid was pretty worthless lazy and couldn't follow through.

But Killeen was something different a man after his own self and Matt Brittman couldn't help but wish from time to time that Killeen was his own flesh and blood. You could stick Killeen on a horse and send him out in a blizzard and he'd stay twelve hours in the saddle trying to save the calves and the cows that got it in the snow and cold so bad their udders froze and the calves just died of starvation and exposure. It made Britt sick to lose a fourth of his calf crop in seventy-two hours when the storm moved down from Wyoming and the snow fell in flakes the size of quarters three feet of it in just two days the worst in twenty years but he'd have lost more lots more if it hadn't been for Killeen working his ass off four days and nights without sleep. He himself lay helpless in his bed raging against the thing which had cut him down the bastard was winning the fight and he could feel himself slipping day by day and he had a hunch his time was almost up had taken his poor body to Eli who with some alarm ordered him to the hospital. He'd refused if the thing was going to take him soon it would be on his own terms and he'd said Eli you haven't forgotten what it is I've asked you to do and Eli said nope I ain't. Britt trembled wondering if he had it coming the next day or the next since Eli was the judge of when he was fit and when he wasn't like a man judging cattle it was a matter of opinion.

By and by it occurred to him that Eli couldn't judge a thing not even if it was going to snow or when it was time to put his summer clothes away Eli after all these years had flipped out over the rim of actuality and was somewhere on the other side of despair. Eli had begun an icy vigil over the life of a man with an incurable disease. And who was to say if he was capable or not or if he was justified in the sense that a hunter of game is justified. So be it Matt Brittman repeated to himself so be it and he resolved to outmaneuver Eli to make it a game of hunter and quarry yes he could pit himself against a man as well as any beast or so he thought the morning that he and Harley and Killeen were working cattle and the temperature stood at ten degrees with the sky a sickly gray promising new snow and everything so still hardly one rabbit running across the fields the creatures knew when to lay low better than some people. The cold was not new to him he had experienced worse he hardly felt the sting only his ears were a little numb and his nose was running the snot blew away in the wind some dropped on the horse's mane he sniffed and dug his heels into the horse's belly.

Harley was coming up hard on his left a hundred feet behind the kid looked nonchalant in the saddle there was something free and easy in the way he rode not at all like Britt who took his riding seriously imagined himself one with the horse he felt his muscles ripple along with Apache's felt the horse's breath along with his own the horse's hooves pounding across the snowy pasture seemed to echo his own footsteps. He felt it all the way it should be. For him riding out across the land was always a fulfillment the distant mountains beckoned him he could reach the top if only the horse had wings he could endure the cold the wind the snow climb to the highest peaks.

Remember the lion tracked there three days solid the lion glimpsed through trees and brush the lion often waiting the lion always moving upward in and out of time in and out of days he did not sleep he went higher and higher after the lion and never got a shot at it the lion earned his admiration for its stealth its cunning its ability to conceal itself and keep moving there was one time he could have shot it when it paused to drink at a stream a clear straight shot across a meadow yet he could not kill it then when thirst and exhaustion had taken over and the match was no longer even. There were times when the lion seemed to be after him the creature often fell behind and pursued the horse's tracks through the wilderness he'd turn and see the lion coming fast and sure through that unearthly silence through two nights spent alone and cold he never slept he was afraid the lion would attack him attack the horse he wondered why the lion did not run off why it was he became less and less certain who was hunted and who was the hunter.

The wilderness did strange things to a man played tricks with all his senses yanked him back to a primordial time stripped him of refinements and left him guided by instinct only. He could not turn back even when he ached with hunger exhaustion pain he pushed on and on to the barren rock and there one morning saw the lion crouching directly above him on a precipice as high as he could go as high as either of them could go and he looking down the way he had come saw it was unbelievably steep and above him was also unbelievably steep and he wondered whether he had caught the lion or if the lion had caught him. There was no way down except to jump the horse from rock to rock the lion was ready to attack yet did not move but crouched like a vicious toy that only needed its spring released. He took his gun and loaded it all the while fearful of the lion poised on the rock looking at him with expressionless eyes giving him time to prepare for an equitable contest between man and beast beast and beast man and man. They had both come to the end and were drained stripped down to their true natures the lion gave him the opportunity which he'd earned. He maintained his wary unmoving position until Britt had him in the sight his fingers curved around the trigger and hesitated. In the split second that it took him to make up his mind the lion made his decision also. He did not lunge for his prey but shot out over his head in an astonishing quick movement that took him across the rocks toward the battleground of timberline the line of demarcation between what could survive and what could not.

The place in which he and the lion had found themselves in the end was no place for man or beast and it was in deference to that that he had not killed the lion or the lion him they went their separate ways in that rare communion between a human and a wild creature possible only when each is part of nature and understands it and respects it and knows when to cool off.

Joe Killeen had worked since sunup moving the yearlings to lower ground with Harley and Britt and his fingers were stiff with cold the climate was a son-of-a-bitch and there was a real longing in him to take off for someplace warm and less tense than the situation he found himself in between Britt and Harley. That was a born loser if there ever was one he could beat the kid at pool and craps and poker and could outride him any day could flatten him if he had to or drink him under the table as he'd done a couple of times already. He resented the runty little bastard come back all of a sudden and making a nuisance of himself just when things were going good between himself and Britt. The matter which had drawn him there in the first place was no longer important he did not really believe anyone that he had spoken to and felt that his parentage would always be vague and obscure each man with his own theory well if Yellow Bird was his birthplace he wanted to put something of himself into that poor old town before she croaked. There was something about Yellow Bird's slow death that got to him he had no religion to speak of anymore ever since he was twelve and drank up the altar wine and chewed up a box of hosts because he was hungry and the priest had turned purple and accused him of devouring the Lord well screw it you could take the church and shove it up your ass he did not believe in God the only thing that mattered was feeling easy with yourself and he didn't in Yellow Bird with the natives getting restless the doctor drinking himself to death Matt Brittman ready to half kill the kid and the weather growing colder all the time.

When you got right down to it the only thing that made him stick around was Meridian Muldoon and wondering when she would tire of the old man. She seemed to have wiped from her mind all that they had shared together and he was hurt and

211

confused about the way the thing had ended with no goodbye and no word of explanation she just up and moved in with Britt and seemed content. Somehow he was not convinced that she felt more than pity for Britt and he had caught her burning stare more than once and though she nearly drove him up the wall he kept his distance while she continued to be a magnet to him and he loved her and sometimes it got so bad that he could not sleep because his mind was constantly on her. To take the pressure off he'd put on fresh Levi's and prance around like a first-rate stud scoot out of town in Daisy and find himself some she stuff down in Coronado a half-breed girl called Whitewater she was very shy and in need of a bath and he'd laid it on her till he could hardly stand up and then he'd gone and got himself a motorcycle for the hell of it and rounded up the bulls the next day it was not the sound they feared it was that he could outrun them all and not break his ass.

Did you ever see a man on fire? Well that was Matt Britt-man standing by the fence watching him on the motorcycle shooing the bulls into the pen all by himself and singing at the top of his lungs the goddamn sky was the color of a sheep and the wind was a blister busting out of mother nature he only wanted to get the work done faster. He had seen Britt waving his arms and wheeled the machine around deliberately so he vanished in the dust and he could hear him screaming at the top of his lungs he only revved up the Suzuki which he had stripped of its stock muffler and then the gun had gone off right above his head a .22 Britt kept across the back window of the jeep that brought him to a halt all right he expected to get canned right then and there but all Britt said was do that again and you're out of a job. He realized then that all he'd ever done was work for another man's pay he was thirty and had nothing to call his own except the miraculous Daisy he wanted to do what all men have a notion to do buy a little land and go into business himself all he needed was a quarter million dollars to buy twenty thousand acres and a couple hundred head he'd wrestle with the

212

land the way a century of cowmen had and grow old in a year-to-year gamble but you wouldn't mind that no sir you wouldn't mind growing old and dying so long as the land itself was like you remembered it at first.

It was a dream he had as idle as those in which he saw himself the captain of a whaling ship a financier giving all his money away a world-famous bull fighter or a man who conquered mountains you could not let go the dream the dream was all you had but every year you got a little older and the dream got a little stale and pretty soon what you got down to was hardcore practicality then you didn't have time to dream anymore you just existed like the rest of the human race you could only believe yourself an individual when you were young. You could do it as an older man only if you were a pickpocket hobo Senator a member of the Supreme Court a psychoanalyst bank robber or a purveyor of cold cash at ten percent per annum you could not do it if you were just plain Joe Killeen adroit drifter pro tempore.

—Want a sandwich Killeen said Harley riding up his face the color of tomato soup the cold wind kept blowing all morning and showed no signs of letting up.

—Yeah said Killeen forgot my lunch again. He got off his horse and tied up at a juniper he stretched out on the ground and felt the cold clear through his chaps god it was a bitch of a day we got fifty head more to move all heifers and calves you know someday somebody is going to streamline this operation you ever figure how much time it takes to babysit a herd well I tried it once and got ten hours a year per head hell a human infant could make out with less. Harley munched his sandwich he was fatigued and dispirited as he looked out across the sloping pasture away to the fringe of sandstone cliffs where the sun broke through now and then and made the walls light up. It's stupid he said the same thing year in and year out you half kill yourself so some housewife in Chicago can have her T-bone rare. Killeen rolled over on his back and stuck a piece of grass

213

in his mouth adjusted his hat and stared up at the sky the dark clouds had split in two and bright blue surged through if you stared up at the sky long enough you got dizzy it blew your mind. He felt small and grand and free with all of it about him the wind whipping the grass and a raven beating its wings so smooth and high and furious a piece of wet black canvas glittering in the coruscating blueness of the sky.

—Still said Killeen spitting out the seeds of an orange it beats working in a city nine to five out here you got a chance with nature look at all that Harley between us and those mountains must be a hundred miles it looks so quiet and untouched you can almost make yourself believe there's not another human being between here and there.

—You know something Killeen said the kid with an edge to his voice it's too damn bad we aren't kin because you are more suited to this ranch than I am and could go ahead and run it.

—You don't like it said Killeen.

—It's a luxury operation said Harley from here on out the land has to be used for profit put houses on it or grow crops nobody can afford to ranch it once my father's gone.

—You mean said Killeen feeling his anger rise you'd let them come and rape the land your father's poured his whole life into?

—There's no choice said Harley besides there's money in it why Happy Hollow used to be Jack Higgins' ranch just look what a nice place they've made it into.

—Harley said Killeen unable to control himself you are a money-hungry bastard.

The kid had it coming all right one week of him had irritated Killeen beyond the brink watching the way he avoided the old man made him sick to his stomach he had forced himself to do nothing but now the time had come the kid was small and soft his reflexes slow he was not quick enough for Killeen who was on his feet in an instant saying get up you little bastard I'm going to beat the shit out of you.

214

Harley Brittman had known it was coming all along had known what he would do and how he would do it he looked at Killeen's face picked clean by the wind a faint arrogance about him an uneducated coarseness common to his kind Harley flicked a speck of dust off his jacket and said coolly you're just a hired hand Killeen.

The words struck Killeen in the teeth he stood there with his legs apart waiting for the kid to get up off the ground but the kid just lay there his face turned toward the sun get on your horse Killeen he said we've got work to do. Harley would never quite remember what happened next for suddenly he was on his feet the taste of blood was in his mouth a burning pain exploded in his head his fists recoiled and struck. He saw Killeen coming again and lowered his head down down down spinning the whole earth was spinning and he was upside down looking at the miserable sky and the dirt was between his teeth and he could not get his breath and he just lay there for a while and felt the pain recede and things come into focus and then Killeen was lifting him up and saying okay kid get the hell on your horse.

—Damn you said Harley wiping his mouth.

—Hurry it up will you.

—You won't get away with this my father—

—Your father's given you the world with a fence around it and you're looking for the gate like some cowardly sheep or other.

Harley stood looking at him his eyes blazing his nerves were all on edge and he did not know what to make of himself he felt ridiculous and out of character it was not his way to fight and call names but sometimes when life got too much you couldn't help what you did you just weren't accountable for your sins was what his father always said. He would have liked Killeen to be his friend he had not had many friends not close ones at any rate and there was something about Killeen that appealed to him at the same time it put him off. He buttoned his jacket around his neck and pulled on his gloves and stood

215

there untying his horse with Killeen next to him looking kind of bemused and not mad anymore.

—I wonder how my father would have turned out if my mother had stuck around.

—Hard telling said Killeen where'd she go?

Harley shrugged and swung his leg across the saddle don't rightly know she sends money at Christmas from some different place birthday gifts and stuff like that I think I saw her once when I graduated from college leastways there was somebody in the back row that looked like this. And he took from his pocket and handed to Killeen the picture he always carried of Billy Deere with her hair done up a pale smile on her lips the picture was fuzzy and creased a twenty-five-cent image taken in a photo booth.

—Nice-looking lady when did she leave?

—I was about four at the time I remember coming in from playing in the yard and my father said your mother isn't going to live here anymore and I said where is she and he said she left on the ten-o'clock bus.

—What made her split?

The kid's mouth was hurting him he scarcely parted his teeth to spit out two words *my father.*

And after that they rode some distance in silence the only sound was the beat of the horses' hooves on the unbroken snow a rhythm that Killeen found compelling and the cries of a whole flock of ravens covering the sky mournful stark and absolute it gave Harley the shivers to see so many all at once a broken blanket of birds so black and hard and ugly. They rode along the creek bed and crossed into a piñon-juniper forest protected from the wind a couple of jackrabbits scurried from behind a fallen tree and suddenly the kid who had brought along his .22 grabbed it from its case tied to the saddle held it to his shoulder aimed and fired and one rabbit exploded into the air. Then very quietly and calmly the gun was put back in its case the kid had remained expressionless only the corners of his eyes drew up as he fired while the rest of him was as immobile as stone. Killeen turned his head and looked at the bloody animal lying in the snow its front paws crossed the little white tail sticking up he shrugged and started to ride on then from behind him he heard a cry and he turned and saw Harley dismount and walk over to the rabbit and bury his face in his hands.

Killeen was off his horse and at Harley's side pleading come on kid we got a lot of work to do.

—I don't know why I did it Killeen so help me God I don't.

—Never mind Harley you got to let it out somehow.

—Not by killing a goddamn rabbit.

—It's okay Harley.

—I can't stand confrontations Killeen and here I am caught in one that there's no way out of.

—It'll work out Harley.

—I have to get the hell out Killeen damn it does the old man have the right to control my life from the grave?

Killeen touched the kid on the shoulder and saw the tears glistening in his eyes he said softly as long as I'm around Harley you ain't going to bug your old man.

—Obligation duty loyalty responsibility and what else don't you know about Killeen like being the biggest disappointment in your father's life go ahead and look at me Killeen and you see the son that never did one thing right and turned out to want to be a lawyer more than anything in the world.

—A lawyer?

—Yeah Killeen I started DU law school last month and I had to quit on account of him and I got to sit here waiting for him to die because I promised see and I don't go back on my word even if it kills me.

—All right Harley grow up so what the hell you can go to law school next year.

—And know that what he spent his life building I just sold to some faceless corporation.

—Then don't do it Harley.

217

—And spend my life doing what I'm doing now riding fences fixing windmills branding calves castrating the goddamn bulls and trying to make the whole thing profitable maybe take on a partner expand the operation. What's the choice Killeen? I can be a fucking cowboy all my life or I can be a selfish bastard and go my goddamn way the question is does reason always prevail over right?

—What's right Harley that you got to decide first I reckon.

—What's right is doing what I got to do according to my own set of values Killeen not somebody else's.

—So do it then.

—I can't.

—How come?

Harley covered the rabbit with snow and with his face in a terrible frown got on the horse again while waiting for Killeen to take a piss into the snow watching the steam rise and then he said I happen to love my old man Killeen.

Britt came riding hard across an open field his face to the wind his chaps flapping his hat pushed back and his skin the color of a stew he was straight in the saddle and bent at the knees and his horse took the ground in long graceful strides the powerful legs moving kicking up the snow in little clouds. Harley shielded his eyes against the sun and watched him coming like a warrior and he said it probably kills him to ride like that but he'll go right on doing it till he drops.

—Harley yelled Britt there's a half-dead calf at the Allison windmill where the hell's its mother?

—I don't know dad.

—Didn't you see it Harley you worked that pasture all morning.

—It must have been lying in the brush.

—Don't tell me where it *was* Harley I'm telling you where it *is* now ride out and find that cow Harley and don't come back till you do.

Harley clamped his mouth shut and touched the horse's

flank with his heel and said yessir between his teeth biting off the words as he rode with his father staring at him with hard blue eyes.

I'm not through with you yet Harley said Britt trying to control a sudden fury that Killeen had noticed before. Was that you that just shot off a gun?

Harley stopped and met him eyeball to eyeball I shot a rabbit he said.

—You shot a rabbit haven't you got enough to do that you got to stop and kill things that ain't never done an ounce of harm to you is that the way I brought you up answer me Harley.

—No it isn't.

—The army taught you how to kill?

—I guess that's it.

—Women and children next?

—Please dad I better go.

The two men faced each other on horseback the horses' breath making steam in the air. A bead of sweat stood out on Britt's forehead and his mouth was drawn in at the bottom as if he had no teeth his face seemed to be cut from a block of beefy ice he searched for something more to say and then at last his eyes lighted on Killeen who was smoking a cigarette and watching.

—Harley said Britt with a sneer why can't you be more like Killeen over there?

—Killeen's better is that what you want me to say?

—Smarter and tougher too.

—I'm sorry I'm not him.

—Me too.

—Now hold on said Killeen joining them Harley here he's doing his best. He examined Britt's face and looked into his eyes there was nobody home. A look of sorrow spread over Harley's face he'd seen it too and knew it was only a matter of time he'd just bear with it.

—And I'll go help Harley if it's okay with you Killeen finished lamely.

—I want you to ride with me said Britt move on Harley I'll see you at the house.

The light powdery snow rose in a cloud and enveloped horse and rider loping silently across the pasture like a movie with no sound track. It was beginning to get cold again a fresh bank of clouds had descended from the north and the wind was working up from the valley it had been a harsh and grueling day.

Britt's voice was strained his shoulders sagged a bit the lines in his face were deeper than Killeen remembered yet he rode on as well as he ever had but at the gate he said I'm tired Killeen as wore out as some old retread six times on the road.

—You've been working too hard Britt.

—I wouldn't have to if Harley'd just shape up I don't know what ails that boy no wonder he can't find a job now Killeen I ask you am I unreasonable with him or not?

—Well Britt it's your privilege.

—I brought him up as best I could wasn't bad or mean or unfair but what it boils down to is that Harley's got his mother in him it's a genetic fact that twenty-five percent of his genes should come from her and twenty-five percent from me and twelve and a half percent from each grandparent but it appears that nature has pulled an aberration out of the hat I see no Brittman blood in him it's the Texas Deeres he takes after those spineless sons-of-bitches.

—Now Britt—

—Let me finish he said as Killeen got the gate and they rode on if Harley was a bull and displayed the characteristics that he does I'd slaughter him because those same characteristics would be perpetuated in whatever calves he sired weakness is inherited any breeder will tell you that.

—Harley's not a bull he's—

—You can apply all the theories of cattle breeding to people Britt went on and what you want to breed into cattle you can breed into people or homing pigeons or race horses it's a matter of selection well I have obviously had no control over what got bred into Harley sometimes I think he ain't even mine.

—Why Britt he looks just like you.

—That don't mean a thing so do you in a way and as a matter of fact I happen to know you came from right here ain't that right Killeen?

—Maybe.

—Goddamn it Killeen I knew your mother stop beating around the bush.

—No bush to beat around Britt.

—The fact that she was what she was don't mean a thing her pedigree was something else I happen to know she came from a highly cultivated stock she was a lady in every sense of the word.

—Don't make me laugh Britt.

—It ain't a laughing matter a girl like that to fall from the straight and narrow but she had her reasons I guess like a young heifer she was when she died not twenty-one years old.

—What said Killeen dazed.

—Maybe twenty-two at most I'm telling you she was an aristocrat.

—Rose Houghton an aristocrat?

—I didn't say anything about Rose Houghton he said irritably I'm talking about Galina Jordan.

—Who's that?

—Your own mother.

Killeen burst out laughing my mother you think my mother was—who?

—Galina Jordan a real beauty Killeen the woman Eli ought to have married instead of that educated imbecile.

—Yeah said Killeen scratching his head that's real nice Britt any notion who my father was?

221

—Me said Britt and rode on.

—Now wait a minute said Killeen catching up I know better understand?

Britt whirled around and his eyes were full of fury his teeth were clenched and when he spoke it was a terrible rasping cry.

—That's it if I say it is by God I know where my seed got planted.

Killeen shook his head look man you're wrong.

—Deny me this Killeen and—

—Harley's your kid Britt not me Harley is and he's fine he's okay he wants to stay here and help you Britt.

—Well I don't want him I'm going to send him away as soon as the hunt's over.

—What hunt?

—Didn't I tell you Killeen we're going after wild horses the eighteenth of this month.

—But Britt that's when hunting season starts.

—So what?

—Well all those guys running around with guns after deer and elk how do you expect to catch a horse?

—You telling me I don't know what I'm doing Killeen you getting like Harley telling the old man he's slipping?

—No Britt no but suppose we get shot at?

—Damn it all Killeen they don't hunt elk and deer where the horses are way the hell up on the mesa they been there for a hundred years the elk are on the mountain and the deer are pretty well cleaned out of this part of the country.

—Are you up to it Britt?

The rancher turned almost purple and his hands shook so hard that the horse reared back and nearly spilled him.

—Just what the hell is going on first Harley then you are you all right dad let me get you a pillow dad now don't overdo dad you insinuating I'm sick you and Harley waiting around for me to die?

—No Britt you just look a little tired that's all.

222

—Never felt better in my life you understand I could ride clear to the top of the peak and down again before you even got to the creek I can outlast you today or any day Killeen I'll show you on that hunt would you like to lay a hundred you play out first?

—I lose when I gamble Britt.

—Twenty to a hundred then you can take the bet Killeen go on and take it.

He saw it was no use to argue so he said okay whatever you want.

—That's better and he snorted me sick that'll be the day I'll live to be a hundred he shouted at Killeen a hundred and you'll be dead and gone because genetically speaking I got a whole lot more than you why I could lay ten women end to end this very minute a young buck like you what could you take on?

—Half a dozen most likely.

—I could go twelve yeah Killeen go get some she stuff I'll show you what I mean.

—There's no contest with you said Killeen if you want to prove you're a stud go ahead and prove it.

—I do every damn night with as ripe a heifer you'd ever want to find.

Killeen winced and getting off his horse to open the gate he thought again of how Meridian let Britt use her why the hell did she take it the old man just wanted his ego lifted he was incapable of real tenderness the kind Killeen was sure he'd given her. Why then did she prefer Matt Brittman?

Women. Killeen unsaddled his horse and knew he was no closer to understanding them than he'd ever been and the way he'd run his life was pretty safe when it came to women he'd just kept them happy and eased off when they got to dropping a rope around his neck and it had worked out every time he could not count the number of women he'd left behind whether married or unmarried rich or poor skinny or hefty some were good lays and some so bad he'd told them they ought to get their

223

holes sewed up. He hung up the bridle and knew the Muldoon girl had got under his skin so bad that he pictured himself hauling her out of there to some quiet place where he'd ball her six times a day if that's what she wanted and he'd build her a house and let himself get tamed and let her work herself into his life so nice and easy that he wouldn't mind the pain of losing his precious freedom. He wondered if he could really take it this business of settling down it made him break out in a cold sweat every time he thought of it and he got after himself for wanting to be like all the rest of the men in the country domesticated and creeping around like house pets.

Matt Brittman seemed to be reading his thoughts as they walked toward the house from the barn he put his arm lightly around Killeen's shoulders and said I know what she means to you Killeen it's something I ain't accustomed to a man mooning around after a heifer and I know she don't love me Killeen even if she says she does but it's kind of nice to let a pretty woman come and take care of you when you need it bad and I can't hardly say no to her selfish bastard that I am.

—It's okay Britt I understand. And he was beginning to in a way though it troubled him and had not the old man meant so much to him he would have pasted him to the wall for messing with his girl.

—A long time ago Britt said I got carried away with a girl and never did again decided then and there emotion is like shit bury it as quick as you can.

—A man like you said Killeen it's natural you should have lived all this time with a woman why haven't you?

Britt came to a stop and watched the darkening sky and pointed with his finger because up there is something I can understand and he kicked at the earth with his boot and down there is something I can understand and all else between the sky and the ground I can understand but women no boy them I pass over like some fearful apparition. He picked up a stone and hurled it through the air and said now I know just where

224

that stone is going to land and I know it can only go so far and I know what it's made of and I know if I get hit with it it's going to hurt but a woman I don't know any of these things about. I only know them in the physical sense you get what I mean and I know that ain't enough to keep them lighted up like a god-damn Christmas tree I know they need more'n that Killeen and I ain't never had the guts to try because I ain't never failed Killeen not at one goddamn thing how would it look on my record if I landed on my face on account of some unpredictable she stuff?

Killeen loved him then and couldn't put it into words would later wish he had but he let the moment pass in silence turning the knob to the kitchen where Meridian was cooking supper.

The aroma of bread baking and cinnamon and apples and a stew bubbling on the stove reached their nostrils as they knocked the snow off their boots and came into the kitchen where the girl with a plastic apron over her Levi's was stirring the contents of the pot.

—Hello Britt hello Killeen she said beaming.

Matt Brittman strode across the room he threw his hat on the table and put his arms around her and kissed her and she dropped the spoon and hugged him close oh Britt oh Britt she said.

—How about me said Killeen turning his cheek to her.

—Oh you she laughed you don't count does he Britt?

—Give him one anyway he's worked hard all day.

She kissed him lightly then pushed them both away don't hinder the cook she said go make yourselves a drink.

—Meridian he said as he was going back to change his clothes it always comes as a surprise to know that you can cook.

—I can't really cook she said tomorrow you may be dead.

Matt Brittman stopped walking and lifted his head but did not turn the gaiety was suddenly gone he said softly well not from that I reckon.

225

Meridian frowned and turned to Killeen is he okay she asked after Britt left the room.

—One minute he is and the next he isn't why are you doing this Meridian?

—Doing what she said sticking a spoon in the stew.

—You're giving him his pound of flesh.

—That's right.

—It must be hell.

She whirled around and snapped it's none of your goddamn business.

—I'm sorry Meridian it's just that I don't want to see you hurt I'm a stupid crazy fool.

Killeen could not help himself he went over and held her close and had the urge to bend down and kiss her but instead he just held her tighter and tighter and tighter let go of me she demanded and he said why should I?

—That's enough Killeen said Britt sharply coming into the room.

Killeen broke away and said I'm sorry Britt and he felt at that moment from the look of Britt that he'd done more than made a pass at what was now Britt's girl he'd stepped out of bounds he was after all a hired hand and he laughed to himself and wondered how it would be if he reminded Britt that he had claimed him as his son well the old man would deny it and who could hold him to anything he said if the thing was eating up his body might it not also destroy his mind? Killeen wiped his hands on his jacket and said I'm going over to the bunkhouse to clean up you want Harley and me to eat separate?

—Hell no you sit right here at the table with the rest of us and Killeen—

—Yes?

—Learn not to cinch the horse that tight and don't get sloppy with the calves again it just don't become a man to do a half-assed job.

Killeen swallowed and bit his tongue he went out and

slammed the door and Britt slipped his arms around Meridian and whispered a nice lad but crude.

—Oh Britt she sighed it's good to see you at the end of a day.

She pressed against him and ran her fingers along his vest and felt the gun and said do you have to wear this thing to dinner my god Britt it's not the nineteenth century.

—I have got to protect myself.

—From what?

—Not from what from who?

—Who then?

—My son he said now I'll let you guess which one.

—Are you crazy who have you got besides Harley?

—Nobody I'm all mixed up now leave the stove alone and come have a drink.

He was on his third bourbon when Harley came in the door his face windburned and his mop of light brown hair tousled he had the look of a small boy with bright and shining eyes as he dropped into a chair and said I found the cow and put the calf with her and listen dad there's a herd of elk moving down from the mountain they're in the Eagle Creek pasture.

—Well get them the hell out of there Harley.

—The snow's forced them down to lower ground there's about fifty head I think they'll probably move on by morning.

—Did you hear what I said Harley exclaimed Britt his voice rising I want you to get them out of there.

Harley shook his head I tried to but they won't jump the fence.

—Shoot at them then you think I'm going to feed a herd of elk for God's sake you think this is some kind of zoo?

—Call the Fish and Game Department they'll have to send some men.

—The Fish and Game Britt said fiercely Harley do you recall the time you and I stood there and watched those bastards kill nine wild horses coming out of the brush?

227

Harley swallowed and looked away to the window where the snow was softly falling yeah I do dad but it seems to me there's no other way to handle it.

Britt's eyes were glazed and he slurred his words as he said listen Harley I am still the boss of this outfit and I say that tomorrow morning you and Killeen and Bob and the boys get the hell in there with .38's and shoot 'em out.

—Kill them?

—No Harley no said Britt in fury his voice high-pitched and shrill just scare 'em good so they'll jump the fence you realize how much those critters eat?

Britt got up and stalked out to the kitchen and when it was quiet Meridian got up from a chair near the fireplace and came around and stood in front of Harley.

—Harley she said I want you to get out of here it just won't work with you and Britt.

His pudding face was red and pensive he said it was all right till you came.

—So you'd like me to leave is that it she said sharply and she remembered how Harley had been jealous of her even as a kid.

His mouth was weak she noticed and he nervously tapped his foot on the floor yeah Meridian he said I think you better go.

—Well I won't she said this is still your father's house.

—And you're my father's whore.

She slapped him hard with all her might and the imprint of her hand was on his cheek his eyes began to water and he hung his head.

—Harley said Britt sharply coming in with Killeen what the hell is going on?

—Nothing.

Britt pointed his finger at Meridian what did he do to you?

—Nothing.

Britt had had too much to drink his mouth was slightly open and his eyes were red and swollen his face was sweaty and bloated and as he made his way toward his son his steps were slow and uncertain only his right arm was sure as it came up like a log and got the kid square in the mouth and sent him staggering back against the stone fireplace. Britt lunged forward again and this time the kid threw his hands in front of his face to ward off the second blow and then Britt's big and heavy boot shot out and struck the kid in the stomach he doubled over and gasped but made no move to fight back or run away.

—See that Britt said triumphantly to Killeen and Meridian he's yellow the color of the Deere blood and he's got a stripe down his back and what you smell is coming from beneath his tail get up you bastard.

There was a stunned silence in the room only the sound of the fire crackling and the wind whistling around the corners of the house and the television coming on with the six-o'clock news made them know that this was not the movies it was now and it was happening in front of them and it was not real.

Harley drew up his knees and his head sank to them and he sobbed uncontrollably Meridian couldn't take it anymore she brushed past Britt who stood with his legs apart waiting for the kid to get up. Meridian knelt beside him and whispered in his ear but the kid remained alone in his despair not moving a muscle trying desperately to control himself but it was beyond all that.

—Come on said Killeen awkwardly come on Britt and have another drink.

Britt pulled away and said you want to fight me Killeen and he made two fists of his hands.

Exasperated Killeen said you'd whip me Britt I know that.

—I can whip him too can't I he said jerking his thumb toward his son.

—Yes Britt you can do that too.

—Meridian he shouted.

—Yes Britt?

—Get the dinner on the table.

229

—All right.

—And after dinner we are going to Coronado and I am taking the bridal suite at the Coronado Hotel and you and I are going to whale has anybody got any objections to Miss Muldoon and me having a little fun? Harley? Killeen? Good he said rubbing his hands together and Miss Muldoon may I have the pleasure of your company this evening?

Furious and ashamed she felt her flesh crawl and humiliation swept across her like the wind and what he had done was to buy her in front of his son and she felt cheap and used and yet she did not cry out no no no she looked at the towering figure of a man gone mad and she remembered what she had said to Eli Wetherill when they shot the dog she'd said they did it because they didn't know what else to do and neither did she and so what could she do except give him what he wanted to make the going out bearable and she would go on doing it until the end she had she figured six months of hell at most and if that did not give her hope it gave her resolution.

She got up and forced herself to smile and in that moment she knew she was in bondage to him for as long as he lived and that he would take her without love because it was too late for that there was only the animal left and the animal was what she accepted on behalf of the man she remembered who was no longer there because death had already begun.

—Sure Britt she said pushing her hair out of her eyes and holding back the tears shall we eat dinner now everything is getting cold.

Time present and time past
Are both perhaps present in time future,
And time future contained in time past.
If all time is eternally present
All time is unredeemable.
What might have been is an abstraction
Remaining a perpetual possibility
Only in a world of speculation.
What might have been and what has been
Point to one end, which is always present.

10

Two days before the start of the Saturday opening of the Colorado deer and elk season two feet of snow had fallen over Yellow Bird driving the elk down from the straight-up-and-down mountains to the flats on the other side of the river. There were two hundred of them in all on state land federal land and in Matt Brittman's Eagle Creek pasture. As more and more snow fell on the town more and more elk drifted down from the mountains and mingled with the cattle and the horses chewing the pale grass that stuck up out of the crusted snow. The Fish and Game Department had come and with trucks and snowmobiles and on foot and horseback tried to drive the herd across the river and up to the high country shooting off their guns to move the animals. Three times they had succeeded in scattering the elk into the timber but each morning they were back again growing tamer and hungrier as each day passed and the word spread to Texas and the Canadian border and carload after carload of hunters crowded up the road from Coronado and waited for the dawn to break on Saturday morning so they could get themselves an elk the easy way. Their voices were heard echoing through the skeletal remains of Yellow Bird and in its one saloon and up and down its muddy potholed streets is it true about all them elk how do you tell a him from a her what kind of license do I need want to put a hundred on me bringing down a buck with one shot like taking candy from a baby one elk is worth five deer hey all you Texans want to team up against us Okies show you what a sure shot is how much longer just thirty-six hours is all.

On that Thursday night more men were crowded into the Yellow Bird saloon than had been there since the last New Year's Eve before the mines shut down it was so crowded that to get from one side of the room to the other required deft maneuvering and nearly fifteen minutes of holding your piss and swallowing a screen of smoke so thick a man could nearly chew it. The hunters had been waiting in town for three nights now watching the hopeless shooing of the elk to higher ground by the Fish and Game men the hunters lined their camper trucks along the road and watched the elk get chased across the fields and across the sluggish river and past the lower end of town where a grove of aspen and spruce and ponderosa unfurled like a forked tongue down the mountainside and then each morning they watched with satisfaction as the elk which had come down again during the night made the Fish and Game guys beat their fists and get grim around the eyes knowing there was no way they could spoil the hunters' fun or save the elk from slaughter. And so here it was just two nights before they'd pick off the elk one by one and be on the road toward home by Saturday noon did a man ever have an easier time getting himself big game and wouldn't it make a trophy to hang above the fireplace some racks I hear are eight feet across with six or seven points and man I feel like Ernest Hemingway let's have a drink.

But the hunters were not the only ones who came to Yellow Bird that final October. There was among the fluorescent orange jackets of the hunters the buckskin outfit of a tiny wiry man who had a set of whiskers and a jagged set of teeth his hair was long and yellowish gray he wore leggings and a pair of leather boots that laced up with thongs he'd cut from the hide of a caribou. He had deep and brooding eyes so dark that you couldn't find the white and no matter how close you looked at him you couldn't tell how old he was or if he'd slept recently or not he was just one of those men who turn up at places where people don't go. He took the last remaining room at the Yellow Bird Hotel the very night the hunters had descended and each night he'd sit and talk to them and get drunk with them they looked all the same to him and so it was on that particular Thursday night as the stranger entwined himself around the bar stool and asked Josie Stringer for a match and a beer that he smiled at her stolid face and recognized a fellow miner. As he opened his mouth Josie shook her head another one of those oh she was used to his kind the harmless nuts found in every gold camp bar in the West who knew where they came from or what they really were in each the tale was different and so she forced herself to listen as he said

—Time has a way of copping out on me now much more than people ever did there's either too much of it or not enough of it and sometimes a combination of both when I have to think hard about something and it stands still only when I'm buying the girl a wardrobe she tells me she doesn't really want or when I dig enough gold in Alaska for the boss mothers that they don't know I've taken a few pieces here and there for decorating my watchband or when I have money to bet on my sons. But the goddamn watch cops out on me if I forget to put it on because it's self-winding and too much of the time I cop out on myself because too much of the time I don't know whether I myself am really truly self-winding or someone has to help me do it. Tick . . . Tock . . . And the boss mothers decided that Colorado needed me more than I needed Alaska and the girl in St. Louis decided that she needed me and I decided that my sons needed me whether they did or not. I decided some after I got here but I haven't decided everything yet. High-country Colorado is not as cold as Alaska but Alaska gold is prettier than Colorado zinc and I don't like people telling me where to live and who my god decorates a watchband with zinc. But now I'm anyway close to my sons and closer to the girl and when I don't want to think about something or need to it isn't so cold this time of year that I can't threaten to take a sleeping bag I don't even own and a bottle of whiskey that I hardly ever buy because I like to drink in bars down to one of the forks of the creek east west or north and spend the night. In Alaska this time of year my piss would have frozen before it hit the ground excuse me lady no matter how much whiskey was in it.

—And I've told Paul and I've told his brother Spider about the girl and Paul just shrugs his right shoulder and Spider just looks at me but not really because his left eye and his right eye go in opposite ways and are always looking at something other than what they're really looking at I think. I sometimes wonder if the little bastard excuse me lady doesn't have two glass eyes and can't really see nothing they're both bastards though real legitimate bastards. They both have a left hook like their old man's and at least I've given them that much and more because I taught them how to play pool though most of the time they're too crazy to admit it but I know they'd like the girl in St. Louis and I have to call her in just a couple of hours. They're good boys my sons. Actually Paul's a much better player than Spider but I laid a hundred bucks on that game in Alaska my money and these locals just have to take one look at Spider's eyes and they know he can't hit shit excuse me lady but I know he can because he's beat me and so has Paul but I don't mind getting beat by my own sons because I taught them. And when they need money to play I give it to them and set up their bets and mine and when I'm playing they watch out for my money and pick it up only to straighten it like shit lady sometimes I wonder. But the girl I have to call in several hours is only twenty-four and I'm as old as the mountains and she kept telling me she didn't really need those clothes she modeled them for me lady in one of the finest stores in St. Louis when I got back from Alaska and in those miniskirts she has an ass and legs that won't quit it's been a long time since I've seen her without any clothes on at all.

—But I have to call my daughter in St. Louis in just a little while and tell her whether she's going to come out here or I go out there because I don't have to work here and I know I can get a job there or I don't have to call her at all it's enough to make me want to take my sleeping bag down to the river and a case of whiskey and piss ice all night excuse me. The boys take off tomorrow and said they won't go to Silverton with me and clean up the yokels there and all this after the way I've taken care of them for the last five days and taught them all they know when they only came up here five days ago to fish and I've only known them for five days my own sons and have taught them everything they know.

—The St. Louis girl looks a lot like you lady and everything's a miracle even if time does cop out on me and fuck excuse me lady I still have the miracle of death left for me but I won't tell you that because you haven't heard a word I've said anyway even if I've said nothing and you don't know that the piss has already frozen in my frozen fucking gut and yeah I'm going down to the creek and my watch is running.

The stranger sucked in his lips and took his watchband with the gold nuggets in it and laid it on the bar lighted another cigarette and stared into the smoke with vacant somber eyes

237

and Josie shrugged and with her thumb and forefinger made a slow circle around the side of her head they're all crazy she said it's got to do with the altitude.

—Hello friend said the Coyote to the stranger mind if I sit down and he set his lunchbox and his radio on the bar and removed a soggy snipe from his hatband.

The stranger shook his head and lighted another cigarette placing it beside the lighted one resting in the ashtray which read Coors beer brewed with pure Rocky Mountain Spring Water the Coyote looked at it and said I used to read but I don't anymore I just read ashtrays and match book covers that's all I got time for.

—Time has a way of copping out on me now more than people ever did there's either too much of it or not enough of it and sometimes a combination of both . . .

As the stranger rambled on the Coyote said you a hard rock stiff I see like me could've went to work for Idarado pulling lead and zinc but hell gold's the only thing worth getting sideways for I remember when I had a placer claim up on Sundog Creek it was winter and forty below so cold. . . .

—High-country Colorado is not as cold as Alaska but Alaska gold is prettier than Colorado zinc and I don't like people telling me where to live and who my god decorates a watchband with zinc. . . .

—I have made a great discovery friend I'm the only one that knows the true whereabouts of Annabelle Lee and she'll make us rich if we handle her the right way grubstake me my friend I don't need much ten dollars' worth of groceries a case of whiskey a sleeping bag . . .

—It isn't so cold this time of year that I can't threaten to take a sleeping bag I don't even own and a bottle of whiskey that I hardly ever buy . . .

—I agree with you about the weather but I got an army surplus tent somewhere upstairs if the landlady ain't pitched it out and I got dynamite too you know real stuff to ball the juice right out of her now friend there's one room where the earth is turned upside down with a blossom rock as pretty as you ever saw a man would've highgraded it out of there but friend there ain't nobody but me knows where she's at and can coax it out of her.

—In Alaska this time of year my piss would have frozen before it hit the ground no matter how much whiskey was in it.

—There's a million easy left in her friend a cool million that them fellers passed by digging out that uranium shit you ever seen uranium ore not worth spitting at it ain't but you take gold there's a look and a feel to it . . .

—Because I don't have to work here and I know I can get a job there . . .

—And friend we can take out all the gold we want for ten years I found enough stuff for that you want to see where I got the stuff hid all over town friend a little bit here a little bit there so's we have it when we need it not all in one place a man's likely to find it in one place and for ten years we got enough stuff to last us if we're careful with it that is . . .

—And yeah I'm going down to the creek and my watch is running and I'll buy you a drink if you open up your lunchbox.

The Coyote and the stranger sat there for a couple of hours not saying any more because they had had such a wonderful conversation together and it was a shame to spoil a new friendship with a lot of unnecessary palaver.

The poker players of the Yellow Bird Hotel decreased by one since the disappearance of Nate Houghton sat in a glum bunch away from the big-game hunters the green felt-covered poker table was in front of them and an unopened deck of cards sat in the middle they had not come to play cards these last three nights but to keep watch the way they did during the day armed with their .44 Magnums and parked themselves opposite the hunters waiting just waiting and watching the tragic situation with the elk. For although each and every one of them had killed elk and deer over the years it was with a certain set of rules they never broke no matter what and for them it was easier to work themselves into a lather hot enough to kill a man than it was to kill an animal who had no chances. A man from Yellow Bird could break a lot of laws but he could not break that one he could hate his neighbor but he couldn't hate a big-game animal he could take out his vengeance on another human being but not on a four-legged animal unless it was a dog that had offended them like that yapping Susie who'd taken a piece from one man's leg you could kill a dog for doing that but a big majestic elk well sir that was something different something sacred and you'd turn your back and walk away rather than kill it like a sheep.

Over many hunting seasons each man had seen the out-of-staters who came in and hunted neither fair nor square and they had watched that too and done nothing over the years not even when that bunch from Kansas went out and shot a herd of eleven elk that was making its way across a narrow rock ledge two hundred feet high so high they knew before they shot that the animals couldn't be gotten out and so they left them there all dead except for one seven-point buck which leapt to his death from the ledge. The men from Yellow Bird had often gone into the forest to put the crippled and dying animals out of their misery tracking a bloody bull elk for fifteen miles through the snow one October before they finally put a bullet through him. Whatever faults an outsider might have found in them they had to grant that the poker players of Yellow Bird were sportsmen in the truest sense of the word they had never once transgressed that ethical code that binds all such sportsmen together for generation after generation the world over a man can be a murderer but he cannot massacre big game and call himself a man was the preamble to their constitution.

The out-of-state hunters were a different breed as the men of Yellow Bird soon realized and they could see what was going to happen. Some of them had helped the Fish and Game guys

240

to drive the elk back up the mountain and some had tried to lure them with a truckload of hay that they scattered through the forest and others had tried patrolling the flats at night to keep the animals out but after three days the elk were nearly tame they did not fear the sound of engines or the guns fired above their heads or even a vehicle headed straight at them. Finally the men of Yellow Bird pounded their fists along with the Fish and Game guys and glared at the out-of-staters and picked fights with them let air out of their tires and siphoned gas from their tanks they had not resorted to violence because they were afraid to pit themselves as marksmen against men who maybe had a perfect aim. Who knew whether or not they were so deadly accurate that one bullet might penetrate two poker-playing chests? There had to be another way and so night after night the sleepless nervous outraged male citizens of Yellow Bird tried to come up with an answer and finding none grew more restless and more disturbed and what could they do when in less than thirty-four hours the hunters would open up on the elk?

The answer came to them slowly and against their will because as they pondered all that Yellow Bird was and had been it became clear to each man on his own that perhaps just perhaps Eli Wetherill might do some good. Now of course the good doctor wasn't good anymore and he had brought to each of them in one way or another some measure of suffering that was not called for as he had brought to each of them in one way or another relief or cure from an ailment that might otherwise have gone undetected and moreover each one of them had at one time or another owed the doctor money and never paid it but had paid him with eggs from his chickens or paint from his store or a quarter of beef from his locker and that was just like money and to a man they remembered the doctor sitting up all night with a sick child at the same time they recalled he halfway killed another child with the wrong medicine or being too drunk to stop a hemorrhage and remember the time Harry's wife was in for a D and C and the doctor went out of the operating room leaving her unattended and she fell on the floor and broke her hip and remember when they wanted to close the schoolhouse down it was him as mayor that took it to the governor and got us reinstated but it was him who refused to allow Pinky to sell his land for a trailer park when he sure as hell needed the money and the dam's his fault and the fact we gotta move is his fault but hell man we did have a hospital here once thanks to him and we had a library too in what used to be Missus Trimbull's House of All Nations and he got the sewage system in and the ball park for the kids but he also did abortions for free no five bucks he charged and when he was a county commissioner he got his share of the pie that was the year he drove a Cadillac remember yeah and let Sue Hickham die but remember that kid of Ralph's who cut his finger off in the door the doc cleaned it off and sewed it back on so good you can't tell where it was separated but poor Nate was crippled all his life thanks to what the doc didn't do for him you still think the doc knows where he's at nah I think Nate just couldn't take no more he loved Rose like nobody's business a man can go insane from grief well let's take a vote how many wants to put the matter to the doc and how many don't unanimous let's go get him Eddie and say I hear that Muldoon girl writes for the Denver paper you suppose she could write something to help us out oh I wouldn't ask that bitch to do nothing but we are in trouble forget what she done we have got to pull ourselves together for the sake of Yellow Bird.

He heard the cars stopping outside and pulled the dirty curtains apart and saw them coming up the path he'd shoveled through the snow and his heart nearly stopped because this time he was alone and they would get him and the telephone wasn't working and even if he had time to go and load his gun he wasn't sure he'd have a chance. He was thoroughly crocked and had been for several days ever since the last snow fell and his spirits went down with the sun and everyone had forgotten

242

him even Britt the son-of-a-bitch was shacking up with Meridian at the ranch and in that condition well he didn't know how Britt could do it and he'd die from it probably but let him what better way to go than balling she stuff like that one Eli only wished he could. His hands were trembling on the curtains he let them drop as the doorbell rang and he heard them shout and begin pounding on the frame and he decided he'd better answer it and be as brave as he could for whatever they'd come to do.

One by one they came through the door shuffling their feet with their hats clasped between their hands they spoke in hushed tones looking at the floor and sweating in a house they'd not been to not once in all those years and they tried not to see how dirty and disheveled the doctor was because they wanted to see him clean and tidy and alert the way he'd sometimes been on important occasions such as this one. They sat on his sofa and on his chairs and some stood against the wall almost out of sight in the dimly lighted room they felt awkward and inarticulate and ill at ease with all these antiques and bric-a-brac oh my the wife must have been a collector I only saw this kind of house once and it belonged to the best madam in Cripple Creek. They shuffled their feet on the carpet moistened their lips chewed their gum smoked their cigarettes and did not know where to begin these sportsmen poker players dog slayers and guardians of morality for Yellow Bird Colorado. And finally they began to get it out word by word sentence by sentence laughing self-consciously and then Eli got out the jug and passed it around and they felt better and more at ease knowing what it was they were trying to say and how each minute their confidence in Eli which hadn't been strong to begin with was coming back all right as it had before on the proper occasions and Eli sat there nodding and saying go on go on and uh-huh un-huh sure until they knew that at last he understood and would do something about it.

—I think said Eli when each man had had his say that the

243

only way to handle this is and they all sat forward on their seats and stood straighter against the wall to call out the National Guard.

—The National Guard they said in astonished unison.

—The only way he said waving his finger at them if the National Guard can handle all these Communist-inspired riots from coast to coast they can handle a bunch of Communist elk hunters.

—But doc the Fish and Game don't have the authority to call in the National Guard.

—Well give them the authority give them all the authority they need.

—The governor has to call in the National Guard or maybe it's the FBI please doc don't make a joke.

—Joke hell it ain't no joke let 'em use mace and tear gas and hand grenades and tommy guns and atomic bombs on those lousy sons-of-bitches.

The group fell silent and one by one they got up and went out the way they came in noticing that the doctor had apparently fallen asleep in his chair a full glass of whiskey held tight in his hand a smile of contentment on his face and then he began to snore loudly with some sign of congestion in his throat and as they took one last look at him they noticed that his mouth had fallen open and that his teeth looked rusty and that his skin looked like a poorly plucked chicken's. Their disgust at the doctor matched what was now a full-blown contempt that had been smoldering for weeks and months and even years he had failed them again and again as far back as they could remember but it was now that he had failed most of all. In him now were all the excuses they'd formed over the years for not having a town that people cared about and in him also was the last outrage: the death of the town for reasons that now seemed to them so pitiful and weak that they wondered why they had simply sat still and let it happen. Then they recalled that Eli Wetherill had told them one by one that you could not stop

244

progress. Whether it was a town or a farm or a mountain that had to be sacrificed for the sake of progress then that was the way it was a country has to destroy as it creates and they could understand that couldn't they? Hadn't they all experienced sacrifice and believed in the first principle of democracy the greatest good for the greatest number and if Yellow Bird's death meant that thousands could enjoy the boating and the fishing and thousands more not get flooded out and who knows maybe they would make a hydroelectric plant and send Yellow Bird's power all the way to New York City. It made sense at the time and one by one they had gone and looked at the World War II honor roll posted in front of the city hall and they looked at the stars in front of certain of the names and they remembered the boys some of them their own sons and neighbor kids they had watched grow up and if that was the kind of sacrifice the doctor was talking about they understood it and would not stand in the way.

But now huddled in a small group on the doctor's front porch they were angry and worse than that infused with the pent-up hopelessness and fear of many years all that they could have become were it not for the doctor turned them sick with regret they questioned their roles as men brave enough to fight for the elk but too weak to do anything about the town where they had lived out their lives. They needed to do something to make themselves feel better and they considered setting fire to the doctor's house right then and there but no they could not live with that on their consciences and besides they might get caught. Then they considered tearing up his office but he didn't go there anymore and all the other buildings that he cared about were torn down so just what the hell do you do to ventilate yourself when the time came to ventilate?

They stood there feeling foolish and at the same time wanting to prove they were not a bunch of sheep scared shitless so one man unzipped his fly and pissed into the snow on Eli Wetherill's porch another took his penknife and carved up the

245

railing another tore off the porch lamp and hurled it with all his might against a tree and they ripped off the railing piece by piece so that Eli Wetherill's house began to have the same look that most of the other places had but still that did not give them the satisfaction they desired. It was dark and getting very cold by then and their fingers were freezing inside their gloves and their feet were growing numb and their ears hurt and god they just felt old and aching and wanting to go back in time to the days when they had honorable work to do and honorable women to love and families to raise and something to look forward to and it was funny how it all ended when you least expected it to leaving you dizzy and scared to go on.

So standing there in the cold and starry night so still you could hear your own voice coming back to you they began to formulate a plan to do justice to themselves and to a town that it was almost too late to show any love for and it was also a plan that would scare off the elk hunters and bring Eli Wetherill to his knees. But they were still afraid and the more they talked in the freezing cold about what they wanted to do the more their teeth chattered and their knees wobbled and they even got a sick feeling in the pits of their stomachs that hadn't been there since the supers forced them back into the mines after an explosion or some such disaster that made them wonder why they had not taken up farming instead. Nobody will go along with it they'll say we're crazy fools we got to get the women and children out by tomorrow noon thirty hours is all we got left now it can't be done just where do you think we'll get the stuff listen I heard the Coyote talking to that geezer from Alaska now you know as well as I the Coyote's crazy as they come besides which he ain't never going to tell where nothing's hid who's to take charge of this here plan how about you Cheepie you served in World War One anybody here had any more recent experience hey Johnnie you was in the second war oh I just played the bugle is all at Fort Dix New Jersey waiting to get sent over I guess I was too old okay Cheepie go and get your uniform on to make it look official shit man it's in shreds it don't fit no more well ain't you got a hat I got a helmet we all got helmets from the mines now hurry up we got to work all night.

11

Ever since Meridian had moved in Matt Brittman had been feeling better his strength which had begun to leave him was slowly coming back and he thought perhaps that he would be all right after all as he lay in his bed his arms around her he wondered if they had been wrong about him. Such things had happened in medicine maybe the growth had just stopped growing or maybe his own system had flushed it out made him resistant to it just like his cattle were resistant to diseases that could wipe out an ordinary herd and he closed his eyes and saw himself not as he was then but twenty years before so firm and lean and strong did he ever think then that he would

248

fail? As he lay with his fingers in her hair and felt her sleeping form so warm and still beside him he saw that he had deliberately chosen this life for himself had always refused to admit weakness the weakness of all men hungering to be free all you had to do was sever human ties. Perhaps he had begun to die little by little as the wounds left by Billy Deere did not heal up and he was left as vulnerable as the next man and twice as bitter.

What was there now with this girl except his masculinity proven now beyond any doubt much to his amazement a man as sick as he who could fuck damn near every night wasn't really sick was proving the doctors wrong was relying on nature to heal him up was experiencing the pleasure of a woman who made neither demands nor trouble. He turned over and reached for the bottle of whiskey he had kept by the bedside every night for over a month he was drinking nearly a bottle a day but it didn't hurt him any in fact it cleared his head and kept the pain away it also made him more keenly aware that he was regaining his human shape through Meridian Muldoon. He who had never felt himself close to another human being now felt an intensity with her that had no name and he would spend his days sharing thoughts with her that he had always kept to himself such thoughts as how he had become a success through hard work and selfless devotion to his cause how he had built his life on perfection and how he could not tolerate change he was a self-made man all right and she seemed proud to know it to stroke his hair as he talked or to sit by the fire and listen to him hour after hour. He let himself be taken care of let himself fall slowly toward her being careful to land always on his feet no woman ever could or ever would take him to the ground.

He was satisfied with what was working out with her even though at times he felt a little foolish indulging himself but she was his means to justify the ruthlessness in his life to build himself up in her eyes and make her believe really believe his sacrifice had been worthwhile. To get all that across to another human being gave him his human form or so he told himself in all sincerity and if he were going to die the very next day he knew it wouldn't be with the uneasiness that had troubled him before. He was more or less at peace with himself although God knows he was not at peace with Harley who was doing things behind his back like giving orders to Bob Wingate the foreman or talking in whispers on the phone or sending a shipment of cows to Denver without his knowledge or permission. He had ordered Harley out of the house the morning after Meridian had slapped his face and he had gone away for three whole days leaving Britt in the most terrible circumstance he had ever found himself. He could not remember what he was to do that day could not recall if the calves had been vaccinated or not if winter was coming or going could not recall the way to Eli Wetherill's house or how much feed the cattle got and he had sweated and kept his mouth shut. How would it look to Wingate to ask him a ridiculous question like how much do we feed the cattle and in what pasture have we left the bulls and how long has it been since Killeen started working here my God you just couldn't be that stupid in front of your own men let alone your woman although Meridian hadn't noticed he ate two breakfasts no he was sure she hadn't. Then the second day came and it was even worse and Killeen had started asking questions while Meridian held her tongue and he remembered having fired Killeen and yet the next day there he was so he couldn't be sure whether he had or not or even if Harley was not in grammar school and Billy Deere coming up from Texas for the summer and he was falling in love for the first time.

It kept getting all mixed up. The past and the present were on a single sheet of paper in a language he couldn't read and what was there except to keep talking to this girl and making love to her and hoping it was a bad dream this stupid business of losing his memory yet he could remember perfectly such things as how he spent his first year in agricultural college and he could see clearly his mother standing at the kitchen stove although it was really Meridian and there was his father standing in back of the truck pitching bales to the cattle only it was Killeen and goddamn it there was a pasture full of elk that looked to him like his own cattle and what the fuck was happening?

Then it came to him in a dream or out of it that he would be ever so much more at peace with Harley out of the way because it was not Harley who had come back it was in fact Billy Deere trying to get the ranch away from him she said it was her money that had got him started and now she was back to collect and what she wanted was half the herd and half the land and all the while she was laughing at him and called him a failure *a failure* when after all these years it was a plain and obvious fact that he was a success in every sense of the word.

The first thing he had done was to move the bulls to the pasture behind the house where he could keep an eye out for them and not let Billy Deere go near and then he'd had a dream about the elk in which they ate down to the ground every last blade of grass in that quarter-section pasture where he'd seen them first. So he had risen early and driven them out on his own only to have them return the following morning and just last night he'd gone to town to get the game warden because these poachers had arrived along with Billy Deere and they were taking the bulls along with the elk and he had got out his Winchester and fired at them but the girl said there was no one there and that what he'd done was to wing one of his own bulls.

Once he had gotten the bulls in the pasture near the house he then waited until it got dark and all by himself so Billy Deere wouldn't see what he was up to he had placed enough poison in the Eagle Creek pasture to kill off all the elk before the hunters came on Saturday he had mixed strychnine with alfalfa pellets and no wild animal was going to get his grass and Billy Deere would not get the cattle either once he was done with her.

251

He was quite relaxed lying in his bed with Meridian he actually felt happier than he ever had having neatly put together the pieces of his life and maybe he should marry this girl in order not to let her get away and so protect her from all the evils of this life. She was good for him this small and slender girl she kept telling him he was all right that he was wonderful in ways that no other man could be and that he was strong and good and beautiful and that no matter what she'd never leave him yet she shed a lot of tears whenever she talked to him in such reassuring terms and sometimes he caught her looking at him with so much sadness that he'd say what's the matter don't I make you happy? Of course you do she'd say. Women. Crying when they were happy well he guessed he could tolerate that weakness just to have her near. He ran his fingers through her hair the way he liked to do she murmured in her sleep and god it was good to press his flesh against hers and feel what he hadn't felt in years and it was just too bad what Harley and Killeen thought.

Harley. In that moment and in other moments from time to time he knew it was his son who slept in the other room knew it was the kid grown up and as strange to him as some aborigine and he knew also that the kid was his sole means of survival in the cattle business and his only kin and it was in those moments that the present was what it should have been. But then when he got to thinking too much about Harley in a way that was like too much darkness he knew he had no time for sentiment and besides he did not trust the kid and then he would drink a lot of Scotch and by and by the image of Harley faded and went away and then he saw Billy Deere and this was the fire that consumed his flesh and made it possible for him to hate. Hate. A word he was not used to. Hate. A word that he connected with something as alien to his nature as voting a straight Democratic ticket. And so he would stop drinking for a while in order to let the hate subside because it was a bad thing to have in you along with everything else. But then he always found hate necessary in order to protect himself and to confirm the fact that he was not slipping after all that nothing was to be taken from him and nothing was to be changed.

Britt lay in a pool of sweat with his hands shaking and he reached for the bottle and found it was empty the dawn was beginning to break and so he got up knowing precisely what had to be done that day a Friday and where he would be the next.

The first thing he did before anyone in the house began to stir was to go to the cabinet where he kept his guns and he took them out one by one examining the finely rubbed wood the gray-blue steel barrels the high-grade alloy receivers with simple designs cut into them and each gun had a particular significance. The shotgun had belonged to his father and he remembered hunting turkeys with it and feeling the trigger he felt his father's hands big like his own but gentler and with a talent for working a piece of wood into the shape of a bird and then there was the Winchester carbine he'd given Harley on his sixteenth birthday and the twelve gauge he'd given him when he was only nine the kid had never fired either but had bought his own .22 when he was eighteen and then his hands rested on the .44 Magnum a gun with no frills just rich wood as smooth as a woman's ass and a barrel that felt warm to the touch he held it in his lap for a long time feeling every inch of it and then he took the cartridges from the box and pushed them into the magazine one by one with his left thumb.

Then he laid the gun carefully on the table and put on his heavy jacket and his Stetson and his warm gloves and picking up the gun he let himself out the back door and the last sound he heard in the house was the clock ticking and the mice scampering behind the wall and the faint coughing of Billy Deere somewhere deep in the shadows. His mind was empty of all things except for a kaleidoscope of colors that went round in his brain in a pleasing design that was like all the shapes of color in the land and they burst now in such profusion and gave him

253

such pleasure that he walked a little more slowly in order to keep it sharp and steady the color and the light enveloped him entirely a warm and wondrous blanket drawing him deeper into itself.

He moved slowly through the snow toward a grove of aspen trees shorn now of all their leaves and the trunks were like white arthritic bodies and the branches crippled from the weather but he did not notice any of it a large rock appeared directly in his path and he sat down on it and turned his head toward town where the first rays of sun were dissolving the shadows and firing the tops of the naked trees and the wind was just coming up and blowing the snow at the top of the peak and a magpie came and screeched at him while the silent birds of morning went delicately along the snow but he did not notice one single thing or hear anything except the roar of color in his head. He put the muzzle of the gun between his teeth and he began to become aware that the taste of metal was not pleasant.

He took the gun from his mouth and noticed that he was sitting on a rock and that the sunlight was striking his body and that he could smell a wood fire going at one of the hunters' campsites. So he got up and went back the way he came putting the coffee on to boil in the dark and empty kitchen it was a cold morning and he needed to be warm.

12

The dog slayers of Yellow Bird were haggard and calm that Friday morning yet despite their weariness they found that each hour brought them closer to accomplishing a goal so impossible that twelve hours before no man would have put odds on the plan's success. Yet here they were having worked all night going from door to door with quiet determination and a kind of strength that the people had not seen before the poker players had never done more than talk and brag about deeds they never accomplished but wished they had and now to a man they knew in their weary bones that the final hours were opening

255

to them a courage they had not known they possessed.

Their numbers now included every able-bodied man left in town less than twenty-four men in all with Eli Wetherill excluded because he was of no further use to them he was their enemy along with the elk killers who waited in the Yellow Bird saloon which had not shut down for three straight days Josie Stringer's liquor license notwithstanding. The poor woman had had no sleep and she remained in a more or less fixed position behind the bar while Charley weaved in and out among the hunters who by that time were drinking their whiskey straight and looking at their watches.

By seven o'clock the next morning they would move in on the elk each man with his hunting license in his inside pocket his gun waiting to be loaded his blood up for a kill the likes of which he was not likely to experience again. As they sat and drank and waited out the hours still other hunters arrived and formed a solid wedge of jeeps and camper trucks between Yellow Bird and the flats across the river and some ventured into town only to be driven back by the hunters who had got there first and so when they could drink no more and were too tired for sleep they knocked out all the windows in each deserted building tore away the porch steps and the railings knocked over the privies shot the locks off all the doors of the deserted houses pulled the front door off the church and smashed the stained-glass window put there by the Masons so many years ago. But they did not touch the places of habitation or molest the strangely silent citizens who seemed to be moving out or going away for the weekend.

It was puzzling all right to a bunch of guys out for a little fun why the local yokels didn't seem to give a damn at all well what could you expect from people who let government come and just take their homes away and put a reservoir where they had lived a hundred years? Now in Kansas we got more pride than that we don't let no road builders dam builders and destroyers of our way of life come through unless we want them to and that is the difference between a Midwesterner and these Coloradans. The only time I ever saw one fight was the time we hunted elk in the Uncompahgre Forest you know the time we cut the heads off and threw the bodies in the creek and them guys from some small town was standing there and fell on us like mad dogs busted my arm in two places. You'd think they'd understand that a trophy is all we come for hell you think we are going to haul eight hundred pounds of meat all the way back to Kansas but you know what it is? Altitude. That's what. Plain and simple altitude that us from the flatlands ain't got thank God else we'd be as weak as them the altitude keeps the oxygen from your brain and cuts down on your ability to have any guts at all like some goddamn tranquilizer. And you put them in this altitude year after year and what have you got guys like those poker players that just watch us all the time what have they got to protect anyhow the elk are free and this burg has seen its day but get those California sons-of-bitches out of here they're blocking the road.

Five men from the State Fish and Game were out now in a last attempt to drive the elk once more across the river and they could see as Friday morning broke with enough warmth to begin to melt the snow that the elk would never leave not when more and more grass was beginning to appear in the rapidly melting snow and some of them bedded down in the flats. So the Fish and Game had radioed for help not caring what kind of help it was. Among their own ranks there were fewer than 125 men all stationed throughout the state for tomorrow's opening of the big-game season and you just couldn't expect them to come running and some of these five men wept remembering a couple of things they'd seen in World War Two and then in Korea and this was like that only it was called sport.

By noon on Friday the men of Yellow Bird had showed up with a plan that did not make sense to the Fish and Game men who were exhausted clear to their bones and were not capable of determining what was rational and what was not. They listened to the men from Yellow Bird who put it to them in such a simple yet convincing way that by God why not you could surely protect an elk herd better if they were all in one spot instead of scattered over eleven different pastures where it would be easy to pick them off one by one and hard for the Fish and Game men to keep track of who was shooting what. Get them together in one state pasture next to Matt Brittman's Eagle Creek pasture because a man ain't allowed to hunt on private land said the dog slayers poker players of Yellow Bird and we can form a flank to the east while you Fish and Game guys form a flank to the west while to the south there is a public road and to the north there are the cliffs no man is going to get himself into and what we can do is put ourselves between them elk and those bastards if necessary. You think they might shoot you guys just to get themselves a trophy? No sir we do not the men of Yellow Bird said there's still some risk involved but what the fuck is life if it ain't a risk?

It was settled then and half of the men from Yellow Bird saddled up their horses and began to drive the elk into the state pasture while the other half brought in all the feed they could find in Carbon County and laid it on the ground and one man put his entire supply of alfalfa there and another his horses' oats and another put out last month's pension check for whatever hay it would buy and it was all in all enough to stuff those elk for many a week to come.

But what the State Fish and Game did not know was that there was another part to the plan to save the elk from slaughter which was the real plan. The dog slayers waited until it got dark and the elk were clustered around the feed some two hundred head by now all tame and quite content in the rapidly melting snow. It was then that one man cut the government-built fence between the state pasture and Matt Brittman's land the Eagle Creek pasture from which he had removed his bulls and mixed the poison with the feed just in case a goddamn elk took a notion to jump the fence again and have himself a meal. But of course the dog slayers did not know about the poison they only saw that Matt Brittman's pasture was empty and that his cattle were no longer there. They were grazing on the adjacent pasture near his house and the dog slayers knew they had to be moved back where they came from so they and the elk would mingle. A man might kill elk on private land but not if they were mixed in with a herd of cattle. All you had to do was cut the fence between Matt Brittman's two pastures but no man had ever tampered with another man's fence you could get arrested for that and even shot now look here we have done enough cutting the state fence in the middle of the night.

The doctor had been roused from his bed that same Friday morning by Harley and Killeen and he thought it was the National Guard called out to save the elk and he felt truly proud of his country in that first waking moment and maybe he ought to paste a flag inside his car window because god the country was really trying to maintain law and order in the best way it could. He was all caught up in it seeing himself in his American Legion uniform although he had never served in a war and he heard the words God Bless America and he was singing them when Harley came through the door and stood over him saying doctor I have got to talk to you.

—God bless America my own sweet home.

—Listen he said his young face fearful his eyes quite hollow you have got to do something about dad.

—Yeah said Eli stretching his arms like what?

—He needs to go to a hospital.

—You a doctor Harley he said yawning.

—He's out of his mind.

—Ain't we all.

—Please Doctor Wetherill he's sick you told me so yourself.

—Did I said Eli propping himself up on one elbow you ought to know better than to listen to me.

Killeen came out of the shadows then and sat on the other

259

side of the bed staring into the doctor's red and puffy eyes Harley's right he said Britt doesn't know what he's doing I think the end has finally come.

—Now listen here both of you said the doctor feeling his face grow hot you two are plotting against him that's what. The man's worked hard all these years and you think you know it all.

Harley bit his lip and sighed it's not that at all I know what dad's got because you told me and you told Meridian too.

—You boys know I never tell the truth your dad's got a little old bleeding ulcer if you really want to know.

Harley shook his head he's slipping fast doesn't remember anything not even what day it is and he imagines all sorts of things and he does the most incredible just yesterday he took all the bulls from the pasture where we'd put them for the winter and he got them to the pasture behind the house where there isn't any grass said it was because of the elk down there on the flats well hell doc the bulls can't stay where they are so I've told Bob Wingate to drive them back into the Eagle Creek pasture tomorrow the elk will have all cleared out.

—Hmm said the doctor what's happening with the elk?

—It's under control I think the hunters will make their kill and go away and that's another thing dad says he won't stay around and watch you haven't heard the worst of it yet. He's leaving for the Powder Creek line camp this afternoon to hunt wild horses.

—At this time of year said Eli in amazement ain't we always waited till hunting season's over?

—He's got it fixed in his mind that it has to be tomorrow and I can't let him go alone so I'm going and so is Killeen and what I want to ask you is to try and talk him out of it.

—Can't never talk Britt out of nothing you know that Harley.

—Then come along.

Come along come along the words echoed in his mind and his blood was stirring in his gut because perhaps the time had really come he had to play it very very cool and hope to hell one of his spells wouldn't come over him and he'd black out the way he had been doing more and more so that he was never really sure if he was in his mind or out of it. And so the first thing he would do was not drink anymore and he took what was left of the bourbon and poured it in the African violets Vera Hayes had given him and then he turned to Harley and said I'll come along on one condition.

—What's that?

—That Killeen sticks by his side.

—Why Killeen said Harley bewildered it's my father and I think I have the right—

The doctor shook his head I know what I'm doing Harley you stick with me two pairs remember that's the way we've always worked it Killeen will ride with Britt and you ride with me now what about the girl?

—Meridian well dad says she can't come and she's mad as hell because she can ride as well as any of us but he put his foot down.

—Good said the doctor I want her out of the way now listen Harley have you got a gun?

—Well yeah my .22 but we never take guns on a wild-horse hunt you know that doc.

—Take your gun Harley and what about you Killeen?

Killeen raised his hands and backed away now listen man I'm no damn good with a gun can't hit a thing no way.

—Can you shoot said the doctor sharply.

—Yeah but—

—See that closet over there Killeen all right get the Remington with the scope.

Harley was exasperated he ran his fingers through his hair and sighed doc my dad will never allow—

—Not only will he allow Harley he will carry one himself.

—I don't believe it.

—You wait and see Harley.

261

—And you doc what are you going to carry an M-1?

—A .44 Magnum with a scope.

—Jesus Christ are you going to kill an elephant?

—Maybe nothing Harley maybe nothing at all I'll see you at the ranch at five o'clock.

And the doctor swung himself out of bed and dressed himself in clean underwear for the first time in three days and went into the bathroom and shaved for the first time in nearly five and when he was through he fixed himself the first real breakfast he had had in many weeks. Harley and Killeen just stared and wondered what had happened to the doc all of a sudden and going back to the ranch the two of them decided it was his nerves and all that booze and just what would they do with Britt and Eli six sheets to the wind and carrying guns and god only knew what would happen next.

13

By late Friday afternoon the dog slayers of Yellow Bird had pushed the elk into the state pasture with the blessing of the Fish and Game guys who had gone back to their trailers to catch a couple of hours of sleep but there was no rest for the dog slayers who were next engaged in removing their families from the little houses in which they had lived for as much as sixty years. There was not much talk as hastily packed suitcases were carried through the melting snow and loaded into car trunks and the women drove away for what they thought was a weekend they left their laundry unwashed and their floors unscrubbed they left with pies unbaked and aprons hanging on hooks behind the doors with shovels stuck in the snow and shelves of preserves in basements and pictures still on the walls and the children and grandchildren cried loudest of all because the televisions were left behind and the toys got buried beneath the junk and why do we have to leave the pumpkins two weeks before Halloween? They waved goodbye to each other believing it was only temporary that whatever madness had come over their men would pass in three days they'd come back again and stay until spring and have a proper farewell the way they meant to with a picnic and a dance and a final service in the church. You don't pull up stakes just like that we're coming back yeah we are coming back real soon.

Driving down the hill from his house to the Yellow Bird Hotel Eli Wetherill saw the straight-faced poker players hurrying down the walks carrying suitcases to the cars saw the obedient women and the balky children the yapping dogs and the cat which would not come down from the roof and he did not know what to make of it where were they going and why and how come he hadn't been told? And so he stopped his car and yelled to one of the dog slayers what's going on and all he got was a shrug and a certain tightening of the mouth oh well let them go their peculiar way what harm can it do they must simply be going off for the weekend.

There was not a single soul he knew in the Yellow Bird saloon that afternoon except the Coyote sitting with his radio and his lunchbox facing an odd-looking chap in buckskin there was Josie quite haggard now and Charley looking just plain confused and there were the elk hunters in a frenzy the juke box blasting the pinball machines shuddering the cue balls snapping together and the hooch was flowing like the good old days but there was nothing good about the scene the men were high on alcohol and excitement they strutted around in their fluorescent hunting jackets and caps buying each other drinks and yelling at the top of their lungs at Josie to hurry up. He did not like the look of them. He did not like the way they treated

Josie. And they kept saying things like fourteen hours till the kill and began placing bets on just how long it would take to wipe out the entire herd three hours no two and a half no exactly fifty-six minutes to kill two hundred elk that's right they only got five of them Fish and Game guys. With them odds anybody can win a war.

The doctor pressed himself between two burly Texans who gave him dirty looks and with his hands clasped over the bar gazed up at the glass-eyed elk with the cigar stuck in its mouth took both of Josie's red chapped hands and whispered in her ear shut down the joint let's run away to the Lesser Antilles.

—I'm making a miserable fortune she said bitterly isn't that what I've been after all these years?

—Take it easy sweetheart you got a ways to go.

—You know something doc she said pushing the hair out of her eyes the fatigue showing clearly in her face when this is over I'm going to amount to something I am going to go ahead and be somebody. She leaned closer her teeth still splendid and big and her breasts like a couple of mounds of dough he ought to give some kneading to and why didn't he just take her now while he was sober and trying to stay that way. I have a plan you want to hear it doc she said pouring a pitcher of beer what I want to do is and then the men began a chant we want more beer we want more beer we want more beer. I'm coming she cried her voice cracking I'm coming honestly doc those fellows are the worst bunch I've seen in Yellow Bird since the union sent those hoodlums in back in thirty-five.

—Josie he said Josie come back I want to hear your plan.

But she was lost in the smoke and the crowd and he stood there wondering if he ought to go ahead and have a drink just one to sort of steady his nerves before he went out to Britt's place and they took off for the hunt and he had a quiet skirmish with himself about it that he won by God he was walking out the door when he ran into Alice Crowley all bulged out and crying oh doc I've been looking all over for you.

—What's the matter Alice you about to foal?

She shook her head I don't think so it's November that I'm due oh Jason's tried to kill me.

—Kill you?

—Yeah he's been drunk for a week and he pitched me out with just that suitcase there and a couple bucks told me to get lost doc where do I go?

—He can't do that Alice you're his wife.

—No I'm not doc that's just the trouble he never married me we just lived together.

—Where are your folks Alice?

—Some place in Chicago the last I heard oh doc I don't even have a bed.

The doctor wiped his forehead and looked at the poor frightened girl it did not seem so long ago that he had brought her into the world and he did not have the heart to turn her out of it so he said now listen Alice the hotel is all filled up with hunters so why don't you go on up to my place and stay I'm going wild-horse hunting for a couple days and when I get back we'll think about what to do with you.

She threw her arms around his neck oh doc you are the most wonderful person in the world and she began chewing very rapidly on her bubble gum as she picked up her suitcase and began walking up the sidewalk.

He ran after her and took the suitcase from her he said you can't carry that in your condition now get in the car I'll drive you up now Alice there is plenty to eat just try and get some rest and keep the doors locked and don't let Jason in for God's sake.

—Yeah she said absently chewing on her gum as they drove back up the hill boy I always wanted to see the inside of your house wow where is everybody going?

—Damned if I know Alice they seem to be in a hurry.

—Yeah they came and talked to Jason but he just laid there in his bed too drunk to talk but I heard them say it's time they all stood up together.

266

—Now don't you worry Alice I reckon they're going to have a shootout with the elk hunters look at them moving women and children out like some grade-B Western movie those men are men you don't take serious now mark my words you ain't got a thing to fear.

The Coyote rubbed his eyes and looked around the bar night was closing in on Yellow Bird and he would not get to sleep again thanks to those sons-of-bitches with the out-of-state tags and he hadn't been able to play his radio either he couldn't turn it up loud enough to be heard above the roar that went on day and night for so long it seemed to him that the hunters had always been there and were never going home. And he was afraid of them so he had emptied the dynamite out of his lunch-box and put it under his bed and had gone to check his hiding places for the other dynamite almost every hour and now he sat there not quite believing that he couldn't find any of it not any of a couple hundred sticks. Nor some thousand feet of cord and he eyed the stranger with suspicion. His own partner a man he'd trusted with a secret he wouldn't tell God and had shown him where everything was everything except Annabelle Lee but maybe the stranger had followed him up there and was waiting for his chance to blow her loose himself and find the blossom rock the room full of gold. The stranger had his feet up and was watching the elk hunters with interest a bottle of beer in one hand and a Camel in the other and he was saying for perhaps the hundredth time to Coyote time has a way of copping out on me. . . .

—Friend said the Coyote the time has come for honesty.
—There's either too much of it or not enough of it.
—So what have you done with the stuff?
—Or when I dig enough gold in Alaska . . .
—You found the gold aha and the blossom rock and there she was so pretty. . . .
—I've taken a few pieces here and there for decorating my watchband. . . .

267

—That's where you got it from I figured all along let me see your watchband friend.

And for perhaps the twentieth time the stranger handed the Coyote his watchband studded with gold nuggets and the Coyote studied it and ran his fingers over it and wet his lips and felt his tongue grow heavy with saliva so now he said turning his radio up and not hearing it above the din so now and he slipped the watchband inside his lunchbox.

—Now listen said the stranger it's all very well for the watch but not very well for the watchband.

—Exactly said the Coyote pressing his ear to the radio.

—When may I have it back?

—Oh eventually.

—When do we eat lunch?

—I can't hear you said the Coyote a smile of joy spreading over his face they are playing our song.

—Tock said the stranger dropping his head back in the chair and letting his eyes just roll around his head and the boss mothers decided that Colorado needed me more than I needed Alaska. . . .

—In the morning the Coyote said we shall visit Annabelle Lee.

—The girl said the stranger suddenly I have forgotten to call the girl oh could you lend me a nickel for the phone.

—Not today said the Coyote and besides it costs a dime.

It was very dark when the Coyote and the stranger set out from the hotel but the Coyote would have known the way blindfolded so familiar was he with each twist and turn of the old road going up the mountain he did not even need a light because the moon was beginning to come up. It was night that he preferred for having spent so many years underground the sunlight made him wince and impaired his vision the sun made him afraid to be out for very long people were always following him in the daylight but nobody at all could track him in the dark not even the stranger who could not see as well as he and who got out of breath very fast a short distance from town.

—It's good to piss in the snow and watch it freeze said the stranger stopping to do just that because the piss is frozen in me to begin with in my frozen fucking gut.

—Isaac was on the crosscut dead but still pissing.

—At the North Pole it's like an icicle coming out and I stood on top of a shaft and pissed one three hundred forty-seven feet long saved it up all day forty-two below.

—The weather report is coming on how am I to know if it is going to snow since I can't find my radio.

—Two hundred feet of it was nothing and zinc is just a pile of shit the gold friend the gold is my own mother.

—A good woman while she lasted.

—Yes and rightly so.

The Coyote and the stranger went on up the mountain together coming out in a clearing just as the first rays of the sun spilled over the peak and struck their gentle faces they had come a good distance by then and could no longer see the town it was the sweetness of their dream that made them glad to be standing almost at timberline breathing in the rarefied air rejoicing in the elk who passed by so close that their tracks steamed in the snow and a cottontail sat on a log and looked at them a squirrel chattered noisily from a tree and even the blue jays welcomed them. From their pockets they took raisins and chocolate and ate it as they walked across a narrow ledge on past a tailings dump and the discarded pieces of mine machinery covered with rust and snow yet to them as lovely as a sculpture the snow was very deep there and it was difficult to push through it required all their energy to move along the vast unbroken stretches toward a primitive scaffolding of bleached-out boards sagging and creaking in the wind. And the Coyote's faded blue eyes danced and he rubbed his hands together and turned to his friend and said with a catch in his voice there she is there's Annabelle Lee.

269

There was of course no way to enter the mine which had been blasted shut there was no way to remove the tons of gravel heaped at the entrance no way to push aside the destruction which man had heaped on Annabelle Lee and with his cache of dynamite gone the Coyote was momentarily stymied but it did not matter no it did not matter at all because he and the stranger from the North Pole spent the day traveling the mine in their heads and one man related to another what was on the other side how rich she was and how pure how the tunnels ran and how large was each room they described the rock to one another and how in this particular place the mountain had been especially kind had a main artery of pure gold flowing from the heart of Annabelle Lee. And for hours and hours they sat as happy as could be working inside a mine feeling the gold with their fingers working the pick with precision as well as love because you did not chop brutally at Annabelle Lee she was a lady and you treated her as such. And then sometime in the afternoon the Coyote began to feel hungry and suggested to the stranger that they return to the hotel and have a meal so they went with tremendous joy arm in arm back down the mountain the Coyote whistling a little tune and the stranger laughing from sheer happiness and he would not go back to Alaska not now with such a rich claim to be worked and he had found a partner and everything was better than it ever was everything was in fact near perfect and to celebrate such a fine and rare occasion the Coyote began stopping at each and every mine shaft along the way and pissing into it and sometimes just a drop or two came out and sometimes a whole stream and he watched with glee it steaming and freezing and began to gobble snow to keep his output going there really was no end to frozen piss if you just remembered that what came in had to go out and thus they traveled down the mountain reaching a grove of aspen trees stripped of their leaves their branches like the gnarled arms of the old enfeebled men and it was here that the Coyote spied a promising mine shaft and cried let me be the

270

one and he hurried to it unzipped his fly and stood at the very edge. And then his small body recoiled and he turned to the stranger in fear the shaft looked as if it went down a long way but in fact it was no more than ten feet deep and there lying face up and still recognizable were the frozen remains of Nate Houghton driver of the school bus and friend to every man.

14

The line camp had not been used in a year it
lay between the mesa and the basin where the land was covered
with piñon and sage and cedar it was where the wild horses had
roamed in diminishing numbers for as far back as any white
man could remember it was a place of cold and wind and disappointment where no one lived and where all that remained of
one man's trying was a crumbling homestead with a split log
fence running around it. They drove up in the truck the four
of them Matt Brittman Eli Wetherill Harley and Joe Killeen
each man silent each man's heart beating fast each man nervously watching the other in silence it was as if they had come

272

to bury some relative or to become monks or take up some other useless pastime. It was dark and quiet with the broken moon just coming up over the low hills the stars were brittle like lights punched through a solid black curtain there was no sound except the faraway cry of an animal catching its prey even the wind was still and there was a breathlessness to the night that made each man speak soft when he had to and not at all when he didn't.

The snow in that particular place had melted nearly off though some of it covered the north side of the hills that did not get full sun and some of it still stuck to the north branches of the trees and to the broken windmill outside the cabin but it was mostly frozen ground that their boots touched as they turned the horses into the corral and carried the gear into the cabin started a fire with wood left stacked from the year before. They began the business of getting ready for the hunt the ropes coiled and uncoiled and coiled again until each rope was exactly the way each man wanted it the dry food placed in the pockets of the heavy jackets a quart of whiskey mixed with a quart of apricot brandy and poured into four separate flasks. The only thing that was different was the guns four of them standing against the wall the barrels glinting in the firelight the boxes of ammunition high on a shelf at the end of the room and as each man took his bedroll and spread it on the cold metal bunk-bed springs he looked involuntarily from the guns to the shells and back again and he lay wide awake with that image firmly in his mind the shape of the gun seemed to be on the walls as well as the ceiling a shape that did not belong in the flickering firelight.

The smell of the smoke was strong in the room and as each sleepless man turned toward the fire seeking comfort in its warmth and pleasant crackling they saw their anger preserved there as well but the anger would not go out with the fire nor would the fire comfort them or relieve the anxiety. For Joe Killeen each snap that the fire made was a punctuation mark lingering and doubtful and he knew it would always be so because he was forever in the present looking neither backward nor forward taking each moment for that moment only. And after the hunt he would quit his job and start running all over again and maybe he'd find an end to the search and maybe he wouldn't and if he tried hard enough he could remember the names of some of the places he hadn't been yet like Moccasin Mohawk Chloride Christmas Crows Landing Chinese Camp Wild Horse Wisdom Ten Sleep Tucumcari all the place names he'd memorized from road maps and he could just keep going forever finding the ridiculous and the sublime. Lying on the top bunk he turned over lifted the edge of his bedroll and peered down through the springs at Britt who lay with his eyes wide open and his arms crossed on his chest but he seemed to be relaxed and maybe this was what he needed after all a couple days out chasing broomtails and maybe the feud with Harley would heal up and he could go away feeling unresponsible for what had or had not happened.

Harley Brittman couldn't take it anymore whatever time his father had left ought to be spent alone with the land and the cattle and Eli Wetherill and Meridian Muldoon all of which seemed to give him more comfort than Harley ever could. He'd just go on back to law school and keep in touch with Bob Wingate to make sure the ranch was running normally and that his father was more or less okay. That was all he could do since now at long last he knew he would never measure up to what Matt Brittman wanted in a son but maybe Killeen could. Maybe Killeen would stick around and be the old man's flunky he did not begrudge him the opportunity to line his pockets and even take his place for he had felt displaced a long time now and god what did you do when you were lonely so lonely your whole body ached. You went along and hunted wild horses with your old man for the last time and you tried to forget you really didn't love him anymore that's what you did and you went on being lonely for as long as you could stand it hoping that time would make you forget that you weren't so bad after all.

Jelly beans and jackrabbits hydrocarbons kill the birds and strychnine kills the elk and nobody gets the grass Billy Deere chopped off my cock with a padlock on every gate the bulls cannot get through one wild horse choked down to the ground a bullet through the head waking up in a strange bed bothers me cold feet a toothache and the parasite is gone wean the calves why don't you and vaccinate the mavericks with DDT I do not remember I do not remember what I am doing here what I am doing here and who are these people with flickering heads and there she is and I said to myself the day she left you walk through the door and I'll plug you dead serving papers on me like I was a criminal guilty of assassinating the Smokey Bear by god nobody does that to me but they are you see they all are and I have to get them first.

Matt Brittman lay in torment tossing in his bedroll the pain was building up again and he had nothing to kill it with had deliberately left his pills at home the booze would suffice and tasted better so he got up and unscrewed the bottle having drunk half its contents before the evening meal it didn't hurt so much being treated his own way spirits of gum turpentine was what his father used on himself as well as critters. It stands to reason a man would benefit from the principles proved on stronger specimens of breathing living animals.

He stood by a grimy window above the sink a small alcove separate from the rest of the cabin. The stove needed more wood and he stuffed it feeling the warmth on his face the dry red hot coals burned without flame until the fresh wood touched them off and he let his head drop forward into the smoke the fascination for the fire was strong in him feeling an irresistible urge to put his fingers to it would it not be good to feel yourself ablaze and not feel the pain because the fire had taken care of it and you would just burn brightly for a time the cold ashes were no concern of yours. He sat down at the table feeling dizzy and uncertain of where he was and why the floor was cold and his feet were covered with heavy socks but the room was not his room and the fire was not his fire and he drank some more of the whiskey he was detached from his body floating around with the smoke and rising with the moon the wind would take him along free free free. He began to laugh then it was very funny to know you had departed from your body and could go wherever you wanted and no more fuel tanks and studded tires and the carburetor jammed in winter it was very nice to fly and not feel the cold nor have to wash your socks.

Harley Brittman decided he had to take a piss outside the door as quickly as he could and the room was so cold he put his jacket on and stuck his feet into his unlaced boots not noticing his father slumped at the table and opened the door softly and stood there sending a stream into the night and the worst of it was his hands were freezing and the goddamn horses were restless. He had better see if it was a mountain lion worrying them and he had better take his gun using the shells in his pocket just three well he could scare off whatever it was with three shots. He approached the corral adjusting his vision to the vague unfamiliar shapes and he paused just in front of the fence his full form outlined in the moonlight and waited and listened just thirty seconds too long.

Matt Brittman moved quickly nothing now except your spirit really free at last warm too and your vision was as wide as the falcon's and you could even see in the dark what was your enemy and what was not. Then what Matt Brittman had left behind in the form of his body took the second gun from the wall and loaded it and fired straight into the night.

Harley.

—Jesus Britt you damn near shot the kid.

—Give me the fucking gun dad what in hell are you doing?

—Now keep away from me both of you didn't you see what was out there didn't you see it move right in front of your eyes I had to kill it I had to Eli.

—What Britt what?

—Evil.

—Tomorrow Killeen the doctor whispered you are to ride with him but about twenty-five yards behind.

—And do what for God's sake?

—He is going to try and kill Harley again.

The cabin was quiet with four men frightened by the sound of their own breathing. The doctor lay in his bedroll knowing that the rest of them would not sleep. He turned his head just in time to see Britt hoist himself up to the bunk that contained Harley and in an instant the doctor's arms were around the big man's waist and he was pulling him to the floor. Matt Brittman smashed the doctor in the side of the face with a solid powerful fist. Then Britt dropped as if from a shot and from his other hand the knife fell to the floor the glint of it caught in the moonlight coming through the window. In a split second Eli covered it with his hand and looking up at Harley's puzzled face knew he had seen it and there was Killeen scrambling to his feet saying I'm getting the hell out of here.

Come back here Killeen said Eli with authority and help me get him into bed.

For Matt Brittman had passed out on the floor his body too heavy for a man to lift and then Killeen was saying I think we ought to take him home.

The doctor shook his head we have come to hunt a horse he said and that is what we are going to do.

—Enough is enough said Killeen the next time he'll get the kid.

—I'm not afraid Harley said quivering in his bedroll I don't really think he would.

—You stupid son-of-a-bitch said Killeen he nearly killed you just now you want to lay there and get it again?

—Let him try Harley said.

Killeen let out a long low whistle your old man's out of his mind.

—I know.

277

—Then let's blow Harley for God's sake we aren't going to get ourselves killed.

Eli laid Matt Brittman on his back and covered him up there were tears in his eyes he said to Harley and Killeen you two trust me or not?

There was no answer and so the doctor repeated the question and finally Killeen said why should we?

—I know what I'm doing said the doctor for the first time in many years.

—And what is that?

—The business of medicine.

—Medicine exploded Killeen you call that medicine leaving a sick man that's out of his mind to kill us all?

—That's right said Eli.

—Count me out said Killeen I'm splitting you coming Harley?

Harley lay there watching the doctor's face and seeing his tears and there was his old man lying still as death in the bunk and the fire was cheerfully crackling incongruous as hell. I think I know said Harley slowly I think I know what has to be done.

Killeen threw up his hands well for Christ's sake clue me in.

—Trust the doctor.

—Trust him trust him said Killeen he's nothing but a—

—A useless drunken old man finished Eli said yes I know give me one chance Killeen just one.

—To do what?

—Practice medicine like I said.

—Oh all right said Killeen irritably I am not responsible.

—Nobody said you were whispered Harley.

—Then what the hell?

—Come on said Eli let's go to sleep.

—You crazy fools said Killeen we'll all be dead shit man do we have to prove we're brave?

Harley doubled up in his bunk felt the beating of his heart

as loud as any drum and fear went crawling down his back like a magnet drawing iron and he bit his lip until it bled and said with complete abandon next time I will let him kill me.

Eli Wetherill wanted a drink more than anything in the world and his body began to heave because he had not touched the bottle going on twenty-four hours. It was about to conquer him he simply had to have a drink just one to sort of steady his nerves just one to give him courage. But that was what he had told himself for many years and the years had stripped him away like some enormous onion until now there was just a rotten core. And so he began to think of baseball each and every play of the last game he had seen on the television screen he watched the baseball game for seven innings and then he did not want a drink anymore he only wanted the dawn to come as quickly as it could.

It was Saturday the 18th of October the day on which he knew that Matt Brittman had to die.

15

At five o'clock in the morning twelve of the dog slayers of Yellow Bird met at the Yellow Bird Hotel rousing Josie Stringer from a deep and well-deserved sleep she came to the door in her bathrobe her hair up in curlers and her round face covered with a thick white cream that had hardened like cement. They were huddled on the sidewalk their faces grim and haggard and as she looked at them through the glass she remembered them as they had been in earlier times and like herself they lived with memories of better days and couldn't speak of what they were giving up. Within each heart was a reverence for the place and you would never know unless you

280

had come from there how deep and strong the reverence was you would have thought them incapable of feeling anything at all. Josie Stringer did not know then or ever that it was these same kindred souls who had killed her dog the death of her dog was due to somebody from out of town running over it the doctor said and he had buried poor Susie himself and placed a cross at her head. She looked annoyed at first she then smiled a little cracking the plaster on her cheek and her fingers undid the lock and she said as she always said when she was particularly pleased and trying to hide it you fellows think this is some kind of cheap hotel to which they replied ain't it the country club we come for a round of golf. She said well so long as you know that the coffee's strong it's just the water that is weak and they said it don't make no difference we are going to drink it all up anyhow.

They shuffled in one by one took off their well-worn Stetsons unbuttoned their sheepskin-lined jackets with the patches on the elbows tracked mud in from the street and removed their stiff fingers from heavy gloves they were a sorry-looking lot those dozen men whose lives had been spent in mines or behind glass counters or out in the pay of the county fixing roads or half killing themselves for the telephone company when the lines went down and some had also worked for the railroad but mostly they were hard rock stiffs who had never allowed a woman underground. They had come to tell her what was happening and it was hard considering the sum total of all the years now finished and the growing tendency to forget what Yellow Bird had never been.

Everybody's gone but us they said the womenfolk and the kids the place is all cleaned out.

—I noticed but resolved to keep my mouth shut said Josie Stringer cooking two dozen eggs on the grill.

The reason being they said we are going to blow up the town.

The coffee was boiling in the big percolator she turned off

281

the heat and said now that strikes me as a little too dramatic.

Can't be helped you see it's on account of them elk hunters that have come down from the mountain and are just laying there and we have got to do something.

—Oh leave it to the Fish and Game.

That's the trouble with you women you don't understand nothing when it comes to hunting elk now you don't like them out-of-staters any more'n we do.

—It's a fact but I don't intend to do no harm.

Us neither just scare 'em good so they run away like sheep.

—It ain't going to scare them elk hunters way across the river a mile from town why they'll laugh their heads off they don't have a thing to lose what's your A-bomb going to prove?

We ain't going to blow your place up Josie and not the houses neither just the stuff that's already vacant and ready to be torn down but that is roughly half the town we figure and it will look like hell itself what with kerosene and all.

She put the eggs on the plates and slammed the dishes on the counter she was angry and plumb sick of their stupidity she said it's my town as much as yours I won't let you do such a silly stupid thing to save some goddamn elk why those hunters are going to laugh at you is that what you fellows want?

They hung their heads and pushed their eggs around with their forks and slurped the bitter coffee and from the tables where they sat they could see the hulks of the empty buildings across the street illuminated by the street lamps and they knew by heart what each and every building looked like and how the town was set to go off at precisely seven o'clock. Right now six other men were working in the dark cutting the second fence where Matt Brittman's bulls were kept and another six were riding up on the far side of the elk. When a single shot was fired at seven o'clock the elk and the bulls would be driven into the Eagle Creek pasture together on Matt Brittman's private land. It was a sound military plan built on the element of surprise that was the collective opinion of all those who had served in the

armed forces and the state militia who had commanded Boy
Scout troops and become addicts of so many Westerns and war
stories that they knew beyond all doubt that their plan was wise.
The enemy would disperse leaving the elk intact.

What we want they said at last is for this place to be remembered.

Josie Stringer felt herself choke up and knew that she was
licked she said well you better let me fix you some food to carry
with you.

We ain't got time it's a quarter to six we got a lot to do now
all we ask from you is if anything goes wrong call the police.

Josie screwed up her face the plaster was flaking off her skin
and she looked like a statue left out in the weather she said
anxiously you sure this dump of mine ain't going up in flame?

This is the only thing that's safe on this side of the block the
old dry-goods store across the street is set to go but it won't take
hardly nothing it's just a shell and we plan to do the theater and
the drugstore and the old bank—

—The bank she said in great alarm that's where the doctor
has his office you can't.

Well he ain't there no more he won't care what's in there
to lose a couple bedpans and a thermometer or two.

—No she cried you have no right to blow up the doctor's
office.

A look of triumph crossed their faces oh yes we have they
said.

—For god's sake let him know.

They were nearly out the door they turned and said oh we
can't hardly do that seeing as how he is hunting broomtails with
that highfalutin friend of his there's nobody here but our kind
Josie we'll get his house as well. And then they ran into the dark
to their places among the ghosts of Yellow Bird to do what had
to be done.

Josie Stringer leaned in silence against the wall for several
moments her hands trembling and then she ran upstairs and

roused her son who gave her a crooked smile and said so what?

She slapped him hard and he huddled under the blankets and began to cry.

—Hush up Charley now get up and get dressed and go get Jed McTavish.

—I can't he whimpered I can't ma.

—What in hell is the matter with you Charley?

—I'm scared.

Josie Stringer was not a woman given to anger or violence she was above all patient and level-headed not once in her life had she felt the urge to strike out particularly against her son who wasn't right in the head and therefore not accountable but what rose in her now was desperation and as her son lay face down sobbing in his pillow she grabbed a piece of iron that lay on the floor beside his bed and with her strong hands wrapped securely around it she hit him in the head. The blood came very slowly from the wound and she guessed it was because he had not much blood there but he was all right she saw with relief as he began to moan so she left him. Next she knocked on the room shared by the Coyote and the stranger from the North Pole but there was no answer and after much knocking and much calling she twisted the knob and went in and found their empty beds and all their belongings scattered about the room.

Then real panic seized her and she raced down the creaking old stairs to the phone and picking it up found it made no sound whatever she banged it against the wall then dropped it the thing was dead and she would have to go to Coronado. She dressed as fast as she could took the curlers from her hair the cement off her face gave herself a slash of lipstick and went out to her car parked behind the hotel. But it would not start no it would not so much as gasp no matter how hard she tried. Her patience was at an end now and she got out of the car and started walking rapidly toward the back of Fred Sweeney's store where he lived with Purvis the old principal of Yellow Bird High. Although she had always avoided their obvious relationship and had never once set foot inside Sweeney's apartment in the back of the store she went there now in fear and determination noticing that her watch said six-thirty and it was still dark and my god all the street lights just went out. Open up Fred she cried open up and by and by he came to the door without his familiar glasses squinting at her through the curtains and mumbling who's there. Josie open up Fred the most awful thing is happening. And she went into the tiny cramped room pretending not to notice Purvis sitting up in the double bed with his pajamas on she refused the chair that Sweeney offered and stood with her hands on her hips and told him what was happening and all the while he kept nodding his head and wetting his lips and Purvis kept one hand over his mouth as if to stifle a cough or laugh. Then Sweeney said I know all about it Josie of course they asked me to help but I have to take care of the store and besides I'm just getting over the flu you understand and as for Eli Wetherill I don't give a damn.

—You bastard she said her eyes afire after all he did for you.

—I can't remember a thing can you Edgar he said turning to the grinning principal who said solemnly not a thing.

She stomped her feet and swore worse than they had ever heard her and they were amazed that Josie Stringer of all people had finally blown her cool.

—You refuse to help she asked turning to go.

—Oh we'll help all right said Sweeney we'll even light the fuse.

Josie Stringer hurried along the main street of Yellow Bird which lay in semi-gloom as the hands of the clock moved toward seven. Not a street lamp was on and not an electric light shone in any window for the dog slayers had seen to it that the power was disconnected it made their task easier to slip around in the shadows of predawn silent and sure. Each man was now in a different position ready and waiting the charges were all in place and since there was not enough of the dynamite to go around they poured kerosene around the foundations of homes

285

they had once lived in or drunk beer in had courted a girl in or buried their relatives from. Each building had a memory but the memory was squeezed out now as they went about their work there was no time for looking back or to wonder if they were doing right they simply had a job to do a job like working in the mines with risk and disaster pending every hour of the shift and after a while you got used to it and knew the odds were with you it was why they had become good poker players sure shots with their guns and victors in the war with the elk hunters. So silent and sure-footed were they as they did their work on schedule and took cover in their appointed places that Josie Stringer saw just shadows moving here and there and calling out could not be sure if it was a man or some stray cow moving through the hollow hulk of a building. Feeling quite cold and tired and knowing there was nothing more to be done she turned at the corner to go up the street to Eli Wetherill's house.

It was then at precisely ten minutes before the hour of seven that the contents of the Coyote's lunchbox placed for safekeeping beneath his unmade bed exploded and blew out the entire front of his room. Josie Stringer turned and nearly fainted she saw a flame burst forth from the old wooden hotel and she remembered Charley and began to run as fast as her legs would take her slipping in the mud and snow screaming the two blocks seemed like twenty miles screaming as one blast after another lit up Yellow Bird the men had simply panicked and set off their charges.

At exactly the same moment guns went off across the river and then the flames rose with a roar up and down the streets illuminating the mountain and that inert symbol of the future the dam intake tower safely beyond the fire at the very edge of the river. She was running hard up the street running to no avail running on legs of iron running as the old buildings toppled one by one running as she thought she heard Charley scream. The hotel was still standing with the flames coming out of the side but the door was open and she ran in and up the stairs halfway because that was all there were just seven stairs and then a gaping hole dark yet jagged dark yet glowing at the bottom and then she felt the heat behind her and turning saw the downstairs was burning also. She plunged down the steps for the last time grabbing one thing off the wall it was a sampler done by her grandmother in 1868 it said it matters not how long we live but how. And with this under her arm she staggered to the street where three of the dog slayers had gathered to watch the hotel burning to the ground and when they saw her they knew that Charley was still inside and not knowing what else to do they led her gently to a truck and put her on the seat and drove through the smoking streets and up the hill to Eli Wetherill's house turning pink in the rising sun.

We couldn't burn it after all they said it was like setting fire to the church we just couldn't do it when the time came I guess we ain't brave men after all and we didn't blast the Muldoon house either the dynamite just run out. She squeezed the hand of a man who had worked beside her husband in the mines and the tears were running down his cheeks as well and he said quietly it's all going to go every bit of it except old Eli's house oh god.

And then they heard in the first light of dawn a sheer wall of sound coming from the flats across the river it was prolonged and rolled like thunder pounding and deep and agonized. The time was seven-ten and the slaughter of the elk had just begun.

16

By five-thirty the six men camped at the
place where the state fence was cut had peeled back the wire
and laid it close to the other side so that the gap was eight feet
wide the distance between two fence posts and then they decided that was not enough to push a whole elk herd through and
so they made another cut and peeled that back. There was in
that group of six not one who had been a cowboy there was a
mucker an assayer the former county clerk and recorder the
man who ran the hardware store a feed and grain dealer and
one retired miner their feeling toward the land was quite different from the cowboys' for they had spent little time meeting the

288

land on a day-to-day basis their experience was drawn from hunting and fishing from camping in the forests and packing in to some inaccessible area where they would go to just let their thoughts collide. To them the elk were as proud and strong as they themselves had once been the elk were what renewed them the elk were as sacred to them as the land was to the cowboys. It did not occur to any of those six that when the chips were down these basic differences between two groups of men would make the scheme absurd and would prove to them what they had suspected all along that cowboys were not all they were cracked up to be they would run like rabbits when you gave them something important to do and would never tell you why they'd let you down in such an awful way.

The motley group went about their work assuming that the cowboys were doing theirs and at the very moment when they were trying to get the elk to move the cowboys were likewise shoving Matt Brittman's bulls through the cut in his fence. The six men fanned out now determined to make as little noise as possible they glanced nervously toward the road where the hunters' camper trucks were all lined up and they heard the hunters' guns go off by accident and heard the commotion saw one man turn his headlights on and they stopped short for fear the lights would be played on them and then they'd have had it out there in the night pulling a dirty trick on a bunch of dirty elk hunters.

Most of the elk were bedded down some with calves and it was hard to get them up and moving harder than they'd thought and just how in hell did you make them run in one direction in the dark? You could see they were going to scatter any old way they pleased and hell you couldn't shout or make one damn noise the way you did in yesterday's daylight getting them into this one pasture that you were now trying to get them out of and just what in hell could six men do with a couple hundred elk? They wished with all their hearts that the cowboys would show up but the cowboys were hard at their end of

289

the bargain or so they thought and god if it wasn't so fucking cold and dark.

By a quarter past six they had only driven about fifty head of elk into Matt Brittman's pasture and it was plain to see they would get very few of the rest the elk were on the run all right climbing toward the cliffs or running off to the north where the hunters would have an even better shot and oh shit here came the elk from Brittman's pasture back over the fence and there was nothing left in Matt Brittman's pasture not even the bulls and what the hell had happened to the goddamn cowboys?

The six who had been chosen to drive Matt Brittman's bulls into the Eagle Creek pasture had been cowboys all their lives they had lived and worked on ranches and they knew the difficulty of rounding up bulls in the dark. They had spent the night in a trailer at the edge of the county road with the horses kept saddled and ready in a van and when it was time they mounted and rode along the fence not speaking at all yet each man humming softly to himself staring up at the sky and sweeping his gaze toward the spots of light coming from the elk hunters' camper trucks and the few lights coming from Yellow Bird across the river. The land began to slope upward and there was a grove of trees toward which they rode letting themselves through two gates until at last they were not far from Britt's house in the pasture with the bulls riding quietly over land that belonged to another man toward animals that belonged to him and they knew they had no business there not one had ever broken into another man's property much less cut his fence or monkeyed with his cattle. The grievous thing which they were about to do hit every man square in the gut they were honest simple cowboys who had always worked for wages who had always had a boss who had always respected another man's rights of property and although they had been chosen for the job because of this experience the experience was why they stopped and looked at each other in the dark and heard the

290

cattle in the dark and saw the sky under which they had all slept in the dark. Their bodies ached they were no longer adventurous no longer responded to the challenge no longer felt it was so goddamn important to save a herd of elk. Long years of habit overtook them all the years and years of getting up in the dark and going to bed with the sun brought out in them a peculiar sense of duty toward an ideal they understood yet could not express. For each man over his lifetime had formed a bond with the land so strong that death was all that would break it. They had worked hard for almost nothing worked till they were raw and had never felt particularly courageous or bold unlike the television cowboys their lot was routine labor of the hardest kind of taking the worst and the best of nature as it came and seeing themselves just going along seeking the solitude and relief from outside pressures that made them cowboys instead of factory workers.

For a very few minutes they sat motionless on their horses and at a quarter past six they turned of one accord and headed back the way they had come rode through the gates and on down the road and back to the horse van. They had not spoken a single word nor seen each other's faces and that was not important they knew they had failed the six men waiting at the place where the state fence was cut but they had not failed each other.

The motley crew were hopping mad and exhausted and tired of the cold and breaking their asses and they knew what was going to happen to the town at seven o'clock just thirty minutes away and already the sky was beginning to get light just what in hell do we do? And the six leaderless leaders huddled together blaming each other for what they had not been able to do and now it was not so much a matter of saving the elk as it was a matter of saving their pride and so with less than thirty minutes left to go they decided what it was they must do with just the assayer disagreeing but in the end they convinced

291

him. They split up and each man went off and found himself a place in the pasture taking cover behind a pile of rocks or within the heavy brush and it was agreed that when they saw the first explosion hit the town they would open fire on the elk killing all that they could before daybreak before the permissible start of hunting season. They watched the elk drift back indistinct shapes thudding across hard ground they were a hundred yards closer to the herd than the elk hunters they were excellent shots and they were fired with anger and despair and the urge to destroy what rightfully belonged to them.

But the cowboys were in addition to being cowboys also men from Yellow Bird and they too felt proprietary toward the elk and so when the horses were loaded in the van they took their guns and set out across the pasture on foot knowing that what they had to do was to shoot down every elk they could find before the day broke over the mountains. They would do it by wandering through the pasture getting as close to the animals as they could and being more accustomed to the dark than any other men in the whole county they could see better and with deadly accuracy could kill at long range nearly anything on legs could kill it in dark as well as daylight. When you got right down to it there wasn't any choice and they would just kill the elk for the same reason that you had to kill a horse you loved that had simply come to the end of its days you could not deliver it to any hands other than your own.

The cowboys kept looking at their watches knowing that at seven o'clock the boys in Yellow Bird would do their duty and it would be wise to hold off till then to make sure the elk hunters literally did not know which way to turn. They were amazed to see that not one elk was in Matt Brittman's Eagle Creek pasture after all. The cowboys walked through the hole in the fence and noticed the elk were all bedded down in their accustomed place with piles of feed still untouched and the cowboys stopped and crouched down on the ground took aim and waited for the minutes to roll by swallowing more and more as their mouths got dry and the backs of their necks got cold even with their collars up and the ground was too damn cold and their hands were so stiff maybe they couldn't pull the trigger after all. They were out there lying in the pasture their guns aimed at the nearby elk and the time was ten minutes before seven. At the moment the cowboys saw a ball of orange burst forth in the blue-black sky over Yellow Bird they squeezed the triggers of their guns again and again and again.

In the same pasture the other six men from Yellow Bird hidden behind rocks and trees were caught off guard by the blast as well as the volley of gunfire. They thought it was the elk hunters out there in the flats and so they did the first thing that came to mind they just began to shoot not caring if it was a man or elk they hit. Those out-of-state bastards had not played fair after all and they had it coming and so they fired again and again and again not hearing the shouts coming from the flats not seeing the elk hunters lined up along the road convinced it was a new batch of hunters who had arrived during the night and jumped their claim to a legitimate trophy planned for many days.

The elk hunters spread out along the fence trying to see what was happening in the pasture but it was not yet light and the game wardens were all along the road with flashing lights so they stood in their positions for almost fifteen minutes and there was no further sound of guns from the flats or the slope beyond it was so very still and silent that the elk hunters began to be afraid that something had gone wrong out there.

Then the light began to break and they saw dimly oh so very dimly the elk careering across the pasture swerving in panic and it was then that each hunter had his moment seeing nothing but those fleeing forms he opened fire an ear-splitting volley from several hundred guns and in tens and in twenties the animals crumpled to the ground while others dropped back crippled but still trying to escape and then these too pitched to the ground and rolled sideways some still some kicking and

293

then another herd came racing out of the trees and the crescendo of bullets rose once again a hideous roar like the earth splitting open and again the elk fell by the score while others raced on spinning and turning in blind sheer panic over the clusters of dead animals on the blood-spattered ground.

And when the light opened out across the flats the hunters many of whom were over the fence and tagging carcasses saw that it was not only the elk which lay dead it was half a dozen men who looked like cowboys.

17

Among the cedar sage and piñon the snow lay in patches and along the north faces of the isolated slopes it remained deep a meringuelike surface broken by the hooves of a herd of wild horses as recently as the dawn. The four men had chased them for perhaps ten miles through the thick and twisted brush along windswept desolate ridges losing their tracks for a time then picking them up again at the bottom of an arroyo where the snow had collected in the shade. From there the trail shot straight up the embankment to an open field where a lone eagle sat unmoving in a pine tree as the four horsemen riding in pairs came past at a determined lope. A covey of sage hens flew up in alarm a couple of cottontails scurried for cover and along the rimrock a slouching coyote crept into a crevice the land was a wasteland and the creatures in it were altered and formed by the hardness as were the mustangs and the handful of men who ran cattle there. To remain very long in so hostile a land is to lose touch with the common world and that is precisely what Matt Brittman intended to do had done over all those years when he and Eli Wetherill came out for as long as a month at a time.

The mustangs like the land were a remnant of all that was free the scruffy mustangs and the scruffy land being neither beautiful nor useful nor easy to get at would be the last to feel the crunch of civilization. In twenty years maybe less the wild horses would be extinct polished off for the sake of grazing land the selling of deer licenses and the drilling for oil shale. The horses served no purpose whatsoever except to sell at thirty bucks a head to some dog-food company and that was pretty good sport for a weekend. By that October there were fewer than two hundred mustangs in Colorado all of them concentrated in the savage land not far from the Utah border. It was a time when the government was putting up fences and the cattlemen were shooting the mustangs dead and the thrill of catching them for the dog-food companies was complicated by the fact that the land in question was very big the horses were very elusive and goddamn it the only way to kill them was to do it from an airplane or a truck in spite of what the law said. Just who in hell enforced it way out there in no man's land?

The wild horse was as the government put it a *non-revenue-producing unit* nobody paid for its grazing fee nobody paid for a license to kill it the parasite just drank all the water and ate all the grass and to hell with the sentimental fools who said the mustang was part of a heritage now listen friend you can't sell heritage. So get rid of those ugly broomtails with a head as big as a mule and legs too short for a goat and tails that touch the ground big bellies and chewed-up hides and a nose like a

Roman emperor the sumbitch ought to be eradicated Progress Prosperity Practicality on the Land of Many Uses. Keep a bunch of cayuses around so some old cowboy can imagine hisself Kit Carson? Man you have got to be kidding who in his right mind goes to all that trouble to catch some runty old dog soldier?

They had been riding four hours already and had not caught a glimpse of the mustangs and now their horses were beginning to play out so they rested in a grove of piñon pines tethering their horses to the branches. They got off and sat on the ground the four loaded guns in cases were strapped to the saddles along with the saddle bags containing food and water and the flasks of whiskey mixed with apricot brandy. Eli Wetherill had stuck close to Harley letting his own hand drop to the gun case each time Britt's large glove-encased hand dropped to his but he was feeling pretty clear-headed now and wondering if last night wasn't all a big bad dream rubbed out by being there on the land which had always made them feel somehow eternal.

The fact that Britt had slipped across the obvious line between rationality and incompetence and had just as obviously recrossed it again had the doctor puzzled. Britt seemed to have regained possession of his senses and was in control of his body as well he outrode them all in a chase that had set Eli's legs on fire Matt Brittman had assumed leadership of that little band swinging his arms in silent command for them to follow him. By examining each step of land he could tell which way the mustangs had gone and how long ago they had passed by and it was his guess now that they were hiding in the burn on the top of the ridge. After lunch Eli and Harley were to chase them out into the open to give Britt his chance to beat them on the run and maybe he would have enough horse and maybe he wouldn't maybe his mind and his body would fail him in front of a shivering horrified crowd.

Eli Wetherill did not want Matt Brittman there he wanted him away from a failing land. In each of the previous years Britt

was like the land itself strong and dry and shaped by the ele-
ments as craggy as one of the outcroppings of rock as stubborn
as the sage as natural as the dirt. But now there was so much
else to see like the land about to be conquered the land about
to be laid out in subdivisions the land about to be destroyed
because the time had come. Yet had not come. Looking around
him Eli Wetherill saw that everything was the same as it always
had been and that was good. You could spend a hunk of your
lifetime out here as he and Britt had done and not notice any
change at all. Except for the fences goddamn it. Well you could
just overlook that. And the tracks of the trucks coming out to
pick off the mustangs. Well maybe they hadn't got many. And
the plastic ribbons of a survey team. Well perhaps they were
just fooling around. You didn't expect this land to change any
more than you expected the moon to drop from the sky. And
that was the difficulty with Britt. Looking at his deeply burnished skin the lines still firm around his jaw his eyes glassy but
able to spot a horse a half mile off his stride limber and quick
his back straight and broad, he did not know that Matt Brittman
was enlivened by the energy of despair or that he no longer felt
any physical pain or discomfort he having given in to hopeless
resignation. Within Matt Brittman's heart burned two things
and two things only one was to capture a mustang the other was
to rid himself of Billy Deere.

The doctor sat munching buckskin jerky and listened to
Britt explain to Killeen what was happening to the wild horses
and doing so with such conspicuous authority that it made the
doctor smile. Britt was a good talker a good rider a good fellow
he was in short a right good hand which was the most you ever
said about any man in that part of the West. He ought to live
Eli Wetherill said to himself he's too good to die.

—You don't get a trophy or anything out of it Britt was
saying to Killeen who was lying on the ground next to him each
man wearing his chaps and Stetson it's just your own satisfaction
that maybe if you haven't deserved that stud you sure as hell

have earned him. Ever figure what it takes to catch a horse that's faster and a whole lot smarter than you if all you got is a rope and a horse not as good as the one you're after? The strong ones don't get caught like that at least not by guys like us but you take a fellow with a gun he could shoot Citation going a hundred miles an hour flat. Well Killeen you got to keep your mouth shut about wild horses and secret places because in a hundred years a man's success won't be measured by money but by how well he can keep his mouth shut about a secret place. And that's what me and Eli have been doing all these years keeping our mouths shut about where the mustangs are and what we know about their habits and where we last saw tracks. It takes a fellow a long time to learn that and if he's a stranger here it's maybe one chance in fifty even if he's got a gun what good is it if he can't spot them? So me and Eli we aim to keep the odds down that's all a man can do and hope his son will carry on that right my boy?

—Yeah said Killeen absorbed in the flight of a raven across the cloudless sky so how come we got guns?

—The reason for that is the oilies he said and Eli let out his breath.

—The what said Killeen.

—Now come on son said Britt you been out here long enough with your old man to know about them weekend cowboys who come out from Rangely and those places up north don't care a hoot for ethics so long as they come back with the goods they ride with their spurs upside down and their Levi's halfway up their ass if they ride at all mostly they come in pickups and just try and crease the mustangs right behind the neck but mostly that horse is as good as dead so what your old man and you are going to do son is run the oilies off.

Harley got up then and went over to the trees and working his fingers among the branches untied his horse swung his leg across the saddle and without a word began to ride toward a line of burned juniper on the top of a ridge he was the very picture

299

of a young man angry and uneasy he dug his spurs into the horse's flanks and rose in the saddle as the animal came to a wash and took the leap pawed the air with his hind legs and as his front legs touched the loose earth on the other side the horse fell but Harley was thrown clear.

Britt shaded his eyes and fury rippled his chin he sputtered rides like a goddamn amateur whoever the hell it is.

The doctor vexed and slowly coming to realize that his hopes were now all wrecked said that there's Harley Britt he took the jump too slow.

Britt wheeled and with unexpected calmness said where are you Eli?

—Right here Britt.

—Can't see you Eli.

The doctor touched Britt's sleeve and he picked up Britt's hat which had fallen to the ground and gave it to him and peered through his glasses into eyes as cold as steel.

—That's better said Britt with the doctor's face thrust against his own it was the sun Eli the sun that blinded me.

But the sun was at Britt's back. A sound rose out of him molten and deadly that blocked out the grimness of his face and left it utterly dark and void the sound rose above his fixed stare and shrouded his head with some terrible halo of hell. Eli and Killeen were at his side in an instant and wrestled him to the ground his powerful body was far from helpless it surged against the combined strength of those two astonished frightened men who gasped and sweated and prayed each in his own way for Matt Brittman to go quietly.

For some minutes Britt lay on his back panting the doctor took his pulse and listened to his heart he noticed certain signs such as the color of his face and the dilation of his eyes and in his saddle bag he had brought two vials and a syringe not knowing until that very moment which vial he would be called upon to use.

—He's done for he said to Killeen take my word for it.

300

Killeen shook his head slightly no he said listlessly no.

The doctor got up very sure of himself he had no time to think as he walked toward his horse calling to Killeen watch him.

Killeen took his eyes off Britt's face long enough to look across the ridge for some sign of Harley and in that instant Britt's foot caught him in the groin and sent him spinning and howling in pain.

—Hold him yelled the doctor.

But Britt was up and running toward his horse ripping the reins from the branch and sliding into the saddle and all the while he kept holding his middle slightly doubled over his legs drawn up clear out of the stirrups yet the horse responded and he was off through the brush screaming back at Killeen come on son come on and follow your old man.

The doctor and Killeen were on their horses so fast that they were only fifty yards behind him. He's gone mad Eli said you can see that for yourself.

—Yes.

—And what we got to do is bring him down.

Killeen's eyes widened and he uttered a little cry kill him?

—Shoot the horse out from under him Killeen.

—I can't.

—He'll get Harley then.

Astride the big palomino Killeen's heart sank and in the vast silence of the wilderness he had the chilling doubt of his own will and his own desire.

I am dying the doctor thought for the pain which had begun earlier in his chest was running down his left arm he was sweating and shivering at the same time he could not catch his breath his whole body had become a medical specimen to be consigned to a first-year class in autopsy. He shoved his tongue between his teeth to keep from crying out and in so doing nearly bit it off his throat was filled with dust and he thirsted greatly unable now to swallow or to feel the inside of his mouth.

But his physical pain as he tore through the brush in search of Britt was something he could bear what he could not bear was knowing that each minute brought him closer to doing what he knew he must do and could not now was the time he knew he could not fail.

He kept glancing at Killeen. After an hour they had found no trace of Britt he had simply vanished into the brush with neither sound nor hoof prints and how in hell could you cover an area the size of Rhode Island in search of a man who had no wish to be found? Killeen was annoyed and weary the whole thing seemed to him disgusting and improbable.

—Listen doc he said reining in his sweating exhausted horse let's go on back to camp.

Eli Wetherill in the saddle resembled some sort of Don Quixote he rode with short stirrups and his elbows were out like chicken wings he held one rein with each hand and let his shoulders droop so tired now that his legs hung loose forsaking the stirrups for the small comfort of being stretched straight out toward the ground.

—Got to find Britt gasped the doctor.

—Just where the hell do you think you'll look growled Killeen.

The doctor shrugged his weary shoulders.

—That's right you don't know and never did said Killeen.

The doctor twisted his face and looked pained.

—You're an impostor and yellow as a dog cried Killeen and began to pull away into the brush leaving the doctor to fend for himself in the wilderness.

—Killeen. The word was drawn out and agonized and turning Killeen saw the doctor with his hand gripping his chest slump forward so that his head touched the horse's mane.

Killeen got him off his horse and did not know what to do with him for the doctor was unable to speak so Killeen poured the brandy and the whiskey between his lips it seemed to help then Killeen peering into his half-closed eyes said go ahead and drink it up and he noticed that the sweat stood in little beads on the doctor's forehead at the same time the doctor shivered as if from cold.

The doctor gripped the flask with both hands and drank slowly feeling the blessed relief he could always count on from alcohol and he had Killeen prop him against a tree all the while rolling his eyes and imploring Killeen not to leave him. Okay okay said Killeen running his hands through his hair he did not know what to do next or even which way to go back to the line camp and maybe the doctor would drop dead and who would believe any of it.

They were on top of a mesa and from there Killeen thought he might be able to catch the lay of the land a little better and he walked a few yards to where the trees parted and looking down he took in every last detail including the dark determined form of Matt Brittman hell-bent for a herd of five wild horses about a half mile to the east and then he saw Harley emerging from the brush about a quarter of a mile to the left of him. Britt didn't notice his son who rode parallel to the horses keeping himself at the edge of the brush giving the old man every last chance to do it on his own.

The wild horse would not be easy to catch and that was the way Matt Brittman expected it to be. During the last hour he had ridden faster and harder and better than Eli or Killeen and had lost them in the brush and by and by he bent down and saw the broken twigs the pressed-down mud the place in the grass where the horses had bedded down the night before he saw their droppings all fresh and shiny and he knew they had gone to the end of the mesa to find water and would eventually come his way. He had plenty of time. He was in no hurry. He sat in the saddle with his hands folded letting the day surround him yet he kept his eyes always to the north from whence the mustangs would come he saw in fact the narrow indistinct trail they had made across the hard and broken land saw it without

303

benefit of snow and prided himself that this was more than any other man could do.

He could not remember exactly where he was now although he knew it was a good place and he could not remember when he had come although he knew that time had nothing to do with it. He sat motionless on his horse and then at last something stirred him he heard the shouts of a man driving horses toward him through the dense piñon-juniper-sage forest on top of the mesa. His pulse quickened and with his right hand he made certain that the rope was exactly as it should be. He strained his ears to listen to the shouts coming to the left of the mesa then down the dry creek bed he strained his eyes to see. He was as drawn and ready as an arrow. It had to be Eli Wetherill driving the horses to him and he chuckled not knowing what year it was but it seemed to him way in the beginning somewhere just him and Eli doing it the hard way and this is where he had caught his first wild stud at the bottom of this very mesa.

They came slowly at first not knowing that a rider waited for them in the brush five wild horses a stallion and his mares exhausted from the long chase through the forest slowed down now crossing the sage field their long tails and manes blowing in the wind. Their heads were up in the proud way peculiar to a wild horse and their bodies were taut and sleek from a summer when the grass was good they came easily and cleanly through the grass their manes spilled over their necks and their tails touched the sage that grew among the grass. As they grazed and came closer to where Matt Brittman waited behind a huge and shaggy juniper their heads went up and down watching listening they came closer and closer the wind at their backs the threat of the man who had chased them for so long now safely past they were hungry and exhausted and they took their time with the grass alert and sniffing their heads tilted at the same angle the sage rustling softly as their hooves brushed past. When they were directly opposite him Matt Brittman took

304

a deep breath and marveled at their grace and beauty as runty and scruffy as they were they were a living chunk of the earth itself.

He had to possess the earth.

From his place behind the juniper he went out like a shot a lasso ready in his right hand his spurs dug so deeply into the belly of his horse that a faint line of blood began to appear on either side. The mustangs saw him then the fine buckskin stallion snorted a warning and the ground erupted into a storm of horse flesh racing toward the safety of the brush they surged in a whirl of color that matched the earth he had difficulty making them out it was as if the earth itself had come to life. He had to give it chase he covered the distance with his horse's hooves barely touching the ground it was only his horse and his own will closing the gap between himself and the mustangs their bodies heaving their eyes wild he saw their desperate run for freedom saw them push their depleted bodies across a draw taking it in one easy leap all except the stallion who fell back. The mares turned briefly then fled for he had given them the signal and they dared not stop or look back once again their hooves kicked up a cloud of dust that the trailing stallion breathed and he doubled his efforts stretching out each muscle past anything he had ever had to do.

And it was likewise with Matt Brittman whose blood had begun to run from his mouth as well as between his legs it was the same for this man no longer a man in whose right hand a rope twirled with exact precision. Twenty feet lay between him and the stallion then fifteen then ten then they were side by side the man ready to make the throw the stallion lunging desperately toward the safety of the brush a hundred feet ahead the brush into which the mares had already vanished. Then the stallion saw another rider coming up hard on his right with Matt Brittman already parallel to his left so he could not turn but depended on his strength to save him and it did not could not the rope was around his neck the other end of it tied to Matt

Brittman's saddle horn. The mustang stumbled in the dirt tasted it and breathed it recoiled violently and attempted to break free and as he did so the rope went tighter and tighter against his neck until at last he fell and all four legs were off the ground he was choked down with his eyes bulged out his powerful lungs using their last free measure of air.

Killeen whistled and held his breath. He had witnessed the most incredible feat of precision and endurance he had ever come across in a man and Britt was truly great and proving it out there in the middle of nowhere with nobody except himself and Harley to see so Killeen just stood and watched it all his love for the man growing and knowing that no one on earth could match him and that really was what it was all about this goddamn thing of calling yourself a man as strong as any mountain.

Matt Brittman with his Levi's soaked with blood sat down on the stallion's head noticing that it was a fine and noble head and that the mustang was the goingest concern he had ever captured and he tied a rope around the stallion's front legs removing the rope from his neck when he was finished. The stallion quivered and snorted and got up wide-eyed and unsteady for thus hobbled he could only move a short distance in an odd jerky gait letting his hind legs fly up as he stared at the man who had licked him the first man who had ever set hands to his flesh. The rancher stood back and admired the horse and he knew that he himself was as good as he ever had been or would be and god he had proved what he had set out to prove in the best way he knew. The stallion and he were about a foot apart and the animal's breath came hard as did the man's and in the eyes of the stallion there was a graceful resignation which was present in the eyes of the man as well and the man had a longing to put his hands on the animal to feel that magnificent flesh to come in contact with what was wholly free. As he stretched out his arms toward the stallion a single shot cracked from the brush and the horse jerked violently lifted his head and with one great convulsion fell dead at Matt Brittman's feet.

Harley.

He knew he had it coming when he saw his old man crimson with fury drag himself to his own horse crawl into the saddle and remove the gun from its case. He began to run turning the horse into the brush and the sound of his father's gun was close so close that one bullet bounced off the trunk of a piñon and tore through the sleeve of the kid's jacket and took away some of the flesh as well. He was counting the shots as he rode one two three and his arm was on fire and he knew what he longed for yet could not stop himself could not let his father catch up he plunged over dead trees and patches of snow he felt himself weak and knew that weak was what he always was and so why not stop and be counted weak yet he could not as he heard the gun going off once more very close and the next shot would be in the back.

The branches tore at his face and he did not care the blood from his arm was soaking through to the outside of his jacket his legs were numb and burned with a terrible ache in the knees and as he rode in his agony Harley decided he would turn around and face his father and let his old man do it looking him in the eye. Britt was coming all right crashing through the brush not a hundred yards behind but then he heard a crashing noise to the left then again to the right and he could not understand as he rode feverishly why his father did not catch up. He was slowing down tired now and so lonely that something like a sob escaped his lips he closed his eyes for a moment then opening them saw it was too late he had reached the fence and his sweaty gasping horse loping across an open stretch could not stop he pitched into the barbed wire and threw his rider sideways out of the saddle. Harley landed on his knees in a cedar as the gun went off once more and he heard his father approaching from the right. He got quickly to his feet and began to scramble up the rocks as fast as he could unarmed now and bleeding he could not hide no matter where he hid the old man would find him and shoot him dead for he had seen in that final look all that it takes for one man to kill another even if it is his son. Harley crouching on a ledge and hidden by the trees saw his old man ride up to the fence and glance from side to side the gun in his hand his finger on the trigger Harley you bastard he cried hoarsely Harley show yourself like a man.

But he couldn't. He sat crying on the ledge until his whole body shook and he vomited on the rocks and then looking down he saw his father slip off the horse in obvious and enormous pain and crawl under the fence and get up again unsteady so that he had to grip the fencepost before he started up the rocks the gun held tight in his hand and Harley knew that his old man knew where he was just as he knew everything and he was coming up the rock to get him and should he try and make a run for it up the rocks and go deeper into the dense forest which might save his life the only question was did he have a life worth saving?

Killeen saw Britt standing by the fence screaming up to Harley and Britt had the gun in his hand and could have shot the kid easy but he just stood there shrieking words that Killeen could not understand and oh god there went Britt under the fence and slowly but surely he was easing himself up the rock toward his son cowering less than fifty feet above. Killeen moved swiftly now and maneuvered himself toward a pile of rocks below the ledge and from there he saw there was not a single obstruction between himself and Harley not a single obstruction between himself and Britt who was down on his knees dragging the gun as well as himself over the brutal rock sliding from side to side yet moving slowly and inexorably upward toward the kid who it seemed had turned to marble who made no move to defend himself he was unarmed yet within reach of rocks large enough to rain down on his father's head.

As Killeen watched the rancher inching toward the kid and the kid sitting frozen on the ledge he noticed that Britt swerved toward the left as if he did not see his son at all as if something were pulling him off course and he could restrain himself no longer he screamed at Harley and he screamed at Britt but the sound of his voice was not heard by either man. So Killeen began to run toward Britt who was trying desperately to get to his feet and could not get up and Killeen kept running and shouting Britt Britt Britt and the closer Killeen came the more of an effort the man made to get up his broad back toward the running figure of Killeen. Before his horrified eyes Matt Britt-man rose on legs that were firm and soaked with blood he stood with the gun pressed to his shoulder his eye against the scope but the weapon was pointed ninety degrees away from Harley and the dying man just stood there with the gun steady and himself steady and he cried out in words not clearly understood where the hell are you Billy Deere?

With a smile on his lips Harley threw back his shoulders and drew himself up to his full height put his hands behind his back raised his face to the sun and called out to his father loud and clear right here.

And the sound was what the life was what the force was what the dream was what the end was and turning the gun with eyes that could no longer see turning the gun precisely on his son Matt Brittman began to move his finger against the trigger felt the metal warm and firm felt the river surging and heard the wings of a butterfly and the turning of a leaf and then he heard no more.

Two bullets hit him at the same moment one from the gun of Joe Killeen the other from the gun of Eli Wetherill who had ridden to the top of the ridge cutting off four miles from the route Killeen had taken he knew the country well it was his secret place and he would always keep his mouth shut.

Without a word Harley came down off the ledge picked up his old man's body and stumbled with it toward his old man's horse which stood patiently on the other side of the fence and then he and Killeen laid him across the saddle with no word spoken between the two all the way back to the line camp.

Neither Harley nor Killeen ever saw Eli Wetherill atop the ridge neither remembered hearing the blast from a second gun and both would swear later that Matt Brittman had been killed by one man only a man who had never killed a human being in his life and this first time only because he had to.

Dropping his gun in the brush Eli Wetherill was thus finished with the present as he knew it and contemplated no visible future he was detached from all about him he was not in time or place his consciousness was manifest only through that mechanical action which brought him to the line camp and put him behind the wheel of Matt Brittman's pickup and propelled him down the road his only goal was to get back to town and that required no further action than driving the vehicle over terrain he did not really see he was for all practical purposes on automatic pilot.

And he would go and keep going go and keep on being a physician but he was not a physician and maybe never had been. He had nothing to live for and knew it as he reached the town at dark and did not see that it was no longer there his eyes only saw what he wanted them to see the familiar outline of his house the familiar bashed-in door of his automobile. He left Britt's pickup parked in what used to be his flower garden and got into his car he had someplace to go alright but the roadmap of his mind was washed out and so he would have to wait a while to know which way Kayenta Arizona was or maybe Mexico. Yes he would go and keep on going in the comfortable dark to a sweet place beneath the trees where he passed out and came to at dawn finding himself at Holdup Hill where he often went to get a view of the town and some perspective of himself as well and then he sat there not believing his own two eyes not

310

trusting his memory or any part of himself and then he began to speak to himself in terms he understood and to remember as well as he could. He was like a man who has nearly drowned. He began walking from the hill through the smoking rubble of the town trying to get hold of himself there on what was left of the old church steps with the broken stained glass glinting like a field of flowers all around him. He was feeling okay until he was aware of Killeen's hands on his shoulders and his haggard face thrust close to his oh Killeen he said pleasantly what has happened to the town?

Killeen staring into the doctor's vacant eyes smelling the alcohol and knowing that what he was about to ask was impossible asked it nonetheless it needs you he said will you come along?

We shall not cease from exploration
And the end of all our exploring
Will be to arrive where we started
And know the place for the first time.

18

There were more of them now poking around the smoldering ruins of the town and walking up the street with Killeen Eli recognized some he had not seen for many years some he thought had died and some who had moved away so long ago that he could not recall their names only their faces and some forgotten shred of their medical records. The ones he had last seen on their death beds were now wholly restored and he smiled knowing that his medicine had brought them through and they were grateful for the gift of life that had been wholly his to bestow and he walked among them gripping their hands and gazing with warmth and affection upon their beaming faces.

313

Killeen had not slept in two nights and the ordeal of the last twenty-four hours had so drained him that he was physically sick his arms felt like lead each step was an effort he was close to breaking down for the first time in his life. Over and over in his mind he saw how he had put a bullet through Matt Brittman and it was only a matter of hours before he would have to account for it and suffer the consequences of an act that might send him to prison for the rest of his days. Yet now with all his dreams busted his sureness of himself was somehow compensating for all that he was guilty of and for once he had no desire to run away or to lose himself in anonymity he was in the midst of a wrecked yet tangible world and he meant to build it up if he could make them understand he would rather have shot Harley for his weakness than Matt Brittman for his strength but had to do it the other way for a man deprived of the last ounce of that strength becomes little more than a burned-out stump of a ghostly towering tree. The doctor mumbled to himself making gestures and now and then he threw back his head and laughed and Killeen knew that this was a different kind of stump upon which a certain kind of fungus had grown and there was no world for the doctor now and what could be done except to make his end hurt as little as possible and so he said in soothing tones it's all right doc.

—What's all right the doctor snapped.

—The end of the place.

The doctor stepped over a pile of rubble and nodded to Fred Sweeney who was sweeping out his store the end of what place he said jovially look there Killeen ain't that a pretty sight the ladies dressed for Sunday service.

Killeen swallowed and guided the doctor around a hole in the sidewalk in front of where the Yellow Bird Hotel had stood the town was filled with people all right the ones who had come to clean up or to collect a souvenir the police were roping off the buildings which had not entirely collapsed a couple of bulldozers were piling up the rubble where whole city blocks had

314

stood. Some of the people who had lived there whose names Killeen did not know some of those who had lost their husbands on the battlefield with the elk were there also standing silently together their hands touching one another and he did not see a single tear nor were they disgraced by death nor diminished by destruction. He had never really known these backward simple people during his brief stay in Yellow Bird they were always hazy yet now they seemed to him the very symbol of a people who had screwed their courage to a sticking place and would not fall.

And he felt he had come home.

And would give them something to remember him by.

But then he was suddenly overcome by the enormity of what he had done and right there in the middle of the destruction in front of strangers rooting like pigs and whole groups of people just watching he flung himself into the doctor's startled arms and began to cry.

—Britt's dead.

—I know said the doctor.

—How could you we just brought him back to the ranch.

—Because I killed him.

Killeen pulled himself away and with a shock realized the doctor's total dissolution his face implacable had a wildness about the eyes and did he not stop and speak to strangers as if he knew them had he not run off from the mesa and driven back to town leaving them all behind and covering up his cowardice with a lie.

—You wouldn't have the guts said Killeen with disgust.

The doctor's lips trembled he looked away to the mountain and his eyes grew misty behind his glasses yes once I did and so I killed him Killeen for thirty seconds I had the guts.

—Goddamn it doctor I shot him I did it *me* he said his voice rising so that people began to stare *me* doctor I have up and killed a man.

—No Killeen said the doctor there was nobody there but

315

me on top of the ridge and he was going to shoot Harley so I had to do it you see in defense of Harley.

—That's not true cried Killeen he was about to kill Harley and *I* shot him he was done for anyway I just finished him off like some crippled animal.

The doctor glanced at the profile of Killeen and it seemed to him a sad and lonely face filled with greater anguish than when he had come barely six weeks before and he remembered what Killeen had come about casting a straw in the wind and hoping to find some shred of himself some reason to belong. Eli Wetherill had not thought much about his own father over the years but he did so now and remembered how the presence of the man was a reassurance in the dark cold days of winter how his hearty laughter filled the drab and drafty house and made him feel all warm inside. But as the years passed and his father no longer came through the door in the evening and his mother no longer smiled Eli began to understand what the presence of his father had meant and he could remember being afraid and dispirited a permanent sadness grew along with his bones and here he was now nearing the end of his own life and he had not arrived at the place he had set out to find. He had become a doctor all right but he was not a physician and he knew the difference and knew it was too late to put whatever talent he had to its right and proper use and he knew he could not then or ever allow Killeen to know that he might be his own son because Killeen deserved better than that. Killeen deserved some solid ground some credentials as good as the Daughters of the American Revolution the Sons of Pioneers the Fathers of Our Nation the Mothers of Invention he deserved the best that Eli Wetherill could give him and that was a lie the best he would ever tell and so studying Killeen's tense young face devoid of heritage and roots and antecedents the doctor took a deep breath and drew himself up as tall as he could and decided to give him what he had missed.

—You could not have shot Britt said the doctor with authority you could not have shot him because he was your father and you were nowhere near.

—My what said Killeen backing away and holding his hands up now wait a minute doctor no more of that shit you wished it and so did he and so did I once upon a time but no man I ain't nobody's kid.

—Killeen said the doctor moving along the broken street oblivious of the roar of machines the running about of people you have earned the right to be from Yellow Bird.

—What said Killeen in astonishment.

—They don't grow horse-shit humans up here Killeen they come like you and him.

—But—

—Shut up Killeen and listen said the doctor trudging along quite rapidly now so that Killeen was obliged to almost run the first summer Billy Deere come up here from Texas she was young maybe fifteen was all and Britt he was maybe seventeen well he knocked her up and she went home and tried to conceal it as best she could but by and by she began to show and her family sent her in care of a maiden aunt to go and get it taken care of well Billy Deere was one spitfire of a woman and she run off from this old witch somewhere in New York State or thereabouts and she come back here begging Britt to do something and he wouldn't see he didn't want no part of her so I took her in. Just finishing up medical school I was didn't even have a license I took her in and delivered her on the kitchen table in this very house you're looking at and you was the reddest most squeezed-up skinnified rabbit I ever saw and of course Billy Deere she shed a lot of tears and made threats but in the end she gave you up see and I took you myself to the nuns in Denver and from time to time checked up on you till you up and run away.

—Christ said Killeen shaking his head Christ—

—You were the first five dollar baby Killeen the very first and I always wondered if the rest might turn out as good as you

317

I knew what you was made of Killeen even when you was a little bitty kid.

—Did Britt know what happened to me?

The doctor shook his head. Nope he never did assumed you was adopted out I guess and that was that he didn't have no more to do with Billy Deere neither till about five years later she come up from Texas again and I could see the hellfire in her eyes and I knew she was going to get old Britt for what he done to her but a man don't place much importance on knocking up a heifer so there he was with his tongue all hanging out when she come back and she chased him till he caught her and there was no way he would listen he just went ahead and married the bitch and she waited and bided her time gave birth to Harley and had another one in the oven when she up and left him and what she told him was that Harley belonged to another man and the one she was carrying away was his so you see—

—Was it true about Harley not being his?

—I never knew for sure but Britt rejected him from that minute on would have stuck him in the orphanage too except that I reminded him that had happened once before and so he was stuck with Harley and Harley was stuck with him and it never worked like oil and water they was and twice as mean.

Killeen bit his lip his head was swimming they were standing in front of Eli's house in the bright sun Killeen gripped the doctor's shoulders and looked into his eyes now quite clear and lucid and he said softly did Britt ever know it was me that had come back did he die knowing I was really and truly his son?

The doctor hesitated his body was sore and close to collapse but he held Killeen close for a few seconds and whispered yes he did.

—Then Harley—

—Britt's mind went like that said the doctor snapping his fingers and he swore to kill them both Harley and Billy Deere though she's been gone nigh on twenty years and as soon as he knew about you he tried to relive his life with Meridian Mul-

318

doon and I expect he'd have killed her too right after he took care of Harley.

—And you knew this all along and just what did you expect to do?

—Do said the doctor why just what I had to do and done it too Killeen you know that now don't you you know I ain't some crazy lunatic?

—I want to believe you doc.

—I ain't never lied to you Killeen said the doctor biting his tongue.

—What did Rose Houghton have to do with all this said Killeen suspiciously. Why did she put the ad in the paper?

—Her well she was my nurse of sorts with her big ass in the way and her mouth sealed shut till she took a notion to die and then her own mistake come out of her and got mixed up with you she would have brought us down Killeen I am in fact the father of one Houghton brat or so I've always believed but she had to dig up ancient history her own mistake and make me out the sucker for some reason I'll never know damn women it's a bad business those five dollar babies I hope to god I never live to see another one.

But I can't believe him said Killeen to himself watching the doctor begin to tremble saw that his eyes were vacant again and that his body which he had held straight all the way through town was drooping now he was like a doll from which the stuffing had fallen out a machine with a corroded engine or one of those car-wash dummies held up by a couple of strings. And yet and yet . . . The possibilities of his parentage were doubling by the week and it amused him to consider the almost endless variations he multiplied and divided until he laughed out loud causing the doctor to turn in some alarm and demand what was so funny. Killeen couldn't explain it couldn't say now listen man it used to matter but it doesn't anymore and I reckon that being Britt's wouldn't have changed me much I'd still be drifting toward a high place I never reach but I keep on trying see and

319

that's what's cool having not one damn thing to live up to nobody to say hey that's Matt Brittman's kid how come he ain't making money like his old man how come he's a lazy son-of-a-bitch how come he didn't turn out as good as his old man? God almighty doctor you think I'd have wanted that kind of liability? So here I am free as a bird got no ties with anyone on earth no family name to carry on like Harley there he's in a heap of trouble being an honest-to-god Brittman he's got to make decisions and money and success and all that shit. Just Daisy and me headed west you know for someplace that's a dot on the map and maybe just maybe I won't go wandering off and maybe just maybe the Muldoon chick'll come along and maybe she won't because I dig her see and what she did for poor old Britt to make the going easier and hell it takes a powerful woman to just up and give herself like that and not hate herself for doing it and maybe just maybe that's what I've wanted all along because hell doc I'm too damn old to get me a mother or a father what I need is a wife yeah I'll say it once again a wife for God almighty's sake.

It would have broken the old man's heart to hear that shit so Killeen just took his arm and guided him up the walk fearing that he was going to pass out cold and he would have given anything to see the doctor all in one piece and he'd give the old man a lift out of town stick him on the seat beside the Muldoon chick and tell him it's okay doc we're taking a little trip and going to see some sights you ain't never seen before.

But Killeen did not get a chance to say that either because as they were going up the creaky wooden steps the door flew open and there was Meridian in a soiled shirt and blood-spattered pants her hair in stringy strands and her poor frail body heaving Doctor Wetherill please come quick we found Alice Crowley in the basement she's unconscious and about to have a baby.

—Where in the hell is my bag said the doctor trying desperately to recall where he'd left his bag and then he said in the car Killeen up there on Holdup Hill and for God's sake be quick.

Killeen went off down the broken street in Daisy and fetched the doctor's bag and knowing it would not be long before they came to get him he made the most of the time he had left time was easy for him now and life was easy no matter what became of it now no matter how he had to answer for killing Britt. *His father.* He said the word over and over tried to believe it and tried to recall any similarities between that man and himself the best hand he'd ever run across yes there was a bond between them Matt Brittman's legacy was the legacy of the land as long as the wind blew there would be some part of him blowing across the land carrying seeds as well as dreams. You could shove yourself into it stake out your claim and know that the land grew better or worse because of you your generation was one of despair the next was the turn of hope ain't that the last emotion Daisy when all else is used up when you have gone so far down there's no place to go but up and hell girl let the town burn and the doctor deliver his baby we got us some going to do.

He drove across the bridge and toward the ranch rattling over the cattle guards and at the Eagle Creek pasture he saw a group of men working over a bunch of bulls laid out flat on the ground and other bulls seemed to be dead and others were wobbling around and as fast as he could he was over the fence and beside Harley and the young veterinarian from town.

—Harley what the hell?

—Poison said Harley his face taut don't ask me how or who Wingate drove the bulls back in here the way I told him to because dad put them up by the house where they didn't belong you know how he was at the end but poison Killeen he sure as hell wouldn't put out poison.

—Jesus said Killeen poisoning bulls what the hell is it he said to the veterinarian.

—Strychnine in alfalfa pellets laid out on purpose in the feed troughs what son-of-a-bitch—

—Killeen please help me said Harley retching into the dirt

321

and Killeen grabbed hold of him and shook him hard get hold of yourself man ain't we had trouble enough.

—McTavish and the whole bunch are at the house I told them Killeen you saved my life but they want to oh Killeen he said his pudding face all pale and quivering it's all dad's work all he was that I hated it's different when you see it dying in front of your very eyes it's him each time one of them keels over and oh fuck it all Killeen I'm done I'm not a man Killeen you saw it a dozen times and you saw it at the end and I'll always wonder why the hell you didn't let him go ahead and shoot me.

—Stand up commanded Killeen to the kid who was doubled up on the ground.

Slowly and unsteadily Harley got to his feet one hand resting on the fence.

—With both hands at your sides Harley and your feet firm and apart like that statue of that huge big Greek.

—Roman.

—Whatever the hell he was stand up straight Harley that's better how many dead?

—Thirteen so far.

—How many sick?

—Nine.

—How many got into this pasture?

—All of them thirty-seven head we don't know yet how many got to the poison.

—Yearling bulls Harley how many you got of them?

—Ninety-three head.

—No sweat Harley all you got to do is breed.

—It'll take years and years and years oh Killeen I wanted to go to law school.

—Make up your mind Harley I ain't got all day.

The kid looked around him at his father's land as far as the eye could see at the sick and dying bulls at the ones already dead at the possibilities of a new herd on the other side of the cottonwoods and he could see his father's face swelling bigger

322

in his head and all that was left now was the makings of a foundation herd and he saw his life used up for the sake of the land and not for his own sake and he knew he had to be his own man and so he said it's not my bag Killeen.

—Goddamn it Harley.

—I can do some good out there if I'm lucky I can try to make some sense of a senseless society not change it Killeen that'll take a hundred lifetimes but just pound the fucking shit out of it please Killeen stay and run this goddamn wreck of a ranch.

Killeen began to laugh and jabbed poor Harley in the ribs and the kid jabbed him back and laughed also and the vet looked up and said cut it out you two your whole goddamn future has just got itself wiped out.

—Yeah said Harley we know.

—How well we know said Killeen.

—You heartless bastards muttered the veterinarian returning to his work.

—Let's go face the law said Killeen and then I got one hell of a fine idea and he began to explain the way Yellow Bird was going to remember him and Harley said you'll never get away with it Killeen.

—The hell I won't you with me kid or not?

—Sure said Harley what have I got to lose?

In the last thirty-six hours she had learned a lot about the town a hell of a lot more than she had during the fifteen years she'd lived there and the score was Yellow Bird eight Los Angeles nothing and she sat on the back porch of the doctor's house smoking a cigarette and listening for the tortured screams of Alice Crowley to begin again she could not stand it anymore and so she had left the kitchen where Eli Wetherill was doing his best and Josie Stringer not knowing what else to do kept boiling water. And just how would she go about putting it all down now that she had said yes to herself and the flame was just beginning to ignite again waiting for permission to burst and set her free but it would be a long time coming and painful too she was now so familiar with death in all its forms and degrees that she found it to be neutral. But she was still alive and she didn't know what it was that had made her suffer a little death along with Britt's when she had not loved him when she had in fact not loved anything except the coal-black boy and Killeen she had finally said yes to herself Christ thinking back to the assurance of a pure and simple fuck and the distinction between passion and love was how many times they could do it and with Britt she had met herself on a wholly animal level and the urge to create had come from the urge to destroy. The stumbling block had always been the recollections of the town itself and what she had witnessed there and what she had chosen to become while there and she always thought maybe it would have been different elsewhere. Her own release was simultaneous with the release of Yellow Bird which knew that it was easier to be content with less than less content with more.

And maybe Killeen will have me after all.

She sat there with the late afternoon sun at her back and it was warm but would go down quickly and leave the corpse of Yellow Bird in utter darkness and the people would come again and look at it in the light of day until at last there was nothing left oh look at it and the snow would fall over the ground covering up the bleeding sores and if you stood a long way off a month from now you might never know that in this place was life.

She was beginning to understand herself as Alice Crowley's voice pierced the air and down below in the town truck after truck was hauling away the bits and pieces of a town which had buried the last of its dead and the sirens wailing probably meant the ambulance coming at last for Alice the siren far across the river and Alice Crowley's screams were what she heard as she took a pencil from her pocket and began to write on a scratch pad the first words she had written in a year *there was a town called Yellow Bird which sat on a dry piece of ground above a muddy river called West Bountiful and there was a mountain rising above the town which had been cleaned out by three generations of gold miners and the mountain died and the town died and the river died too when they built a dam and the river was forced to retreat against whatever will it might have had which was like the town's will which somehow had to be broken and the way they did it is perhaps best symbolized by a man who was a physician as useless and obsolete as the town which*

—Jesus Christ Josie push down on her stomach.

—And bust it out of her?

—Hang on to Josie's ass Alice and bear down bear down goddamn it girl you want it in there forever?

—Three hours of this doc and that kid ain't moved an inch.

—It's coming Josie it's coming bear down Alice now real hard like this unhhhh like you were sitting on the pot that's good Alice get some more towels Josie hurry up.

—There ain't no more clean ones you want sheets?

—Yes anything now Alice I know it hurts here grab a hold of this grapefruit it's all I've got I'm sorry.

—Am I going to die gasped Alice lying in a puddle of blood and sweat on Eli Wetherill's kitchen table.

—You ain't going to die Alice we are going to have you in a hospital before long.

—When doc when?

—They'll be here soon Alice now give me a couple good ones yes yes yes!

Alice Crowley's white-knuckled hands closed in on the grapefruit and burst it and she brought her teeth down on it and was halfway off the table before Josie Stringer rushing into the room with an armload of sheets dropped them and took the girl's writhing moaning body and held it fast to the table pinning it down with her powerful arms her two sacks of breast pushed down into Alice's sweating grimy face honey she cried honey it's all over.

—Scissors Josie said Eli calmly lifting the wet and slippery newborn child with strong and steady hands lifting it with his fingers between its feet lifting it upside down and delivering a hearty smack to a red and wrinkled bottom and then the frail tiny lungs filled with air the mouth opened and a thin wail could be heard at the same time there was an angry insistent pounding at the front door.

—See who the hell that is said Eli working rapidly now and tell them I'm busy I'm a doctor do you hear and I'm busy. And he took the infant and wrapped it in a sheet and laid it beside Alice across whose face a flash of serenity crept well Alice he said you got yourself a girl about five pounds I reckon.

The girl's parched dry lips parted her eyes were blurred with tears just two words came from her mouth thank you she said.

—What are you going to name her Alice he said engrossed once more in his work.

—Hope she said faintly.

—Hope he said well that beats Gertrude Hope he said again shaking his head ain't that a hell of a name for the last five dollar baby?

—The what she said raising her head.

—Oh nothin' Alice a little joke I play on myself now and then but this is the last time Alice on account of I ain't funny anymore.

Josie Stringer pale and trembling came into the room and whispered in his ear it's the law McTavish and a couple deputies doc they say you got to come right now.

Eli wiped his head with his sleeve and his glasses were streaked tell those bastards he said firmly tell those bastards I'll be there when I can then come back here Josie I need you real bad.

And when she left the room he said Alice you okay on this table the house is pretty cold but with that stove you'll stay warm and nice.

—I'm okay she said sleepily I feel empty like a jack-o'-lantern is all.

Eli Wetherill came into the room with his clothes spattered with blood he came straight and tall and with a quickness to his stride his hands had not failed him nor had his head and it was with enormous pride that he pushed open the door to the living room and to the group of standing grim-faced men announced friends I have just delivered a right good baby.

Jed McTavish cleared his throat and stepped forward there was a piece of paper in his hand and as he unfolded it the three deputies fingered their guns the tragedy of the elk had resulted in no arrests just an accident was all it was they were worn and frustrated the grim relief of placing Eli Wetherill under arrest brought only fleeting satisfaction. They were not smiling they looked as if they had convicted him and he smiled wondering where they had come from and why they should be so hostile and why Mac of all people ought to be addressing him in such a frigid tone and with his hand also on his gun and god didn't they know he had just delivered a baby against all odds and it would live because of what he'd done under the most primitive conditions? Now he would have a drink to celebrate and he reached for the bottle on the table only to have a deputy grab his wrist and then Eli's fist recoiled and he hit the deputy in the head only to find himself held hand and foot by two burly deputies who said under their breaths bastard son-of-a-bitch motherfucking ass.

—I charge you said McTavish staring at the rug I charge you with the murder of Nathaniel Walter Houghton.

—What said Eli dazedly what?

—Whose body was found at approximately four o'clock yesterday afternoon in the vicinity of the Baritone Wonder and I will advise you of your rights Eli as it is my duty to do.

327

—Mac you old fart—

—As sheriff of Carbon County said McTavish in a loud voice you do not have to answer any questions you are entitled to the right of counsel and—

—Call off your dogs Mac said Eli struggling to break free and we'll have us a snort.

—You are under arrest Eli and you are to be taken to the county jail pending your arraignment.

—My what said Eli Mac for god's sake what is this?

—You are being arrested.

—For what said Eli trying to see through his smeared glasses.

—For the murder of Nate Houghton.

—Oh said Eli thoughtfully oh that well he done it himself Mac in front of my very eyes.

—Tell it to the judge.

—But what I wish to do is to confess to the murder of Matt Brittman that is the man I killed at four o'clock in the afternoon in cold blood staring him in the eye I blowed his head off Mac with a .44 Magnum.

McTavish shook his head he was becoming impatient you didn't kill that son-of-a-bitch that was trying to kill his poor unarmed boy that Killeen feller had the honor I wisht I'd of done it myself.

Eli shut his eyes his head drooped then all of a sudden he exploded into action and with all his strength used his force on the two men who held him and spit in the face of Jedediah McTavish who stood coolly letting it drip down his cheek you oughtn't to have done that Eli. And then he punched him in the stomach with his fists. The last thing Eli heard was the frail uncertain wail of a child named Hope.

He came to in the car and saw that his hands were manacled and that was strange considering who he was but he decided not to ask about it because he was too busy watching out the window at the throngs of people of Yellow Bird going by and they waved at him and a low cheer went among them spreading from man to man and it surprised him considering that they had not voiced their approval of him before but then they were a rather reserved bunch going to and from the mines with scarcely a word and there came the shrill blast of the mine whistle blowing the changing of the shift and in another five minutes the Almighty Dollar will be filled with drinking men and lunchboxes with high-grade ore concealed in the peanut butter and the sweet soft voice of Nellie Brown dressed in shimmering cloth soothing the troubled heart and easy on the eyes the slick flip of cards you'd placed your wages on coming up deuces wild and craps shot on the hardwood floor snake eyes baby and Miss Galina Jordan accepts with pleasure your invitation of the twenty-second and the train tickets folded up back and forth into a neat stack one coupon good for a trip to Salt Lake from there to the City of the Angels and on down to Mexico clip clip clip and he saw the train pulling into the depot and the men getting off carrying suitcases with straps wearing suits with vests and you never trusted a man who wore suspenders and a belt and one train going out with the mother lode in seventy-two cars and why did that whistle sound the way it did sending chills up his back like hearing it for the first time and the sign hanging in front of the livery was swinging in the wind and there was Tom Pazulla his back permanently bent from shoeing horses whistling his little tune and waving his hammer the only dago in Yellow Bird everybody liked him for his smile. And more and more people were rooting for him and calling him by name and they were pressing against the car so that it had to go very slowly and he tried to wave but both hands came up and he felt foolish so he just nodded his head and then the car turned the corner toward the bridge and he wondered where they were going but decided not to ask about it because he was too busy turned around in his seat watching the surging throbbing life of Yellow Bird spilling all over him and across the river and across the plains to the mountains looking like somebody had spilled ice cream on top. He had never felt so good before listening to the laughter and the whistles blowing and the baby crying on and on and on

At midnight when every last person had left Yellow Bird when there was no further need for the town to be watched or waited upon or guarded or picked over when it was an inky velvet dark with the stars thrown out upon an endless sky when the only sound was the wind whistling up the sullen half-frozen river when all was peaceful and bathed in the loveliness of the night the finish was put to it by a man who wanted to be remembered and another who wanted to be forgotten. They had worked for many hours and then at last from their perch on Holdup Hill where Bessie Pilcher had once paid a quarter to see a boy have an erection one of them pressed down on a handle and began to count as was his habit to count so many things. He had barely reached the count of five when the flash seared their vision but they saw almost as if by day the dam intake tower with the word CUNNINGHAM in raised red letters on the top then the ground rocked beneath their feet and they saw the tower wobble for an instant and then slowly and majestically it fell into the place cut out by the river fell and was silent fell and was dark and all was as it was in the beginning long before some man had stuck his shovel in the earth.

But a mile or so up the mountain where the snow was beginning to pile up for the winter two men heard the explosion and scrambled from their tent and a warm fire and stood shivering in the night peering down at the nothingness and the Coyote turned to the stranger and said it must be them fellers from Cripple Creek on the shift at the Yankee Doodle Dandy. His gold tooth gleamed in the moonlight and from the band of his straw hat he carefully removed a snipe.

—Time has a way of copping out on me said the stranger.

—Come to think of it said the Coyote scratching his head they ain't worked the Yankee Doodle Dandy for a while so maybe

—There's either too much of it or not enough of it
—Maybe they mean trouble for us my friend when
—I have to think hard about something
—Maybe we ought to go down and kill 'em shoot 'em just say when
—When I dig enough gold in Alaska
—On second thought friend maybe we ought to go to bed
—They don't know I've taken a few pieces here and there
—Nobody knows but us we're all that's left and goddamn it friend I wish I had my radio and my lunchbox.

They went to sleep in the little warm tent with the stove giving out a gentle fire that kept them snug they dreamed about the blossom rock and a room that was filled with gold and their crippled fingers wore smooth the handle of the axe and the wheelbarrow wore down its wheel and the little gray burro wore down its shoes and the darkness inside the mountain became thick with the dust of their progress and it was the kind of thing a man would give his life for to go about taking a part of the mountain's life in the right way being as careful with her as you could it would be as near to heaven as any man could get and so they dreamed on through the cold and silent night of how when morning came they would make a wise and proper beginning.

Nancy Wood, who was born in Trenton, New Jersey, in 1936, came to Colorado Springs when she was 22 and has been there ever since. She lives with her four children and a foster child in a large old house; hikes, backpacks, rides and climbs when she is not writing or listening to classical music; and is a passionate conservationist who has written outspoken articles for such magazines as *McCall's, Audubon, American Heritage* and *Woman's Day* on the changing West, and the impact of such deadly incursions into its survival as the AEC, highways and the desecration of public lands. She is the author of a new book on the deforestation of America published by the Sierra Club in the fall of 1971.

The Last Five Dollar Baby had its origin in a non-fiction book on Colorado which Nancy Wood wrote during 1967–1968. As she traveled 24,000 miles within the state, noting the disappearance of small towns and an entire way of life, she decided that what was really happening there could best be told in fiction. After long and thoughtful planning, the book came to life in an intensive spate of work at an isolated ranch in Watrous, New Mexico. Many of its events are rooted in reality—the wild horse hunt, saloon talk, the mood that runs time—past, present and future—together. But the imaginative formulation of this time, this place and these people are uniquely her own.